# For the Love of You

*Love's Divine Book II*

Ava Freeman

*For my Family*

Also by Ava Freeman

**After Hours Series**

Four Letter Word

Four Letter Word 2

Fire We Make

Belong to You

**Friends & Lovers Series**

Friends & Lovers

Games We Play

Lovers Rock

**Rapture of Love Series**

A Taste of Remy

A Touch of Desire

The Look of Love

**Love Divine Series**

Love's Divine

# Also by Ava Freeman

**Standalone Novels**

The Makings of You

Sweetest Taboo

# Chapter One

"Damn it, has anyone seen my shoes?"

Genesis spun in a circle inside of her office, now glam suite, so named by Kenzie, searching for her heels.

"I've got them," Lucy sang, appearing in the doorway, heels in hand.

"Oh, thank God. I don't know what I'd do if you all weren't here." Genesis kissed Lucy's cheek and grabbed the shoes.

Lucy winked at her and pushed her into her office chair. "I'm not sure either, but sit down so I can do your face. We're cutting it close."

Genesis obeyed and did her best to sit still as Lucy began applying her makeup. This wasn't the big day, far from it, but she knew how important their engagement party was to Zuri. She was loving all the attention and excitement surrounding their upcoming nuptials but Genesis found herself a touch overwhelmed.

Shannon came into the room munching on a bag of chips. "Hey Gen, you got any red Gatorade? I looked all over the pantry and couldn't find any."

"Seriously, Shannon? Why are you bothering this woman when she has a party in her honor to attend?" Lucy gave Shannon a side eye before returning to her task.

"Hey, I'm here for moral support," Shannon said, wiping crumbs from her shirt.

Kenzie appeared in the doorway. "Yeah, and to make a mess everywhere," she teased, snatching the chip bag from Shannon's hands. "Come on, let's go raid the fridge and leave these two to finish getting ready."

Genesis chuckled as Shannon and Kenzie disappeared down the hallway, their playful banter fading into the distance. She took a deep breath, trying to calm her nerves.

"You okay?" Lucy asked, pausing her makeup application to study Genesis's face.

Genesis hesitated, her eyes darting to the doorway to make sure Shannon and Kenzie were out of earshot. She let out a shaky breath and met Lucy's concerned gaze.

"It's all happening so fast. Don't get me wrong, I love Zuri with every fiber of my being. She's my soulmate, my everything. But this whirlwind of parties and planning and attention... it's a lot." Genesis fidgeted with the hem of her robe. "Sometimes I wonder if I'm cut out for all of this. Zuri comes from such a different world than I do. Her family is so... grand. And here I am, just a small-town girl who fell in love with a Baker."

Lucy set down her makeup brush and knelt beside Genesis, taking her hands. "Hey now, don't sell yourself short. You're amazing and Zuri loves you for who you are."

"She does, but it doesn't help that I don't have family to be here with me, not like Zuri. Kenzi and Shannon are great, but I want my parents."

Lucy squeezed Genesis's hands, her eyes full of understanding. "Oh, honey. I can imagine how hard it must be without them here. But remember, family isn't just blood. Myself, Rain, and your other friends are your family too, and we're here for you every step of the way."

Genesis nodded, blinking back tears. "You're right. I'm being silly."

"It's not silly at all," Lucy assured her. "Your feelings are valid. Have you talked to Zuri about this?"

Genesis shook her head. "I don't want to. She's so excited about everything."

Lucy raised an eyebrow. "Something tells me that Zuri would be interested in your emotional state."

Before Genesis could respond, her phone chimed with a text. She picked it up, a smile spreading across her face as she read the message.

"It's Zuri," she said with a smile. "She says she can't wait to see me and that she loves me more than all the stars in the sky."

Lucy grinned. "That woman adores you. Now, let's finish getting you ready so you can go see your fiancee."

Lucy had a point. Maybe she wasn't from Zuri's world, but Zuri had chosen her, and that was worth celebrating.

The sounds of Shannon and Kenzie's laughter echoed from the kitchen, reminding Genesis of the family she had built around her. She closed her eyes, allowing Lucy to work her magic.

A gentle knock on the door frame startled Genesis out of her reverie. She opened her eyes to find Rain standing there, a garment bag draped over her arm.

"I've got your dress," Rain announced, her eyes sparkling with excitement. "And let me tell you, Zuri is going to lose her mind when she sees you in this."

Genesis experienced a flutter of anticipation in her stomach. "Ooh, let me see!"

Rain unzipped the bag, revealing a stunning burgundy

gown with details that shimmered in the light. Genesis gasped, her earlier worries forgotten.

"It's perfect," she breathed, reaching out to touch the silky fabric.

Lucy finished up the last touches on Genesis's makeup and stepped back to admire her work. "Alright, Miss Thing, you're all done. Let's get you into that dress."

With Rain and Lucy's help, Genesis slipped into the gown. It hugged her curves in all the right places, the burgundy color was a beautiful contrast against her dark skin. As she looked at herself in the full-length mirror, she felt a surge of confidence.

"Wow," Shannon whispered from the doorway, where she and Kenzie had reappeared. "Gen, you look incredible."

Genesis smiled at her reflection, then at everyone else. "Thank you all so much."

As Genesis stood there, surrounded by her friends and their excited chatter about the dress, her mind drifted to Zuri. She thought about their first meeting in Barbados, the way Zuri had captured her heart with one look. Genesis was drawn to her so easily, and now they were getting ready to commit to each other. She wasn't someone who believed in fate, but their connection made her a believer.

The beginning of their romance had been unconventional, but once they became a couple, it was like something out of a fairytale. Late-night walks through the city, stolen kisses in the back of taxis, long conversations over cups of coffee that grew cold because they were too engrossed in each other to remember to drink. Genesis smiled to herself, recalling how Zuri surprised her with a weekend getaway to a quaint bed-and-breakfast in northern California, where they spent hours exploring the nearby hiking trails and evenings curled up by the fireplace.

There was so much they had done together, and so much more for them to explore, but there was that small seed of doubt buried deep inside. It made her question her place in Zuri's world, but also her own life. Going from her parent's home to college and then becoming a parent to her sister and Shannon's wife, she wondered where she was in all of that. Had she given herself time to grow as her own person before committing, or was she once again just following someone else's lead?

Genesis attempted to dispel the doubts creeping in. This was supposed to be a joyous occasion, and she was determined to focus on the love she and Zuri shared.

"Hey," Rain said, noticing the slight change in Genesis's expression. "You okay?"

Genesis nodded, forcing a smile. "Yeah, I'm fine. Just... thinking."

Lucy squeezed her hand. "It's normal to be nervous, honey. But remember, this is Zuri we're talking about. The woman who looks at you like you hung the moon and stars."

"She's right," Kenzie chimed in. "I've never seen two people more perfect for each other." Shannon coughed. "I mean, more perfect for each other now."

Everyone laughed as Shannon leaned on the door frame. "I remember the girl I married, and she's still inside, but you're an amazing woman. You deserve all the happiness you can stand and I think Zuri can give that to you. Don't question it Gen, just let her love you and you love her."

A lump formed in her throat at Shannon's words. She blinked back tears, not wanting to ruin her makeup. "Thank you, Shannon. That means a lot."

"Alright, enough of this mushy stuff," Lucy declared, though her voice was thick with emotion. "We've got a party to get to, and a certain fiancée who's probably climbing the walls waiting for you."

Genesis smoothed down her dress. "You're right. Let's do this."

She grabbed her clutch and followed her friends out of the room, her heels clicking against the hardwood floors.

As they made their way downstairs, Genesis's phone buzzed with another text from Zuri:

"You're the best thing that's ever happened to me. 🤍."

Reading those words, Genesis felt genuine love. Whatever doubts she had, whatever challenges they might face, she had complete certainty that her love for Zuri was real.

* * *

When they entered the event space, Genesis couldn't help but feel emotional as she took in the sight before her. Everything was as she and Zuri had envisioned it. Even though this was just an engagement party and not the wedding, the attention to detail was impeccable. The grand ceiling was festooned with delicate strings of lights that cast a soft, golden hue over the gathered crowd. Swathes of plum silk draped down the walls, matching with the table runners and clusters of deep violet hydrangeas that adorned each table.

Genesis moved through the crowd, accepting congratulations and well-wishes. She felt good in her outfit, and couldn't wait to see how Zuri's came out. When she spotted her future wife across the room, it was like time stopped. She wore a striking suit in a rich maroon shade, tailored to fit her perfectly. The color complimented her caramel skin and Genesis' darker burgundy lace gown. Her heart swelled as she watched Zuri, happy and carefree.

Then, Zuri turned and their eyes met. The world seemed to fade away as Zuri's face lit up with a radiant smile. She excused herself from the group she was talking to and made her way towards Genesis, her eyes never leaving her fiancée's face.

As Zuri approached, Genesis felt a wave of love that momentarily pushed aside her earlier doubts. Zuri reached out and took Genesis's hands in hers, her eyes roaming over Genesis' form.

"You look breathtaking," Zuri murmured, leaning in to place a kiss on Genesis's cheek. "I'm the luckiest woman in the world."

Genesis blushed under Zuri's intense gaze. "You're not so bad yourself," she teased, running her hands along the lapels of Zuri's suit. "We make quite the pair, don't we?"

Zuri laughed, the sound warming Genesis from the inside out. "That we do, my love. That we do."

It was like a dream as Genesis and Zuri made their way around the room, greeting guests and accepting congratulations. As they moved through the crowd together, Genesis marveled at how effortlessly Zuri navigated the social scene. Her fiancée greeted each guest, her charisma drawing people in like moths to a flame. Genesis found herself content to stand by Zuri's side, offering smiles and nods, letting Zuri take the lead in conversations.

The night progressed in a whirlwind of congratulations, toasts, and well-wishes. Genesis floated along, carried along by the tide of celebration. She savored Zuri's hand in hers, the gentle pressure a constant reminder of their connection amidst the chaos.

After lots of dancing and mingling, Genesis took a bathroom break and afterwards found herself on a balcony, watching the party unfold inside. She leaned against the railing, taking a deep breath of the cool night air. The sounds of the party drifted out to her - laughter, the clink of glasses, soft music. For a moment, she closed her eyes, trying to center herself.

"There you are," Zuri's voice came from behind her. "I was wondering where you'd disappeared to."

At the sound of Zuri's approach, Genesis turned to face her. She had two flutes of champagne in her hands and offered one to Genesis.

"I missed you," Genesis said simply. It was a statement, a sigh of relief, a proclamation of love all rolled into three words.

"Babe, you were gone for like five minutes," Zuri responded with a grin.

"Well, it was five minutes too long."

Zuri smiled, her hand brushing away a stray curl from Genesis' face. "Afraid I'd run away?" she teased.

A playful smirk danced on Genesis' lips as she leaned into Zuri's touch, her own hand capturing Zuri's and holding it against her cheek. "Run away? From me? You couldn't if you tried. I've got you wrapped around my little finger."

Zuri laughed, pulling Genesis closer. "Is that so? And here I thought I was the one calling the shots."

"Oh, honey," Genesis cooed, reaching up to straighten Zuri's collar. "You keep thinking that."

The sounds of their guests interrupted their playful banter as they yelled out their approval at the DJ's song choice. They walked back inside to people watch.

"Isn't this place beautiful?" Zuri asked, holding Genesis closer.

"It is. Monique did her thing with the decor. I wasn't expecting it to be so elaborate," Genesis admitted, her gaze sweeping over the room. The large French doors were thrown open, offering a glimpse of the shimmering pool and lush gardens beyond.

"It reflects you," Zuri replied. "Elegant, extravagant in its simplicity, and breathtakingly beautiful."

Genesis chuckled, shaking her head as she nudged Zuri. "You're so corny."

"But you love it," Zuri countered, her voice certain.

"Maybe..." Genesis conceded, as she leaned in to whisper in Zuri's ear. "But only sometimes."

Zuri laughed, a rich sound that echoed in the grand space. "Only sometimes? I guess I'll have to up my game then," she said, her tone light.

"If you're this sappy now, what's going to happen at the wedding?"

Zuri shrugged. "You'll just have to marry me and find out, won't you?"

Genesis nibbled on her lip and gave her a little smirk before she wrapped her arms around Zuri's neck and pulled her in for a tender kiss. "I can't wait," she murmured, her voice breathy as they broke apart.

Elijah and Reggie chose that moment to intrude, their boisterous laughter echoing around them. "Are you two ever not making eyes at each other?" Elijah quipped, a genuine smile on his face.

"I don't know, are you ever anything less than annoying?" Zuri shot back causing Reggie to break into laughter.

Turning to Genesis, Reggie offered a smile. "Congratulations Gen, we're so happy for you both."

Genesis' face lit up. "Thank you, Reggie," she said before turning towards Zuri with a teasing smile. "Did you hear that? He's happy for us, even if Elijah here is grumbling."

Reggie elbowed Elijah. "Don't worry, he's just mad that Zuri and I beat him to the altar."

"Alright, alright. Jokes aside, I'm also happy for you two," Elijah conceded with a sigh, though his smile was genuine. He clapped Zuri's shoulder in an affectionate gesture.

Zuri looked at Genesis. "Yeah, I'm pretty damn lucky," she affirmed, reaching out to take Genesis' hand.

"And don't you forget it," Genesis added, her thumb softly brushing over Zuri's knuckles.

"I wouldn't dare," Zuri assured with a playful wink before turning back to her cousins. "I'm going to take my beautiful fiance out on the dance floor if y'all don't mind."

Reggie and Elijah both chuckled, stepping back to allow the couple room. "Enjoy yourselves," Reggie said, as he clapped Zuri on the back.

Elijah gave a mock bow, stepping aside with a flourish. "The dance floor awaits."

Genesis rolled her eyes playfully at their antics but allowed Zuri to guide her towards the dance floor. The strains of a slow song filled the room, the melody weaving around them like an intimate spell. Zuri wrapped her arms around Genesis' waist, pulling her close as they began to sway to the music.

"You know," Genesis began, her voice gentle as she rested her head on Zuri's shoulder. "It's been fun getting to know your cousins. They're like the brothers I never had."

"Good, you want to take them off my hands?" Zuri asked with a smile.

"Seriously, you're lucky to have them and all of your family."

Zuri looked around at her relatives scattered about the room. She tightened her grip around Genesis' waist. "And you are part of that family now, Genesis. We're in this together."

"That's a sweet sentiment, but I'll always be an outsider. It's okay, I've accepted that," Genesis said, her voice barely above a whisper.

Zuri pulled back, her brow furrowed as she looked into Genesis' eyes. "Hey, what's this about? You're not an outsider. .

You're the woman I love, the one I've chosen to spend my life with. My family adores you."

Genesis sighed, averting her gaze. "Yes, they like me, Zuri, but it's not the same. You all have these shared experiences, inside jokes, family traditions. I'm still learning all of that. I think it wouldn't bother me so much if I had that too. Shannon was like me. She didn't have any other family. This is so new for me."

"Why didn't you tell me sooner?"

Genesis looked down before settling back on Zuri's concerned face. "I didn't want to burden you with my shit and dampen your joy."

Zuri's eyes held a mix of love and sadness swirling in their depths. "Gen, your feelings could never be a burden to me. We're partners, remember? That means sharing the good and the bad. It's okay if you feel uncomfortable. This is all new for you. But I can guarantee that my family is excited to add you into the fold and even if they weren't, it wouldn't matter. It's you and me, always."

"You promise?" Genesis asked, unable to hide the tears she felt pricking her eyes.

"Every day for the rest of our lives," Zuri replied earnestly, cupping Genesis' face gently, brushing away a stray tear with her thumb.

Genesis smiled, the corners of her eyes crinkling. "I look forward to it," she said , leaning in for another kiss.

Their world fell away, and for a moment, it was just the two of them swaying to the music. The laughter and chattering of the party guests faded into a murmur in the background.

A chuckle from Zuri broke the moment as she rested her forehead against Genesis'. "We're going to make quite a pair at the altar, aren't we?"

The song ended, and the DJ announced they would be stopping so that guests could toast the couple.

"Let's go grab our seats, babe, so our friends and family can tell us how amazing we are," Zuri said, grabbing her hand.

Genesis grinned, following Zuri's lead as they navigated through the throng of people. She let her hand rest on Zuri's thigh once they were seated. The act of touching her provided Genesis with a sense of being grounded.

Reggie stood with a champagne glass in his hand. "Alright, folks," he began, drawing attention towards him. "I've known Zuri since we were kids running around in our grandmother's garden. And I've known Genesis for... less than that." He winked at Genesis, causing a bout of laughter. "But in the short time, I've come to see how truly special she is. I've never seen Zuri as happy as she's been these past few months. And it's all thanks to Genesis."

At his words, the room erupted into applause. Genesis blushed and fought the urge to look away. Instead, she turned to Zuri, who smiled and set her at ease.

"Now," Elijah chimed in, standing next to Reggie with his own champagne glass raised high, "I have a toast of my own. To Genesis and Zuri, for showing us that love comes in the most unexpected forms, and when it does, it changes everything. Here's to a future filled with happiness and all the good things in life. Cheers!"

There was a clinking of glasses throughout the room, and the sound of laughter swirled in the air. Genesis savored the moment, her heart thumping with joy.

More people stood up to toast them, but the biggest surprise was her sister. Kenzie had a hard time when she discovered that Genesis and Shannon were most definitely not getting back together. But, after a few months, Zuri won her over and now she was their biggest fan. It allowed for them to bridge a gap in their relationship that had been widening for far too long.

"Um, hey everyone, I'm Gen's sister, Kenzie," she began, her voice trembling slightly. The room fell silent, all eyes on her. "First, I would like to say how proud and happy I am for my sister. She is deserving of all the love and joy life could offer," she said, her voice growing stronger. "I'm grateful to see Genesis so in love and to see that love returned with equal measure by Zuri. And to Zuri, welcome to the family. We're pretty close knit, so you better stay on your P's and Q's."

Everyone laughed and raised their glasses. Genesis brushed at the tears in her eyes. When her vision cleared, she looked across the room and froze. Coming through the entrance was someone who bared an uncanny resemblance to her dead mother. Older but very much sporting a face she was sure she'd never see again.

She looked for Kenzie to make sure she wasn't going crazy, but her sister was grinning and running over to what she had almost thought was an apparition.

"Surprise, baby," Zuri whispered in her ear.

Genesis looked over at her, still confused. "I don't understand."

Zuri's smile faltered a bit when she saw her expression, but she caught herself and grabbed her hands. "I wasn't sure if I should keep it a secret, but Kenzie insisted. I know how long you've been wanting to get in touch with your family and…"

"What did you do?"

"I found them," Zuri confessed. "I found your aunt and uncle. You always talk about them, and the connection you lost."

Genesis could only gape as she watched Kenzie hug her mother's sister Rachel. Her husband Leonard was beside her, just as jolly as she remembered, only now his beard was peppered with gray.

Genesis swallowed over the lump in her throat and the room began to spin.

"You had no right," Genesis spit out before jumping up from her seat.

# Chapter Two

Genesis dashed towards the private bathroom, dodging people trying to offer their congratulations. Luckily, it was in the opposite direction from where her aunt and uncle had appeared. As she slipped through the heavy oak doors and into the tranquility of the lavatory, she leaned against the cool marble walls, bringing her hands to her face. A rush of hot tears burned her eyes, but she fought hard to stifle them. Didn't she want this? Hadn't she longed for some sort of connection to her roots for a long time now? Yet, the shock of it all overwhelmed her.

Her thoughts were racing as she tried to process what had just happened. The muffled sounds of the party outside seemed distant now, like a fading dream. She caught a glimpse of herself in the ornate mirror above the sink - her wild curls slightly disheveled, her brown eyes wide with a mix of excitement and fear.

"Get it together, Gen," she whispered to her reflection.

She smoothed her hands over her dress, the silky fabric cool against her trembling fingers. The weight of the moment pressed down on her shoulders. Meeting her aunt and uncle after all these years - it was supposed to be a joyous occasion. So why did she feel like running?

Genesis closed her eyes, remembering her aunt's smile, the proud glint in her uncle's eyes. They had looked at her with such love, such familiarity. As if they had known her all along.

She heard a soft knock on the bathroom door, and then an unexpected voice.

"Genesis, sweetheart, it's Veronique. Can I come in?"

Hearing her future mother-in-law's melodic voice made her anxiety ease up. Veronique's kindness was like a sweet embrace that filled the void of missing her mother.

After grabbing some tissue to dab at her eyes, she went over to let her in. "Hi Veronique. I'm sorry, I shouldn't have run out like that. Everyone must think I'm a total mess."

"Oh, I doubt that. We all adore you and Zuri and just wants you to be happy. She told me why you reacted the way you did and I can't say I blame you." She sat on a velvet chaise lounge, pushed against the wall and patted the space beside her. She pulled Genesis into a side hug when she sat down. "Does she resemble your mother?"

Genesis sighed. "How'd you guess?"

"You looked as if you'd seen a ghost. I don't know what it's like to lose a mother at a young age, but I'm familiar with grief. It's a shock to the system, isn't it? Especially when the person who's gone was such an important part of your life," Veronique said, her voice filled with understanding.

Genesis nodded, a sense of relief washing over her. "I never thought I'd see anyone who reminded me of her again. And then, out of nowhere, there she was."

Veronique squeezed her hand. "I can only imagine how overwhelming that must have been. Especially with all these emotions going on right now. But you know what I think?"

Genesis looked at Veronique, hanging on to her wise words. "What do you think?"

"This is a gift, Genesis. A chance to reconnect with a part of yourself and your history that you thought you'd lost. It's scary, but imagine the stories and memories they can share with you about your mother." Veronique's eyes were encouraging as she spoke.

Genesis bit her lower lip, considering this. "You're right... I guess I just panicked."

"My daughter meant well, but this should have been a discussion instead of some sort of grand gesture."

Genesis nodded. "I guess it's because I told her I don't care for material things. Now, she tries to show her affection in other ways."

Veronique smiled and stood up. "Sounds like she took what you said to heart. Come, let's fix your makeup."

As the pair spent the next few minutes retouching Genesis' makeup, they chatted about Zuri's childhood mishaps, making Genesis laugh and relax. By the time Veronique declared her ready to go back out, she felt better than she had moments ago. The older woman had a calming effect on her, something that still surprised Genesis considering the short time they'd known each other.

"Thank you, Veronique."

"You're welcome, my darling. Now," Veronique started, her voice slightly amused, "knowing Zuri she'll be worried sick about you."

Genesis chuckled at that, picturing Zuri pacing outside the door to the ladies' room. "She's having a panic attack herself, I'm sure."

Just then, there was a light knock on the door. Veronique smiled at Genesis once more and went to open it.

Zuri entered, her worried brown eyes opened wide. "Gen,

I'm so sorry, I didn't mean.." she began, but her mother cut her off.

"Sweetie," Veronique placed a hand on her shoulder, "Give Genesis a chance to speak, okay?"

"Yes, mother," Zuri replied, chastened.

Veronique left them alone. Genesis' gaze found Zuri's. Sincere remorse furrowed Zuri's brows. It touched a soft spot in Genesis' heart and she reached out to hold Zuri's hand.

"Zuri, it's okay."

"But... I screwed up. I wanted to surprise you, and..."

"You did surprise me," Genesis cut in, "Just not the way you expected."

"I'm sorry, baby." Zuri reiterated, her eyes shimmering with unshed tears.

Genesis' fingers traced the back of Zuri's hand before kissing it. "This was a lot. But it doesn't mean that I'm mad at you or that I don't appreciate what you tried to do for me."

Zuri nodded, absorbing every word Genesis spoke. "I should've talked to you about it first instead of assuming it would make you happy. When Kenzie said she was on board, I figured she would know better than me if you'd be okay with it."

"I would have been, but with a heads up." Genesis stood up with a sigh. "How about we say hello to my family?"

"Are you sure, Gen? You don't need a bit more time?" Zuri asked, her eyes still filled with concern.

Genesis nodded and picked up her clutch purse. "Yes, I'm ready. No time like the present. But I need you with me."

"You don't even have to ask," Zuri said, pulling Genesis into her arms. Burrowing into the comfort of Zuri's embrace, Genesis heaved a sigh of relief.

They walked out front and she could see Kenzie and Shannon chatting with her aunt and uncle. Her heart squeezed a bit in her chest as she took in her aunt's face again, so familiar and yet so foreign. She looked so much like her mother–or at least, like the woman she remembered. Her big brown eyes, her smile; it was all there.

"Here goes nothing," Genesis murmured under her breath, leaning into Zuri for support.

"Deep breaths," Zuri whispered back, pressing another kiss to Genesis' temple.

They approached the small group, and Shannon stood up. "Here Gen, take my seat."

"Thanks Shay," Genesis said, squeezing her arm. She faced her aunt and uncle's smiling faces. "Hi, Aunt Rachel and Uncle Lenny. It's been a while."

Her aunt's eyes shimmered with tears. "Too long Genesis. My goodness, you look just like Lynn." She wiped at her eyes with a tissue.

"It's so good to see you again, sweetheart," her uncle said with a genuine smile.

"I'm happy you're both here."

Kenzie looked as if she was going to burst with excitement. "Gen, they have four kids. They're having a family reunion too in three months. We have to go."

Genesis blinked at her sister. "Four?" she echoed, looking back atRachel and Lenny. The shock must have shown on her face as her uncle chuckled good-naturedly.

"Yes, four. There's Grace, who you knew, of course, but we had three more after you... after we last saw each other," he said, his voice trailing off awkwardly.

Genesis could hear the unspoken words hanging in the air - after you all disappeared from our lives.

"Wow," Genesis said before her aunt stepped in.

"They're all grown now, of course," she added, eager to shift away from the sensitive topic. "But they're very excited to meet you two. The whole family is thrilled to get reacquainted , but especially your grandmother."

Genesis' eyes widened. "Granny Lee is still alive?"

Uncle Lenny laughed out loud. "Alive and keeping us all in line, even at 90."

"I may or may not have been told how I better keep her granddaughter happy over the phone," Zuri said, making everyone laugh. "This trip was too much for her, but she wants to come to the wedding, if that's alright with you?"

Genesis smiled and nodded. "That's more than alright with me."

The conversation flowed after that, the initial awkwardness melting away as Lenny and Rachel shared more stories with Genesis and Kenzie. As they talked, she looked over at Zuri, who was just as absorbed in what was being said. Her love for her at that moment was so big, a tidal wave of happiness and gratitude.

* * *

The evening wore on, filled with laughter, tears, and countless stories. Genesis found herself leaning into Zuri, drawing strength from her presence as she navigated this unexpected reunion. Her aunt and uncle seemed eager to make up for lost time, sharing anecdotes about her mother that made Genesis' heart ache with a bittersweet mixture of joy and longing.

As the night drew to a close, Genesis felt a strange sense of peace settling over her. She squeezed Zuri's hand, silently communicating her gratitude. Zuri squeezed back, a silent "I'm here" that Genesis felt deep in her bones.

"We'd love to have you both visit us soon," Aunt Rachel said, her eyes full of hope. "If you and Kenzie come to the reunion, you can stay with us. It would give us a chance to catch up properly, away from all this..." she gestured vaguely at the opulent surroundings.

Genesis hesitated, feeling the weight of the invitation. It was one thing to reconnect here, in the safety of her engagement party, but to step fully back into that world? She glanced at Zuri, who gave her an encouraging nod.

"We'd love that," Genesis heard herself say, surprising with the steadiness in her voice. "Right Kenzie?"

Kenzie nodded enthusiastically. "Absolutely! I can't wait to meet the rest of the family."

Uncle Lenny beamed. "Wonderful! We'll send you all the details. And Genesis, don't worry about a thing. We'll take it slow, at your pace."

As they said their goodbyes, Genesis felt a whirlwind of emotions. She hugged her aunt and uncle, the familiarity of their embrace both comforting and overwhelming. When they pulled away, Aunt Rachel cupped Genesis' face in her hands.

"You look so much like your mother," Rachel said. "She would be so proud of the woman you've become."

Genesis did her best not to cry. "Thank you," she whispered.

As they watched her aunt and uncle leave, Zuri wrapped an arm around Genesis' waist. "You okay, love?"

Genesis leaned into her, taking a deep breath. "I think so. It's just... a lot to process." She stepped back and gazed into Zuri's eyes. "But, you did good."

"I'm just glad you're not upset anymore. I really thought I'd ruined everything."

Genesis shook her head. "You could never ruin anything, Z. You just... you have a way of shaking up my world in the best possible ways."

They stood there for a moment, lost in each other's eyes, until Kenzie's voice broke through their bubble.

"Hey lovebirds, I hate to interrupt, but Zuri, would you mind if I speak to Gen alone real quick?"

"Of course." Zuri kissed Genesis quickly on the lips. "Love you baby."

Genesis watched as Zuri walked away, then turned to face her sister. Kenzie's eyes were shining with mix of excitement.

"So," Kenzie began, fidgeting with the hem of her dress. "That was... intense."

Genesis let out a shaky laugh. "You can say that again. I still can't believe they're here."

"Are you really okay with all of this?" Kenzie asked, her voice unsure. "I mean, I know I got excited about the reunion, but if you're not comfortable..."

Genesis took a deep breath, considering her sister's words. "Honestly? I'm not sure. It's like... opening a door I thought was locked forever. But maybe it's time, you know?"

Kenzie nodded, reaching out to squeeze Genesis' hand. "I get it. And hey, whatever you decide, I'm with you. We're in this together, sis."

"Thanks, Kenz," Genesis said, feeling a rush of affection for her sister. "I don't know what I'd do without you."

They hugged tightly, and as they pulled apart, Genesis noticed Kenzie's eyes darting around the room. "Looking for someone?" she teased.

Kenzie blushed. "Maybe. That cute bartender from earlier... I thought I saw him again."

Genesis laughed, grateful for the lightness of the moment. "Go get him, tiger. I'll be fine."

As Kenzie scurried off in search of her potential conquest, Genesis found herself alone for the first time since the unexpected reunion. She took a deep breath, allowing the events of the evening to wash over her.

Genesis smiled to herself, thinking about how Zuri had

orchestrated this reunion. It was so typical of her fiancée - grand gestures with the best intentions, even if they sometimes missed the mark. But that was one of the things Genesis loved most about Zuri - her willingness to go all out for the people she cared about. Z was most definitely her person and Genesis hoped she made her feel as loved as she did in that moment.

# Chapter Three

"Are you there yet?"

Zuri did her best not to let out the annoyed sigh that was desperate to leave her lips as soon as she answered her cousin's call. Elijah had been texting her all morning about the meeting she was about to have.

"I am a few blocks away. Is there a reason you've been bombarding me with text messages? You are aware that I can close this deal, right?"

"Yeah, yeah, of course."

Zuri took a deep breath and massaged the bridge of her nose. Ever since she mentioned wanting to get rapper William Brody, a.k.a. Flo Easy, for their movie with Phillip Minor, Elijah had been nagging her nonstop. He was a fan in every sense of the word and thought he should be the one to bring him on. Both she and Reggie dismissed that idea because Elijah was highly talented in many respects, except for his lack of finesse when handling celebrities.

"I was just wondering if you remembered what I asked about yesterday?" Elijah said, panting.

Zuri sucked her teeth. "What are you doing that has you breathing so damn hard in my ear?"

"Sorry..running..treadmill," he squeaked out before asking her to hold on.

Zuri rolled her eyes and looked out the window. The studio where William worked was in a less than desirable part of town. She had hoped to get him out to their offices or at least a nice restaurant, but he insisted they meet where he made his music. It was a total power play, and she grudgingly respected him for it.

Her friend Devin McKinley was meeting them there as well for a photoshoot. To entice William to work with them, she asked Devin to shoot some photos for his feature in The Culture magazine's Leaders of the New Class issue, which focused on up-and-coming stars in the music industry.

Through a few conversations, it was clear that Flo Easy would not be easy to convince. While he had never acted before, he had done some in his music videos and she could tell he had raw talent. She wasn't always fond of singers and rappers acting since most of them were mediocre at best, but there was something about him that showed true potential. After reading the script for Minor's film, she couldn't picture anyone else in the part.

Elijah returned to the call, his breathing more controlled. "Sorry about that, Z. The setting changed and had me running harder than I expected."

"Eli, if you want an autograph from Flo Easy, you're gonna have to get it yourself. I am not asking this man to sign a damn t-shirt."

"It's not just any t-shirt, it's from his first world tour. I'm sure people ask him to sign that stuff all the time."

"We're here, Z," her driver said as he pulled alongside a nondescript building.

"Thanks Drake. Eli, I am not going back and forth with you about this. If he agrees to do the film, you can get him to sign the shirt."

"Zuri, wait..."

She hung up the phone and shoved it into her bag. Drake looked at her in the mirror with a smirk. His deep-set hazel eyes never missed a thing.

He was a recent hire and had been driving for her for over six months. Having a driver always seemed pretentious and wasn't something she ever considered, but Genesis wasn't comfortable with the number of late nights she had to do and insisted on her getting one. After some searching, an acquaintance of hers put her in touch with Drake's agency and the rest was, as they say, history.

"Elijah pushing your buttons again?" he said, his deep timbre filling up the car.

"Isn't he always? I almost wish I hadn't told him until I was sure we could get this guy to work with us." She looked outside, surveying the street. What she saw was less than appealing.

It had the kind of quiet that felt eerie, the stillness broken only by the distant hum of traffic. Zuri noted the cracked sidewalk, glancing around at the derelict buildings that lined both sides of the road. Faded signs hung from rusted metal posts, their messages long obscured by grime and years of neglect. Debris cluttered the sidewalks—old flyers flapped lazily in the breeze, shards of glass glittered in the fading daylight, and graffiti was scrawled across boarded-up windows.

She spotted the music studio wedged between two crumbling structures, the building's red brick exterior having turned a dull brown and the metal door rusted, its peeling paint revealing the name of the place in crooked, hand-painted letters. A grimy window sat next to it, too filthy to see through. Above, a flickering neon sign buzzed weakly, casting a sickly glow over the entrance. Abandoned cars, long forgotten by their owners, sagged at the curb, their flat tires and shattered windows a testament to the street's decay.

"I think I should go inside with you," Drake said as he also took stock of where they were.

Zuri contemplated taking him up on his offer. She had little information about Flo Easy, and her familiarity with the people he associated with was even lower. "I'm not sure the car should be left unattended. God only knows if it will still be here when we come back. I'll go in alone and if it doesn't seem right, I'll call you.

Drake nodded and kept his eyes glued to the building. Zuri removed her jewelry and had him place it in the glove compartment. Despite coming from money, she wasn't stupid.

Zuri stepped out of the car, her boots landing with a soft crunch on the cracked pavement. She straightened up, brushing a hand through her locs as she glanced around, eyes narrowing while she gazed down the street. Other than a few people who shuffled by, it was empty. The only store open was on the opposite side of the street, a liquor store with a faded sign.

As she walked toward the studio, her footsteps echoed in the quiet, the click of her boots sounding against the weathered concrete. She reached the rusted door, lifting a hand to ring the one button that seemed to work.

No one responded, but the door suddenly jerked as the buzzer sounded, indicating it was now open. Upon stepping inside, she discovered that it was much brighter and cleaner than she had expected.

"Sup, can I help you?" a lanky guy asked. He sat at a desk that appeared to be security of some sort.

"Yes, I'm meeting with William." He looked at her, confused. "I mean Flo Easy."

"Oh, he's upstairs, second floor. You gotta sign here," he said, jabbing at a binder with a sign-in sheet.

Zuri filled it out and offered a smile which wasn't returned.

He pulled the binder back towards him and nodded behind her. "You gotta take the elevator."

"Thanks."

Zuri eyed the elevator warily as she approached it. The old metal cage looked like it had been there since the building's early days, its once-polished surface now rusted and covered in grime. The sliding gate rattled as she pulled it open, the sound sharp in the otherwise quiet hallway. Inside, scuffed linoleum covered the floor, worn thin in places and revealing patches of the concrete underneath. A single bare bulb flickered weakly overhead, casting jittery shadows across the narrow, claustrophobic space.

As she stepped in cautiously, the entire elevator creaked under her weight as if it hadn't been used in years. The control panel was an antique—a small box with oversized buttons, their numbers barely visible from years of wear. Zuri pressed the button for the second floor, and the elevator jerked to life with a sudden lurch that made her grip the railing. The cage door slid shut with a metallic clang, and the elevator groaned as it ascended.

The ride was anything but smooth and eventually she made it to the next floor. She approached the gate to open it, but it was stuck. Even pulling with all her strength couldn't extricate it from its locked position.

"Oh, come on," Zuru mumbled under breath. "Hello?"

She called out, hoping someone was around, but from what she could tell, the hallway was empty. The only sound came from one room: muted bass and treble.

"Fuck this." Zuri jabbed at her phone and dialed Devin.

"Z, what's up?" Devin yelled. She could hear the music in the background.

"Please tell me you're in there with William."

"Yeah, he was just playing some tracks for me. You're almost here?"

"Oh, I'm here," she said, looking around the dingy elevator. "But I'm stuck in this piece of shit elevator."

"Oh shit, I'll be right there."

Zuri placed her phone back into her bag and, without thinking, leaned on one wall of the elevator. It groaned in protest as she jerked away from it, fearful she'd plummet to the floor below. If she didn't need a win so badly with this film, she would have already called it quits and headed back to her office. But Zuri wasn't one to give up, especially with business.

Devin appeared just as she was about to curse out the dilapidated box. "Oh thank God."

"I'm here to save the damsel in distress," Devin said with a cheeky smile.

Zuri gave him a death glare while he reached inside and flicked a mechanism that allowed him to open the gate.

"A little trick I learned when I arrived earlier."

"A warning might have been nice. This place is a piece of shit. What's an award-winning rapper doing making music here?"

"Authenticity. This is where he recorded his mixtapes and the album that got him those awards.Oh, and he owns the building."

As Zuri stepped out of the elevator, the hallway surprised her. Unlike the dilapidated exterior and the rickety elevator, the corridor was well kept. The floors were polished hardwood, and the walls, painted a muted charcoal gray, were smooth and clean, with only a few framed album covers and band posters hanging in neat rows. Each professionally mounted piece showcased the studio's history of successful projects and collabo-rations.

The air smelled of fresh wood polish, a pleasant contrast to the grime she had expected. Doors lined the hallway, each one marked with a small, engraved plaque naming the rooms—"Recording A," "Editing Suite," "Vocal Booth"—each door sturdy and solid, with silver handles that gleamed under the light.

Now and then, faint muffled sounds seeped through—snip-pets of a guitar riff, a few lines of vocals, the soft hum of conver-sation—but nothing loud enough to disrupt the calm. The space exuded sleek professionalism, creating a stark contrast with the building's exterior and giving the impression that the heart of the studio had fiercely shielded itself from the decay that surrounded it. Despite what it seemed, William cared for this space immensely.

Devin led her to Recording C and held the door open for her. Designed for high-end production, every inch of the immaculate and state-of-the-art studio space was carefully crafted. The floors were sleek, dark wood, polished to a shine that reflected the ambient lighting overhead. Soundproofing panels lined the walls, their geometric patterns adding a modern touch to the otherwise minimalist décor. In the center of the room, a large, high-tech mixing board dominated the space, its array of dials, switches, and glowing LED displays looking like the control panel of a spaceship. Behind it was a wide window, revealing the recording booth on the other side, lit and lined with cutting-edge microphones and equipment.

William and his entourage occupied the sleek leather couches along the back wall. He leaned back, his presence commanding even as he sat relaxed, dressed in a crisp designer tracksuit with a gold chain draped over his chest. His trademark sunglasses rested on his nose, even though the lighting was dim, and he wore a cap tilted to the side. Around him, his crew was deep in conversation, some scrolling through their phones, others laughing as they passed around bottled water and snacks. A couple of them nodded their heads in sync to the low beat playing from the studio's speakers, a track Flo Easy had likely just laid down.

"Zuri, it's a pleasure to meet you in person. You are," William gave her a once over. "Exquisite."

He stood to shake her hand, and she was thrown by both the compliment and his bright, dimpled smile.

"Thank you, but I'm going to have to ask that you keep the compliments to a minimum," Zuri said as she shook his hand.

"And why is that? Am I not allowed to appreciate a beautiful woman?"

Zuri raised an eyebrow, her hand still resting in his as she matched his gaze with steady confidence. "You're allowed," she replied, her voice cool but firm, "but I didn't come here for compliments. I came here to talk business."

William's smile didn't falter, but there was a flicker of amusement in his eyes. "Business, huh? Well, I respect that." He released her hand and took a step back, folding his arms. "Straight to the point. I like you already."

"Good," Zuri said, crossing her arms as well, keeping her tone professional. "Because I don't waste time, and I'm sure you don't either."

Zuri had gotten used to being in male dominated spaces and one thing she learned was to demand respect right out the gate. If she gave an inch, they would try to take a mile, so she gave nothing and made sure she came out on top in the end.

"You are right about that. Time is money. And it seems you want to make some with me. So how about we let Devin take his pics, then we can talk some more about this film of yours?"

Zuri glanced at her watch. "I do have somewhere I need to be, so.."

"I got you. Let me just play this track we laid real quick."

William went over to one of the guys at the mixing table and asked him to play a song called 'Get Over'. String instruments began playing over a swelling melody that launched into a pulsing beat.

*Click. Click. Click.* Devin leaned back and snapped a quick succession of photos before maneuvering to the other side of the music studio.

Will and his friends mouthed the words as the track played, their heads bobbing in sync with the infectious rhythm. Zuri found herself tapping her foot, impressed by the polished sound and clever wordplay. As the song reached its crescendo, William's eyes met hers, a knowing smile playing on his lips.

The track faded out, leaving a charged silence in its wake. "So, what do you think?" William asked, his gaze fixed on Zuri

She nodded appreciatively, maintaining her professional demeanor. "It's good. Very radio-friendly, but with depth. I can see why you're in such high demand."

Will's smile widened. "You contacted me for a reason right? Yo Ray, play the next one."

Zuri attempted to protest but Devin shook his head and leaned in. "This has been me all morning. You gotta just rock with it."

Zuri suppressed a sigh, realizing she'd have to play along if she wanted to make any progress. She settled into one of the plush leather chairs, crossing her legs and leaning back slightly. "Alright, let's hear it."

"Yo, Devin, can you make sure not to take any pictures with my face on the left side? I low-key hate that angle. It always makes me look like I have a double chin." William showed him a photo on his phone as he nodded to the music. "Last time I did a photoshoot, I swear that dumb-ass photographer only took pics from that angle. I'm tryna give Tupac. Can't do that if my shit isn't on point. You feel me?"

One guy from his entourage, Ricky, burst into laughter. "Tupac? Have you looked in a mirror? It's like someone used the DNA of Michael B Jordan and mixed it with the predator."

Zuri stifled a laugh, covering it with a cough. William shot daggers at Ricky, while the rest of the guys broke into raucous laughter. After spending a couple of hours with the group, she was now used to the constant jabs they took at each other. To an outsider, it might have looked malicious, but it was all in good fun. They had known each other for years and were closer to each other than most of their families.

"I believe Will meant he is trying to channel the energy of Tupac, not his exact look, right?" Devin asked and Will nodded his head. "What you guys don't understand is this." Devin brought his camera over to William and showed him the picture. "A good photographer can get you whatever shot you desire."

"Damn, this is nice," Will said, snapping his fingers.

Devin stood off to the side while Will passed the picture around. Everyone agreed he struck the perfect balance. From experience, Zuri could tell the shot would be his profile picture for the magazine. Devin had a serious talent for choosing photos for his celebrity spreads, which made him much sought after.

"Told you he was good, Will. He did an amazing job shooting photos of my cousins and I," Zuri said, giving Devin a pound.

Will smiled wide, his diamond encrusted grill sparkling in the light. "Thanks for putting me on Z. I like what we've got so far."

Devin took back his camera. "I'm glad you like it. We have a session for more traditional pictures, but I think this is the one. I've got another shoot to run to, but I'll see you soon." After shaking hands with Will, Devin leaned in and kissed Zuri's cheek. "And thank you for setting this up."

"Of course, we're family. Let me know about that dinner with Marisa."

Devin gave his last farewell and left the room. Zuri smiled and noticed most of the guys were on their phones. It was a task to hold their attention for longer than the average TikTok.

"So, Will, have you thought some more about what we talked about or..."

Will looked up and signaled at his crew with his hand. "Yo, we need some privacy."

Ricky and the rest of Will's entourage filed out of the room. Will lit up a joint that had been lying dormant while he shot pictures. He offered it to Zuri, but she declined.

"Here's the thing, Z, I'm not sure this role is for me. Like it's solid writing, but I don't know if I have the level of talent to pull it off."

One of the first lessons Zuri learned in the early days of running the studio was how to be diplomatic. Finding the words to convince an actor to take on a role was an art, and she had taught herself to become Picasso.

"Are you aware of the reason I selected you to be the lead in this film?""

Will shook his head. "Honestly? Nah."

"There was a scene in the movie Juice where Tupac and Omar Epps are in the hallway, and Epps tells him he doesn't want to be a part of his crew anymore and calls Tupac crazy," Zuri saw Will's eyes light up and she knew she was going in the right direction, "And Tupac says that famous line, 'I am crazy, but you know what else..."

"I don't give a fuck," Will finished for her. "Bro, I love that movie. He was so good. It gave me chills the first time I saw it."

"It's like he wasn't acting. But did you know Tupac attended a school for the arts? It's part of why he was so damn good. Now you? You've got raw talent, and I'm rarely wrong about the people I choose for my films. Plus, you get the opportunity to work with Phillip Minor. If this succeeds, you could be the next Pac. Acting, rapping and playing in the major leagues. There are actors who would kill for this role, so I am not offering this lightly."

Will sat back in his chair and stroked his goatee. Although his crew was making fun of him earlier, he was a handsome young man. He had a head full of beautiful locs and blemish free brown skin. The gym was his second home besides his music studio and it showed in his muscular build. At 6 '2 he was the perfect height, weight and look for an actor without the polish, but she knew a diamond when she saw one.

He still looked unsure, so she tried a different angle. "Have you seen any of Phillip Minor's films?"

"Maybe like one or two, but I'm not that familiar with his work."

"I bet you know it better than you think." Zuri pulled out her phone and showed him some iconic scenes from Minor's films. His face lit up with recognition.

"Yo, I had no idea some of that stuff was from his movies. There are memes and shit based on those clips."

"He's been working for decades creating amazing black cinema. Having him come to our studio to make his next film is major. You're sitting at the precipice of your career. If you feel a pull towards it, why not do it too?"

Will leaned forward, his eyes intense as he focused on Zuri. "You think I could be that good?"

Zuri nodded. "I wouldn't be here if I didn't. Will, this role was made for you. It's gritty, it's real, and it's going to put you on the map. This year The Culture, next year Vanity Fair."

It wasn't explainable, but there was always a subtle shift when an actor or musician took on a role. Zuri had seen it countless times, and she saw it now in Will's eyes. The hesitation melted away, replaced by a spark of excitement and determination.

"Okay, you've been in my ear enough. I'm down to do it."

"That's what I'm talking about." Zuri put out her fist to give him a pound. "You won't regret this. Phillip wants you to audition for him, but it's just a formality. I promise."

"No doubt," Will said, unable to hide his smile. "Listen, I'm having a listening party next Saturday. I'd love it if you came. It's gonna be a good time and I can introduce you to some people I know."

Flo Easy's music was mumble rap to her, the work of a generation that she didn't get. A Tribe Called Quest, Heavy D, and LL Cool J were some of the old school artists she still had on rotation. She was oblivious to what was popular, but she would never miss a chance to network.

"Thanks, Will, that sounds great. Send me the info and I'll be there." Her phone buzzed in her pocket and Genesis' name popped up. She excused herself and went into the hallway to answer. "Hi, honey, is everything okay?"

Genesis sighed. "It would be better if you were here in bed with me."

A grin spread across Zuri's face as she leaned against the wall. "You know I would much rather be there with you and not in a room full of weed smoking pseudo intellectuals. What is it about marijuana that makes people think they're so clever?"

"Without having ever studied it, I would guess that cannabis functions like other psychoactive drugs. It opens your mind, you become relaxed, and you find clarity in your thoughts that differ from when your brain chemistry isn't altered. Hence, the popularity of hallucinogens. Whether it enhances anything, the likelihood is slim."

Zuri took a moment to bask in Genesis' voice and intelligence. "God, you are so sexy when you talk like that. Maybe I should leave here early and meet you at your place."

Genesis groaned in agony. "I wish, but I already agreed to an early dinner with Lucy. It's been months since we've been able to hang outside of work," she said. "But you could let yourself in and we can hang out after."

They had exchanged keys to each other's homes. Since they both owned their properties, moving in wasn't simple, so they compromised by giving each other access to their spaces. Zuri had yet to take advantage because she had been busy, but her schedule was opening up.

"That sounds like a plan. So, did you just call because you missed me or..."

Genesis let out a husky chuckle, and Zuri already knew where the conversation was going. She walked down the hall, trying doors until she found a studio space that wasn't being used. Once inside, she locked the door and settled into a cushioned chair by a mixing table.

"Are you over there having fun without me?" Zuri asked with a smirk.

"You left so early, and when I woke up, I needed your hands on me. But you weren't here, so I had to take care of myself," Genesis said with a moan.

Her heart racing, Zuri leaned forward in the seat and asked, "And what are those hands doing right now?"

Genesis responded with another moan, this one deeper, and Zuri could picture her spread eagle on her bed. Her voluptuous body writhing against the sheets while she caressed and teased herself.

"Oh baby, they're caressing my thighs. I'm imagining your lips dragging against them like you do, right before..."

"Before what?" Zuri asked, knowing what she would say next but longing to hear her say it, anyway.

These phone sessions had become a regular part of their relationship and while it took getting used to, Genesis loved it. They were busy women and sometimes spent weeks apart because of Zuri's work. Genesis was reminded of why things had worked so long with Tracy because she had a similar schedule. But unlike her ex, she did her best to be there for Genesis. Whether it was phone sex, or making sure to always take her call, Zuri wanted the woman she loved to feel that love.

Genesis' breath hitched as she continued to pleasure herself. Zuri swallowed and tried to remain calm, even as she felt wetness gathering below. She had to seal this deal, but damned if she didn't want to leave early and head to Genesis' place.

"Mmmm, before you put your mouth on me. I love it when you tease me," Genesis said, her voice cracking. She went quiet, and for a moment Zuri thought maybe she'd gotten distracted. That was put to rest when she released a deep groan of ecstasy. She mumbled Zuri's name over and over as her breathing slowed down.

"I love listening to you," Zuri said, her voice dropping an octave lower as she leaned back against the chair, letting the subtle tones of pleasure reverberating from Genesis wash over her like a warm tide. "I wish I could be there to see your face, to touch you."

"I wish you were here, too, but I must share you with the world. I should let you get back to work. Wouldn't want Flo Easy to get annoyed with you."

Zuri laughed. "Oh please, 'Flo Easy' is about as harmless as it gets. Trust me, I've met some of the big dogs who are about that life. It's all for show with most of these new rappers, but that's not my business. I'm just here to get the next breakout star for my movie."

"And you do a wonderful job."

"Thanks sugar. By the way, William invited us to a listening party for his new album. Are you down to go?"

Genesis sucked her teeth. "Am I down to go? I'm not a total nerd, okay? Ride or Die is my jam." She started spouting off lyrics from Flo Easy's latest release and it had Zuri doubled over with laughter. "What? I can't only listen to jazz and classical music. I'm multifaceted."

Zuri wiped the tears of laughter from her eyes. "That you are, baby."

Ricky's deep baritone followed a swift knock on the door. "Ay yo Zuri, you in there?"

"Yes, I'll be right out." Zuri clutched the phone and made kissing sounds. "I love you, but I have to go."

"Mmmm, I felt each one of those kisses on me. I love you too, Z. Can't wait to see you later."

"Same here, babe."

When she swung the door open, Ricky stood there laughing at something on his phone. He acted as one of Flo Easy's body-guards and had the stature to back it up. At 6 ′5 and 300 pounds, most of it muscle, he was intimidating. But once you got to know him, you soon found out he was a big teddy bear. Still, he wasn't afraid to pop off if the situation called for it.

"Yo, you ever watch this dude, Trey? His videos are hilarious," Ricky said as they began walking back to the studio.

"I've watched a video or two. His skits are like a modern day Jackass but with Black guys."

"What's Jackass?" Ricky asked as he held the door for her.

Zuri shook her head. She always forgot how young the crew was. The oldest had just made 25. "I'll show you after we finish the shoot."

"Cool." Ricky went and took up residence in the corner he'd been occupying.

Zuri went through her phone and looked for some documents that she needed to send to William. "Okay Will, let's talk more about how we can help you get your Tupac on."

"Sounds good, but I'm thinking we should go out to dinner to celebrate. It's already that time, anyway. You down?" Will turned to her, waiting for an answer.

Zuri hesitated for a moment, weighing her options. She had plans to meet Genesis later, but there was still time before that. Plus, this was a prime opportunity to solidify the deal and build rapport with Will.

"You know what? That sounds great."

# Chapter Four

A few days later, Genesis stood on the sidewalk outside of the restaurant La Rosetta, the summer breeze tousling her wild curls. She smoothed down her flowy sundress, a vibrant yellow that popped against her skin. Her fingers tapped a restless rhythm against her thigh as she scanned the street for any sign of Kenzie's car.

The anticipation of seeing her aunt and uncle after so many years had Genesis' stomach in knots. She had hoped that Zuri would be with her that morning, but she was in Las Vegas meeting with investors. The night they were supposed to meet up, Zuri went out celebrating with Flo Easy and his crew. By the time they were done, it was early morning and Zuri didn't want to disturb her, so she had gone home instead. Genesis understood, but she felt a twinge of disappointment. Five days had passed since they last kissed, touched or been in each other's presence. It was five days too long.

A familiar blue sedan pulled up to the curb, and Kenzie emerged, her face a mirror of Genesis's nervous excitement. The sisters embraced, drawing strength from each other.

"What took you so long? I couldn't go inside without you."

Kenzie pulled out a stack of papers from her bag.

Genesis raised an eyebrow as Kenzie presented one of them. "What on earth is that?"

"So, I told you I had a lot of questions, and I know you said that maybe I shouldn't bombard our aunt and uncle with too many. But then I couldn't figure out what I should ask. So I typed out all the questions I was thinking about, and I added bullet points for the things that might need clarification. If you look, "Kenzie pointed to the top of the first page," I left the most important ones on here."

Genesis laughed, shaking her head at her sister's thoroughness. "Kenz, you're something else. But maybe we should ease into things before whipping out the interrogation, huh?"

Kenzie nodded sheepishly, tucking the papers back into her bag. "Oh by the way ," she said, her eyes suddenly lighting up, "I meant to tell you earlier, but with all the excitement about today, it slipped my mind. Remember that glitch in the payroll system at the firm? The one that was causing all those discrepancies in the overtime calculations?"

Genesis nodded, her brow furrowing at the memory of the headache-inducing problem that had plagued their accounting department for weeks. "Don't tell me you cracked it?"

Kenzie's smile widened, a hint of pride in her eyes. "I did more than crack it, sis. I completely overhauled the entire system. You know how I've been taking those coding classes on the side? Well, I put my newfound skills to the test."

Genesis listened in amazement as Kenzie detailed her solution, describing how she had identified a flaw in the original coding and rewrote entire sections to create a more efficient, error-proof system. Genesis felt a swell of pride for her sister's accomplishment.

"Damn, it sounds like you need a raise because that is amazing. I don't know what we would do without you Kenzie, seriously."

Kenzie smiled, but Genesis saw a flash of emotion that she couldn't pinpoint.

"Thanks, sis. I'm glad to help. Anyway, I think we've kept them waiting long enough," Kenzie said, holding the door for Genesis.

The brassy jingle of the door chime announced their arrival, the sound weaving through the bright and open space. Genesis paused just inside the threshold, her eyes taking in the elegant interior of the restaurant. The aroma of garlic and fresh basil wafted towards her, a culinary prelude that did little to ease the fluttering sensation in her stomach.

"Come on," Kenzie urged, her fingers brushing against Genesis's arm, grounding her.

Genesis nodded and followed Kenzie's lead, her body rigid with a cocktail of emotions. She allowed her gaze to travel over the tables draped in crisp white linens, past the waitstaff, who moved with an almost choreographed grace between patrons, their trays laden with colorful dishes.

"Are you okay?" Kenzie's voice was a gentle nudge, pulling Genesis back from the precipice of her thoughts.

"Uh-huh," she nodded, though her smile didn't quite reach her eyes. There was a rawness to this anticipation, one that the usual comforts couldn't temper. Zuri's reassuring words played in her mind, but she was still on edge.

"Let's find them," Kenzie said, no sign of fear whatsoever.

Kenzie had been only five the last time she saw their family. Her age seemed to make it easier for her to accept and want to embrace them faster. Genesis wished for that same ease, the childlike ability to forgive and forget in order to indulge in simple joys.

She saw them seated at a corner table bathed in soft sunlight filtering through the large windows. Aunt Rachel was mid-laugh, tossing back her head, her gray hair catching the sun's rays. Uncle Lenny's smile was infectious, crinkling around his eyes and revealing laugh lines that spoke volumes about a life lived with joy.

Kenzie was already halfway there when Genesis came out of her brief stupor and followed her.

"There you two are. We wanted to wait for you before ordering," Rachel said, giving them both a kiss.

Lenny grinned at them. "We were discussing ordering tea."

"What's so special about tea?" Kenzie asked as she picked up a menu.

Rachel began digging in her bag. "Your mom used to make her own special brews. The reason we were laughing is she refused to buy tea in a store, and acted like it was worse than dishwater." She withdrew a small tin box, worn with age, and placed it on the table. Genesis leaned in closer at the sight of it. "She'd mix different herbs and flavors, always experimenting. It was her little hobby."

Genesis' heart tightened at the mention of her mother's forgotten passion. In the stringent confines of their religious community, her mother had been allowed few individual pursuits outside of family care and devotion to faith.

Kenzie touched the tin. "This was hers?"

"Yes! The last one she made before everything changed."

Genesis reached out, her fingertips brushing the cool metal of the tin. A rush of memories entered her mind - her mother's smile over the brew, the comforting smell filling their modest home, and the soothing taste that never failed to turn a bad day around. It was a fragment of the mother she remembered before their isolation - free-spirited, creative, and full of love.

"There's enough in there for the two of you to share. When

you're ready, it might be nice to share a cup and remember her," Lenny said.

Genesis nodded, her eyes welling up with the unexpected rush of emotions, and she closed her hand over the tin. The physical contact seemed to draw out the memories trapped within its confines, and she took in a shaky breath as her heart thrummed with a mix of sadness and joy.

Rachel reached out, laying her hand atop Genesis's. "We don't mean to upset you girls. Just thought it might be a nice way of reconnecting."

"No," Genesis assured her, shaking her head and managing a small smile. "It's...it's perfect."

She glanced at Kenzie, who mirrored her sentiment with a teary yet resolute nod. "Thank you, Aunt Rachel."

"Well, that's one way to start lunch," Rachel said, wiping away tears of her own.

"Let's order, shall we?" Lenny interjected then, lightening the mood.

After perusing the menu, everyone placed their orders. Genesis sensed Kenzie's restlessness as she tapped her foot. Her sister had a million questions, but now that they were face to face, it seemed she didn't want to overwhelm them. So Genesis took the lead, wanting to bring order to the emotional chaos swirling around them.

"Aunt Rachel, Uncle Lenny," she began, her voice steady and firm. "I hope you know how much it means to us that you're here. Even after all these years, it's a gift."

"We were always there in spirit, Genesis," Rachel said. "We never stopped loving you girls."

"The distance never mattered," Lenny added with a shrug. "You were always in our hearts."

"Can I ask you something?" Kenzie piped in. They both nodded. "What was mom like when she was a kid?"

"Oh, Lynn was a firecracker," Rachel said with a chuckle. "Always full of energy and ideas. She'd dragged me into many adventures."

"Really?" Genesis leaned forward, intrigued.

"Oh yes," Rachel continued, looking into the distance. Your mother was always coming up with these grand schemes. One summer, she decided we were going to open a lemonade stand. But not just any lemonade stand - she wanted to make it the fanciest one in the neighborhood."

Lenny chuckled, shaking his head. "I remember that. She had us all running around collecting flowers to decorate the stand."

"And she insisted on using actual glasses instead of paper cups," Rachel added. "Said it would make us seem more 'sophisticated'."

Kenzie glanced at Genesis, her eyes saying that she was trying to reconcile this image of their mother with the reserved, serious woman she had known. But Genesis had known that woman, and it was her she mourned every day.

"What happened?" Kenzie asked.

Rachel's laughter filled the air. "Well, we set up our fancy stand, complete with a lace tablecloth and flower arrangements. But about an hour in, a gust of wind came through and knocked everything over. Glasses shattered, lemonade everywhere - it was a disaster."

"Oh no," Genesis gasped.

"Your mother, though, she didn't miss a beat. While I was ready to pack it in, Lynn just looked at the mess, put her hands on her hips, and declared, 'Well, now we have a story to tell!'"

The image of her mother as a spirited, resilient young girl made Genesis happy. It was a side of Lynn she had known briefly that was eventually buried beneath years of strict religious observance and isolation.

"She sounds so... different," Kenzie said, voicing Genesis's own thoughts.

Rachel's smile turned bittersweet. "She was. Your mother had such a zest for life, always ready with a joke or a crazy idea. It was hard to see that spark dim over the years."

Genesis swallowed hard, fighting back the lump forming in her throat. "When did you first notice the change in her?"

Lenny and Rachel exchanged a look, a silent conversation passing between them. Finally, Lenny spoke, his voice gentle but firm.

"It was gradual at first. Your father had always been more serious, more inclined towards religion. But Lynn balanced him out, kept things light. Then, bit by bit, she started pulling away. Stopped calling as much, declined invitations."

"We tried to reach out," Rachel added, her eyes glistening. "But each time we did, it appeared as though we were creating more distance between us."

Genesis nodded, reminiscing about the discomfort that would fill the house whenever extended family was mentioned. The way her mother's shoulders would tighten, her smile becoming forced.

"Did you ever try to..." Kenzie hesitated, searching for the right words. "I don't know, intervene?"

Rachel's eyes clouded with regret. "We did try, a few times. But it only seemed to make things worse. Your father saw our attempts as attacks on their faith, and your mother...she just retreated further into herself."

"The last time we saw you girls," Lenny continued, his voice thick with emotion, "it was at a family barbecue. You were so little, Kenzie. And Genesis, you were this bundle of energy, always dancing and twirling."

Genesis smiled, remembering her childhood love of movement that had blossomed into a love of dance.

"Your mother seemed almost like her old self that day," Rachel added. "Laughing, joking around. But when it was time to leave, something changed. She hugged us tight, like she knew it would be the last time. And then...they were gone."

The table fell silent, each lost in their own thoughts and memories. A mixture of grief and anger bubbled up inside of Genesis - grief for the years lost, the relationships severed, and anger at the circumstances that had torn her family apart.

Kenzie broke the silence, her voice small but determined. "But we're here now. We can make new memories, right?"

Genesis spoke, gripping her sister's hand. "Yes, of course we can do that, Kenz. It's what she would want."

The rest of their lunch passed in a ripple of shared stories and laughter from the past, each memory knitting together the torn fabric of their family history. Genesis' initial discomfort ebbed away, replaced by a sense of serenity she hadn't known this reunion could bring. The love that bloomed around that table was palpable, and Genesis laughed along with Kenzie and their aunt and uncle at a story about their mother's fearful encounter with a garter snake.

"You've got your mother's feistiness, Kenzie, I can tell," Rachel said, pointing a finger at her with a hearty chuckle. "And you," she added, turning to Genesis, "you've got her gentle strength."

Genesis had always strived to embody the strength and resilience of their mother, who, despite the confines of their old life, had left indelible impressions of love on her children.

Their conversation continued to meander between tales of the past and their present lives. Lenny and Rachel expressed genuine delight over Genesis' upcoming nuptials.

"She's quite a woman," Rachel said, referring to Zuri. "You're lucky, Genesis."

Genesis beamed at her aunt's sentiment and echoed it with a nod. "I am, aren't I?"

When they said their goodbyes in the late afternoon, Genesis experienced a sense of fulfillment that had evaded her for years. The void left by their parents' decision to cut them off from the rest of the world had been filled in a way she hadn't thought possible. Hugs were exchanged, as well as promises to keep in touch. Genesis reached for Kenzie's hand as they watched them drive away.

# Chapter Five

When she got home, Genesis received a text from Zuri that she was coming over to her place straight from the airport. She smiled at her phone, her heart fluttering with anticipation. Then she took one look around the house, suddenly aware of the clutter that had accumulated over the past few days. With a burst of energy, she sprang into action, determined to make the space presentable before Zuri's arrival.

She flitted from room to room, gathering stray books and magazines, straightening throw pillows, and whisking away dirty dishes to the kitchen. As she loaded the dishwasher, she hummed a tune from a dance routine she'd watched at Beacon, her body swaying to the rhythm.

With the living areas tidied, Genesis turned her attention to the bedroom. She made the bed with crisp efficiency, smoothing out the wrinkles in her favorite purple duvet. A spritz of lavender linen spray added a touch of freshness to the air.

With the house looking more presentable, Genesis glanced at the clock. Zuri's flight wouldn't land for another hour, which left her with some time to kill. Feeling restless, she decided a workout might help calm her nerves and pass the time.

She changed into her favorite leggings and sports bra, pulling her wild curls into a messy bun atop her head. Genesis rolled out her yoga mat in the center of the living room, the late afternoon sun streaming through the windows and warming the hardwood floors.

Twenty minutes later, she licked the bit of sweat gathering on her upper lip, her eyes glued to the window as she held herself steady in a warrior pose. When she released, she felt a twinge of pain in her abdomen, signaling the pain to come after the intense workout she had just completed. It was a small price to pay to keep herself in shape. She was grabbing her water bottle from the counter when she heard her phone ringing. A quick glance told her it was a call from Andrea. They hadn't spoken in a while, so this was a pleasant surprise.

During her drama with Zuri, Andrea had played many roles, confidante, cheerleader, and voice of reason. Meanwhile, she had also been juggling her own relationship and getting her business off the ground. Somewhere during the time of Genesis doing the same, their connection slipped. Andrea broke off her engagement with her girlfriend Natalie, and Genesis had been so caught up in her own whirlwind romance that she'd barely registered the pain her best friend must have been going through. But she did her best to be there for her.

A year later and they still hadn't talked about the change. They were both tiptoeing around what needed to be said. Genesis had won Zuri, but somehow had lost her best friend.

"Hey stranger," Genesis said after picking up. She placed the phone against the wall of the breakfast nook so she could take a seat and wouldn't have to hold it.

"Ooh girl, you're breathing like you just ran a marathon. Are you still doing that workout routine you've been texting me about?" Andrea asked, speaking over whatever she had just placed in her mouth.

"Yes, and what did I tell you about calling me while you eat?" Genesis asked, clucking her tongue.

There was a brief pause while she chewed and swallowed. "I'm trying to be efficient. I've been making calls all day, so I saved the best for last."

Andrea was a graphic designer and in high demand, so it touched Genesis that she was making time for her.

"So kind of you to put me in your rotation," she said sarcastically.

"You're welcome," Andrea replied, ignoring her tone. "So, how is life? The short version because I have about," she looked down at her watch, "fifteen minutes."

"A time limit?"

"Efficient."

Genesis laughed. "I've been good. Work is... work. Having some issues with a new hire."

"They're likely intimidated by you. When I was still working for other people, almost every person I had a problem with took issue with the fact that I was not only good at my job, but better than them. Once I became my own boss, it was such a weight off my shoulders."

"Yeah, I think it's just me getting used to being in charge of staff. It's still surreal."

"You couldn't pay me to manage people, so more power to you. But it's your business, so if someone is stepping out of line, then you need to remind them who's in charge. If they can't handle that, they can go."

"Zuri said the same thing, but she's been at this a lot longer, so she has no qualms about laying down the law."

Genesis enjoyed working for herself and knew that she could never go back to being under someone else's thumb in a corporate setting. Going into business on her own was harder than she had thought, as Zuri let her know in a not-so-subtle way in the beginning, but she had no regrets. This was what she wanted.

"How is Ms. Zuri? I've been seeing your lovey dovey pictures on social media."

Genesis' mind flashed to her last post. A picture of them after dinner at Nobu. It was a good night and their smiles matched just how happy they felt inside. But that date had been over a month ago, and the most they'd been able to manage were late night hookups and movie dates at home. Genesis loved spending time with Zuri no matter what they were doing, but she wasn't ready to admit how much she missed their more elaborate dates and quality time together. The whirlwind of their romance had settled into a comfortable routine, which Genesis appreciated, but there was a part of her that longed for their early days.

She sighed, her fingers tracing the rim of her water bottle. "Things are good with Zuri. It's just..." she trailed off, struggling to put her feelings into words.

"Just what?" Andrea prompted.

Genesis bit her lip, choosing her words carefully. "I love our life together, I do. But sometimes I miss the spontaneity, you know? The surprise dates, the long talks that would last until dawn. Now it feels like we're just... existing side by side sometimes."

She thought back about the impromptu dancing in the kitchen, the midnight picnics on their balcony, the way Zuri would surprise her with little gifts or notes hidden around the house. Those gestures hadn't disappeared entirely, but they had become less frequent as work and life responsibilities piled up.

"Have you talked to her about this?" Andrea asked, her voice gentle.

Genesis shook her head. "I don't want her to think I'm unhappy or ungrateful. Because I'm not. I just... I guess I'm worried we're falling into the trap of comfortability."

"The honeymoon phase doesn't last forever, girl. But that doesn't mean the love isn't there. You just have to make time for each other."

"I know, I know. It's just sometimes I worry that our lives are moving in different directions. Zuri's always jetting off for work, and I'm here trying to build my business."

"Gen, honey, communication is key. You can't bottle this up. Zuri loves you, but she's not a mind reader."

Genesis didn't fail to notice the parallels between her statement and what was happening between them.

"I don't think I ever felt this way before. So worried about saying and doing the wrong thing. Not even with Shannon, and I put up with so much from her."

"That's because you had to sacrifice yourself for Shannon. She was all about her wants and needs. Zuri treats you the way you deserve to be treated, with respect and love."

"You're right, but it scares me a little, Andrea. The way I feel about her. I've given so much before and.."

"You're scared that you'll get lost in her, and she might not reciprocate those feelings?"

"Something like that," Genesis said, nibbling on her bottom lip.

"You can't worry about what-ifs. Zuri shows you she loves you by her actions and that is what's important. Besides, you shouldn't get lost in anyone. Remember, you are a fully realized woman on your own and if she was gone tomorrow, you would still be Genesis. Love isn't about becoming one with someone and disappearing. It's about two people loving and supporting each other to grow and become something greater than you are alone."

Genesis placed her hand over her heart. "That was poignant. When did you get so wise?"

"Shit, let my mom tell it, I know nothing and she swore I was going to die an old maid. I told her mom, then I'll die an old maid. I'm not out here trying to have anyone run over and through me like Marie."

Genesis grimaced at the mention of Andrea's sister. Married since her mid-twenties, Marie had been to hell and back with her philandering husband, Omar. They had four kids together, and she always wondered how she continued to smile and appear happy when everyone knew he had an entire other family and treated her like shit.

When Andrea and Genesis met in college, she remembered Marie visiting the school, always a kid in tow. She would arrive on campus, looking exhausted but still managing a smile, a toddler perched on her hip and another child clinging to her leg. Even then, there were whispers about Omar's infidelity, but Marie never spoke of it. Instead, she'd regale them with stories of her children's latest antics, her eyes lighting up as she described finger-painted masterpieces and first words.

"I can't believe she's still with him. How does your mom find that acceptable?"

"She thinks it's noble, Marie being this long-suffering wife that maintains her home and has raised her kids to be studious and polite. Meanwhile, I'm trying to create a genuine and happy life and all she can do is ask when I'm going to give her grandkids. It's ludicrous."

"Internalized misogyny runs deep in some women, especially from the older generation," Genesis said with a sigh. "Anyway, how is Rebecca?"

"Driving me crazy with planning my birthday party. She has lots of grand ideas."

"Well, it's your 40th. Are you okay with that?"

"Whatever my lady wants, I'm good with."

Genesis nodded and gave her a smile, but she wondered if it was true. Andrea had always been opinionated, but ever since she met Rebecca, there had been a subtle shift. She was reluctant to say anything because the change could be attributed to maturity as much as Andrea's desire to please the woman in her life. Genesis kept her thoughts to herself, not wanting to project her insecurities onto her friend, who seemed happy.

"How's rock climbing going? I remember you talking about getting your guide's certification and everything."

"Yeah, I decided not to do it."

Genesis blinked in surprise. Rock climbing had been Andrea's passion for years. She'd drag Genesis out of bed at ungodly hours on weekends in college, determined to catch the first light on the cliffs. Andrea used to say there was nothing quite like conquering a challenging route. The rush of adrenaline as she reached the top, the world spread out beneath her.

When she moved to Colorado, one of the first things she did was check out the climbing scene. Most of her friends were from the climbing group she joined.

"You loved it so much. What happened?" Genesis asked, trying not to sound judgmental.

"Things change. Rebecca's not into outdoor stuff like that. She prefers yoga and spin classes. We've been trying out Cross Fit as well."

"You could still go on your own or with other friends."

"I guess," Andrea said. "It's just... Rebecca worries, you know? She thinks it's too dangerous. And, with work, I don't have much free time, anyway."

"Well, as long as you're happy," Genesis said. "That's what matters."

"I am sweetie. Very much so. By the way, I am so excited to see you and meet Zuri for my birthday."

Picking up that she wanted to change the subject, Genesis put on a cheerful voice. "One more month and I get to hug you in person again. It's been too long."

"Way too long." Andrea let out a sigh. "I hate that we weren't able to make it to the engagement party. Covid had my ass laid out for over a week. How was lunch with the family?"

Genesis leaned back in her chair, a smile creeping onto her face as she recalled the afternoon. "Amazing. Awkward at first, but after that... it felt like home, you know?" She ran a finger around the rim of her coffee mug, lost in thoughts of the connection she had rekindled with Aunt Rachel and Uncle Lenny.

Andrea's eyebrows rose in surprise. "That good, huh? I mean, it's been what - twenty-five years?"

"I didn't realize how much I missed them or even needed them until they were right there in front of me."

"Well, Gen, this is just the beginning. You've got a whole new chapter ahead with Zuri and your family. I'm excited for you."

"Thanks, Drea. It helps that I have an amazing chosen family as well."

Genesis expected an immediate response, but silence greeted her. Her heart dropped until Andrea spoke.

"You know I love you too, girl.

Genesis felt a lump form in her throat at the affection in Andrea's voice. Maybe there was still hope after all.

"On that note, I have to go, sweetie. Give Zuri a hug for me."

Genesis ended the call with Andrea, a mix of emotions swirling inside her. The conversation had left her feeling both comforted and unsettled.

Unlike her local family and friends, she and Andrea couldn't just grab a cup of coffee and hash things out. This was going to require a bit more finesse.

Her phone buzzed, and she checked it to find a message from Zuri. Her flight had arrived early, and she was on her way.

Genesis' heart fluttered with anticipation at Zuri's message. There was something about seeing her name on the screen that always elicited an instant reaction from her.

"Looks like it's going to be a good evening, Kuma," she said, rubbing her dog's head, as she got up to prepare for her lady's arrival.

# Chapter Six

Around 8pm, Zuri arrived via car service in a black Lexus. She stepped out clutching a bouquet of lilies and pink roses, their vibrant petals a stark contrast to the gloomy evening sky. The driver got her duffle bag from the trunk and handed it to her with a hearty goodbye.

She stood there for a moment, inhaling the crisp night air and glancing around at the quiet neighborhood. The small paper bag next to the flowers in her hand held the cinnamon bun she'd picked up from their favorite bakery on the way. Its sweet aroma hung in the chill air, making her taste buds dance in anticipation. It was good to be home after a grueling few days meeting with investors in Las Vegas.

Zuri made her way up the gravel pathway, the crunch under her boots a comforting sound. She smiled, already imagining Genesis' animated tales about how Kuma had knocked over another flower pot or how her dance students had improved. Sometimes Gen thought she talked too much and would clam shut, tilting her head, eyes wide as she'd ask, "Am I boring you yet?"

Zuri would only chuckle, shaking her head and murmuring

a fond 'No', eager to hear more of Gen's stories that brought a spark of simple joy to their lives.

As she approached the wooden front door, the house seemed quiet, too quiet. But as her fingertips brushed the cool brass of the doorknob, music trickled from somewhere inside. She inserted the key into the lock and the moment the door opened, Kuma came rushing at her, wagging her tail.

"Hey my sweet girl." Zuri placed the flowers and treats on a side table and she got down to her knees, dropping the duffle bag with her. She scratched Kuma behind the ears. The dog's appreciative whines and wagging tail were a welcoming balm.

"Alright, alright." She laughed, extricating herself from the furry onslaught, and stood up, brushing off her pants.

The sultry strains of Sade's "No Ordinary Love" wafted from the bedroom upstairs. A smile tugged at her lips as she recognized the song. It had been on repeat from a playlist that Genesis created a few months into their relationship that they had been adding to for the past couple of years.

After not showing up at the house the other night due to partying with William and his friends, Zuri was still contemplating how to make amends. She let the excitement of getting Will for the film trump spending time with Genesis, and that wasn't something she wanted to make a habit of doing.

Zuri grabbed the flowers and the bag of sweet bakery delights, then began her ascent up the carpeted staircase. She paused outside the bedroom door. The music was louder now, Sade's words a murmur that filled the quiet hallway. Drawing in a deep breath, Zuri pushed it open.

The sight that unfolded before her elicited a gasp of surprise. The room was awash in the glow of candles flickering from various spots, casting shadows that danced against the walls and ceiling. Vanilla and lavender filled the air, adding to the sensual ambiance Genesis had crafted. But none of that could compare to the sight of Genesis herself.

She was sitting on the edge of the bed, her curls falling free around her shoulders. Her lithe body was draped in satin and lace. The caramel tone of her lingerie contrasted vividly with her dark skin, making Zuri's pulse race. Genesis' pink lips quirked into a smile as she observed Zuri's wide-eyed surprise from beneath heavy lashes.

"Well, well, what do we have here?" Zuri asked, arms folded as she leaned against the doorway.

They shared their respective locations via their phones, so Genesis knew where she was as soon as she landed, down to the minute. She had used her time wisely.

"I thought I might surprise you," Genesis answered, her voice a low purr. The light of the candles reflected in her eyes, bringing out the depths of her dark brown gaze. She moved toward Zuri, her hips swaying with every step.

Zuri's heart pounded in her chest as she watched Gen approach, all lithe grace and quiet confidence. Noticing the items in Zuri's hand, Genesis smiled. "What's this? For me?" she asked, gesturing to the bouquet.

"Of course," Zuri replied, handing them over. "I'm glad to be home."

Genesis took the flowers, inhaling their intoxicating fragrance before placing them on the chest of drawers. She also grabbed the paper bag, peeking inside with a squeal of delight. "Mmm, from our bakery? I have been craving this so bad."

She wrapped her arms around Zuri's neck and leaned in for a sweet kiss. Zuri responded by holding onto her waist. The world outside ceased to exist in that moment; it was just Genesis and her.

"I missed you," Genesis murmured, peppering her neck with kisses.

"And I, you." Zuri confessed, her breath hitching at the feel of Genesis' lips on her skin.

Genesis pulled back, her eyes filled with tenderness and desire. She took Zuri's hands, leading her further into the room. "I want you to get comfortable and tell me all about your trip."

"Can I include anything else with my recap?" Zuri asked as she followed behind her.

"Well, that depends on what you have in mind."

As Genesis climbed onto the bed, Zuri attempted to follow, but she encountered a foot against her chest. "I know you're not trying to get into my bed with your outside clothes on."

Zuri laughed, a rich, throaty sound that echoed around the room. "Well, when you put it like that," she retorted playfully, stepping back to strip. Genesis watched with an appreciative gaze. Tossing her clothes over a chair, she joined Genesis on the bed. "I'm going to take a shower, but I wanted to feel your body against mine first."

"Hmmm," Genesis mumbled as she pulled off a piece of cinnamon bun. "Is that the reason, or did you just not want me to eat all of this pastry alone?"

Zuri leaned forward and sucked the glaze off of Genesis' fingers, eliciting a yelp of surprise. "A little of both."

"How was your trip?" Genesis asked as she handed her a piece.

Zuri chewed on it and shrugged. "It was okay. Shareholders always believe they should have a say in how things are run. You invested because you saw our worth, but now you want to undermine the work we're doing?" She let out a sigh and snuggled closer to Genesis. "It's all because of this stuff with Francis. They just don't want to say it."

Genesis frowned. "They're just scared, babe," she said, patting Zuri's hand. "They see all the headlines and panic, not understanding that this is a storm that will pass."

"But it's such an unnecessary storm, Gen," Zuri groaned, burying her face in Genesis' shoulder. "All because one man wanted to take advantage of the little power he wielded."

"It's a tale as old as time."

Pulling away, Zuri leaned back on the pillows. "And yet it never fails to poison everything it touches."

Genesis hummed in agreement. "But that's all back there now," she reminded Zuri, wrapping her legs around hers. "Right here, right now...it's just you and me."

Zuri sighed, melting under Genesis' touch. "You're right, as usual," she admitted with a hint of amusement in her voice. "I assume you aren't trying to burn this house down just to play therapist. What did you have in mind tonight?"

"Is it too much?" Genesis said, looking around the room. "I just hate how if you light too few candles, you can't see, so I lit all of them, but it does look a bit..."

"Romantic, it looks romantic, my love," Zuri said, cutting her off. "I'm going to go shower and you just lay here and keep being beautiful."

Genesis laughed at her compliment. "Alright, if you insist." She replied, leaning back against the pillows and crossing her arms behind her head. Zuri chuckled, pressing a quick kiss to Genesis' forehead before sliding out of bed and heading for the bathroom.

Zuri took her time in the shower, letting the hot water wash the remnants of her time away. She masked her worry for Genesis' sake, but deep down, concern gnawed at her about her film company's future. When shareholders got scared, the board of directors would go into crisis mode as was happening now. They had flown her out there and told her in no certain terms that the company needed to make sure that her godfather's scandal didn't impact them. They were lucky that Rain's film had been doing amazing domestically and overseas, and getting Phillip Minor to agree to work with them had been another enormous boost. There had also been several smaller films they released that received critical acclaim. Despite all this, Francis's actions were casting a long shadow over their accomplishments.

Chairman of the Board, Robert Smith, had pulled her aside after the meeting and convinced her to go to the bar of the hotel for a drink. Zuri had been reluctant but Robert had always been a friend and would tell her the truth, not what she wanted to hear.

"You know, Zuri," he began, swirling the amber liquid in his own glass, "I've watched you, Reggie and Elijah work so hard to build something truly amazing. Your studio is like the little engine that could. It's small but always produces stellar films that make an impact. But this situation with Francis..." He trailed off, taking a sip of his drink.

Zuri nodded, understanding the unspoken implications. "I know it looks bad, Robert. But we're doing everything we can to distance ourselves from him and his actions."

Robert leaned in closer, his voice low. "It's not just about distancing, Zuri. The board is worried about the long-term repercussions. We need something big, something to shift the narrative completely."

Zuri frowned, her mind racing. "What are you suggesting?"

"Have you considered bringing in new blood? Fresh faces that aren't associated with any of this mess?" Robert asked.

Zuri felt a pang of unease. "You mean like selling shares?"

Robert nodded slowly. "It's not just about the money, though that would certainly help. It's about changing the perception. New investors, maybe even a merger with a larger studio. It could give you the boost you need to weather this storm."

The suggestion had left Zuri feeling conflicted. On one hand, it could solve their immediate problems. On the other hand, it felt like giving up control of the company she and her cousins had worked so hard to build.

"What if I came at it from another angle?"

Robert raised an eyebrow. "I'm listening."

"Phillip Minor has never won an Oscar even though everyone knows his work has been phenomenal."

"It's in part because of his reputation."

"Yes, but I can tell you now, this movie we're going to produce with him is some of his best. It has Oscar written all over it."

Robert leaned back in his chair, a thoughtful expression on his face. "An Oscar, huh? That would certainly be a game-changer."

Zuri nodded eagerly, her eyes bright with excitement. "Exactly. Imagine the headlines: 'Ellis Films Leads Phillip Minor to Long-Overdue Oscar Win.' It would completely shift the narrative away from Francis and onto our accomplishments."

"It's an ambitious plan," Robert mused, stroking his chin. "But Phillip Minor is notoriously difficult to work with. How do you plan to manage that?"

Zuri leaned forward, her voice low and confident. "I've already had several meetings with him. He's... challenging, yes, but he respects our vision. And more importantly, he's hungry for this recognition. I think he knows this might be his last real shot at an Oscar."

Robert nodded slowly. "It's a wild card, but it might just work."

They parted ways and all the confidence in Zuri during the conversation deflated. She knew what she was angling for could be the solution but like Robert said, it was a wild card and there were no guarantees.

Her hands scrubbed at her skin as if she could wash away

the stress. The implications of this scandal could have far-reaching consequences, from losing investors and talented filmmakers, to facing possible legal action. The shower didn't wash away her fears, but it provided a brief respite, the steady drumming of water soothing her tense muscles.

Zuri allowed herself one deep sigh, watching as the steam rose from her skin, before pushing those thoughts aside. This was her time with Genesis, and she needed to focus on her.

Wrapping herself in one of Genesis' plush towels, Zuri headed back to the bedroom. She found Genesis sprawled across the bed, eyes closed. Zuri paused there, admiring her for a moment.

"You're staring," Genesis pointed out without opening her eyes, a smile twitching at the corners of her mouth.

"And if I am?" Zuri shrugged off the towel, letting it drop into a puddle of white at her feet before sliding back into bed.

Genesis cracked an eye open, raking her gaze over Zuri. "Then you're doing what I want."

Zuri chuckled, pulling Genesis against her once she had settled under the covers. She buried her nose in Genesis' hair, inhaling the sweet scent of strawberries left over from her shampoo. When they were away from each other, she'd taken to using it herself to keep Genesis with her.

"I take it you approve of my surprise?" Genesis asked, running her long, lean fingers along Zuri's arm, tracing patterns she knew always drove her wild.

"I'll let you know after I've fully assessed the goods," Zuri teased, nipping at a sensitive earlobe.

Genesis' head fell against the pillows, her body shuddering underneath Zuri's ministrations. "I think you're biased," she teased.

"No such thing as bias when talking about perfection," Zuri

purred, her hand slipping beneath the hem of the silky top piece and finding heated skin.

"Oh, I can agree with that," Genesis moaned in response, arching into her touch.

With a sultry laugh, Zuri leaned in and captured Genesis' lips in a deep, slow kiss, her tongue brushing the seam of her parted mouth. As their tongues danced together, Zuri pulled her top off, revealing Genesis' luscious skin. She trailed kisses down Genesis' neck and along her shoulder blade before moving to her breasts, sucking on a nipple. A needy gasp escaped Genesis as she arched into the touch, pressing herself further into Zuri's mouth.

"Mmm, that feels so good," she moaned.

With deft fingers, Zuri removed the rest of the outfit, sad to see it go. Genesis looked beautiful, but she was eager to touch the body she had been craving for days.

She traced a line down Genesis' stomach with her tongue, stopping at the patch of dark curls covering her mound. Zuri inhaled, taking in the scent that was uniquely Genesis before dipping her head lower. She lapped at the folds, teasing the sensitive nub before diving in to taste more of her favorite fruit.

Genesis' hands plunged into Zuri's hair as she moaned her name, throwing her head back in pleasure. "God, baby. Yes," she panted, her hips bucking up against Zuri's face.

Zuri kept going, taking Genesis higher and higher, only stopping to brush a few stray strands of curls away from her face. "You taste so good," she purred, before descending on her again with renewed vigor.

Genesis could only moan in response, shuddering under the onslaught of sensations overwhelming her body. Her cries echoed in the dimly lit room as Zuri continued her assault. It seemed like an eternity since they had last been together like this, and she was determined to compensate for lost time.

"Zuri, I'm close." Genesis' voice was raspy with desire. "Oh god I need...need..."

Zuri slid two fingers inside of Genesis as she continued to tease her clit. A groan left Genesis' mouth as her body tensed before shattering apart in Zuri's arms.

It took a moment before she could form coherent thoughts. Her eyes were hazy when she opened them, locking onto Zuri's gaze. "Your turn," she said huskily.

Zuri allowed herself to be guided onto her back, her body humming from the orgasmic aftermath. Genesis straddled Zuri's hips, looking down at her with darkened eyes.

"You are so beautiful," Genesis whispered before parting Zuri's legs and settling between them with a hungry moan.

There were lots they discovered they enjoyed in the bedroom. Genesis was especially eager to explore after spending years having her sexual urges stifled by her ex. But there was something simple and pure about tasting each other and bringing such pleasure to one another with their mouths.

Genesis' tongue slid along Zuri's elongated clit, her hands caressing Zuri's thighs as she mapped every inch of her silky folds. Zuri's hips arched off the bed, her eyes sliding closed as she lost herself in the pleasure of Genesis' talented tongue. God, she had missed this.

"Keep," she panted, "doing that," she ordered between gritted teeth.

Genesis moaned as she complied, her tongue swirling around the bundle of nerves before sucking gently. She slid inside of Zuri, and the sensation had stars exploding behind Zuri's eyelids. Soon enough, her back arched and she cried out Genesis' name as she shuddered, her toes curling in pleasure.

Genesis lapped the wetness off her own fingers before kissing Zuri's dazed lips. "I love you."

"I love you too," Zuri said, her voice hoarse with desire.

They lay there afterwards, limbs entwined on the sweat-soaked sheets. Zuri stroked through Genesis' curls while she caught her breath, a contented smile on her face. "I've missed this," she said, kissing the top of Genesis' head. "I've missed you."

Genesis yawned and cuddled closer, tucking herself into the crook of Zuri's arm. "Mmmm me too, baby." She leaned up and pressed a feather-light kiss to Zuri's lips, the scent of strawberries lingering between them. "I don't know if I'll ever get used to having to be apart from you."

"Me neither, but I'm glad we're together now," Zuri muttered, smiling as she drifted off to the sound of their synchronized breathing.

# Chapter Seven

*There's nowhere to hide when love is callin' your name, yeah.*

Zuri's eyes fluttered open as the sounds of Kem infiltrated her sleep. She shifted in bed and noted the space where Genesis should have been.

She stretched, her muscles pleasantly sore from the previous night's activities. The scent of coffee and something sweet wafted up from downstairs, coaxing her out of bed. She slipped on Genesis' silk robe, tying it around her waist as she padded barefoot down the stairs.

In the kitchen, Genesis swayed to the music, her curls piled atop her head. She wore nothing but an oversized t-shirt, her long legs on full display as she flipped pancakes at the stove. Zuri leaned against the doorframe, drinking in the sight of her.

"Good morning, beautiful."

Genesis turned, a bright smile lighting up her face. "Hey, sleepyhead. I was wondering when you'd join the land of the living."

Zuri crossed the kitchen and wrapped her arms around

Genesis from behind, nuzzling into her neck. "Mmm, what time is it?"

"Almost noon," Genesis chuckled, leaning back into Zuri's embrace. "I figured you needed the rest after your trip. And, well, after last night."

A lazy grin spread across Zuri's face as memories from their passionate reunion flooded her mind. "Last night was... incredible," she murmured, pressing a kiss to Genesis' shoulder.

"It was," Genesis agreed, turning in Zuri's arms to face her. She cupped Zuri's face in her hands. "I'm glad you're home."

Zuri leaned in, capturing Genesis' lips in a slow, languid kiss. The pancakes sizzled on the stove, momentarily forgotten as they lost themselves in each other.

"The pancakes," Genesis murmured, her eyes still closed.

"Right," Zuri chuckled, releasing her. She moved to pour herself a cup of coffee while Genesis returned her attention to the stove.

"So, what's on the agenda for today?" Zuri asked, leaning against the counter and sipping her coffee.

Genesis flipped the last pancake onto a plate and turned off the stove. "Well, I didn't know you'd be free."

Zuri swallowed a mouthful of coffee. "I cleared my schedule so we could spend some time together. I thought maybe we could go for a walk in the park later, weather permitting."

As she placed the plate of pancakes on the table, Genesis looked at her with eyes full of hope. "Wow, I didn't expect that."

Zuri raised an eyebrow. "You didn't expect me to make time for you?"

Instead of answering, Genesis busied herself bringing over syrup and fruit. "Before that walk, would you like to join me in my pottery class?"

"Pottery class? I didn't know you were taking one!"

Genesis beamed, her smile as bright as the morning sun

streaming through the kitchen window. "I started a couple of weeks ago. It's been so much fun, and I've been dying to share it with you."

Zuri had no interest in pottery. She wasn't what anyone would consider artistic, but the excitement in Genesis' eyes decided for her.

"I'd love to join you," she said, smiling. "Though I warn you, I'm not artistically inclined."

"Don't worry, babe. It's not about being perfect. It's about having fun and getting your hands dirty."

As they sat down to enjoy their pancakes, Genesis launched into an animated description of her pottery adventures. Her hands moved expressively as she spoke.

"Babe, you're going to love it," she gushed. "There's something so therapeutic about molding the clay with your hands, feeling it take shape beneath your fingers. And the instructor, Mara, is wonderful. She has this calming presence that just puts you at ease, even when your pot looks more like a lopsided fruit bowl than the vase you intended."

Zuri chuckled, captivated by Genesis' excitement. She could almost feel the cool, damp clay beneath her own fingers as Genesis described the process.

"And the studio itself is like something out of a dream," Genesis continued. "It's in this renovated warehouse with these enormous windows that let in the most beautiful natural light. There are plants everywhere, and it's been one of my favorite places I discovered recently."

After clearing the dishes, they got ready for the day. Genesis insisted on dressing Zuri in old clothes, assuring her that things were bound to get messy.

When they arrived at the studio and stepped out of Genesis' car, Zuri took in the pottery studio. The building was indeed a renovated warehouse, its brick exterior weathered but well-maintained. Large, arched windows dominated the facade, offering glimpses of the creative hub within.

The moment they crossed the threshold, Zuri understood what Genesis meant about it being dreamlike. Sunlight streamed through enormous windows, casting a warm glow over the space. The air was thick with the earthy scent of clay and the faint aroma of coffee brewing somewhere in the back.

Potted plants of all varieties lined the windowsills and hung from the ceiling, their verdant leaves creating a lush, natural canopy. Unfinished clay pieces in various stages of completion dotted the wooden shelves lining the walls, a testament to the creativity flourishing within these walls.

The studio was buzzing with activity. People were already sitting at the wheels in the studio, using their hands to shape lumps of clay with varying degrees of success. Laughter and chatter filled the air, creating a welcoming atmosphere that put Zuri at ease.

"Genesis! You made it!" A tall woman with silver-streaked hair pulled into a messy bun approached them. As she drew near, she wiped her clay-stained hands on a well-worn apron.

"Mara!" Genesis exclaimed, giving the woman a quick hug. "This is Zuri, my fiance."

Zuri melted at the pride she heard in Genesis's voice as she introduced her. *God, I love this woman.*

"Nice to meet you Mara," Zuri said while shaking her hand. "I have to warn you. I'm terrible at making art."

Mara's eyes crinkled with amusement as she shook Zuri's hand. "Nonsense! Everyone has an artist inside them, waiting to be unleashed. We just need to coax it out sometimes."

She led them to an empty workstation, gesturing for them to take a seat. "Now, let's start you both off with a simple project. How about a bowl?"

Genesis nodded while Zuri tried to mask her apprehension

with a smile. Mara placed a lump of clay in front of each of them and showed the basic technique for centering the clay on the wheel.

"Remember," Mara said, her voice soothing, "it's not about perfection. It's about the process, the feeling of creation."

As Genesis settled in beside her, Zuri felt a flutter of nervousness. She watched as Mara showed how to center properly, her practiced hands making it look effortless.

"Alright, now you try," Mara encouraged, stepping back.

Zuri placed her hands on the cool, damp clay, trying to mimic Mara's movements. The wheel started spinning, and immediately, the clay wobbled off center.

"Whoa!" Zuri exclaimed, struggling to control the unruly lump.

Genesis giggled beside her, her own clay already forming a neat cylinder. "You've got this, babe. Just relax your hands a bit."

Zuri took a deep breath, loosening her grip. Slowly, the clay cooperated, centering itself on the wheel. A triumphant smile spread across her face.

"There you go!" Mara praised, nodding approvingly. "Now, let's start shaping that bowl."

Zuri followed Mara's instructions, pressing her thumbs gently into the center of the clay to create a shallow depression. As she worked, she got lost in the rhythmic motion of the wheel and the cool, malleable clay beneath her fingers.

Beside her, Genesis was in her element. Her hands moved with graceful precision, coaxing the clay into a symmetrical bowl. Zuri admired the look of intense concentration on her fiancée's face, the tip of her tongue peeking out between her lips as she focused on her work.

"You're a natural," Zuri commented, distracted from her own less-than-perfect creation.

Genesis looked up. "Thanks, babe. How's yours coming along?"

Zuri glanced down at her bowl, which was lopsided and had several finger-shaped dents along the rim. She chuckled sheepishly. "Well, let's just say it has... character."

Genesis leaned over to inspect Zuri's work, her curls brushing against Zuri's shoulder. "I think it's beautiful," she said sincerely. "It's uniquely you."

Zuri placed her hand over her heart and turned her head, catching Genesis' lips for a quick kiss.

As they continued working on their bowls, Zuri relaxed into the process. She may not have been creating a masterpiece, but there was something satisfying about shaping the formless lump into something recognizable.

Genesis, meanwhile, had moved on to adding delicate details to her bowl. With deft fingers, she carved intricate patterns along the rim, her brow furrowed in concentration. Zuri marveled at her fiancée's natural talent and the pure joy radiating from her.

"Time to glaze!" Mara announced, clapping her hands together. She guided them through the process of selecting colors and applying the glaze to their creations. Genesis chose a deep blue that reminded Zuri of the ocean at twilight. Zuri opted for a vibrant yellow she hoped would disguise some of her bowl's imperfections.

As they painted their bowls, Zuri chuckled at the contrast between Genesis' precise, even strokes and her own haphazard approach. "I think I might have missed my calling as an abstract expressionist," she joked, holding up her bowl for Genesis to see.

"I love it. It's going to get a prime place on the mantel in my house."

"Oh no, you don't," Zuri said, moving it closer to her.

Genesis raised an eyebrow, a playful smirk tugging at her lips. "Oh? And why not?"

"Because," Zuri said, cradling her lopsided bowl protectively, "this masterpiece is going on display in my office. It'll be a conversation starter."

Genesis burst into laughter, the sound echoing through the studio. "Well, in that case, I insist on making you a matching set. Can't have your office looking unbalanced, can we?"

Zuri's heart swelled with affection. Even in this moment of playful teasing, Genesis was thinking of ways to support her. "I'd love that," she said.

As they finished glazing their bowls, Mara came around to collect them for firing. "These look wonderful!" she exclaimed, examining their work. "You'll be able to pick them up next week. And Zuri," she added with a wink, "I hope to see you again soon. You've got a natural flair for... unconventional design."

Zuri laughed, shaking her head. "I think that's the kindest way anyone's ever told me I'm terrible at something."

After cleaning up their workstations and washing the clay from their hands, Zuri and Genesis stepped out of the studio into the afternoon sun. As they walked hand in hand towards the car, Zuri felt a lightness in her step that hadn't been there before. The stress and worries that had been weighing on her seemed to have melted away, at least for the moment.

"Thank you for sharing this with me," Zuri said, squeezing Genesis' hand. "I had no idea pottery could be so... freeing."

Genesis beamed at her. "I'm so glad you enjoyed it! I was a little worried you might find it boring."

"Boring? With you there? Never," Zuri chuckled, pulling Genesis close. "And listen, I know things have been hectic with work and Beacon. I'm going to do my best to free up my time so we can do more of this. Okay?"

As Genesis stared deep into her eyes, Zuri was taken aback by the sight of tears forming. "Yeah, babe, I'd like that," she said, her voice slightly trembling.

Before Zuri could ask what was wrong, she kissed her cheek and walked to the driver's side of the car. Whatever it was, she didn't want to talk about it, but when they pulled up to the house, she had to say something.

"Gen, is everything okay?" Zuri asked, reaching over to place a hand on Genesis' thigh.

Genesis glanced at her, a flicker of uncertainty in her eyes before she masked it with a smile. "Of course, just thinking about some things I need to do when I visit Beacon tomorrow."

Zuri nodded, not convinced but willing to let it go for now. "How about we have dinner at a restaurant tonight? There's a new Korean barbecue place I thought you'd like."

Genesis' face lit up, her earlier pensiveness forgotten. "Oh yes! Let me just change into something more comfortable, and we can head out."

They entered the house, greeted by an excited Kuma, who bounded up to them, tail wagging. Genesis knelt down to scratch behind the dog's ears, cooing affectionately.

"Hey, sweet girl. Did you miss us?" She looked up at Zuri. "Would you mind taking her out for a quick potty break while I change?"

Zuri grabbed Kuma's leash from the hook by the door. As she followed alongside Kuma, watching her sniff around the grass, Zuri couldn't shake the feeling that something was bothering Genesis. She hoped they could have a genuine conversation because she wanted to make sure she didn't repeat the mistakes of the past. What they had was too important for her to mess up.

# Chapter Eight

Monday morning, Genesis stared at the sweaty man seated on the other side of her desk. She had heard of stress sweat before but never seen it in action. Henry Thomas was experiencing it in spades.

"So, see, here's the thing, I file my taxes every year," he said, dabbing at his forehead with a cloth.

"Yes, you do, Mr. Thomas, but you have failed to include the income you earn by renting out your yacht for several years in a row."

"Please, call me Henry. And is it that big of a deal? It's just a little side money."

Genesis looked down at the paperwork she had gone over multiple times. "According to your own records, you made over a million dollars in the last five years from it. You can see why the IRS might not take kindly to you not claiming this income, right?"

Henry waved his hand. "What is that to the IRS? I pay my fair share of taxes."

Trying not to let out an exasperated sigh, Genesis stacked the papers that she collected from him on his tax history.

"Here's the deal Henry. I'm an accountant and a damn good one. I've built this business up to be the best here in LA, and I work with some very rich and famous people. One thing I will never do is lie to you, but I will also never cheat the US government on your behalf."

Henry sputtered and shook his head vigorously. "I would never ask that of you. I'm an honest man."

"Well, in this instance, I think we have different definitions of honesty. But going forward, we do everything on the up and up. Do you understand?"

"I do. I'll make sure everything is on the up and up." He mumbled. "Thank you for not throwing me to the wolves, Ms. Malone."

"Genesis, and it's what you're paying me for." She gave him her most disarming smile. "My assistant will give you a breakdown of what we need from you and any fines or penalties we can expect to see. You've been a good client. We will do everything in our power to make this right."

He stood up and shook her hand. "I appreciate it."

"No problem," she replied as she escorted him out.

Kenzie directed him to another small office so she could inform him of his next steps. Genesis brought her mug of cold coffee to her lips and winced at the taste.

"I told you to stop microwaving it."

Genesis startled and spun around, liquid sloshing over the rim. "Damn it, Lucy, don't sneak up on me like that."

"Oh hush, you know you love me." Lucy swiped a napkin from the dispenser. She handed it to Genesis, who blotted at her blotchy blouse. "Who was that?"

Genesis shrugged and sat on her desk. "Another wealthy individual who was unaware of the necessity to declare all of his earnings."

"So, our usual clientele?"

They both laughed. Genesis was happy that her business had become successful enough that she could bring Lucy and a few others on to work with her. Thanks to Reggie, her list of clients had been growing and there was no way she could have handled it without help. It was a good problem to have.

Lucy scanned the stack of files on Genesis's desk. "You have a way with people, Gen. You take the worst situations and make them manageable."

Genesis chuckled, crumpling the now coffee-stained napkin and tossing it in the bin. "That's why they pay me the big bucks."

Lucy leaned against the edge of the table. "Speaking of big bucks, how is Zuri?"

"Really, Lucy?" Genesis let out a chuckle.

"What? I love Zuri, but let's not pretend she isn't rolling in money."

Genesis lifted a brow at her friend. "Zuri is more than just her bank account," she defended, leaning back in her chair.

"I know, I know. She's got the whole philanthropist thing going for her too. Plus, she's easy on the eyes," Lucy retorted with a cheeky grin.

Genesis rolled her eyes but couldn't refute the truth in Lucy's words. Zuri was indeed beautiful in ways that still left Genesis breathless.

The mention of Zuri made Genesis check her watch. She had to leave soon to oversee dance classes at Beacon. Seeing those youthful faces lit up with the power of expression never failed to make her day.

They heard a knock on the open door and both turned to Kenzie standing there looking annoyed. "Mr. Thomas is gone and can I say that one's going to require a lot of work?"

Genesis leaned forward, clasping her hands under her chin. "Tell me about it," she groaned. "He's been on the IRS radar for a while now. Let's hope we can wade him through without any more waves."

"Good thing we have an amazing assistant working here. Kenzie, you have been a godsend," Lucy said sincerely.

Kenzie started at the office several months after Genesis opened the firm. Her first assistant had been bright, but overwhelmed with the job. When Kenzie asked if she could come on and help, Genesis had been skeptical. She loved her sister, but they had only recently started consistently getting along at the time and she thought it would put pressure on their already fragile relationship. Instead, Kenzie turned out to be extremely efficient. She handled the mountain of paperwork well, keeping everything ordered and streamlined.

Genesis was relieved, not only for her help but also that their relationship had grown stronger for it. She smiled at her younger sister. "You've been doing an amazing job, Kenzie."

Kenzie huffed out a laugh. "Thanks to you both. It's been a blast working with you." Her face became serious when she turned to Lucy. "Lucy, do you mind if my sister and I speak alone?"

"Not at all," Lucy said, jumping up from her seat. "I've got a few clients to follow up with."

Once Lucy had left, Kenzie stepped into the office and closed the door. Genesis frowned, anxiety fluttering in her belly. "What's up, Kenzie?" she asked.

"Don't worry, it's nothing bad. I just wanted to share with you that I will be enrolling in law school.

Genesis blinked, speechless. "Law school?" she echoed, "That's... that's amazing!"

Kenzie shifted on her feet, a hopeful smile tugging at her lips. "I was scared to tell you. I didn't want you to think I'd be abandoning you or the company."

Genesis held up a hand. "No, don't even worry about that.

This is about your future. We can always hire more help. But you only get one life and it's up to you how you live it."

Relief washed over Kenzie's face, and she slumped onto the chair opposite Genesis'. "Oh, thank God," she exhaled. "Things have been going so well between us. I was afraid my leaving would disappoint you."

"Kenzie," Genesis started, leaning forward with a reassuring smile. "Your life is not about my approval or disapproval. You are an amazing woman and making decisions for yourself doesn't mean you are disappointing anyone."

Kenzie smiled. "You think I can do it?"

Genesis chuckled. "I don't think, I know. You've got the brains and the determination for it, for sure. If the way you advocated for Shannon and I getting back together is any indication, you are going to fight to the death for your clients." Genesis walked over to give her a hug. "Have you been studying for the LSAT?"

"Day and night. Zuri got me into a competitive program. The techniques are so helpful."

"Zuri was already aware of this?" Genesis asked, pulling away.

"Yeah, when we first started discussing it, she encouraged me to tell you, too. She's been pushing me to follow my dreams and believe in myself."

Genesis' heart swelled with love for Zuri. Always supportive. Always helping others believe in themselves. "Sounds like her," Genesis said with a smile. "Well, if you need anything from me, be it study support or just someone to rant to when the coursework gets frustrating, I'll be here."

"Thanks, Gen. Zuri offered the same. She said to aim high for the schools I applied to because she would cover tuition for wherever I decide to go."

"Oh, she did?" Genesis asked, freezing in place as she

processed Kenzie's words. "Offered to pay for your tuition? All of it?"

Kenzie nodded, looking both sheepish and grateful. "Yeah. She's amazing, just like you said."

"Yeah, that she is." Genesis glanced at the clock on the wall. "I'm sorry to cut this short, Kenz, but I have to head to Beacon." She kissed her cheek. "You keep me informed on what's going on with your school applications and tests, okay? We're in this together."

Kenzie nodded with a grin. "Absolutely, Gen."

Genesis gave her sister one last hug before grabbing her bag and heading out the door. The streets were bustling with people and cars. Her phone buzzed in her pocket, a message from Rain appearing on the screen. She smiled as she read it, Rain inviting her and Zuri to meet her new boyfriend. Genesis made a mental note to ask Zuri about it before replying.

As she got in her car, her mind drifted back to her conversation with Kenzie. Genesis sighed as she turned the vehicle on. A swirl of emotions stormed inside her. Zuri, ever the benefactor, was always putting others before herself. Yet Genesis felt a bit hurt. She was Kenzie's sister; shouldn't she have been the first to know about such a momentous decision?

Zuri had assumed a role that Genesis should have taken on. Yet, there was an unmistakable thread of gratitude weaving through her confusion. The truth was, she wouldn't have been able to offer Kenzie the opportunity that Zuri was providing. Zuri's heart was always so full for those she cared about. That she included Kenzie in that circle made Genesis love her even more. But she thought it might be worth having a talk about boundaries again.

What happened over the weekend didn't help to ease her irritation. Instead of talking to Genesis, like Andrea suggested, about their relationship, she had avoided the topic entirely.

Genesis shook her head, trying to clear her thoughts as she navigated through traffic. She couldn't let this fester. They needed to talk, and soon.

When she arrived at Beacon, her entire mood lifted. No matter what happened between her and Zuri, she would never forget how she brought dance back into her life.

Ariel, the young woman who worked at the welcome desk, greeted her with a big smile. "Hey Mrs. Malone...I mean Ms. Baker."

"Oh, you got jokes today I see," Genesis laughed, giving Ariel a playful wink before heading towards her office.

She could hear the rhythmic beat of music as soon as she headed downstairs, the energy of young dancers in training seeping out into the corridor.

"Genesis, there you are. I was hoping we could have a chat."

The sound of Lea, the director of the Beacon program, behind her sent the hairs on the back of Genesis's neck standing on end. She turned, forcing a smile onto her face as she faced the older woman.

"Lea, always a pleasure," Genesis said, her voice laced with an undercurrent of apprehension.

Ever since their first meeting, when she could tell that Lea had a thing for Zuri, Genesis had written her off as a thorn in her side but harmless. Then Lea became her boss. Of course, in the role that Zuri had created, she was given an enormous amount of leeway and autonomy, but that didn't mean she was free from Lea's attempts to assert dominance.

"What can I do for you?" Genesis asked.

Lea's smile had a forced quality to it. "I would like to talk about the dance program. Nothing too serious."

"Okay, walk with me to my office," Genesis said, continuing down the stairs. "I'm listening."

"I've been hearing about some changes you've made?"

Genesis frowned at the question. The 'changes' that Lea referred to were improvements she had thought out and implemented. Incorporating more diversity in dance styles, balanced training routines, and an increased focus on mental resilience.

"Yes," Genesis confirmed, her tone steady. "I believed that they were necessary enhancements for our students."

They entered her small but stylish office and Genesis placed her bags down, then took a seat behind her desk. Lea looked around and noted the art and plants decorating the space.

"I see you've made yourself at home here," Lea said, her tone neutral.

"Of course. I plan on being here for a while, so I want my space as comfortable as possible," Genesis replied, the faintest hint of a challenge in her words.

Lea gave a stiff nod, sitting in a chair across from Genesis. "As I was saying, the expectation was that our program wouldn't be so non-traditional."

"I see." Genesis took a moment to compose herself before speaking. "And by non-traditional you mean...?"

"Hip-hop. Break-dancing. Reggae, Samba," Lea listed off. "The kids should be learning modern dance, but these styles are outside of the original vision of our program. Our students need to be well-versed in classical styles, ballet, and contemporary. This is a stepping stone towards professional dance careers for most of them. Not some street competition."

Genesis' eyes narrowed as Lea concluded her speech. She understood the reasoning behind Lea's words, but the narrow-minded perspective was old-fashioned.

"Lea," Genesis began, her tone patient and cool, "I appreciate your input. And while classical styles are indeed important, the world of dance is vast and diverse. Not incorporating these 'non-traditional' styles into our curriculum would be unfair to our students.

Lea seemed taken aback by Genesis's firm stance.

"Moreover," Genesis continued, "these styles aren't as 'street' as you make them out to be. They are respected forms of dance with deep cultural roots and they also require discipline and technique much like ballet or contemporary."

"I...understand your point," Lea conceded, though it was clear she wasn't pleased.

"Good," Genesis responded, hoping that would be the end of the matter. "Rest assured, they will be learning traditional dance as well. I personally studied it and understand its significance for one's professional journey. But traditional means something different to these young women, and I believe we should honor that."

Lea didn't speak for a moment, her brows furrowed in deep thought. "Alright..." she finally breathed out, a reluctant concession in her voice. "We'll see how it goes. I have faith in your ability to handle this.

Genesis nodded, her heart rate returning to normal. She could tell the conversation was far from over, but for now, she had won this round.

"Great," she said, her voice steady. "I appreciate you putting your trust in me."

With that, Lea got up and left Genesis alone in her office. As soon as the door closed behind her, Genesis took a deep breath.

With the day's drama behind her, Genesis allowed herself to relax into her surroundings again and focus on why she was there in the first place — the kids. She loved every minute of work with them, seeing their confidence grow as they mastered new dance moves and absorbed the history of each style.

* * *

After responding to some emails, Genesis headed to do the thing she enjoyed most; watch the teens at work. The beats of a vibrant Afro beat song echoed off the walls and dance students moved across the floor in Studio One. The class was given by an amazing teacher named Kem, whom Genesis had brought on board to broaden the students' understanding of African dance forms.

Kem moved with an ease that could only come from years of practice. Her body twisted and turned, feet pounding in time with the drumbeats. The students attempted to mimic her movements, some with more success than others.

Genesis sat at the back of the class, watching with keen interest as Kem put them through their paces. She marveled at how effortlessly the teens moved, their movements fluid and full of life. Even though they were still beginners, their dedication and passion were clear. It took her back to a time in her life when she had the same feelings. Taking part in giving these young people the chance to explore their own passion brought joy to her heart, and that was a cause she would always be ready to defend.

Kem bounced over to her side of the room and dropped beside her on the floor. "These kids have such boundless energy.

Genesis smiled. "They do. It's amazing to watch them throw themselves into it with such enthusiasm."

"You should join us," Kem said with a grin. "Show these kids how it's done."

Genesis laughed and shook her head. "Oh no, I couldn't possibly keep up with them now. My dancing days are behind me."

"Nonsense," Kem replied, nudging Genesis with her elbow. "Once a dancer, always a dancer. It's in your blood."

Before Genesis could protest further, Kem was on her feet, pulling Genesis up with her. "Come on, just one dance. For old times' sake."

The girls all stopped practicing their moves and cheered when they realized Genesis was going to join in.

"Ms. G, can we see you dance?" Katie, one of the younger students, asked, her voice full of excitement.

Genesis hesitated, but the excited faces of the students and Kem's encouraging smile broke through her reservations. "Alright, alright," she conceded with a laugh. "But don't expect too much. It's been a while."

Kem's face lit up. "Trust me, it'll come back to you." She turned to the class. "Alright, everyone! Let's show Ms. G how we do it!"

The music changed, the pulsating rhythms of a popular Afrobeats song filling the studio. Kem took her place at the front, her body already swaying to the beat.

"Okay, Genesis," Kem called out. "We'll start with something simple. Watch my feet."

Kem began with a basic step, her feet moving in a quick, syncopated pattern. Her hips swayed, arms loose at her sides. Genesis watched and broke down the movements.

"Now you try," Kem encouraged.

With a deep breath, Genesis moved forward. At first, her steps were hesitant, but as the rhythm took hold, muscle memory kicked in. Her feet found the beat, matching Kem's movements with increasing confidence.

"That's it!" Kem cheered. "Now let's add some arms."

Kem demonstrated a fluid arm movement, hands rotating at the wrists as they moved from shoulder height down to her hips. Genesis mirrored the movement, her body falling into the familiar patterns of dance. The students watched in awe as their composed director transformed before their eyes, her movements becoming more fluid and confident with each beat.

"Now let's put it all together!" Kem called out, her voice barely audible over the pulsing music.

Genesis felt a rush of exhilaration as she surrendered to the rhythm. She closed her eyes, losing herself in the music and the sheer joy of movement. For a moment, she wasn't Genesis the accountant or Zuri's fiancé, she was just Genesis, the dancer.

The students cheered and clapped, their enthusiasm infectious. Genesis opened her eyes to see them attempting to follow along, their expressions filled with excitement and admiration.

As the song ended, Genesis found herself breathless but grinning from ear to ear. The surge of endorphins left her with a sensation of dizziness and bliss.

"See? It never leaves you," Kem said, patting Genesis on the back.

The students crowded around, their voices overlapping in a chorus of praise and questions.

"That was amazing, Ms. G!"

"Where did you learn to dance like that?"

"Can you teach us those moves?"

Genesis laughed, her cheeks flushed with exertion and embarrassment. "Thank you, everyone. I haven't done anything choreographed in years," she admitted, her breath still coming in quick pants.

As the adrenaline faded, Genesis felt a twinge in her lower back, a reminder that she wasn't as young as she used to be. Still, the joy of dancing outweighed any discomfort. She watched as the students continued to practice, their movements more enthusiastic than ever, inspired by what they had just witnessed.

The rest of the class flew by in a blur of music and motion. When it was time to wrap up, the students were reluctant to leave, still buzzing with excitement at Genesis's impromptu performance. They gathered their things, chattering amongst themselves about the unexpected treat they'd received.

"Ms. G, you've got to dance with us more often!" exclaimed Jasmine, a talented fifteen-year-old with dreams of Broadway.

"Yeah, please?" chimed in Katie, her curly hair bouncing as she nodded emphatically. "It was so cool to see you in action!"

Genesis smiled at their enthusiasm. "We'll see," she replied, not wanting to make any promises she couldn't keep. "Now, don't forget to practice at home. I want to see improvement in the next class!"

The students filed out, their voices echoing down the hallway as they continued to discuss the day's events. Genesis watched them go, a sense of nostalgia washing over her. She prayed the girls got to follow through with their dreams.

Kem grabbed her bag and approached Genesis with a knowing smile. "That was something else, Gen. You've still got it."

Genesis chuckled, shaking her head. "Not quite. I'll definitely be experiencing the effects of it tomorrow.

"But it was worth it, wasn't it? Did you see their faces? You inspired those kids today."

"It felt good," she admitted. "I'd forgotten how much I missed it."

"I'm gonna need you to dance with us more often," Kem said matter of factly. "The kids would love it, and I think you would, too." She said goodbye, but then turned back around. "Any chance you like dancing at a club?"

Kem's smile lit up her entire face. Genesis had noticed how attractive she was when she hired her, but she had been primarily interested in her skills as a dancer. Now she couldn't tell if this was a friendly invite or something else. Sometimes it was hard to tell with femmes.

"A club?" Genesis repeated, her curiosity piqued. She hadn't been out dancing socially in ages, not since before she and Zuri had gotten serious.

Kem nodded. "Yeah, there's this great spot called Velvet. They play all kinds of music. Everything from old school R&B to the latest Afrobeat's. The dance floor is always packed."

Genesis hesitated, her mind racing. Velvet, she knew that name. It was a well-known lesbian bar in the area.

"I'm not sure," Genesis said, trying to read Kem's expression. "Clubs were never my scene and I haven't been to one in ages."

Kem's smile didn't falter. "All the more reason to come! My friends and I are going on Saturday night. It'll be fun, I promise. No pressure to stay late or anything."

"Okay, let me think about it."

"Sure. Then I can show you some more moves." With that, Kem bounced out of the room, leaving behind a trail of her woodsy scented perfume.

Genesis went about straightening up the room and was startled when she turned and saw Kem poking her head in the doorway.

"I just wanted you to know that was an innocent invite. I'm aware of who your lady is, and I'd like to keep my job. It's just exciting to meet some fellow sapphics. Later."

Genesis chuckled to herself as she watched Kem leave. She felt a mixture of relief and amusement at her clarification.

As she tidied up the studio, Genesis hummed along to the lingering echoes of the day's music. Her body still thrummed with the residual energy of dance, a sensation she hadn't experienced in far too long. Kem was right. It was about time she started moving again.

# Chapter Nine

Zuri cruised down the highway, heading to Beacon to meet with Lea and the other upper management staff, including Genesis. They tried to keep their relationship separate from their work lives, but it wasn't always easy. Especially when Genesis would catch her eye during meetings and flash that irresistible smile.

Her phone rang, and she clicked over to the Bluetooth in her car. "Alma, don't tell me you're calling to flake on me this weekend?"

A deep sigh filled her car and made her chuckle. "Unfortunately, I mentioned it to Nathan and he can't wait."

Nathan and Alma had been dating for over a year. After years of being single, her best friend had found the man of her dreams, according to her. Zuri liked him and he was the perfect sunshine to Alma's grumpy nature.

"Hard to turn down a listening party for the hottest rapper in the game. I promise you'll have fun."

"From your lips to God's ears. Anyway friend, I was calling to get your opinion on something. If a man asks for your ring size, do you think that means he's planning to propose?"

Zuri let out a celebratory yell, then stifled it. "Sorry about that."

Alma let out her own laughter. "For once, I agree. Z. He's the best thing that's ever happened to me. And this is coming from the most cynical person on earth."

"I think you just hold your heart close to your vest, Alma, nothing wrong with that. I'm glad you found someone who makes you happy."

"Look at us, in grown up relationships and happy. Anyway, when are we going dress shopping? I want to make sure I set it aside because Nathan loves to make plans in advance. It would be sickening if I wasn't so touched."

Zuri hesitated because she hadn't even been thinking about going dress shopping. The engagement party took up most of their extra time over the last few months, so jumping into other aspects of planning wasn't at the front of her mind. She didn't want to admit it, but with all the work she had put in for the party, she had assumed Genesis would have stepped up regarding the wedding.

"Let me talk to Gen because we haven't even settled on a date for the wedding."

"You're kidding me, right?" Alma's voice held a note of surprise. "You guys are so in love, I thought you'd elope by now."

"No, we haven't eloped, yet," Zuri said, her lips curving into a smile as she pictured Genesis in a beautiful white dress. "But don't worry, you will be the first to know when things are more concrete."

As she pulled into the parking lot, Zuri took a deep breath, steeling herself for professionalism. She grabbed her laptop bag and strode towards the building, her heels clicking on the pavement.

Just as she reached for the door handle, a familiar voice called out, "Hey there, gorgeous!"

Zuri turned to see Genesis jogging up, her curls bouncing with each step. "I thought that was your car pulling in," Genesis said, out of breath.

"Good afternoon," Zuri replied, fighting to keep her tone neutral despite the flutter in her chest. "Ready for the meeting?"

Always ready. But first…" Genesis glanced around, then leaned in to place a quick kiss on Zuri's cheek. "For luck," she whispered.

Zuri wanted to pull her close. It had been a few days since they saw each other in person, but she had to wait until later when they had dinner plans. Even though everyone knew they were a couple, it was important to her they respect Genesis.

"You are killing me in that outfit," Zuri said, as they walked inside the building.

Genesis grinned, smoothing her hands down the sides of her outfit. "Oh, this old thing?" she teased, but Zuri could see the pleasure in her eyes.

Zuri allowed her gaze to trail over Genesis's ensemble. The plaid pencil skirt, perfectly hugging her curves, accentuated her figure with its high waist. A sophisticated mix of muted forest green and deep navy was seen in the pattern, with a subtle pop of color created by thin lines of burgundy. Just below her knees, the skirt revealed a tantalizing glimpse of her toned calves.

Genesis had paired the skirt with a crisp white button-down shirt, its sleeves rolled up to her elbows in a casual yet professional touch. The top two buttons were undone, offering a hint of her collarbone and drawing Zuri's eyes to the delicate gold chain that rested there. The shirt was tucked neatly into the skirt, emphasizing her waist.

Sleek, pointed-toe pumps in a rich cognac leather adorned her feet, complementing the earthy tones of her skirt. There was something about her in heels that drove her crazy. *Focus Zuri,* she thought to herself. These days of being apart were really getting to her.

They headed towards the conference room, where Lea and the rest of the staff had already assembled. They parted, and Zuri went around greeting everyone. Lea looked especially happy to see her.

"Z, you made it. We weren't sure you were coming this time around," she said, leaning in for a hug.

Zuri returned the hug, noticing that Lea held on a beat longer than necessary. As they pulled apart, Lea's hand lingered on Zuri's arm.

"I wouldn't miss it. The quarterly review is too important."

Lea nodded, massaging her arm. "Well, I'm glad you're here. Your insights are always invaluable."

Zuri's eyes darted to Genesis, who was busy chatting with another colleague. She noticed the slight furrow in Genesis's brow as she glanced their way. Clearing her throat, Zuri stepped back from Lea.

"Thanks. I'm excited to hear everyone's updates," Zuri said, moving towards her seat at the conference table.

As she settled in, she caught Genesis's eye across the room. Her fiancée raised an eyebrow, a silent question in her gaze. Zuri gave a small shake of her head and mouthed "Later" before turning her attention to the meeting at hand.

The next hour flew by as they reviewed budgets, discussed upcoming projects, and brainstormed new initiatives for Beacon. Zuri found herself impressed by Genesis's contributions. She had a way of seeing connections others missed, and her passion for the arts was clear in every suggestion she made.

As the meeting wound down, Zuri's mind drifted to their dinner plans. She was looking forward to some alone time with

Genesis after days apart. Maybe they could discuss setting a wedding date.

"Zuri?" Lea's voice broke through her thoughts. "Do you have a moment to go over the finances for a few of our new initiatives?"

Zuri blinked, refocusing on the present moment. "Of course," she replied, gathering her papers. She glanced at Genesis, who was packing up her own belongings. Their eyes met, and Genesis gave her a small, understanding smile.

As everyone filed out, Zuri followed Lea to her office. It was a nice, compact but airy space, with large windows overlooking the city skyline. Lea gestured for Zuri to take a seat in one of the plush chairs across from her desk.

"So, about these new initiatives," Lea began, shuffling through some papers. "I'm a bit concerned about the budget for the youth outreach program. It seems like we might be stretching ourselves thin."

Zuri leaned forward, her mind shifting into problem-solving mode. "I've been pondering on that. What if we partner with local schools? We could offer after-school programs that would allow us to reach more kids without increasing our costs."

"That's brilliant. This is why we need you here more often. Your ideas are always so... innovative."

Lea moved to sit beside Zuri and show her some of the other plans they were considering. As they pored over the documents, Lea's chair inched closer to Zuri's. Their shoulders were nearly touching now as Lea pointed out various figures on the spreadsheet.

"And here," Lea said, her finger tracing a line of numbers, "is where I think we could really optimize our resources."

Her hand brushed against Zuri's as she reached for another document. The touch lingered a moment longer than necessary, and Zuri felt a prickle of unease.

Back when she first hired her, Lea had shown clear signs she was available to Zuri. Little flirtatious remarks, lingering touches, and suggestive glances had all been part of Lea's repertoire. The attention flattered Zuri, and she indulged in it. With Tracy gone half the year and not always available, even when she was around, it had been nice to have someone who made her feel appreciated. There had been many late-night dinners making plans for Beacon and one night it crossed into something else.

Zuri's mind drifted back to that night. They had been working late, poring over grant proposals and curriculum plans, their minds focused on work but their bodies buzzing with something more. Empty wine glasses littered Lea's living room coffee table, evidence of their attempts to relax after a long day.

"Oh my God, I think my eyes have crossed," Lea said with a laugh, falling back on the couch.

Her blonde curls pooled behind her head, the lamplight bringing out the golden highlights. Lea's eyes, bright with intoxication, locked onto Zuri's.

Zuri stretched and sat back in her cushioned chair. "Yeah, we've got some great donors coming through, so the work is worth it. But I am exhausted."

"You should stay over tonight. I'd hate for you to drive home if you're tired."

Zuri felt a flutter in her stomach at Lea's tone. She knew she needed to leave, but the wine and the late hour had lowered her defenses. "I really should get going," she said halfheartedly.

Lea sat up, leaning closer. "Stay," she murmured, her hand reaching out to touch Zuri's knee. "Please."

Zuri was drawn in by Lea's intense gaze. Before she could think better of it, Lea closed the distance between them, pressing her lips to Zuri's in a tentative kiss. Zuri's breath hitched as their lips met, quickly gaining hunger and urgency.

As they explored each other's bodies, hands roaming freely and eagerly, Lea's perfume and the taste of wine overwhelmed Zuri's senses.

For a moment, Zuri allowed herself to sink into the kiss, her loneliness and desire overriding her better judgment. Tracy had been preoccupied with work and likely another lover. She always wanted to keep things between them as casual as possible and because it suited her lifestyle, Zuri had allowed it. But by that point, she had fallen for the other woman and it got harder to ignore how lonely she had become. It was like Lea had picked up on that signal and seized the opportunity.

Soon they were stumbling towards the bedroom, shedding clothes along the way as if it was a race against time. Zuri's skin tingled wherever Lea touched her, sending waves of pleasure through her body. The hazy fog of lust clouded Zuri's thoughts as they fell onto the bed in a frenzy of limbs.

But then reality crashed down on Zuri as Lea's fingers slipped beneath the waistband of her underwear. She was Lea's boss. This was wrong. With a sudden rush of clarity, Zuri pulled away, gasping for air as she tried to regain control of her racing thoughts.

"I'm sorry, I can't do this," she said, scrambling off the bed. "This is...it's not right. I'm your boss."

Lea's face fell, a mix of confusion and hurt in her eyes. "I don't care about that. We're both adults and we're attracted to each other."

Zuri shook her head, trying to ignore the ache between her legs. She knew she had to leave before things went any further. "It's not just that," she said, pulling on her clothes. "I have a rule about not getting involved with colleagues or employees. It never ends well."

Lea stood up from the bed, wrapping a sheet around herself

as she reached out for Zuri's hand. "But there's something between us," she pleaded.

Zuri pulled away, experiencing a mixture of guilt for leading Lea on and frustration with herself for succumbing to temptation. She grabbed her bag but paused at the door and turned towards Lea, who stood in her bedroom doorway, her face creased with heartache. "Let's just... let's pretend this didn't happen. I'll see you at work tomorrow."

She fled into the night, shame and regret churning in her gut. The next day, they had an awkward conversation where they agreed to forget about it and remain professional. But things were never quite the same after that.

Zuri banished the memory. After she began seeing Genesis, Lea fell back. Yet there were moments like now where it was obvious that Zuri could have more if she so desired.

"Speaking of innovation, I'm loving some changes that Genesis has made to the dance program."

At the mention of Genesis, Lea's expression cooled noticeably. "Yes, Genesis has brought a fresh perspective to the program," she said, her tone polite but lacking enthusiasm. She shuffled some papers, avoiding Zuri's gaze. "But let's get back to the budget, shall we?"

Zuri nodded, trying to refocus on the task at hand. As they continued to go over spreadsheets and projections, she noticed the shift in Lea's demeanor. The casual touches had stopped, replaced by a professional distance that bordered on chilly.

After about thirty minutes of number-crunching, Zuri glanced at her watch. "I think we've made good progress here," she said, gathering her things. "I have plans with Gen, so I have to get going."

Lea's smile tightened almost imperceptibly. "Of course, don't let me keep you. Enjoy your evening."

Zuri hurried down the hallway, her mind still buzzing from

the meeting with Lea. As she rounded the corner, she nearly collided with Genesis, who was leaning against the wall, scrolling through her phone.

"Hey, you," Genesis said, her face lighting up. "I was starting to think Lea had kidnapped you."

Zuri laughed, and kissed Genesis' hand. "Sorry about that. The budget review took longer than expected."

"No worries. I used the time to catch up on some emails. Ready for dinner?"

As they stepped out into the evening air, guilt washed over Zuri. She hadn't told Genesis about her history with Lea, and now it was a secret hanging between them. However, if she revealed the truth, that would entail the difficult decision of letting go of someone incredibly skilled at their job.

Zuri hesitated, then pushed those thoughts aside for now. She held hands with Genesis while they walked to their cars.

"Wanna just take mine and come back for yours?" Genesis asked.

"Sure, you know I love being your passenger princess."

Genesis chuckled as she opened the passenger door for Zuri with an exaggerated bow. "Your chariot awaits, Your Highness." She settled into the driver's seat and glanced at Zuri. "I was thinking of The Corkscrew."

The Corkscrew was one of their favorite restaurants and it had become something of a tradition between them to eat there at least once a month. It was nice that they had reached the point in their relationship where they had a special place to share.

Zuri waited until Genesis pulled out to start a conversation. "How are things at Beacon? I know you hired a couple of new people."

Genesis let out a sigh. "The teachers are outstanding, really knowledgeable, and I can tell the students are loving the new mix of dance styles. But Lea and I have been clashing about some of my choices."

Zuri thought back to her lukewarm response to her mention of the changes. "Really? That's unusual, because she's fairly open to new things."

"Yeah, with you."

Zuri's lips parted in surprise, but she did her best to be careful with what she said next. "What does that mean?"

Genesis shrugged. "She deals with you differently than she does me. I don't think she's happy about me working there. It's obvious she wants you Z, let's not pretend otherwise."

"Genesis, I..." Zuri began, but found herself at a loss for words.

"It's fine Z. I just... I needed to say it out loud. I see the way she looks at you, the touching for no reason."

Zuri cleared her throat, unsure of what to say. She didn't realize Genesis had even noticed any of it. "I won't lie and act like it's not there, but I just ignore her flirtation. If she's making you uncomfortable because you're with me, that's a problem."

Genesis sighed, her grip tightening on the steering wheel. "I don't want to make a big deal out of it. It's not like she's done anything. But she questions my decision making more than some of the other department heads."

"Well, then we need to have a talk," Zuri decided, her tone firm. Genesis opened her mouth to protest, but Zuri cut her off gently. "Not about us, Gen. Professional boundaries and respect in the workplace is a non-negotiable."

"I'm fine with you doing that if she gets out of line. Right now, it's a lot of conjecture on my part. She is, after all, my superior and doing her job. I just question her motives."

"If you want me to keep out of it, I will, for the moment. But promise me that you'll let me know if anything else comes up." Genesis nodded, but Zuri wasn't sure whether she would. That meant she had to monitor it from her end. "And for the record, I love you. Lea can wish all she wants, but it doesn't change the fact that you're the one I want."

Genesis smiled at that. "I know, baby."

The ride was quiet as they both listened to the music on the radio. Zuri could tell the attraction was still there for Lea, but she had let it go because she had yet to cross a line, but Genesis' discomfort was a different matter.

A familiar fear churned inside her at the thought of losing Genesis. She swallowed hard and brushed it aside. Gen wasn't like the other women she'd been with. They had trust and understanding. Their relationship was a far cry from any of the nonsense she had to deal with from Tracy or anyone who came before that.

She longed to confess everything, but the words caught in her throat, held back by the suffocating grip of fear. What if Genesis didn't understand? What if this secret, this one little omission, shattered the beautiful connection they'd built? Zuri's mind raced with possibilities, each more devastating than the last. She imagined the hurt in Genesis' eyes, the disappointment clouding her usually bright expression.

"We're here," Genesis called out as she pulled into the restaurant parking lot.

The sight of their favorite haunt brought a smile to their faces. When they reached the entrance, Zuri pulled open the door for Genesis.

"After you, m'lady," Zuri said with a slight bow.

Genesis giggled and winked at her. "Such a gentlewoman."

They entered the restaurant and the all too familiar aroma of herbs and spices mixed with the scent of fine wine welcomed them. The low hum of chatter from happy patrons and soft strains of jazz created a relaxing atmosphere. Decor was a blend of vintage chic and modern comfort. Cushioned seats lined up against brick walls, while stained glass lamps hung down from the ceiling.

"Good evening, ladies!" The owner, Roberto, greeted them. He was a hearty man with an infectious laugh, olive skin dotted with freckles and graying hair that he kept slicked back. His ever-present bright red apron bore stains from a hard day's work. They'd come to know him well over their frequent visits.

"Roberto!" Genesis responded enthusiastically, giving him a quick hug.

Zuri watched as Genesis conversed with Roberto, her laughter echoing around the restaurant. It wasn't hard to see why everyone fell in love with her spirit. She had this way about her that made people feel like they were the most important person in the room. Zuri felt it too, that irresistible force that drew her to Genesis. She hoped she made Gen feel the same, because she meant the world to her and Zuri would do anything to maintain what they had.

# Chapter Ten

Friday night, Genesis stepped out of their car, and found Zuri's hand as as the pulsating beat of the music washed over her. She had been looking forward to Flo Easy's listening party, mostly for the chance to unwind.

The club entrance glowed with neon lights, bathing the crowd of stylishly dressed party-goers in an electric hue. Genesis smoothed her fitted black dress, the fabric hugging her curves. Zuri wore a sleek, off-the-shoulder emerald green jumpsuit that accentuated her toned arms. Genesis felt a flutter in her stomach as she admired her girlfriend's stunning silhouette. While her woman wasn't vain, she had a reputation to uphold, and after being with Shannon in the spotlight, Gen knew it was important for them to look the part of a power couple.

It had been a couple of months since they attended any kind of formal event. Zuri's work had far fewer movie premieres and parties than Genesis expected. Much of what she did was at the office or studio, places Genesis couldn't really be.

The film company was in the midst of a major project, and Zuri had been putting in long hours at the office. Genesis understood the demands of her girlfriend's career, but that didn't make it easier.

Nights that were once filled with laughter and shared meals had become quiet affairs, with Genesis eating alone or reheating leftovers for Zuri when she finally stumbled through the door, exhausted. Their weekend plans had been repeatedly canceled or cut short due to urgent conference calls or last-minute script revisions. Even their usual morning routine of sharing coffee and stealing kisses before work had become a rushed affair, with Zuri often dashing out the door before Genesis had even fully woken up.

"So, I'll see you tonight, right?" Zuri had asked that morning as she ran around getting dressed.

Bleary eyed and half awake, Genesis nodded, letting out a loud yawn.

"Oh, my babe, this is why I hate waking you up." Zuri kneeled on the bed and kissed her forehead. "Get some more rest. I left breakfast for you on the stove."

Genesis didn't even get a chance to say thank you before Zuri was out the door. Breakfast was great, but she wanted them to share it together more than once a week.

"This dress is stunning on you, baby," Zuri said, her waist-length dreads swaying as she turned to press a kiss to Genesis's cheek. "Ready to head in?"

Genesis inhaled, excitement and nerves tingling in her belly. She needed to be present, and appreciate these moments. "More than ready. Let's do this."

Hand-in-hand, they made their way inside, the heavy bass thumping through Genesis's chest. The energy was infectious, bodies undulating on the packed dance floor, laughter and chatter rising above the music. Smiling, Genesis let the rhythm flow through her, hips swaying to the beat. She recognized the song as one of Flo Easy's first hits. Her mind was grappling with the fact that she got to meet and hang out with people who, before meeting Zuri, she only saw on tv or listened to on her phone. Her time married to Shannon was nothing compared to the world she was in now.

Zuri led them towards a VIP section, her fingers squeezing Genesis'.

"Zuri, over here!" A man with flowing locs and a megawatt smile waved them over. Genesis recognized Flo Easy from his music videos. Zuri was right, he was movie star handsome.

Flo Easy rose from his plush seat as they approached, his grin accompanied by the shine of a diamond encrusted grill on his top teeth. His gave off a youthful fun-loving glow that was at odds with his intense lyrics. He shared a quick embrace with Zuri, whispering something into her ear that made her chuckle. Then he turned his attention to Genesis.

"You must be Genesis," he said, offering a hand for her to shake. "Zuri told me all about you."

A blush crept up her cheeks, but she stood straight and met his gaze. "All good things, I hope."

"Only the best," he assured her. "Zuri's lucky to have you."

Genesis thanked him, her heart fluttering in her chest. She wanted to pinch herself. Was this her life?

"What y'all want? It's all on me tonight." Flo Easy yelled, loud enough to be heard over the music. Everyone in VIP answered back in celebration.

"Um, well Flo, I..."

"You can call me Will."

Genesis blinked in surprise, but quickly recovered, giving him a grateful smile. "Alright, Will. In that case, can we get some champagne?"

He grinned and signaled for the waiter. "I'll do you one better. How about a bottle?"

"Oh, well I don't think..."

Before she could protest, he had already requested a bottle of Dom Perignon. Genesis looked at Zuri, her eyes wide with surprise. Zuri burst into a fit of laughter and leaned in close to her ear.

"It's fine, babe. He can more than afford it. He's being extra generous because he and I are about to make a lot of money together. Let him show his appreciation."

Genesis was still trying to get used to the way people in Zuri's circle spent money. She took a deep breath and reminded herself that this was her life now.

"Okay, I'll be a good girl."

"Will you?" Zuri asked. She leaned in closer, this time letting her lips drag against Genesis' ear. "Did I mention how hot you look?"

Genesis sucked in a shaky breath. "Yes, but I don't mind hearing it again."

Zuri's eyes danced with heat. "I think I need to keep reminding you."

She pressed a lingering kiss to Genesis's lips before kissing a trail along her neck, sending a shiver down her spine. Heat pooled between her thighs and for once she was glad that people surrounded them because otherwise she might have let Zuri have her right there on the spot.

"Zuri," she breathed out, trying to regain some semblance of control.

Zuri pulled back with a mischievous glint in her eye. "What? I'm not allowed to show my appreciation?"

Genesis bit her lip, trying to suppress a moan. She could feel the heat rising in her cheeks as their eyes met.

"Hmm, I think you're trying to drive me crazy," Genesis said with a shaky voice.

Zuri leaned in and kissed her again. This time it was slow and sensual, filled with all the passion that built up whenever they spent time apart. Genesis melted into it, letting herself get lost in the feel of Zuri's lips against hers.

The surrounding music faded into white noise as they deepened the kiss. Everything else disappeared from their minds as they focused only on each other.

When they pulled away for air, Genesis noticed some members of Flo Easy's crew watching them with interest. She felt a flush creep up her neck, self-conscious.

Zuri followed her gaze and smirked. "Let them watch," she whispered. "They just wish they were me."

Genesis laughed, some of her nervousness dissipating. "You're so bad."

"That's what makes it fun," Zuri replied with a wicked smirk, her hand sliding down to rest possessively on Genesis' thigh.

Although she had never been one for public displays of affection, that all went out the window with Zuri. Genesis couldn't deny the thrill that ran through her at Zuri's possessive touch. She leaned into her, reveling in the closeness of her body.

Will approached them with their champagne. "You two seem to be enjoying yourselves," he said with a knowing smile, filling up their glasses. "I didn't mean to interrupt anything."

Zuri shrugged. "Don't worry about it. We were just catching up."

A subtle grin played at the corners of his lips, hinting at his amusement, but he let it drop. Instead, he turned to Genesis. "So tell me about yourself, Genesis. Zuri is a dynamic lady, so I can only assume you two are equally yoked."

Genesis chuckled. "Equally yoked? Someone grew up in the church. I haven't heard that term since attending myself."

Will raised his tattooed hands. "You got me there. I'm not a church boy anymore, but I still follow a lot of the teachings. This rap game is just a means to an end."

"Yes, pretty soon you'll be adding movie star to your list of accomplishments," Zuri said, raising her glass.

Nervous about having the spotlight on her, Genesis shrugged. "I'm just an accountant with a very cute husky. The most exciting thing about me is my book collection."

"Sounds like you underestimate your charm," Will countered, laughter blossoming in his eyes. "But I have to ask, what's your favorite book?"

Genesis pondered a moment before answering, "I'd have to say 'The Alchemist' by Paulo Coelho. It taught me a lot about listening to my heart and following my dreams."

"Nice. I just finished The Four Agreements, and it was the same for me."

Finding out that the young rapper whose most famous track to date was about his love for getting high had the mind of a scholar was a pleasant surprise.

As they continued their conversation, Genesis sipped her drink, her eyes glancing at Zuri as she mingled with Flo Easy and his entourage. Zuri was in her element here, confident and poised, body language open and inviting.

"Hey everybody."

All eyes turned to Elijah as he entered the VIP area. He was dressed in his best version of hip- hop gear. He sauntered over, his eyes wide with excitement as he spotted Will.

"Yo, Flo Easy!" he exclaimed, his voice rising an octave higher than usual. Genesis watched in amused disbelief as Zuri's normally composed cousin transformed into a starstruck fan before her eyes.

"Bro, I've been following your career since day one," Elijah gushed, clasping Will's hand in both of his own and shaking it vigorously. "Your first mixtape? Fire. Absolute fire. I played it on repeat for months."

Will chuckled, clearly flattered but a bit taken aback by

Elijah's enthusiasm. "Thanks, man. Always good to meet a day one fan."

But Elijah was just getting started. He launched into a detailed analysis of Will's discography, rattling off obscure song titles and quoting lyrics with the fervor of a devoted scholar. "And that verse in 'Midnight Hustle'? Pure poetry, my man. The way you layered those metaphors? Genius."

Genesis glanced at Zuri, expecting to see amusement mirrored in her girlfriend's eyes. Instead, she found Zuri's cheeks flushed with embarrassment, her lips pressed into a thin line as she watched her cousin's fanboy moment unfold.

Undeterred by the growing awkwardness, Elijah pulled out his phone. "Yo, can I get a selfie?"

Will obliged and Zuri rolled her eyes. Genesis stifled a laugh when Zuri mouthed, 'so embarrassing'.

As Genesis went back to people watching, it was then that she saw her.

Tracy was holding court in a corner of a different VIP section, accompanied by a group of beautiful people. Despite being in the same industry, Zuri had avoided Tracy and vice versa, but they were bound to run into each other at some point. Genesis glanced at Z who was engrossed in a conversation with Will. She debated whether to alert herto Tracy's presence or let her enjoy the evening unaware.

Before Genesis could decide, Tracy's gaze landed on her. Recognition flashed in her eyes, followed quickly by a stiff smile. Genesis tensed as Tracy whispered something to the young woman beside her. Her new girlfriend, if the gossip sites were to be believed. The woman's eyes widened as she looked in their direction, her expression a mix of curiosity and something Genesis couldn't quite place.

"Hello, hello."

Genesis broke eye contact and smiled when she saw

Alma walking towards them, her boyfriend Nathan following behind her. From their first time meeting, Alma and Genesis clicked as if they were old friends. She greeted Alma with a hug, grateful for the distraction. "Hey girl, you look amazing!" she exclaimed, admiring Alma's sleek red dress.

"Me, what about you? I'm so jealous of the way you're filling out that dress. Isn't she gorgeous, Nathan?"

Nathan raised an eyebrow and leaned over to kiss Genesis' cheek. "That sounds like a trick question, so I'm going to defer answering and just say all of you ladies are stunning."

Genesis chuckled. "I like a man who knows what not to say."

Alma nodded in Zuri's direction. "I see Z is over there holding court, as usual."

As if on cue, Zuri glanced over and caught sight of Alma and Nathan. She excused herself from Flo Easy's group and returned, her face lighting up.

"Y'all made it!" Zuri said, embracing them both. "Thanks for getting my girl out of the house, Nate."

"I wasn't going to miss out on meeting one of my favorite rappers." He leaned into Zuri. "Any chance you can introduce me?"

"Of course, come on."

Alma shook her head as she sat down beside Genesis. "This is all he's been talking about since I told him. You already know how I feel about clubs."

Genesis nodded as she poured her some champagne. "Yes, but it's sweet that you're accommodating him."

Alma took a sip and sighed contentedly. "That's what love is, I suppose. Compromise and all that jazz."

"To an extent. If I've learned anything, it's that you can't compromise who you are at your core," Genesis said, her eyes drifting to Zuri across the room. "But finding someone who brings out the best in you? That's the real magic."

"You're right. I just worry I'm not exciting enough for him, you know? He's always wanting to go out, try new things. And here I am, content with a night in and a good book."

"Hey, opposites attract for a reason. You balance each other out. And from what I've seen, Nathan adores you just the way you are." Genesis looked over at where Tracy sat, her eyes darting between Genesis and her friends. "At least you don't have the ghost of a past relationship still haunting you."

Alma looked in the same direction and laughed out loud when her eyes landed on Tracy. "Who? Tracy? Please Gen, she is not anyone to be worried about. That was a relationship that passed its expiration date. What you have with Zuri is real. In all the years I've known her, she hasn't been as happy as she is now."

Genesis smiled, grateful for Alma's reassurance. Zuri returned, sliding into the booth next to her and wrapping an arm around her waist.

"Sorry about that, babe. Nate's like a kid in a candy store meeting Flo."

Genesis leaned into Zuri's embrace, breathing in her familiar scent. "No worries. Alma is always great company."

Zuri's eyes flicked between the two of them. "Everything okay? You seem a little tense."

Instead of answering, Genesis nodded in Tracy's direction. Zuri's body stiffened, but then she relaxed. When she faced Genesis, her eyes were full of love.

"It was going to happen at some point," Zuri said, brushing a loose piece of hair from Genesis' face. "You good?"

"I'm good if you're good."

Zuri sipped some champagne and settled into the couch. "Never been better."

# Chapter Eleven

Zuri was not good. She had noticed Tracy out of the corner of her eye when they first arrived, but didn't want to make Genesis uncomfortable. There were still some intense emotions about how things went down in the past and the last thing she wanted was for their night to be ruined because of her ex. But now her presence was throwing off what was supposed to be a fun night out for them.

After kicking Tracy out of her home and moving on with Genesis, the other woman had faded into the background. She attempted to contact Zuri after the breakup, but she had blocked Tracy on every platform she had and when she called the job, Zuri's assistant had her perpetually "unavailable". It may not have been the most mature approach, but Zuri had never experienced such betrayal from someone she loved.

Years wasted on a woman who only saw her as a retirement plan. That made her look like a fool to the world as she did what she liked, and Zuri stayed in the background. She still couldn't believe that she had been so desperate for love that she allowed herself to be treated that way.

"I heard she's dating some musician named Songstress. Such an original name," Alma remarked with a hint of disdain. "Anyway, she's hot right now, and has three songs in the top ten on Billboard. It made sense that Tracy would attach herself to someone like that."

Zuri just nodded in response, her eyes on Tracy and her new girlfriend. Songstress was younger, in her early 30s, and ripe for the picking. Tracy still had enough star power to make anyone she was with shine brighter with her name recognition. They looked happy and in love. Zuri never thought Tracy was that great of an actress. Her looks made up for much of what she lacked, but the way she could make people fall in love with her was a talent.

"Well, whoever she's with will never compare to what she lost. She dropped her dime, and I picked it up," Genesis said, stroking Zuri's leg.

Zuri looked into her eyes and smiled. Genesis leaned in and planted a kiss on her lips, drawing her attention away from Tracy and back to the present moment. Genesis' touch and the tenderness in her eyes eased her spirit.

"You're right," Zuri said, squeezing Genesis' hand. "I've got everything I need right here."

Alma raised her glass. "To new beginnings and better choices!"

They clinked glasses, the sound of laughter and music from the club enveloping them. Zuri allowed herself to relax, sinking into the plush booth and letting the rhythm of the bass wash over her. She watched as Genesis swayed to the music, her curls bouncing with each movement.

"Dance with me?" Genesis asked, extending her hand to Zuri.

Without hesitation, Zuri took it, allowing herself to be led onto the dance floor. The music pulsed through the club, and

Zuri let the rhythm take over her body. Genesis moved with fluid grace, her dancer's body in perfect sync with the beat. Zuri matched her movements, letting go of her usual reserve and losing herself in the music and the moment.

Genesis spun Zuri around, pulling her close. Their bodies moved together, the heat between them rising with each beat of the music. Zuri's hands found Genesis' waist, and she marveled at how perfectly they fit together.

As the song transitioned to a slower tempo, Zuri wrapped her arms around Genesis' neck, pulling her closer. They moved together, lost in their own world, amidst the crowded dance floor. Zuri breathed in Genesis' scent, an intoxicating mix of jasmine and vanilla, and closed her eyes, savoring the moment.

"It's okay if you're still upset, babe. Tracy hurt you."

Zuri opened her eyes to find Genesis gazing at her.

"I'm not upset," Zuri said, her fingers playing with the soft curls at the nape of Genesis' neck. "Not in the way you might think. I don't have any feelings for Tracy, but seeing her reminds me of how far I've come. It's a reminder, not a wound."

"That's a beautiful way to look at it."

Zuri laughed lightly, shaking her head. "I'm telling it like it is." She leaned in, pressing her forehead against Genesis's. "And having you here makes everything better."

The song ended and Zuri kissed Genesis's hand before sending her back to VIP while she made her way to the bathroom. Like always, there was a line for the women's restroom. While she waited, she scrolled on her phone and moved out of the way when she felt a presence in front of her. When the person didn't walk by, she looked up and into Tracy's penetrating dark eyes.

"So, this is what we're doing now? Accosting people on their way to the bathroom?" Zuri asked as she slipped her phone into her pocket.

Tracy blinked, a small frown creasing her forehead. "No... I was hoping we could talk, Z," she said, the old nickname slipping out like a plea.

Zuri rolled her eyes as she crossed her arms and shifted her weight onto one foot. She raised an eyebrow, daring Tracy to continue, but said nothing. She had lost the privilege of casual conversation with her, and Zuri wasn't going to make it easy for her.

"Look... I know you're still mad at me and I get it," Tracy said quickly. "I wanted to say... I'm sorry. For everything."

Zuri's right eyebrow joined its twin in a high arch. "Sorry? Really?" she scoffed, lips twisting in a skeptical smile. "Now, isn't that something?"

Tracy shifted uncomfortably under Zuri's steady gaze. She opened her mouth as if to say something more, but seemed to think better of it.

"It's not like you've made it easy to speak to you. An apology is long overdue. Did you even read the letter I left you?"

Zuri remembered after she returned from Paris and found the hand-written letter on her bed. She never opened it, choosing to toss it in the trash without a second glance.

"No, I didn't read your letter," Zuri replied coolly. "I had no interest in anything you had to say."

Tracy's eyes widened, a flicker of hurt crossing her face before she composed herself. "I understand. I thought... maybe with time..."

"Time?" Zuri interrupted, her voice low but sharp. "Time doesn't erase what you did, Tracy. It doesn't change the fact that you used me and never loved me."

Tracy flinched at Zuri's words, her gaze dropping to the floor. "I know I messed up, Z. I was selfish and scared, but I never said I didn't love you."

Zuri shook her head, a mirthless chuckle escaping her lips.

"Right, just that you weren't in love with me despite five years together. And now what? You're with Songstress and you've found your conscience? Please." She shook her head, her dreadlocks swaying with the motion. "Save your apologies. I don't need them."

Tracy's eyes flashed with a mix of hurt and frustration. "I'm trying to make amends here. Can't you see that?"

"Amends?" Zuri scoffed. "What are you trying to make amends for? For wasting five years of my life? For making me believe in a future that would never happen? Or for treating me like I was your personal ATM?"

Tracy winced at the accusations. "It wasn't like that, Z. I cared about you, I still do."

"You have a funny way of showing it," Zuri retorted, her voice dripping with sarcasm. "Don't worry about me. You said what you had to say."

Zuri turned to continue waiting on line and was ready to ignore Tracy, but she spoke again.

"I see you and Genesis are together. Guess I shouldn't be surprised, since it was clear there was something between you two when I went to Barbados. I wish you could have been honest with me."

Zuri's breath hitched at Tracy's words. She turned back to face her. Her eyes flickered with an emotion she couldn't name, but it seemed different from what Zuri was used to seeing. Was that regret in Tracy's eyes?

"Are you implying that I cheated on you?" Zuri asked, her voice low "Because if you are, you're more delusional than I thought."

Tracy flinched, looking down at her feet. "No, I'm saying..."

"I don't care what you're 'saying', Tracy." Zuri cut her off, her anger simmering below the surface. The audacity of this woman was astounding. "Do not come here and try to twist things around to make me the bad guy. You were the selfish one who betrayed our relationship."

A few people near them glanced their way. Tracy looked embarrassed, her gaze darting between Zuri and the surrounding people.

As if on cue, Songstress appeared at Tracy's side, slipping an arm around her waist. "Everything okay here, babe?" she asked, her eyes flicking between Zuri and Tracy.

The young woman was tall, slightly towering over Tracy. Her skin was dewy and smooth, the color of mocha. Her black hair shimmered under the light, artfully braided into a high bun, her smooth, round face framed by massive gold hoops.

Tracy looked up at her girlfriend and nodded. "Yeah, we were just talking."

"Really?" Songstress looked at Zuri with a smirk on her glossy lips. "Because it didn't sound like you were just talking."

Zuri shrugged, not eager to entertain another scene. "We're done here." She cast one final glance at Tracy before turning back to the line for the restroom.

When she emerged a few minutes later, Tracy and Songstress were nowhere to be seen. Zuri was relieved. She needed air to put distance between herself and the emotions that threatened to suffocate her.

Once outside, Zuri took deep breaths, trying to calm the storm inside her. She hadn't expected the encounter with Tracy to affect her this much, but the memories of the pain and betrayal were still raw.

She needed a moment to herself and didn't want Genesis to see her like this.

"Z, everything okay?" Alma asked as she walked up to her. "I saw you and Tracy chatting while I danced with Nathan."

"Everything's great. Tracy needed me to know how sorry

she was. Can you fucking believe that? As if saying I'm sorry would erase what she did to me."

Alma's brown eyes widened, and she reached out, touching Zuri's arm with a comforting hand.

"Oh babe... she's still the same old person. All talk, no substance. Please don't let her ruin your night," said Alma, her voice filled with sincere concern.

Zuri sighed, raked a hand through her dreadlocks, and shifted her gaze to the sky. "I'm not letting her ruin anything, Alma. It brought up some old feelings, you know?"

"Understandable," Alma said, offering a supportive squeeze before releasing Zuri's arm. "But remember who you're here with tonight."

Zuri's gaze shifted from the stars to Alma's face, her friend's words sinking in. Memories of the past couple of years with Genesis flooded her mind. The way Genesis' whole face lit up when she laughed, the gentle touch of her hands as they danced together in Zuri's living room on lazy Sunday mornings, the passionate debates they'd have over books and movies that always ended in playful tickle fights.

All of this angst, that wasn't the type of relationship they had. Other than when they first got together, most of their time had been full of love and laughter. Genesis had brought a light into her life that Zuri hadn't even realized was missing. Now, she couldn't live without it.

"Yeah, I need to get my head right. Thanks for coming to check on me. I'll come back inside in a few, I promise."

Alma gave her a small nod and a reassuring smile before walking back towards the entrance, leaving Zuri alone with her thoughts.

Zuri took a deep, cleansing breath. Her heart still was heavy, but she'd survived worse. This encounter with Tracy was an unfortunate blip in an otherwise perfect evening.

She headed back, her mind set on one person; Genesis.

The flicker of joy that incited in her heart was enough to banish the last of her tumultuous feelings. That part of life was over and despite her anger at Tracy approaching her, it gave her a sense of closure. She could move forward and leave her ex in the past where she belonged.

# Chapter Twelve

When Zuri returned to the VIP area, Genesis greeted her with a smile, pressing a glass of champagne into her hand.

"Will is about to perform some songs from the new album," Genesis said, doing a little happy dance.

Zuri laughed out loud. "I can't believe how much you like this music."

"Just because you only prefer the classic stuff doesn't mean everyone else has to!" she teased. "There's enjoyment to be had in all forms of music, love."

Will took the stage and transformed into his persona, Flo Easy. Gone was the young man who loved books and spirituality and before them stood a powerful lyricist, owning the room with his authoritative presence. His velvety voice filled the space, drawing people from their cocktails and conversations towards him. The new songs had some great beats, and everyone in the club was moving along, some already able to recite the words.

Zuri swayed to the rhythm, her fingers tapping against the crystal flute holding her champagne. Genesis watched her and smiled. Seeing Zuri let loose and enjoy herself was a rarity, and Genesis relished such precious moments, especially considering what she'd just seen between her and Tracy.

"Now that's more like it," she teased, bumping her shoulder into Zuri's. Zuri laughed, rolling her eyes good-naturedly in response.

As Flo Easy's set ended, applause thundered throughout the room, none louder than the ones coming from their VIP section.

When Will rejoined them, he was beaming, his face glistening with a sheen of sweat from the performance.

"That was amazing! Those new tracks are so good!" Genesis exclaimed, bouncing on her toes.

Will laughed. "Thanks, Gen. I'm glad you enjoyed it."

Zuri offered a more subdued but heartfelt congratulations, giving Will a brief hug. "You killed it out there. The crowd was eating it up."

"You would think I'd be tired, but," Will climbed on a couch, "who's ready for another round?"

"I know I am," Elijah yelled out before everyone else.

Everyone laughed then yelled out their agreement, the excitement of the night still coursing through their veins. Genesis soaked up the infectious energy. She glanced at Zuri, who looked ready to call it a night.

"One more drink, babe. We never get to hang out." She batted her eyelashes and did her best version of puppy dog eyes. "I'll make it worth your while."

A slow smile spread across Zuri's face. "Well, when you put it like that..." She pulled Genesis close, whispering into her ear. "You better make good on that promise."

Genesis grinned, her heart fluttering at Zuri's touch. "Oh, I intend to."

Zuri excused herself and went to talk to Will and his

friends. She dropped back into the seats beside Alma and Nathan and joined in on their conversation.

Despite her best efforts, her mind kept returning to the confrontation she saw between Tracy and Zuri. That it happened didn't bother her, but Zuri's response did. It's possible that she was being absurd. After all, there had been no signs she regretted ending their relationship, but the look on her face as she and Tracy spoke had not been one of someone who was over it. She looked very much like she was still in pain.

Had they gotten together too soon after Zuri ended things with Tracy? Their first year was a whirlwind and at the end, she proposed. Genesis knew all too well how hard it could be to get over someone you gave years to, but her desire for Zuri had over-ruled her common sense. Now she wondered if she would always be competing against the ghost of what could have been.

A couple of hours later, they made it back to Zuri's house. Zuri had broken down and gotten a driver when Genesis found out how late she would sometimes get home from premieres and various events. It was a worthy expense and set Gen's mind at ease but was also a godsend on nights like this.

Genesis leaned into the window on the passenger side as soon as they exited the car. "Drake, you're amazing."

Drake chuckled, his hazel eyes crinkling at the corners. "Just doing my job, Genesis. You two have a good night now."

"You too, Drake. Get home safe," Zuri called out, her arm wrapped around Genesis's waist.

As they walked to the front door, Zuri stumbled, giggling as Genesis' grip tightened around her.

When they reached the door, Zuri fumbled with her keys.

Genesis giggled at the sight of her usually composed girlfriend struggling with such a simple task.

"Need some help there, love?" Genesis teased, taking the keys from Zuri's hand.

Zuri huffed, but there was no real annoyance in her voice. "I'm capable of opening my door. Thank you very much."

Genesis raised an eyebrow, amusement dancing in her eyes. "Oh, I'm sure you are."

She unlocked the door, pushing it open with one hand while the other found its way to the small of Zuri's back. After they stepped inside, Genesis hesitated and Zuri turned towards her.

"You got something to say to me, Ms. Malone?" Zuri asked with a smirk.

Genesis moved toward her and stroked her collar bone. She smiled when she saw the slight shiver that ran through her. In that moment, she felt a surge of emotion—love, desire, and a hint of uncertainty. She wanted to voice her thoughts, to tell Zuri how much she craved more moments like this. More lazy mornings tangled in sheets, impromptu dance parties in the kitchen, nights where they could just be together without the world demanding their attention.

Zuri kissed her forehead. "Talk to me, baby."

Genesis nibbled on her lip. "I had a delightful time tonight, and I want more. More of this," she said, pulling her closer, "more of you."

Zuri's gaze filled with affection. She reached up, cupping Genesis' face in her hands. "You have me, Gen. All of me."

Genesis couldn't stop the tears that welled up in her eyes. She was tired of holding back her feelings. "Oh baby, I wish that was true."

"Hey now, don't cry." Zuri pulled her into a tight hug. "Is this why you got so quiet on Sunday after pottery?"

Genesis nodded, unable to speak, fearing her voice would

betray her emotions even more. She took a deep breath, trying to compose herself.

"Gen, I..." Zuri started, then paused, collecting her thoughts. "I'm sorry. You're right, I have been busy, but that's no excuse. You mean the world to me and I don't ever want you to feel you're not getting all I have to give."

"I miss you. I miss us." She shook her head. "It seems silly even bringing this up now. We had so much fun tonight."

Zuri cupped Genesis' face gently, her thumbs wiping away the tears that had fallen. "There's nothing silly about you expressing yourself. I want to know these things."

Genesis leaned into Zuri's touch, closing her eyes. When she opened them again, she saw nothing but love and sincerity in Zuri's gaze.

"I've been so caught up in work and everything else, but I have been trying babe." Zuri continued, her voice low and earnest. "You and the life we're building together are important to me." She took Genesis' hands in hers, intertwining their fingers. "I promise you to be more aware. I love you, and I want us to work through this together."

Genesis let out a deep sigh. She hadn't realized how much she'd been holding in until this moment. "I love you too, Z. So much."

"Good. I'm glad we're on the same page then," Zuri said with a wink. Genesis smiled. "There's that beautiful smile of yours. Need more of that, less of the tears. How about we go upstairs and relax? I'm exhausted."

As they made their way upstairs, her mind drifted back to the argument she'd witnessed between Zuri and Tracy. The image of Zuri's pained expression flashed in her mind again.

Zuri began leading her upstairs. "You sure know how to sober a girl up."

Genesis chuckled as they climbed the stairs, her hand still

grasped in Zuri's. "Sorry about that. Not the romantic end to the night I had in mind."

"Please, don't ever be sorry for being honest with me." They stepped into the bedroom and Zuri pulled down the zipper of her jumpsuit, letting the bottom half hang on her waist, before plopping into a cushy chair in the corner of her bedroom. "I'll tell you one thing, I am getting too old to hang at the club."

"Oh, stop it," Genesis took off her shoes and tossed them aside. "You're only as old as you feel."

Zuri stifled a yawn, her eyes trailing off to the side. "Yeah, and right now I feel like I'm a hundred and two." Her statement was followed by another yawn, this one too powerful to be hidden behind a polite hand.

"Good grief!" Genesis chuckled and shook her head. "You need a good night's rest." She moved towards the chair where Zuri settled down, kneeling in front of her.

Genesis undid the intricate knots that held Zuri's dreadlocks away from her face. Her fingers moved with practiced ease, untying each knot and letting the long dreads cascade down Zuri's back. They were beautiful up close, she thought, as beautiful as the woman herself.

Zuri leaned back and let out a contented sigh. She massaged Genesis's hands and brought them to her mouth, kissing both palms.

"Thank you for coming out with me. I know you work so hard during the week and having another obligation is the last thing you want..."

Genesis cut her off by placing her finger against her lips. "I don't care how tired I am. If you need me, I'll be there."

Zuri pulled Genesis closer, their foreheads touching. "What did I do to deserve you?" she whispered.

Genesis felt a twinge in her chest, the earlier doubts

creeping back in. She pushed them aside, focusing on Zuri's breath against her skin. "You're you. That's more than enough."

Their lips met in a tender kiss, slow and languid. Genesis savored the taste of champagne on Zuri's tongue. She melted into her, her fingers tangling in Zuri's dreadlocks. As they pulled apart, she studied Zuri's face, searching for any signs of hesitation or regret. But all she saw was love and contentment in those brown eyes.

"Come on, let's get you to bed," Genesis murmured, helping Zuri to her feet.

They moved together towards the king-sized bed, shedding the rest of their clothes along the way. Genesis pulled back the plush comforter, then thought better of it.

"I believe I promised to make staying out longer worthwhile. How about we have a nice shower and then lay down?"

Zuri perked up, her fatigue forgotten. "I think that sounds like an excellent idea," she purred, her gaze roaming over Genesis's body.

Genesis took Zuri's hand, leading her into the spacious ensuite bathroom. The room was a marvel of modern design, with sleek marble countertops and a walk-in shower big enough for four people. Genesis flicked on the lights, dimming them to create an intimate atmosphere.

She turned on the water, adjusting the temperature until steam filled the air. After grabbing a shower cap for her hair, she put Zuri's locs up into a bun with a large band and placed her oversized shower cap over. The rainfall showerhead poured water over them, the glass enclosure fogging up around them. Genesis reached for Zuri's favorite lavender body wash, squeezing a dollop onto a loofah.

Genesis washed Zuri's body. Her hands moved in slow, sensual circles, massaging away her stress from the long night.

"You take such good care of me," Zuri murmured, her eyes closed.

Genesis smiled, pressing a kiss to Zuri's shoulder. "It's my pleasure," she whispered, her hands gliding down Zuri's arms.

As she continued, Genesis marveled at the smooth expanse of Zuri's caramel skin, glistening under the water. Her fingers traced the curve of Zuri's hips.

"Turn around," Genesis instructed gently.

Zuri complied, her eyes meeting Genesis' with a smoldering intensity that made her breath catch in her throat. The steam swirled around them.

Genesis's hands glided over Zuri's collarbone, down the swell of her breasts, and along the flat plane of her stomach. Zuri's breath hitched, her eyes fluttering closed as Genesis's fingers dipped lower.

Genesis' hands continued their exploration, eliciting soft moans from Zuri. She savored every touch, every gasp.

Unable to resist, she leaned forward to capture one erect nipple in her mouth, sucking it hard between her lips. Zuri cried out, arching her back even further as Genesis switched to the other breast, sucking and licking with abandon. Her hand slipped down to Zuri's lower belly, her fingertips teasing her before dipping further below. A strangled gasp escaped from Zuri as Genesis found her wetness and began stroking her with an artful mix of tenderness and force.

After years of being on the receiving end of pleasure, Genesis loved the way Zuri responded to her touch. It was addictive and for the first few months of their relationship, she couldn't keep her hands to herself. Now, they had reached a nice equilibrium where their love making was far less urgent, but the desire she had for Zuri wasn't. She was always hungry for more. Her taste, her touch, the very essence of her.

As Genesis continued to explore Zuri's body, her own desire

built as well. She could feel the wetness between her legs, craving Zuri's touch as much as she was giving it. Slowly, she brought her wet fingers to Zuri's lips, inviting her to taste herself. Zuri's eyes darkened with lust, and she opened her mouth. Moaning, she licked every trace of her arousal from Genesis's fingers before pulling her in for a deep, passionate kiss.

Water rained down on them as Genesis returned to teasing her with slow, purposeful strokes. She took her time, worshiping Zuri's body with her mouth and hands. She reveled in the way Zuri gripped her, the way her breath came in short, ragged gasps.

Genesis' hands on her hips were strong and sure, holding her steady as Zuri's body trembled with pleasure. The sensation of Zuri's nails digging into her back sent shivers down Genesis' spine.

Zuri's hips bucked against Genesis's hand, urging her on. Her grip tightened even more as the pressure increased, matching Genesis's slow strokes with frantic thrusts of her own. The water splashed around them, and the sound of their heavy breathing filled the air.

Genesis couldn't get enough; she wanted to taste every inch of her skin, to devour her like the sweetest dessert. She kissed down her neck and shoulders, nipping gently, causing Zuri to squirm with pleasure. Her hands cupped Zuri's ass, pulling her closer still. Then, Genesis pushed another finger inside her wetness as she claimed Zuri's mouth once more.

With a cry of delight, Zuri arched her back and moaned into the kiss. This time, when they broke apart for air, they were both panting heavily.

Genesis looked into Zuri's eyes and saw her own arousal mirrored there. The connection between them was palpable, as if they could read each other's minds. She had never felt so close to anyone else before; it was both exhilarating and terrifying.

As they gazed at each other, Zuri's body tensed up and contracted around Zuri's fingers as she came apart, her orgasmic cries muffled by the sound of the waterfall shower head.

"God, Genesis," she gasped, her eyes hazy with desire. "I love you."

Genesis smiled and leaned in to kiss Zuri's forehead. "I love you too," she whispered against her damp skin. "Now, how about we get out before we both melt into puddles on the floor?"

"You sure you don't want me to reciprocate?"

"Pleasing you did more than enough for me, baby. But we can revisit this conversation in the morning."

Zuri chuckled softly, her eyes still heavy with desire. "I'll hold you to that promise."

They finished their shower, washing away the remnants of the club night and their lovemaking. Stepping out, Genesis wrapped Zuri in a fluffy towel, drying her off with tender care.

When they returned to the bedroom, they slipped under the covers, their bodies gravitating towards each other. Zuri nestled into Genesis's side, her head resting on her chest as she stroked her back.

"Thank you," Zuri murmured.

"For what?"

"For being you. For loving me. For reminding me what's important."

Genesis turned in Zuri's arms to face her, their noses almost touching. "You don't have to thank me for that."

Zuri's eyes searched hers, a hint of vulnerability in their depths. "Of course I do." She pulled back a bit and rested on an elbow, keeping her other hand on Genesis. "I spoke to Tracy while I was waiting to use the bathroom."

Genesis' heart skipped a beat. She tried to keep her voice neutral as she asked, "Oh? How did that go?"

Zuri sighed, her hand caressing her thigh. "It was... strange. Awkward. She apologized for how things ended between us."

Genesis swallowed hard, willing herself to remain calm. "That's... good, I suppose. Did you two clear the air?"

Zuri was quiet for a moment, and Genesis could almost hear the gears turning in her head. "I think so. It was closure, in a way. But it also made me realize something."

Genesis held her breath, her mind racing with possibilities. "What's that?"

"How incredibly lucky I am to have you."

Relief washed over Genesis, but a small part of her still held onto doubt. "Are you sure? I mean, seeing an ex can stir up old feelings..." She regretted the words as soon as they left her mouth, but the only way to know the truth was to be honest.

Zuri cupped Genesis's face with her free hand, her touch gentle but firm. "Gen, listen to me. What Tracy and I had is in the past. Yes, it was a significant part of my life, but it's over. You're my present and my future. You're the one I want to wake up next to every morning."

Tears pricked the corners of Genesis' eyes. She blinked them away, not wanting to let her emotions overwhelm her. "I saw you two talking earlier, and you looked so intense. Perhaps I should have said something, but..."

"Oh, love. I'm sorry you had to see that. It was intense, but not in the way you're thinking. Tracy was trying to apologize, to explain herself. I was angry, hurt even, but not because I wanted her back. I was upset because I realized how much time I wasted."

Genesis nodded, letting out a shaky breath. "I understand. It's just, I worry I rushed you into this. Maybe you didn't have enough time to heal before we got together."

Zuri shifted, pulling Genesis closer. "Gen, you didn't rush me into anything. Did you forget I came to you and asked you out?"

The memory of Zuri appearing at her house and how determined she was to take her out still made her blush. "I could never forget that."

"You helped me heal. You showed me what genuine love looks like. What it is to be cherished and respected. Every day with you is a gift, and I wouldn't change a thing about how we got here."

Genesis leaned in, kissing Zuri's lips. "I'm sorry for doubting, even for a moment. You mean everything to me, Zuri. The thought of losing you..."

Zuri silenced her with another kiss, this one deeper and more passionate. When they parted, Zuri pulled Genesis into her body and held on tight.

"You won't lose me. I'm right here, and I'm not going anywhere."

Genesis let her mind wander as sleep claimed her. The gentle rise and fall of Zuri's chest was like a lullaby, soothing away the last vestiges of her earlier worries.

# Chapter Thirteen

"He wants what in his trailer?"

Elijah looked down at his phone for confirmation. "Brand new carnations, every morning. He said he finds them inspirational."

Zuri looked at her cousin and rolled her eyes. She couldn't do anything but say yes. This was, after all, The Phillip Minor, world famous director, and they were supposed to feel lucky just getting to work with him. His outrageous demands were just the tip of the iceberg.

Monday morning was feeling very much like the beginning of a hellish week.

"Alright," she sighed, "tell him he'll have his carnations. Anything else?"

Elijah squinted at his phone again, scrolling through the endless list of requests. "He wants the trailer stocked with bottled rainwater from Oregon, vinyl records from the 60s, and..." He paused, an incredulous look on his face. "And a masseuse on call."

Zuri's eyes twitched. A masseuse on call? Was the man serious? She resisted the urge to throw something at her cousin. It wasn't his fault, after all. But Phillip Minor was turning out to be more than a handful, even before they started production.

"I swear," she muttered under her breath, "this movie better win every award known to humankind."

"Did you say something, Zuri?" Elijah asked, looking up from his phone with a puzzled expression.

"Just thinking aloud." Zuri waved him off. "Okay, add those things to the list and see that they're arranged. Anything else?"

Elijah scrolled further, then gave a low whistle. "He wants a private chef skilled in cooking Mediterranean cuisine, vegan of course, and a selection of aged white wines. Oh, and every day at 11:56 am, he must have a cup of matcha tea prepared with the aforementioned Oregon water."

Zuri pinched the bridge of her nose, the beginnings of a headache building. "It's like we're organizing a luxury spa retreat rather than a film shoot. Alright," she agreed, "add that to the list too."

Just when she believed that Phillip Minor's demands had reached their peak of insanity, Elijah voiced the final request. "Oh, and he wants a harpist to play soothing tunes each evening before he goes to bed.

Zuri stared at Elijah for a moment before she broke into laughter. Her cousin joined her, both doubling over, tears rolling down their faces. It was downright absurd and if she didn't laugh, then she would be crying.

"It does not say that, Eli."

"No, it doesn't say that but he would like a harpist available during his lunch hour to provide a peaceful environment for him to create," Eli gasped out between fits of laughter, "and it specifies the harpist must be a world-class performer with at least one Grammy nomination!" He collapsed against the doorway of her office, clutching his stomach as waves of laughter overtook him.

Zuri shook her head, breathless from laughter. "Well, we better start scouting for Grammy-nominated harpists then!"

As their laughter subsided, Zuri glanced at her cousin. She sighed deeply, biting her lip in apprehension as she considered how to meet Phillip Minor's extravagant demands. His reputation as a difficult director was well-earned. However, she was aware that beneath the quirks and eccentricities, there lived someone her own father regarded as a "genius" capable of selling out theaters and attracting unparalleled audiences.

"Alright," she said to Elijah. "Let's get these things sorted out."

Elijah nodded as he took a seat. "I have to admit, I never considered this part of things. It was just exciting to have him on board."

"I spoke to my dad about him, and he mentioned his penchant for outrageous requests. The good thing is, he is a worthy investment. He creates award winning work and we are getting to work with him in the prime of his career. Also, I heard he's angling for an Oscar within the next five years, so if the man wants sandwiches prepared on Kilimanjaro, we will get them."

Elijah chuckled. "Kilimanjaro sandwiches it is, then. But, Zuri, are we ready to handle... this?" He motioned to his phone screen.

Zuri leaned back in her chair, her gaze drifting towards the window and the Hollywood skyline beyond. Their studio had begun as an underdog, one manned by what others considered nepo babies, therefore there was an expectation that they would fail within the first five years. And yet, here they were, ten years later, at the top of their game. No one could take away that accomplishment from them, least of all Phillip Minor, with his eccentricities and crazy demands.

"Are we ready?" Zuri echoed Elijah's question, shifting her gaze back to him. She offered a smile. "We are more than ready.

We've dealt with difficult actors before... although none quite like Minor. But we'll manage. We always do."

Elijah let out a low chuckle as he pocketed his phone. "That's the spirit, Zuri," he said, rising from his seat. Before he left, Zuri stopped him.

"One more thing, Eli. We're not just doing this for us or the studio," she said, her tone turning serious. "We're doing this for grandma Hazel. She went through hell during her lifetime to be accepted and taken seriously as an actress. It is our duty to carry on that legacy and ensure that her hard work is never forgotten.

"That's right cuz. We are our ancestor's wildest dream." Elijah walked over and kissed her cheek before heading out. "I'll hit up, Reggie, and get him up to speed."

"It can wait. He's on his honeymoon."

Reggie and his girlfriend Delilah had tied the knot the weekend before at a beautiful wedding venue in LA. They were now on their honeymoon in Greece. While she was ecstatic about her cousin and his lovely bride, it made her ponder if she and Genesis were taking too long to get married. They had already been engaged for a year and a half, and yet they hadn't found the time to plan their wedding. Following the proposal, it seemed as though Genesis had become less enthusiastic about the idea and Zuri wasn't sure why. She understood that already having a divorce under her belt had its own set of baggage, but she wasn't Shannon and hoped they could move past the pain of the past. After their talk a few days ago, it seemed like they were on the same page, so she figured it was the right time to see where Genesis' head was at.

"I'll give him a couple of days before I add to his post-wedding stress," Elijah chuckled, closing the door behind him.

Left alone in her office, Zuri sighed, rubbing her temples as she contemplated the enormity of what lay ahead. Despite the madness that was Phillip Minor, despite having to manage the studio without Reggie, despite wrestling with her pending nuptials, this was the life she loved. The thrill of creating magic on screen, the rush of working with talents like Minor... she wouldn't trade it for anything.

Her phone buzzed on the desk, pulling her out of her thoughts. She picked it up and smiled when she saw Genesis's name flash across the screen.

Check your email

Happy to have something else on her mind besides Minor and his weird requests, she opened her mailbox. Genesis had sent her a link to an article about an exhibition at the city's art museum - 'The Art of Love: Paintings of Passion Through the Ages'. Her heart fluttered as she read her accompanying message.

Date night on Saturday?

When have I ever said no to you?

I can think of a couple of times

Those weren't indefinite no's, more like maybe another time.

Good to know! How was your day?

Not bad, got a bunch of work done, but it will be better when I come home to you.

Hmmm, perhaps you should open your office door.

Zuri raised her eyebrows in surprise. Before she could

respond, there was a gentle knock on her office door before it creaked open. Her heart fluttered at the sight of Genesis standing in the doorway with a bouquet of roses in her hand.

"Surprise," Genesis said, walking over to Zuri's desk. "I figured you had a tough day, baby and wanted to lighten the load."

Zuri blushed at the gesture. Genesis always had a knack for making her feel special, she mused, accepting the roses. After setting them aside, she walked around her desk, and wrapped Genesis in an embrace.

"You always brighten my day."

Genesis hummed in response, wrapping an arm around Zuri's waist and using the other hand to massage her back. "I must admit, it was a selfish act because I didn't want to wait and see you at home. So, I thought I'd bring you dinner," she said, motioning to a bag near the doorway.

Zuri recognized the restaurant's logo. "Is that from Chez Violette?" she asked, her mouth already watering at the thought of their favorite French restaurant.

Genesis nodded with a grin, disentangling herself to fetch the bag. "But of course! Can't handle Minor and his major demands on an empty stomach, can we?"

Zuri chuckled, following Genesis to the small meeting table set up in her office. As Genesis lay out their meal, coq au vin for Zuri and ratatouille for herself, a wave of gratitude washed over Zuri. Despite juggling her own demanding career as a new business owner and supporting Zuri in her high-pressure job, Genesis always made it work.

"Wine too?" Zuri watched Genesis pull out a bottle and two clear plastic cups.

Genesis threw her a wink as she opened the bottle and filled the cups. Once she was done, she sat down and made herself comfortable. "So, what did Mr. Minor ask for today?"

Zuri ran down the list of his demands. "I'm pretty sure there's going to be more once we go into production. I'm aware that he's considered the best and all that, but it's a little excessive. If I wasn't aware of his reputation already, I would think he was fucking with us."

"Artists and their quirks. Seems to come with the territory. From the outside looking in, the more eccentric an artist is, the more people respect them. I wonder if it's because we associate unusual behavior with people who are accomplished."

Zuri considered her words, twirling her fork around the browned chicken. "Maybe," she agreed. "But to me, it just seems like manipulation of perception. They act outlandish and when their behavior is questioned, it's passed off as some artistic temperament or genius quirk, making them more interesting in the eyes of the public. But hey, I guess we can't complain too much. Their madness brings us the content we love."

Genesis laughed. "That's a pretty cynical view, Zuri. But then again, you do have a front-row seat to all the drama."

Zuri chuckled. "That's true. If I was on the outside looking in, I'd find it all fascinating, too. The thing that bothers me most is women get labeled as divas and difficult, but the men exhibit the same behavior. The only difference is that the public doesn't perceive it as a character flaw when it comes to men.

"It's similar to how rich people who display peculiar behavior are seen as eccentric, whereas regular people like us are branded as crazy."

"Exactly."

They sat in comfortable silence for a few moments, each lost in their thoughts as they enjoyed their meal. Zuri was the first to break the silence.

"I was thinking about where we should have our wedding. Reggie and Delilah's location was beautiful," she said, swirling the wine in her cup.

"It was..."

Zuri waited for Genesis to say more, but she didn't, so she continued with her train of thought.

"California would make the most sense, but a destination wedding in Barbados could work too."

Genesis looked thoughtful. "Barbados would be nice since it's where we fell in love."

"It would be like coming full circle."

Genesis nodded, playing with her glass. "But we'd have to consider our guests, too. Traveling to Barbados might be a bit much for some."

Zuri considered this, nibbling on a piece of bread. Genesis was right; a destination wedding could cause logistical issues for their families and friends. But something about the idea of exchanging their vows on the sandy beaches of Barbados sounded so right.

"We'll make a list and consider everyone's schedules and finances. And if it doesn't work out... then we'll find somewhere else."

Genesis locked eyes with her and leaned onto the table. "What if we just went to city hall?"

Zuri stopped mid-bite, her eyes widening as she read Genesis' lips, hoping she had misheard her. "City hall?" she said, her voice barely a whisper. "You mean... like a... quickie wedding?"

Genesis shrugged, her expression casual but eyes serious. "Well, not a quickie wedding. I mean, it would be just as special. Only difference would be the location," she pointed out, watching for Zuri's reaction.

"But..." Zuri began, floundering for words. Her dreams of a grand wedding had been on her mind for months, a beautiful vision of the love they shared and nurtured together. Suggesting a city hall wedding felt like replacing that vision with something less... grand.

"But what?" Genesis prompted, reaching across the table to cup Zuri's hand in hers. "Just think about it, Zuri. We could avoid all the unnecessary drama and stress that comes with planning a big wedding."

"Maybe I want that drama and stress," Zuri countered, her eyebrows furrowing together as she attempted to process Genesis' words. "Maybe I want...the grandeur, the celebration, recognizing our love in the presence of those who matter most to us."

"I'm not suggesting that we deny ourselves that, but a big wedding can often turn into a spectacle. More about the presentation than the bond being celebrated. And I just...I want this to be about us."

Zuri felt a lump forming in her throat. She understood Genesis' perspective, but the idea of a small, quiet ceremony was in stark contrast to the vibrant, joyous celebration she had envisioned.

"I hear you, but I always imagined our wedding as this beautiful moment where we could share our love with everyone who's important to us. My family, your family, our friends... all coming together to celebrate us. I only want to do this once and get it right." Genesis flinched at the comment and Zuri found herself scrambling. "I'm not judging you for the fact that you were married before, honey."

"I know you're not judging, Zuri. And I understand your vision. I want to celebrate our love too. It's just..." Genesis paused, searching for the right words. "After my first marriage, I realized that sometimes the grandeur can overshadow what's important."

Zuri's heart ached for Genesis. She knew the pain of that failed marriage still lingered. "But this is different," she said gently. "We're different. Our love is stronger."

Genesis smiled, but there was still a hint of uncertainty in her eyes. "I just don't want to get caught up in the spectacle and lose sight of what matters."

Zuri wasn't convinced. "I get that. But can't we have both? The intimacy and the celebration?"

Genesis smiled. "Of course we can. I'm just throwing ideas out there. Whatever we decide, as long as I'm marrying you, I'll be happy."

Zuri leaned across the table, pressing a gentle kiss to Genesis' lips. "Okay. Let's table this for now and revisit it later. We don't have to decide everything tonight."

Genesis nodded, relief evident in her eyes. "By the way, Rain wants us to meet this new guy she's seeing. Brick is his name. When she said it the first time, I thought she was joking, but apparently not."

Zuri allowed a small chuckle. "Brick?"

Genesis shrugged. "Perhaps his parents were into The Flintstones."

"Or Cat on a Hot Tin Roof," Zuri chimed in, continuing with the playful banter.

"You would come up with the classic movie reference."

"I know you're not trying to call me old when you pulled out The Flintstones."

Their laughter filled the small space. For a moment, they forgot about the unresolved issue of their wedding and reverted to their normal dynamic, lighthearted and comfortable.

"When does Rain want us to meet him?" Zuri asked after their laughter had subsided.

"Soon," Genesis replied, checking her phone for the exact date and time. "She said Brick's got a boxing match in a couple of weeks and wanted us there for support."

"From pretty boy Jackson to a boxer. Our girl has interesting taste. I don't love the sport, but I'm down to go. Someone's gotta look out for her."

Genesis nodded, her fingers brushing over the smooth screen of her phone. "That's the plan. Plus, I'd like to see what kind of guy is named Brick."

Zuri chuckled again. "Maybe he's ruggedly handsome."

"Or as dumb as a brick." Genesis added, and they both dissolved into laughter once more.

After finishing their food and most of the wine, they began cleaning up. Zuri stopped midway and looked at Genesis with a loving gaze.

"Even though we have differing opinions on our wedding, you know I love you, right?"

Genesis grinned. "I know. And I hope you know I love you too, regardless of what we decide."

Zuri nodded as she considered Genesis' words. She understood Genesis' concerns. The memory of her first marriage, which had ended so painfully, still cast a long shadow. The idea of a grand, elaborate ceremony might bring up uncomfortable memories or fears .

Yet, as she stacked the empty containers, Zuri couldn't quite shake the vision she'd been nurturing since childhood. Dreams of a fairytale wedding, complete with a flowing white gown and hundreds of flowers. Those dreams had evolved as she grew older, but the core remained the same. A day filled with love, laughter, and the joining of two families.

Zuri glanced over at Genesis, who was humming as she packed up the leftovers. One of the things Zuri cherished the most about her fiancée was her serene disposition. Perhaps a quieter, more intimate ceremony would better reflect their relationship. But this woman, with her quiet strength and boundless compassion, was her soulmate. Didn't their love deserve to be shouted from the rooftops?

"Come on," Genesis said, knocking Zuri out of her thoughts.

"Let's finish this up so we can get home and cuddle on the couch."

Zuri chuckled, her heart feeling lighter despite everything. "You just want to watch reruns."

"Busted," Genesis admitted with a grin before she tied up the bag of food. "But you're the only one I want to watch them with."

Zuri smiled, reaching out to squeeze her hand. "And you're the only one I want to watch them with, too."

They continued in silence, falling into the familiar rhythm of their shared routine. As they gathered their things to leave, Zuri's phone buzzed with a text from Elijah.

"Oh, for the love of..." she muttered, her eyes scanning the message.

Genesis raised an eyebrow. "What now?"

"Mr. Minor has added to his list of demands," Zuri sighed, rubbing her temple. "He now insists on having a personal yoga instructor who specializes in 'laughter yoga' available on set."

Genesis let out a snort of laughter. "Laughter yoga? Is that even a real thing?"

"I guess we're about to find out," Zuri replied, shaking her head in disbelief. "Here's hoping we have a box office hit with this one."

Genesis pulled Zuri close. "Hey, look at it this way. At least you'll have plenty of entertaining stories to tell at our wedding reception. Whether it's at city hall or on a beach in Barbados."

Zuri leaned into Genesis' embrace, allowing herself a moment of comfort. "You're right. We should invite Mr. Minor to the wedding and have him entertain our guests with his laughter yoga."

Genesis laughed out loud. "Now that would be a sight to see. Let him lead a session right after the vows."

The image of Phillip Minor, in all his eccentric glory,

leading their wedding guests through a laughter yoga session was too much. Zuri burst into genuine laughter, the stress of the day melting away as Genesis joined in.

They gathered their things and headed out of the office, hand in hand. As they walked to the elevator, Zuri's mind drifted back to their earlier conversation. She knew they still had a lot to discuss, but for now, she was content to enjoy this moment with the woman she loved.

# Chapter Fourteen

A week later, on a Saturday, Genesis found herself at home and restless. She wished she could spend the weekends with Zuri, but there was no guarantee they would see each other. While her job had strict weekday hours, something she upheld, Zuri never knew when something might come up or events that she couldn't miss. This weekend she was in New York at the Tribeca Film Festival where three of the studio's films were premiering.

Genesis sighed, running her fingers through her hair as she paced the kitchen, munching on fruit. She'd already tidied up, meal prepped for the week, and even squeezed in a quick yoga session. But the day stretched before her, empty and uninspiring.

She checked her phone again for the fifth time that morning but still no message from Zuri. Genesis asked that she text her once she landed whenever she traveled but that didn't always happen. It was one of those frustrating behaviors that no matter how many times she brought it up, Zuri would forget.

"Kuma, come here, girl." Her huskie came running, jumping up for scratches and cuddles. "Let's go for a walk."

Genesis got the leash and grabbed a bottle of water. Although it was only 10 in the morning, the California sun was already burning hot in the sky. She slipped into her flip-flops, clicked Kuma's leash onto her collar and out they went.

As she walked along the familiar cobbled paths of her neighborhood, her mind wandered back to that morning and her conversation with Zuri. Phone sex had become a regular part of their love life since they both had become so much busier in the past several months. It was a way to stay connected, sure, but it was also a testament to the emotions they could evoke in each other, even when separated by days, miles and sometimes time zones. Genesis had long left behind the shy woman she once was, who was afraid to ask for what she wanted in bed.

However, as much as she loved every aspect of who she was becoming, a small part of her felt neglected in other ways. Zuri did her best to be present, but even when they were together, there were phone calls and emails and deadlines. It was like some sort of interruption, work or otherwise, that took Zuri away from her, punctuated every moment. It made Genesis wonder if this is what the rest of their relationship would be like. Endless bouts of waiting followed by fleeting periods of togetherness.

Long gone were the days when she and Zuri would decide to go on late-night drives or weekend hiking trips. Now, they had to schedule time for each other during their busy lives. Genesis couldn't pretend like her life had not also become a whirlwind, but it was manageable, especially now that she had a team working under her. Every day, the distance between paths seemed to grow larger, with Zuri always at the top of her game, while Genesis waited for a phone call or a date.

She hated that she couldn't just come out and tell the truth when they had dinner at Zuri's office the other night. While she had no regrets about proposing, it had been an impulsive move and now that she had a full picture of what their life would be like together, Genesis felt a twinge of uncertainty. She loved Zuri, but was love enough to sustain a relationship where one partner always seemed to play catch-up?

Then there was the money factor. Even though Shannon had a successful career, it was different because they grew together. Zuri was born into a level of wealth that some only dreamed of, and while Genesis reaped the benefits, it didn't stop her from feeling out of place.

A couple of months before, Genesis joined Zuri at a fundraiser for the foundation her mom Veronique ran along with her lifelong friend Agnes, called Covenant House. It was their contribution to trying to end homelessness by building tiny homes for unhoused individuals. It was a noble cause and Genesis was more than happy to show her support, but what she wasn't looking forward to was the party.

Having a wealthy girlfriend had its perks but nothing could make you feel smaller than hanging around people whose net worth was more than your entire extended family's combined. Genesis had tugged at the hem of her borrowed designer dress, feeling out of place among the glittering socialites and business tycoons who filled the ballroom.

Zuri squeezed her hand reassuringly. "You look stunning," she whispered, into Genesis's ear. "Everyone's going to love you."

Genesis managed a small smile, but her stomach churned with anxiety. No matter how much time passed, she still felt like an imposter in Zuri's world of galas and champagne toasts.

Veronique spotted them and waved them over, her face lighting up. "Zuri, darling! And Genesis, how wonderful to see you both."

They hugged and Veronique made Genesis do a spin as she admired her dress.

"Is this the new Roberto Cavalli?"

"Yes," Zuri answered for her. "And she refused to let me buy it, so I had to resort to sneaking it into her closet."

Genesis felt her cheeks warm. "It's just a loan," she murmured. "I'll return it tomorrow."

Veronique waved a dismissive hand. "Nonsense, darling. It looks far better on you than it ever would gathering dust in some boutique. Now, come meet Agnes. She's dying to meet you both."

As Veronique led them through the crowd, Genesis felt Zuri's hand settle on the small of her back, a comforting presence amid the sea of unfamiliar faces. They approached a statuesque woman with silver hair coiled atop her head like a crown.

"Agnes, dear," Veronique called. "This is Genesis, Zuri's fiance."

Agnes turned, her hazel eyes sparkling with interest. "Pleased to meet you. Veronique says you've been doing a marvelous job at Beacon."

Genesis swallowed hard, willing her voice not to shake. "It's been incredibly rewarding. The kids are so talented and eager to learn."

As she spoke about the program, Genesis felt some of her nervousness melt away. This was her element, after all. She might not know the difference between Gucci and Prada, but she knew dance.

"And this is why I hired her," Zuri said, her voice full of pride.

Everyone smiled and Genesis joined in. She began to relax and found common ground with Agnes over their shared passion for the arts. The older woman's eyes lit up as Genesis described some of the innovative programs they were implementing at Beacon.

"You must come see our next showcase," Genesis said, her

enthusiasm bubbling over. "The kids have been working so hard on a piece that blends hip-hop with classical ballet. It's really something special."

Agnes nodded approvingly. "I'd love that. Perhaps we could discuss ways Covenant House might collaborate with Beacon. Many of our young people could benefit from creative outlets."

Genesis felt a surge of excitement at the possibility. "That would be amazing. I've actually been thinking about starting a dance therapy program for trauma survivors."

As she elaborated on her ideas, Genesis noticed Zuri watching her. Their eyes met, and Zuri gave her a subtle wink that made her heart flutter.

The evening progressed, and Genesis found herself swept up in conversations about art, philanthropy, and social justice. To her surprise, she was holding her own, even impressing a few of the more intimidating guests with her knowledge and passion.

When she made her way to the bar, a woman stood there sipping on a martini. The woman turned, her eyes roving over Genesis with a mixture of curiosity and disdain. She was tall and willowy, with perfectly coiffed blonde hair and a designer gown that probably cost more than Genesis's yearly salary.

"Well, well," the woman drawled, her voice dripping with false sweetness. "You must be Zuri's... companion. I'm Vivian Ashcroft."

Genesis forced a polite smile. "Genesis Malone. Nice to meet you."

Vivian's perfectly plucked eyebrows arched. "Malone? I'm not familiar with that family. Old money or new?"

Genesis felt her cheeks warm. "Oh, um, neither actually. I'm not—"

"Ah," Vivian interrupted, her lips curving into a smirk. "I see. How... quaint. And what is it you do, dear?"

"I'm an accountant," Genesis replied, trying to keep her voice steady. "And I also work with Zuri at Beacon Arts."

Vivian's laugh tinkled like ice in a crystal glass. "An accountant! How practical. I suppose someone has to balance the books, don't they?"

Genesis felt her spine stiffen at Vivian's condescending tone. She opened her mouth to retort, but before she could speak, a warm hand settled on her lower back.

"There you are, my love," Zuri's voice purred in her ear. "I've been looking everywhere for you."

Genesis turned to see Zuri's radiant smile, her eyes flashing with a mixture of adoration and protectiveness. Zuri pressed a soft kiss to Genesis's cheek before turning to Vivian with a cool smile.

"Vivian, I see you've met my fiancée. Isn't she stunning?"

Vivian's smirk faltered slightly. "Fiancée? I wasn't aware you were engaged, Zuri."

"Oh yes," Zuri replied, her arm sliding possessively around Genesis's waist. "We're keeping it quiet. How's Cliff doing? I heard he's in Europe?"

A sour look took over Vivian's face. "Yes, he's opening a store in Italy."

"Amazing. Well I hear the third time's the charm. Now, if you'll excuse us, I need to steal my fiancée away for a dance." Zuri whispered into her ear as they walked away. "Cliff is her third husband and he's supposedly shacked up with a model in Italy."

Genesis gasped. "No way?"

"Way," Zuri said, sending her into a spin.

Zuri had saved her like she always did, and she loved her for that. But she didn't look forward to a lifetime of those types of encounters. And what would happen when Zuri wasn't around?

Kuma tugged at the leash, pulling Genesis from her

thoughts. She noticed the husky's attentiveness towards a squirrel that scurried around the bushes nearby so she happily let Kuma explore.

They had walked for a few blocks when a familiar car pulled up beside them. Shannon stepped out wearing a casual short set and large sunglasses. Genesis had forgotten that she mentioned stopping by for a bit. When she asked, it had been a bit of a surprise since they rarely hung out now that Shannon had a new woman in her life, but it was nice to have some company.

Genesis regarded her with a hand on her hip. "Okay super-star. Why does it always look like you're about to walk down a red carpet?"

Shannon flashed a dazzling smile, pushing her sunglasses up onto her head. "I can't help it. Just comes natural to me."

"The arrogance, I can't," Genesis said with an eye roll.

Kuma bounded over to Shannon. "Hey girl, you miss me? Huh?" She looked up as she petted her. "How have you been?"

"Same old, same old. Work's been keeping me busy."

Shannon nodded, her eyes searching Genesis's face. "And Zuri? How's that going?"

Genesis hesitated, unsure how much to share with her ex-wife. "It's... good. She's in New York right now for a film festival."

"Ah, the glamorous life," Shannon said, a hint of teasing in her voice. "Must be exciting, dating a big shot film producer."

Genesis laughed, but it sounded hollow even to her own ears. "Yeah, it's alright."

Shannon's brow furrowed. "Hey, you okay?"

Genesis sighed, running a hand through her curls. "It's nothing. Just... adjusting to the new normal, I guess."

Shannon leaned against her car. "Want to talk about it? I've got time if you want to grab a coffee or something."

Genesis hesitated, weighing her options. On the one hand, talking to her ex about her current relationship felt strange. On the flip side, Shannon had a deeper understanding of her than nearly anyone else.

"Yeah, that'd be nice," Genesis said. "There's a little cafe just around the corner. We can sit outside with Kuma."

They walked over and caught up a bit. While they weren't at the stage of hanging out, they kept in touch often enough to be knowledgeable about each other's lives.

"Did Kenzi tell you about her plans to become a lawyer?" Genesis asked as they were seated.

"Yeah, kind of came out of nowhere, but I'm glad she's figured out what she wants to do with her life. I think we did a great job raising her, considering the circumstances."

"We did an amazing job."

As they settled into their seats, Genesis thought about the new found ease between them. It was a far cry from the misery that had dominated the end of their marriage.

"So," Shannon said, stirring her iced latte, "what's going on with you and Zuri? And don't give me that 'it's fine' nonsense."

Genesis sighed, petting Kuma, who lay at her feet. "Everything's moving so fast with her career, and sometimes I feel like I'm struggling to keep up."

Shannon nodded, her expression thoughtful. "That sounds tough. Has she been making time for you?"

"She tries," Genesis admitted. "But there's always something. A last-minute meeting, a crisis on the set, a networking event she can't miss. I get it, I do. But…"

"But you're not a priority," Shannon finished for her.

"Is that selfish of me? To want more of her time when I'm aware of how important her work is?"

"I don't think that's selfish at all, Gen. Have you talked to her about how you're feeling?"

Genesis shook her head. "I don't want to add to her stress. She's already juggling so much."

"As someone who was once married to you, let me just say that bottling up your feelings never ends well," Shannon said with a knowing look. "You've got to talk to her. Before it festers and becomes something bigger."

"You're right. But I feel needy."

"Being honest about your needs isn't being needy," Shannon pointed out. "It's being a partner. Relationships are about compromise, remember?"

Genesis nodded, a small smile tugging at her lips. "When did you get so wise?"

Shannon laughed, the sound soothing and familiar. "Therapy and a lot of self-reflection. Plus, dating someone with kids puts things into perspective. Relationships take work, Gen. You know that better than anyone."

Genesis smiled. "We learned that the hard way, didn't we?"

Shannon chuckled. "That we did. But look at us now. We're sitting here, having a civilized conversation about your love life. Who would've thought?"

Genesis laughed, feeling herself calm down. "Life's funny that way, I guess. How are things with Melissa, is it?"

Shannon smiled. "Melanie. And things are great. The kids are warming up to me, too. It's been a learning curve, but I'm enjoying it."

Genesis felt a pang of something. Not quite jealousy, but a wistfulness for the easy companionship she and Shannon once shared. "That's wonderful, Shan. I'm happy for you."

"Thanks," Shannon said, her smile genuine. "Talking to you like this reminds me of how good we were together before things got complicated."

Genesis nodded, a bittersweet smile on her face. "We had some good times, didn't we?"

"The best," Shannon agreed. "Listen, I stopped by because I need to ask a favor."

Genesis raised an eyebrow, curiosity piqued. "Oh? What kind of favor?"

"Well, I need a place to stay and I hate to ask you, but would it be possible for me to stay with you?"

Genesis blinked in surprise, surprised by Shannon's request. "Stay with me? For how long?"

Shannon shifted in her seat, looking uncomfortable. "For a few months." She saw Genesis's facial expression and switched up her request. "Or maybe just three months, max."

"What about Melanie? Couldn't you stay with her?"

"That's... complicated. Things are still new with us, and with the kids... I don't want to rush into living together, even temporarily. Too much, too soon."

Genesis hesitated, her mind racing. Having Shannon stay with her would be complicated, to say the least. Having her ex-wife as a houseguest seemed like a recipe for disaster. They had done this before and that was before they ever got involved, so while Zuri didn't love it, she made do. This was a different scenario.

"What happened to your condo?"

Shannon's eyes dropped to her hands, fidgeting with the straw in her drink. "To be honest, things haven't been going so well with work."

Genesis leaned forward, concern etching her features. "What do you mean? I thought your sports analyst gig was going great. You were always talking about how much you loved it."

Shannon let out a bitter laugh. "Yeah, well, loved is the operative word there. Past tense." She took a deep breath, her shoulders slumping. "The network cut costs and chose not to renew my contract. I've been freelancing, picking up gigs here and there, but it's not enough."

Genesis's eyes widened. "Oh, Shan. I had no idea."

"I didn't want anyone to know," Shannon admitted, her voice barely above a whisper. "Thought things would turn around. But between the mortgage on the condo, catching up after my treatments, and just... life, I've been drowning in debt."

The weight of Shannon's words hung heavy in the air between them. Genesis remembered how proud Shannon had been when she landed her analyst job, how excited she was to have a career that combined her love of sports with her natural charisma. To see her now, defeated and struggling, made Genesis's heart ache.

"I've been trying," Shannon continued, her words tumbling out now. "But the condo is in foreclosure, and I have to be out in a couple of weeks. I would rent something, but my credit is shit at this point."

Genesis felt a surge of empathy for her ex-wife. Despite their past issues, she couldn't bear to see Shannon struggling like this. "Why didn't you say something sooner? I could have helped, or at least listened."

Shannon shrugged, a wry smile on her face. "Pride, I guess. And a little shame. It's difficult admitting you've failed, especially to someone who's known you at your best."

Genesis reached across the table, squeezing Shannon's hand. "Hey, you haven't failed. You're going through a rough patch, that's all. It happens to everyone."

Shannon nodded, blinking back tears. "Thanks, Gen. That means a lot."

Taking a deep breath, Genesis knew what she was about to say could complicate things.

"You can stay with me. But only for three months, alright?"

"Thank you so much, Gen." Shannon jumped out of her seat and wrapped Genesis in a tight hug. "You have no idea how much this means to me. I promise I'll be the best houseguest ever. You won't even know I'm there."

Genesis patted Shannon's back, acutely aware of the curious glances from nearby patrons. "Okay, okay. Let's not get carried away. Remember, it's just three months."

Shannon pulled back, wiping at her eyes. "Of course. That's more than enough time for me to get back on my feet."

Genesis couldn't shake the nagging feeling that this was a mistake. "Look, Shan, we need to talk about some ground rules. This can't be like last time."

Shannon nodded. "Absolutely. Whatever you say goes."

Genesis took a deep breath. "First, you'll need to contribute to groceries and utilities. I know money's tight, but even a little would help."

"Done," Shannon agreed.

"Second, I need you to respect my space and my relationship with Zuri. No late-night heart-to-hearts, no impromptu dance parties in the living room at 2 AM."

Shannon chuckled. "Those were some good times, though."

Genesis shot her a warning look. "I'm serious, Shan. Things are different now. I'm engaged, and I need you to respect that."

After taking her seat, Shannon crossed her heart. "You're not gonna have a thing to worry about, I swear. I won't overstay my welcome. And I'll help around the house, do chores, whatever you need."

As Genesis and Shannon walked back to her house, Kuma trotting alongside them, a combination of emotions stirred inside her. On one hand, she was glad she could help Shannon in her time of need. On the other hand, she knew this was going to be a hard sell to Zuri.

"So, when do you want to move in?" Genesis asked, trying to keep her tone casual.

Shannon ran a hand through her hair. "Well, I need to be

out of my place by next Friday. Would it be okay if I moved in then?"

Genesis nodded, her mind already racing with all the preparations she'd need to make. "That should work. I'll clear out the guest room this week."

When they got close to the house, Shannon stopped, placing a hand on Genesis's arm. "Gen, I just want to say again how much I appreciate this. It's not an ideal situation, but I promise I'll do everything I can to make it as smooth as possible."

Genesis managed a small smile. "I know you will, Shan. Just... please remember what I said about boundaries, okay?"

"Absolutely. It'll be like I'm not even there."

As they said their goodbyes and Shannon drove off, Genesis stood on her front porch, watching the car disappear around the corner. She took a deep breath, steeling herself for the conversation she would need to have with Zuri.

* * *

After she finished cleaning the house and getting the guest room ready for Shannon's return, Genesis found herself with nothing to do on a Saturday night. Staying in and watching a movie was a possibility, but she was tired of the same routine.

Genesis smiled when she remembered Kem's invitation to hang out with her friends at Velvet. On impulse, Genesis grabbed her phone and dialed Kem's number.

"Hey girl, what's up?" Kem's cheerful voice came through the speaker.

"Well, I'm alone with no plans and thought maybe..."

Kem let out a squeal of delight. "Yass! I have been waiting for you to say you would come out."

Genesis laughed at Kem's enthusiasm. "Alright, alright. What time should I be there?"

"We're heading out in about an hour. Meet us at Velvet around 9:30?" Kem suggested. "And it's just me and like two of my homegirls, so it should be a fun time."

"Sounds perfect. I'll see you then."

After hanging up, Genesis felt a surge of excitement. It had been a while since she'd had a proper girls' night out. She headed to her closet, rifling through her outfits. Her eyes landed on a slinky red dress she hadn't worn in ages. Perfect.

An hour later, Genesis was putting the finishing touches on her makeup when her phone buzzed. It was a text from Zuri.

> Hey babe, just got out of the last screening.
> Wish you were here. Miss you.

Should she tell Zuri about her plans? About Shannon? One of those things seemed simple enough, the other not so much.

> Going out dancing with Kem from Beacon.
> Hope you're having fun at the festival. Miss
> you too.

She dropped her phone in her bag and finished getting ready. It had taken everything in her not to question why she hadn't heard from Zuri all day.

The ride to Velvet was quick, and soon Genesis stood in line outside the club. The bass from inside thrummed through her body, and she could feel the energy of the crowd.

"Genesis! Over here!"

She turned to see Kem waving, flanked by a couple of women. Genesis made her way over, greeting everyone with hugs and air kisses.

"Genesis, this is Donna and Renee. My ride or die friends."

Genesis smiled as she took in Donna and Renee. Donna was a petite woman with a shock of vibrant purple hair styled in an edgy pixie cut. Her olive skin glowed under the neon lights of the club's entrance, and her dark eyes were lit with mischief. She wore a fitted black jumpsuit, paired with towering stilettos that made her almost as tall as Genesis.

Renee was statuesque, over six feet tall, even without heels. Her rich mahogany skin seemed to shimmer, adorned with intricate gold jewelry that caught the light. Her hair was styled in long, sleek box braids that fell past her waist, swaying as she moved. She wore a flowing white maxi dress with daring side slits that revealed glimpses of her long legs.

"Nice to meet you both," Genesis said, feeling at ease with Kem's friends.

Donna grinned, revealing a dimple in her left cheek. "Kem told us so much about you! We've been dying to meet the infamous Genesis."

Renee nodded in agreement, her voice a smooth, rich contralto. "Seriously, we were starting to think you were a figment of Kem's imagination."

Genesis raised an eyebrow and looked over at Kem. "It's like that?"

"When we first met, you were so self-assured and bad ass, which intimidated me, but then you were so nice on top of it.

Genesis laughed, flattered at the compliment. "Well, I'm very real and very excited about a night out. It's been too long since I've hit the dance floor."

"Oh honey, we're gonna change that tonight," Donna said with a wink. "Hope you're ready to shake what your mama gave you."

As they made their way into the club, the dance floor was packed, bodies moving in sync to the rhythm. Colorful lights flashed across the crowd, creating an almost dreamlike atmosphere.

"First round is on me, ladies!" Kem shouted over the music, leading them towards the bar.

Genesis settled onto a barstool, taking in the club's energy. It had been ages since she'd been out like this, and she could feel the excitement bubbling up inside her.

"So, Genesis, Kem tells us you're engaged. Where's the lucky lady tonight?" Renee asks.

"She's in New York for work. Film festival stuff."

Donna's eyes widened. "Ooh, fancy! What does she do?"

"She's a film executive," Genesis explained, a hint of pride in her voice despite her mixed feelings. "Her company has a few movies premiering at Tribeca."

"Damn, girl, you did good," Renee said, snapping her fingers.

Kem chimed in. "Her lady is the big boss at Beacon."

Renee and Donna looked at her in awe. It was clear Kem must have told them about Zuri too.

"So, what's it like dating a hotshot exec?" Donna asked, leaning in with curiosity. "Do you get to go to all the fancy Hollywood parties?"

"Sometimes, yeah. It's... interesting. Not what I'm used to."

Kem must have sensed Genesis's discomfort, because she changed the subject. "Alright ladies, enough chit-chat. We came here to dance, didn't we?"

The others cheered in agreement, and Genesis was glad for the distraction. As they moved to the dance floor, she relaxed. The pulsing beat of the music filled her senses, drowning out her worries and doubts.

As they found their spot on the crowded dance floor, Genesis closed her eyes and let the rhythm take over. Her body moved in time with the music. For the first time in weeks, she felt free.

Donna and Renee flanked her, their energy infectious as they danced. Kem was a whirlwind of movement, her laughter ringing out over the music. Genesis laughed too, caught up in the moment's joy.

They danced for what seemed like hours, switching between fast-paced tracks and slower, sultry songs. Genesis' skin was glistening with sweat, her curls wild and free.

During a high energy song, someone bumped into her from behind. She turned, ready to brush it off, when she found herself face to face with a striking woman.

"I'm so sorry," the woman said, her voice husky and low. She placed a hand on Genesis's arm, steadying herself. "Didn't mean to invade your space."

Genesis felt a jolt of electricity at the woman's touch. She was tall, with smooth cocoa skin and piercing eyes. She had short hair that framed her face in waves.

"No worries," Genesis said, very aware of how close they were standing. "It happens."

The woman's eyes roamed over Genesis's face. "I'm Imani. You want to dance?"

Her instinct was to say no, but one little dance couldn't hurt. As soon as yes came out of her mouth, the other woman pulled their bodies close and moved.

Genesis hesitated for a moment, feeling a mix of excitement and guilt as Imani's body pressed against hers. The music seemed to sync with her racing heartbeat. She glanced over at Kem and the others, but they were lost in their own world, dancing.

Genesis took a deep breath and let herself enjoy the moment. She began to move with Imani, their bodies finding a shared rhythm. The music pulsed around them, the bass thrumming through Genesis's chest.

Imani's hands rested on Genesis's hips, guiding her movements. Their eyes locked, and Genesis was surprised at the flutter of excitement in her stomach.

"You're an amazing dancer," Imani said, leaning in close to be heard over the music.

Genesis smiled, a blush creeping up her cheeks. "Thanks. You're not so bad yourself."

Imani laughed, the sound rich and inviting. "I try. But I have to say, you make it easy to look good."

As the song transitioned into a slower, more sensual beat, Imani pulled Genesis closer. Their bodies pressed together, moving as one to the rhythm. Genesis could feel the heat radiating between them.

For a moment, Genesis forgot about everything else. Her worries about Zuri, the complications with Shannon, the stress of work. All that existed was this moment, this dance, this connection with a beautiful stranger.

But as Imani's hand slid lower on her back, reality came crashing back. Genesis stepped away, breaking their connection.

"I'm sorry," she said. "I can't do this. I'm engaged."

Imani's expression shifted from surprise to understanding. She took a step back, giving Genesis space. "No harm done."

Genesis nodded, flustered. "I should have said something sooner."

"Hey, we were just dancing," Imani said with a gentle smile. "But I get it. Your fiancée is a lucky woman."

"Thanks. I should get back to my friends."

Imani put her hands up and winked at Genesis before walking away.

Genesis watched her disappear into the crowd, then turned to find Kem and the other ladies.

On her way over to them, she felt a mix of emotions swirling inside her. The excitement of dancing with Imani still lingered, but it was being overtaken by guilt and confusion.

A few hours later, Genesis was home and somehow made it up what seemed like an endless flight of stairs to her bedroom.

She collapsed onto her bed, the room spinning from the combination of alcohol and dancing. After kicking off both heels, she snuggled into the bed and relished the cool sheets against her skin. Despite her exhaustion, a smile played on her lips as she replayed the night's events.

The energy of the club, the music, and the company of Kem and her friends had been what she needed. Then the memory of her dance with Imani popped up, and she groaned.

"What is wrong with me?" she said out loud, into the darkened room.

Kuma popped her head up from her bed and tilted it in Genesis' direction.

Genesis sighed, rubbing her temples. "Nothing's wrong, Kuma. Mommy's just being silly."

She fumbled for her phone, squinting at the bright screen. There were a couple of missed calls and texts from Zuri. Guilt gnawed at her as she read through them.

> I can picture you dancing! Wish I could be there with you.

> Just finished the last screening. Heading to bed. Call me tomorrow?

Genesis buried her face in her pillow. She'd been so caught up in the night's excitement that she hadn't even thought to check her phone. The weight of everything she was juggling suddenly seemed overwhelming.

Was this what self-sabotage felt like? She rolled onto her back, staring up at the ceiling. The room was still spinning, and her mind was racing. She couldn't shake the feeling that she was on the verge of messing everything up.

Genesis thought about calling Zuri, but a glance at the clock told her it was past 3 AM in New York. Plus, what would she even say? 'Hey babe, sorry I didn't call earlier, I was too busy grinding with a beautiful stranger at the club'. The thought made her stomach churn.

Instead, she forced herself to sit up and do her bed time routine because she knew it would set her at ease. Tomorrow was another day. And for at least a few blissful hours, she'd forgotten about her worries with Zuri, the impending arrival of Shannon, and all the complications that came with both.

# Chapter Fifteen

Zuri bounded through the sprawling labyrinth of LAX airport, her heart hammering in sync with the steady beat of her leather boots against the polished tile floor. Loud chatter, competing intercom announcements, and the rumbling echo of departing flights filled the air.

Clutching her smartphone in hand, she weaved through a bustling throng of passengers, narrowly avoiding a collision with a harried businessman and his precariously balanced carry-on. Her phone buzzed against her palm.

Reggie and Elijah's faces filled the screen as her cousins' video call connected.

"Make it quick, fellas. I'm already running late."

Elijah let out a low whistle. "Cutting it close there, cuz. Isn't your flight in ten minutes?"

Zuri's laugh was breathless, the sound absorbed by the echoing sounds of the airport. "Wouldn't be me if I wasn't running late, now would it?"

Reggie shook his head, his expression half admiration, half dismay. "I swear, Zuri. You amaze me with your ability to pull off miracles."

She winked at him as she dodged a hasty couple rushing towards what Zuri presumed was their departure gate. "You act like you've forgotten the time I handed in that twenty-page paper for Dr. Lorrison's class ten minutes before the deadline."

Elijah chuckled at the memory. "He might have forgotten Zuri, but I didn't. Especially since you snagged an A on that beast."

"Exactly. Anyway, what's going on with the Minor project?"

Reggie sighed, rubbing his temples in a familiar gesture of frustration. "That's why we called. The man's a genius, true, but he's also unpredictable."

"How unpredictable?" Zuri asked, side-stepping an airport security officer.

"Let's just say he's decided he wants a complete script rewrite ten days before shooting begins."

Zuri gasped, nearly tripping over the hem of her dress. "What? You can't be serious!"

"As a heart attack." Elijah grimaced. "He says the current script doesn't 'capture his vision'."

"I can't believe it," Zuri exclaimed, as she reached her gate just as the final boarding call was announced. She gave her cousins a firm nod. "Alright, pull together all the writers we have available. Make them aware that it's going to be a long night.

She hung up without waiting for their response and took a deep breath, staring at Genesis, who stood at the gate tapping her watch.

"What? I'm here, baby, right on time." Zuri pulled her into a deep kiss, then apologized to the flight attendants as they showed their boarding passes.

Walking down the passageway towards the plane, Genesis shook her head and laughed as she looked over at Zuri. "Right on time? I think your watch is a little off, babe. My parents always told me, 'if you're early, then you're on time, and if you're on time, then you're late.' So I think our concepts of time are different."

Zuri chuckled, looping an arm around Genesis's waist. "In that case, I suppose I'm perpetually late. But you love me anyway."

"I suppose I do," Genesis responded with a teasing smile, rolling her eyes in mock exasperation.

Once they were in their seats, Zuri reached into her tote bag and pulled out her laptop. With a swift click, the screen lit up, and she began typing.

Genesis watched from the corner of her eye before asking, "I thought this trip was supposed to be a break for you, babe?"

Zuri glanced at Genesis, her fingers hovering above the keyboard. *What am I doing?* She closed the laptop and slipped it back in her bag, and then stood up to place it in the overhead compartment.

When she sat back down, she turned to Genesis, offering an apologetic smile. "You're right. It's just hard to turn it off sometimes."

Genesis reached over and took her hand. "I understand," she said, giving Zuri's hand a reassuring squeeze. "Always remember that it's okay to take a break. You've earned it."

Zuri kissed Genesis' cheek and laid her head on her shoulder. Not for the first time, Genesis reminded her why she had fallen for her in the first place. She was everything Zuri had always needed, but never knew she wanted until they met.

"I'm excited about meeting Andrea in person. If she's anything like the times we've talked on video calls, she and I will get along just fine," Zuri said.

"That's my girl. She's always been a bit of a wild child, but I'm happy that she's found someone who gets her."

"How did you two meet again?"

Genesis grinned at the memory. "Sophomore year in the student lounge. She was playing an acoustic cover of Metallica's 'Enter Sandman' on her guitar, of all things. I was excited to meet another black girl who was into rock music. Once we started talking, we discovered our upbringings were similar, and we bonded over that. Soon, we became inseparable. People used to joke that we were like twins, because we shared so many interests but had such different personalities. She was always loud and bodacious and I was an introvert."

Zuri chuckled at the description. "That sounds familiar."

Genesis gave a gentle laugh. "Well, someone has to keep their head when the one they love is racing around like a madwoman."

Zuri smirked, her fingers dancing along Genesis' hand. A flight attendant requested everyone's attention for the safety briefing, and Genesis released her hand to buckle up. Zuri watched Genesis dutifully follow each instruction the flight attendant laid out and was one of the only people to raise her hand with questions. It was as if she had never been on a plane before. She loved these little moments. Her sense of responsibility and care was something Zuri admired and found endearing.

"You really gonna ask that lady about these masks like you don't know what we have to do?" Zuri whispered in a teasing voice.

Genesis turned to her with her finger over her lips. "Shhh, maybe you'll learn something."

Zuri made a funny face and dodged Genesis' playful tap.

Shortly after, the aircraft rumbled beneath them, and with a jolt, they were airborne; the cityscape shrinking beneath them as they ascended into the sky.

"Seriously though," Genesis said once the seatbelt sign

blinked off and the flight attendants began their rounds offering beverages and snacks. "You're going to love Andrea. And she's looking forward to meeting you, too."

"What about the woman she's marrying? You haven't told me much about her. Rebecca, right?" Zuri asked, leaning into her.

Genesis shrugged. "She's fine."

Zuri raised an eyebrow. "Fine? That makes me think she is very much not fine."

"Stop," Genesis said with a laugh as she pushed her away. "We've never met, only communicated during phone calls but my best friend loves her, and that's good enough for me."

Zuri urged her on. "Right, but..."

"But, this relationship kind of came out of nowhere. Andrea was engaged to Natalie, I told you about her. She was great, then they broke it off. Drea was miserable for months and I did what I could to support her. Then, out of the blue, Rebecca was in the picture. I guess I'm worried that she's rebounding."

"Have you talked to her about this?"

Genesis groaned. "She's in love. What I have to say doesn't matter."

"Really? That's not the vibe I get between you two."

"You're right, I guess I just don't want to alienate her. She seems happy." Genesis caressed her face. "But thank you for caring, babe."

Zuri leaned into her hand. "Anytime."

As the flight attendant passed by their row, Zuri asked for two glasses of champagne. She noticed Genesis' curious gaze on her, but she just smiled, biding her time until the flight attendant set the shimmering liquid in front of them.

"What's this for?" Genesis asked as Zuri handed her a flute.

Zuri held up her glass, the light from above catching the bubbles fizzing inside. "To us." She clinked her glass against

Genesis', the sound echoing gently around them. "For every late arrival and every early morning, for finding balance amidst chaos and confusion. And to many more adventures together."

Genesis' lips curled into a tender smile. "To us," she echoed back, raising her own glass before taking a delicate sip of the bubbly champagne.

They settled into a comfortable silence, punctuated only by the low hum of the plane's engine and the occasional chime from the seatbelt sign overhead. Zuri allowed her gaze to wander, taking in the expansive blue of the sky outside their window, the fluffy clouds below them creating a surreal, dreamy landscape.

"You're so beautiful when you're lost in thought," Genesis admitted.

Zuri's eyes flicked back to Genesis', a blush creeping onto her cheeks. "What was I thinking about?" she countered.

"How to solve some complex problem that us mere mortals couldn't even grasp," Genesis teased. "Or perhaps you're excited about all the new food you'll discover in Denver?"

Zuri laughed lightly at that. "In truth, I was appreciating the view."

"The view or the company?" Genesis quipped, her smile broadening at Zuri's responding laughter.

Zuri studied Genesis for a moment before she leaned over and kissed her on the cheek. "Both," she murmured against her skin.

Genesis grinned before pulling Zuri closer for a proper kiss.

Their lips met, a spark igniting between them, as it always did. Even after all this time, their connection seemed to intensify rather than diminish.

The chime of the seatbelt sign interrupted them, pulling them out of their shared bubble. Genesis pulled away, but not before stealing one last peck from Zuri's lips.

Zuri fiddled with the television in their section, hoping to find a movie for them to watch.

"Babe, I have something to tell you, but you have to promise not to get mad."

Zuri paused and raised an eyebrow at the statement. "Kind of hard not to be concerned when you put it that way." Genesis gave her a pleading look. "Fine, I promise I won't get mad."

Genesis fidgeted with the edge of her seat. "Shannon stopped by a few days ago. We were catching up and, turns out, she's been having a ton of financial issues and lost her home."

"Oh, I'm sorry to hear that," Zuri said, her body relaxing a bit.

Genesis nodded, her eyes flickering with concern. "Yeah, it's been rough for her. She lost her analyst job, and then couldn't keep up with the mortgage payments." She paused, taking a deep breath before continuing. "She asked if she could stay with me and I said yes."

Zuri's heart skipped a beat, her breath catching in her throat. She forced herself to maintain a neutral expression, even as her mind raced with a thousand thoughts. "Oh?" she managed, her voice controlled. "For how long?"

Genesis bit her lower lip, a telltale sign of her nervousness. "Three months," she said, her eyes searching Zuri's face for a reaction. "It's not ideal, but she has nowhere else to go."

Zuri nodded, her fingers tracing patterns on the armrest between them. She felt a knot forming in her stomach, a mixture of jealousy and unease that she tried to push down. "Right, of course," she said, her voice sounding distant even to her own ears. "That's very kind of you."

The last time Shannon had been in Genesis' home, she had been hoping to make amends and try again. If Zuri hadn't seen the truth of who Tracy was, it was very possible that Genesis and Shannon would have gotten back together.

Once Zuri and Genesis became a couple, Shannon took a step back, but they would often do activities together because of Kenzi. She understood the concept of found family and why Genesis still felt a deep attachment to Shannon, but that didn't make it easier.

She closed her eyes, memories flooding back. The way Shannon had looked at Genesis when they'd bumped into her at the farmer's market last month. The lingering hug that had made Zuri ill at ease. Inside jokes they shared, reminders of a history Zuri wasn't part of.

Then, as they were planning their engagement party, Genesis handed Zuri her guest list and near the top was Shannon. She resisted the urge to request Shannon's removal. It felt petty, so she kept her thoughts to herself. Now, so soon after, Shannon was once again popping up like an unwanted houseguest. Literally.

Genesis reached out, placing her hand over Zuri's. "Babe, I promise there's nothing to worry about. Shannon and I are long over, you know that. This is just me helping an old friend."

"An old friend you were once married to. Let's not act like this isn't something that shouldn't bother me. Imagine if this were me and Tracy."

"That's not fair. Your relationship with her was nothing like Shannon's and mine."

"Exactly."

Genesis looked away, sheepish. "You're right, we should have discussed this before I said yes."

"I understand you want to help," Zuri said, turning to face Genesis. "But this isn't just about you anymore. We're together now, and decisions like this affect both of us."

"I promise, it's just temporary. She'll be out as soon as she finds a new place."

Zuri was quiet for a moment, weighing her thoughts. How

often was Shannon going to be seeking Genesis' help? Was she planning on turning to her every time she had a crisis? Zuri understood that both Genesis and Shannon didn't have much family, but this was getting ridiculous.

She couldn't find a way to express this without sounding like a jealous jerk, so Zuri decided to let it go, for now.

"Okay," she said finally. "But I have some conditions."

Genesis perked up, relief washing over her face. "Anything."

"First, we set a firm move-out date. No extensions," Zuri stated firmly. "Second, I want to be there when she moves in. And third, we need to establish clear boundaries."

Genesis nodded eagerly. "Of course, already on it. Whatever you need to feel comfortable."

As the plane soared through the clouds, Zuri tried to focus on the movie she had chosen, but her mind kept drifting back to the conversation about Shannon. She glanced at Genesis, who was engrossed in the film, her profile illuminated by the glow of the screen. Zuri basked in her beauty, even as a twinge of unease settled in her stomach.

She knew Genesis loved her, but the thought of Shannon being in her space, even temporarily, was unsettling. Her mind swirled with scenarios, but she did her best to push the thoughts down. They were happy, and nothing, not even Shannon, was going to change that. Not if she could help it.

* * *

They arrived at Denver International around 5pm and made their way towards the exit. Andrea was going to drive them to their hotel and then take them out to her favorite barbecue restaurant. Zuri was excited to indulge. She could already taste the smoky, sweet sauce on her tongue, her mouth watered at the thought of ribs and cornbread.

Genesis was busy reading messages on her phone as they stepped onto the curb, while Zuri looked around and spotted Andrea in the sea of drivers waiting in their cars.

"Hey, isn't that Andrea over there?" Zuri pointed, tapping Genesis's arm and gesturing toward a sleek black car adorned with an array of colorful bumper stickers.

"No, I don't think that's... holy shit."

Zuri looked between the two of them, her face etched with confusion as Andrea squealed and made her way over. She could tell Genesis wasn't happy about something, but couldn't decipher what.

"Son of a bitch," Genesis mumbled.

Those were the only two words that left her mouth before she put on a fake smile and pulled Andrea into a hug. Zuri sighed. There went that peaceful weekend she was hoping for.

# Chapter Sixteen

*What the hell is this...* Genesis tried her best not to show what was running through her mind as Andrea and Zuri hugged, but it was hard. Andrea, her sister from another mother, stood in front of her looking like a different person. Gone were her beloved waist length locs, bohemian clothes, and even the multiple piercings in her ears.

"Is that a fade?" Genesis blurted out before she could stop herself.

"Yeah," Andrea said, running her hand over her head. "It was time for a change. Do you like it?"

"I..." Genesis began and faltered. She was still grappling with the sight before her. Her thoughts were all jumbled up, and she wasn't sure what to say.

"I think it looks great. Locs hold energy, I've been told, so people who want to move on to another phase cut them," Zuri said with a smile.

"Exactly." Andrea gestured for them to follow her to the car. "Rebecca saw how much work it had become to maintain them and thought I'd be happier letting them go. She was right, as usual."

Genesis followed Andrea's gaze to her car. A shiny, black, luxury sedan that seemed worlds apart from the old VW Andrea had been driving as long as Genesis could remember.

"What happened to Buggie?" Genesis asked. Zuri looked at her with curiosity. "That was what we called her car."

Andrea threw her head back and laughed. "Buggie? That was a lifetime ago! She's long gone, sweetie. Auctioned off on eBay to a hippie dude in Oregon."

Genesis had a pang of nostalgia. The swift passage of time displayed so vividly through the changes in Andrea. It wasn't only her friend's physical appearance or the new car; even her laugh seemed different. Less carefree, more measured.

Andrea gave Genesis a sympathetic look. "It's a lot to take in. We haven't seen each other in a while and things...well, things change."

"I can see that," Genesis muttered under her breath.

When Andrea moved to Denver, they swore they would see each other as often as possible. They were only a two-hour flight away from each other, unlike when Andrea stayed on the east coast and Genesis moved west. Andrea met Natalie four years ago, and that changed their plans. Despite that, they remained close, speaking to each other every day, and Genesis wouldn't have made it through her divorce if not for her friend.

Guilt welled up in Genesis and threatened to overwhelm her. As they followed Andrea towards her freshly waxed car, she glanced at Zuri. She was quiet, observing the interaction between the long-time friends. Genesis was filled with an overwhelming sense of gratitude for her presence.

"Anyway," Andrea started, the keys jingling in her hands as she fiddled with them, "I thought we could start with dinner and catch up more properly. There's that barbecue place that Rebecca and I adore."

Genesis nodded, her emotions still tumultuous beneath her

calm exterior. Her eyes strayed to Andrea's fingers, no longer adorned with stacks of eclectic rings but featuring simple, elegant bands. Another sign of change.

They placed their luggage in the trunk and Zuri stepped closer to her.

"You okay?" Zuri asked, her hand finding its way to Genesis' back.

"Yeah..." Genesis mumbled as they walked to the car.

As they entered, she noted the plush leather seats, a stark contrast to Buggie's worn-in upholstery.

Andrea started the car, the engine humming quietly, and drove downtown. Genesis marveled at how much more adept Andrea seemed at navigating the drive. In the beginning, she had clung to her boho lifestyle, professing her disdain for the city's pace and noise. Now, she maneuvered through the traffic, her fingers tapping on the steering wheel to some pop tune playing on the radio, not the indie folk music that was her signature.

After about fifteen minutes, they made it to the city proper and arrived at the hotel.

"Here we are," Andrea announced as they pulled up in front of a sleek glass building with the name Hotel Zanzibar emblazoned on the front. "How about I come back and pick y'all up around 8?"

"Sounds great," Zuri said, trying to sound extra cheerful.

Genesis moved to get out of the passenger's seat and Andrea grabbed onto her hand. "I'm so happy you're here."

"Me too Drea. I've missed you," Genesis said, looking deep into her eyes, hoping she understood how much she meant it.

Andrea gave her hand a comforting squeeze before letting go, "I've missed you too, Gen."

A lump formed in her throat, but Genesis swallowed it down and forced a small smile, stepping out of the car.

The door shut behind Genesis and Zuri with a soft thud, leaving them standing in the cool evening air. Zuri grabbed their luggage and closed the trunk.With one last wave, Andrea drove off and left them alone. Genesis stood for a moment in silence, watching the car disappear around the corner.

The sense of estrangement from someone she had once been so close to was proving difficult to shake off.

Zuri tugged on Genesis's arm. "Come on, love. Let's get inside and settle before dinner."

As they walked into the lobby of the hotel, Genesis' eyes widened at its opulence. The marble floors, chandeliers, and plush furniture all screamed luxury. It was the kind of place Zuri loved.

After checking in, Zuri led them to the elevator and pressed the button for the top floor. As they rode up in silence, Genesis wondered what was going through Andrea's mind. Was this change what she wanted? Did she regret where their friendship had ended up or was Gen something else from her past she needed to shed?

The elevator dinged, and they stepped out onto a private floor. Zuri led her to a penthouse suite with floor-to-ceiling windows overlooking the city skyline.

"Wow," Genesis breathed out as they stepped inside. The suite was even more luxurious than the lobby. A large living room with plush couches and a grand piano greeted them, while a dining table set for four sat nearby.

"It's a bit extravagant," Zuri said sheepishly while guiding her to the couches. "But I wanted to make this visit special."

Genesis was touched by Zuri's gesture. She settled onto one couch while Zuri poured them each a glass of wine from a nearby bar cart.

"Here, love, I think you need this," Zuri said as she handed Genesis her glass.

"One or several," Genesis remarked before taking a generous sip. "I'm so confused. We might not talk as often, but I didn't expect this to happen within a year. It's like some sort of pod person replaced my best friend."

Zuri nodded in agreement. "Sometimes that's how it is. I had a friend who I was close to, Nadia. We attended film school together and had plans to work with one another when we graduated. She went away for the summer and came back, never talked to me again. Ghosted me. I still don't know what happened, but I had to accept it."

Genesis let the words sink in, swirling the deep red liquid in her glass. "We're still friends and she invited me out here, so I guess I should stop being so dramatic."

"Let's enjoy dinner," Zuri suggested. "You'll catch up, reminisce. It'll feel more like old times."

Genesis looked at Zuri with a small, grateful smile. "You're always so optimistic," she said.

"Sure, if you catch me at the right time," Zuri replied with a grin. "Now let's get ready for dinner so we can meet Rebecca."

With an eye roll, Genesis nodded and allowed herself to be pulled up from the couch. She prayed things went well because she couldn't take anything less.

* * *

A few hours later, Andrea, Zuri and Genesis sat at a round table in Roland's World Famous Barbecue on Restaurant Row, waiting for Rebecca. Genesis was doing everything she could to break free from her funk and enjoy the evening. She was not only seeing her best friend for the first time in years, but it was her birthday! It was a time to celebrate, not mope about changes in Andrea. If she liked it, Genesis would have to learn to love it.

"Everything here is good, but my favorites are the brisket with the mac and cheese," Andrea said, excitement in her voice.

Genesis did a happy dance. "Oooh, you know I love a good mac and cheese. It's so hard to find places that make it right."

Zuri shrugged. "Mac and cheese is pretty basic. I don't think it takes much for it to be good."

Andrea and Genesis both turned simultaneously and gave her a disbelieving stare.

"Zuri, love, you don't understand what it takes to create the perfect mac and cheese," Genesis rebuked.

"She's right, Zuri. It's not about throwing together some pasta and cheese." Andrea chimed in as she picked up her menu. "It's about the proper consistency, the creaminess, the blend of cheeses. It's an art."

"Mac and cheese is not 'basic'. It's comfort. It's childhood. It's... it's home."

Zuri raised her hands in surrender. "Okay, y'all are doing The Most," she declared with an eye roll.

Genesis and Andrea exchanged a triumphant glance before they both broke into laughter. In that moment, it reminded her of the times in the past when they used to have fun debates about any and everything. Perhaps Zuri was right, and time together was what they needed.

As their laughter faded away, a woman walked through the restaurant doors. Genesis recognized Rebecca right away from their video calls. Her silky jet-black hair spilled down her back in a waterfall of glossy waves, complimenting her tanned skin. She wore a plum-colored blouse under a fitted black leather jacket that accentuated her curves. Black skinny jeans with high-heeled boots that gave her petite frame a couple of extra inches completed the outfit.

Rebecca touched her hand to her heart as she saw them, crossing the room with a big smile. "Hi, guys."

Andrea stood and waved her over, a similar bright grin lighting up her face. The two shared a quick hug before pulling away. Rebecca turned to Genesis and Zuri.

"Genesis, it's so nice to see you in person. I'm a hugger. Hope you don't mind."

"Same here," she lied as they hugged.

Zuri smiled. "Nice to meet you," she said, leaning into a quick hug. "We're excited to celebrate Andrea."

"Thanks, me too. And can I say, you're even prettier in person."

Andrea rolled her eyes. "She did a bit of internet stalking when she found out Genesis was dating you."

Rebecca waved her off. "Don't act like you didn't, too." She leaned into Zuri. "Are you aware that Andrea is obsessed with your mom? We've watched her movies so many times."

They all laughed, and Zuri nodded. "I have heard about Andrea's admiration for my mother. Don't worry, you'll get to meet her at our wedding."

"Really? That's incredible! I can't wait. I mean... not that I'm star-struck or anything," Andrea blurted out, her eyes wide with excitement.

"We are all aware of just how star-struck you are. It's okay," Genesis teased, bringing another round of laughter circling the table.

The server arrived to take their orders and Genesis snuck a peek at Andrea and Rebecca as they interacted. Rebecca caressed Andrea's head in an affectionate but possessive way.

Genesis experienced a twinge in her chest, realizing she was not only trying to accept the change in her friend, but also this new relationship. Andrea seemed happy, more than happy, she seemed at peace. *Am I jealous?*

"How are your wedding plans going? I'm excited to have an

excuse to visit Cali," Rebecca said, grabbing some bread from the table.

Zuri glanced at Genesis, and spoke for them. "We kind of pushed planning to the back burner. With work and everything, it hasn't been feasible. But I've looked at a few venues. There's one in Napa we like, right babe?"

Genesis blinked, realizing that she was being addressed. She offered a slow nod, managing a small smile. "Yes, it's breathtaking."

Rebeca clapped her hands together happily. "Napa, that sounds so romantic!" She turned to Andrea, her voice brimming with enthusiasm. "Doesn't that sound super romantic, babe?"

Andrea chuckled, wrapping her arm around Rebecca's shoulders. "Yes, it does," she said, pressing a light kiss on her temple. "How about we order?"

While looking through the menu, Genesis noticed the way Andrea's eyes lit up when she found her favorite dish. "Oh, the brisket and mac and cheese are calling my name," Andrea said with delight.

But before Andrea finalized her decision, Natalie reached out and touched her arm. "Honey, remember what Dr. Patel said about your cholesterol? We might want to consider something a little healthier tonight.

Genesis watched as Andrea's smile faltered. "Oh, right," she said, her enthusiasm dampening. "I guess I forgot."

Rebecca's fingers trailed down Andrea's arm, intertwining with her hand. "How about the grilled chicken salad? It looks delicious, and it's much better for you."

Andrea nodded, a resigned expression crossing her face. "You're right, of course. The salad it is."

Genesis frowned. The Andrea she knew would have laughed off any suggestion to change her order, especially on her birthday. She remembered countless nights of indulging in greasy takeout and decadent desserts, with Andrea always proclaiming that life was too short not to enjoy good food. An irritated groan involuntarily slipped from her lips.

Zuri, sensing the shift in mood, interjected. "Well, I'm getting the brisket. Genesis, want to split an order of mac and cheese with me? I know how much you love it."

Genesis hesitated for a moment, her eyes darting between Zuri and Andrea.

"You know what? I think I'm going to pass. I'll have a chicken salad too, so Andrea doesn't feel alone." Andrea looked at her, gratitude in her eyes. " But I will steal like a forkful," Genesis said, turning to Zuri.

They all laughed, and the conversation flowed more easily after that, as they reminisced about old times and shared updates on their lives. Genesis relaxed a bit, enjoying the familiar cadence of Andrea's laughter and the feel of Zuri's hand on her knee under the table.

"So, Genesis," Rebecca said, turning her attention to her, "Andrea tells me you're quite the dancer. How did you get into that?"

"Oh, I've been dancing since I could walk," she said with a laugh. "My mom used to say I came out of the womb doing pirouettes."

Andrea jumped in with an anecdote. "Gen's being modest. She's incredible. We used to put on these impromptu performances in college. Remember that time we danced on tables at that dive bar?"

Genesis burst into laughter, the memory flooding back. "Oh god, I'd forgotten about that! We were so drunk on cheap tequila."

"And you still managed to nail every move," Andrea added.

For a moment, it felt like the good old days. Genesis caught

Andrea's eye, and she laughed when Andrea made a goofy face. The hint of her old friend put her at ease momentarily.

Rebecca's voice broke the moment. "Ugh, thank God you stopped drinking."

Genesis felt her smile falter at Rebecca's comment. She glanced at Andrea, expecting to see her usual playful defense of their wilder days, but found her friend nodding in agreement.

"You're right, babe," Andrea said, squeezing Rebecca's hand. "I'm so glad those days are behind me. I shudder to think of all the damage I was doing to my body."

Genesis blinked, taken aback by Andrea's response. In the past, she would have been scheming on how to recreate their table top dancing. This new, serious Andrea felt like a stranger.

Zuri steered the conversation in a different direction. "So, Rebecca, Andrea mentioned you work in finance. How did you two meet?"

As Rebecca launched into the story of their first encounter at a charity gala, Genesis found her mind wandering. She watched Andrea hanging on Rebecca's every word, nodding along and adding context. It was clear they were deeply in love, but Genesis couldn't shake the feeling that something was off.

"Oh, it was quite the meet-cute," she began, grabbing Andrea's hand on the table. "I was at this stuffy charity gala for work, feeling completely out of place among all these uptight finance types. And then, across the room, I spotted this dapper woman in a burgundy suit."

Andrea blushed, ducking her head slightly. "You make it sound so romantic. I was a mess that night."

"Nonsense," Rebecca insisted, giving Andrea's hand a squeeze. "You were breathtaking. Anyway, I couldn't take my eyes off her. She was laughing with some friends, and her whole face just lit up. I knew I had to meet her."

Genesis found herself leaning in, despite her mixed feelings. She had to admit, Rebecca was a captivating storyteller.

"So, I grabbed two glasses of champagne and made my way over," Rebecca continued. "But just as I got close, I tripped over my own feet - curse those heels - and ended up spilling both glasses all over Andrea's beautiful suit."

Andrea laughed, the sound rich and warm. "I thought she'd done it on purpose at first. I was ready to give her a piece of my mind."

"Can you blame me?" Rebecca said with a wink. "It was the only way I could think of to get you out of those clothes."

"Why were you at a charity gala?" Genesis asked, turning to Andrea.

Andrea's smile faltered slightly at Genesis' question. "Oh, well...I was there representing the company I worked with at the time. We'd recently made some charitable donations and were invited to attend."

"I see." Genesis didn't push further but she remembered when Andrea would have railed against representing a Fortune 500 company that only gave money to charity for tax breaks, let alone representing them at an event.

As Rebecca continued to describe their whirlwind romance, Genesis noticed how different it sounded from Andrea's past relationships. Gone were the tales of spontaneous road trips and wild nights out. Instead, Rebecca spoke of elegant dinners, art gallery openings, and weekend getaways to exclusive resorts.

"And then, on our third date, Andrea surprised me with tickets to the symphony," Rebecca gushed. "I knew right then that she was the one."

Andrea beamed at Rebecca, squeezing her hand. "I just wanted to impress you," she said.

"That's so romantic," Zuri chimed in. "You two seem perfect for each other."

"I like to think so. We also have something else to share. Babe tell them the other good news!" Rebecca practically squealed.

"I can't believe I forgot to mention it earlier. Rebecca proposed last month. We're thinking of a spring wedding next year."

Genesis felt a jolt of surprise. Engaged? When did that happen? She looked at Andrea, who was beaming as Rebecca held up her left hand, showcasing a sizable diamond ring.

"Congratulations," Genesis said, her voice sounding hollow even to her own ears. "That's... wonderful news."

"Don't worry, I'm sure ours will happen way after yours," Rebecca assured them. "How about we take a group picture to remember this night?"

As Rebecca fussed with her phone, trying to get the perfect angle for their group selfie, a wave of sadness hit Genesis. She plastered on a smile as the camera flashed, but inside she was reeling. How could Andrea have forgotten to mention something as monumental as an engagement? Before, Andrea would have called her screaming with excitement the moment it happened.

"Oh, this one's perfect!" Rebecca exclaimed, showing the photo around the table. "We all look so happy."

Andrea turned to Genesis with a guilty look. "I'm so sorry I didn't tell you about the engagement sooner, Gen. Things have just been so busy with work and wedding planning. But I'm so glad you're here now to celebrate with us."

Genesis nodded, not trusting herself to speak. Zuri squeezed her knee, a silent gesture of support.

"So, tell us more about the wedding plans," Zuri prompted, trying to keep the conversation flowing.

* * *

Back at the hotel, they began their bedtime routine almost as soon as they got back. They had plans to meet Andrea and Rebecca in the early afternoon for a workout and lunch. In the evening was the big birthday celebration.

As Genesis removed her makeup, she could feel Zuri's eyes on her.

"You want to talk about it?" Zuri asked, coming up behind Genesis and wrapping her arms around her waist.

Genesis sighed, leaning back into Zuri's embrace. "I don't know. I just... I feel like I've lost my best friend. The Andrea I saw tonight isn't my Andrea."

Zuri nodded, her reflection in the mirror showing understanding. "People change, love. Sometimes drastically."

"I know, but this is different," Genesis said, turning to face Zuri. "It's like she's become a different person to fit into Rebecca's world."

"I know it's hard to see someone you love change so much. But this is who Andrea wants to be now. Maybe this version of her is happier and healthier."

Genesis shook her head, frustration clear in her voice. "But she didn't even tell me she was engaged, Zuri. We used to share everything. Now it's like I'm just an afterthought in her life."

Zuri pulled Genesis closer, rubbing soothing circles on her back. "I know it hurts, babe, but tomorrow's another day. Find some time alone to talk and catch up. All relationships go through rough patches."

She nodded, burying her face in Zuri's shoulder. "You're right. I'll try to talk to her alone tomorrow."

Genesis wasn't sure it would matter, but she hoped that some one-on-one time with Andrea might help bridge the growing gap between them.

# Chapter Seventeen

Genesis' eyes fluttered open, adjusting to the morning light filtering through the sheer curtains of the hotel room. She reached out expecting to find Zuri, instead her hand met an empty space.

Frowning, she propped herself up on her elbows, scanning the room. Her gaze settled on Zuri, her silhouette appearing as a breeze blew the curtain in from the balcony. She slipped out of bed, padding across the plush carpet to join her.

"Hey beautiful," she said, leaning against the balcony door.

Zuri turned to her and gave her a small smile. "Hey. I didn't mean to wake you. It's early."

Genesis yawned and stretched. "It's okay. I'd rather be awake with you than sleep alone." She moved closer, wrapping her arms around Zuri. "What's on your mind?"

"You want to order breakfast?"

Genesis didn't miss that Zuri had avoided the question, but she let it go. "Breakfast sounds perfect. Maybe some French toast and fresh fruit?"

Zuri nodded, placing a gentle kiss on Genesis' forehead before heading back into the room to call for room service. After placing their respective orders, she heated some tea and brought two steaming cups out to the balcony.

"For you, mademoiselle. They had your favorite, ginger and lemon." She placed the cups on the small table and settled into her seat. "One thing about this place is the air is always so crisp."

Genesis took a sip of her tea. "You've been here before?"

"Yeah, my dad liked to come out here to ski. My mom hated it, but she liked the outfits, so she would oblige him. It was one of the few things we did as a family."

"That sounds nice. It must have been fun to come here as a kid."

Zuri smiled wistfully, her eyes focusing on a distant point beyond the balcony. "It was. Those trips are some of my favorite childhood memories. We can come back here in the winter sometime. I'd love to show you the slopes."

Genesis raised an eyebrow, a playful smirk tugging at her lips. "You? On skis? Now that I'd pay to see."

"Hey!" Zuri laughed, reaching out to swat Genesis' arm. "I was quite the ski bunny back in the day."

"Mm hmm, sure you were," Genesis teased.

A knock at the door interrupted their laughter, signaling the arrival of their breakfast. Zuri rose to answer it.

The aroma of freshly made French toast and fruit filled the air as Zuri wheeled the cart onto the balcony.

"This looks amazing," she said, reaching for a strawberry.

Zuri settled back into her seat, spreading a napkin across her lap. "Let's dig in before it gets cold."

They ate in comfortable silence for a few minutes, enjoying the view and each other's company. Genesis let out a moan of delight, savoring each bite of syrupy French toast.

Zuri was on her phone, something she had taken to doing more when they were eating. She didn't like it, but Genesis didn't want Zuri to feel like she was finding fault in every little thing she did. She tried instead to engage her in conversation.

"Everything okay at the studio?" Genesis asked, popping a grape into her mouth.

Zuri looked up, a flicker of guilt crossing her face as she put her phone down. "Sorry, I was checking some emails, but everything is fine at the studio. Same old stuff. However, there is something I wanted to talk to you about."

Genesis paused mid-bite, her fork hovering in the air. She set it down, her full attention now on Zuri.

Zuri returned to her phone, and slid it over to Genesis. At first, she couldn't figure out what she was looking at, then she saw the headline and looked at the picture again. It was a photo of her and the woman she met at the club, Imani, grinding on each other.

Genesis experienced a sinking sensation as she gazed at the image on Zuri's phone. She looked up at Zuri, her eyes wide with panic. "Zuri, I swear it's not what it looks like. We were dancing, nothing more."

Zuri took her phone back. "I'm curious why you never mentioned it to me?"

Genesis' throat tightened as she struggled to find the right words. She reached for her tea, taking a sip to buy herself a moment. Of all the things she wished she had said, this omission had come to bite her in the ass.

"Honestly, I didn't think it was worth mentioning. We danced for a couple of songs. You know I would never be with anyone else."

Zuri's expression remained neutral, yet Genesis detected a flicker of hurt in her eyes. "I do know that, but this looks... intimate. And it's all over social media now."

Genesis leaned forward, reaching for Zuri's hand. "Baby, I

promise you, it was nothing. We were having fun, blowing off steam after a long week."

Zuri pulled her hand away, running it through her locs instead. "I get that. I do. But it still hurts to see. And to find out about it like this..."

Genesis felt a pang of guilt. She should have told Zuri about that night and dealt with the repercussions then. "I'm sorry. I should have mentioned it to you, but I didn't view it as something newsworthy."

"You're not only an accountant anymore, Gen. You're my girlfriend and with that comes more visibility. The media loves to latch onto anything they can spin into a story, especially with someone at my level." She gestured to the phone with her free hand. "Pictures like this... they can be misconstrued. And if there is anything I don't like, it's being caught off guard."

Genesis nodded, processing Zuri's words. She felt a mix of emotions. Guilt for potentially causing problems, and a touch of resentment at having to monitor her behavior.

"I understand," she said, her eyes downcast. "I'll be more careful in the future."

Zuri leaned forward, gently lifting Genesis' chin with her finger. "Hey, look at me. You haven't done anything wrong. This is part of the territory when you're in the public eye. It takes some getting used to. I only ask that you always be honest with me, even if you think I won't like it."

Genesis met Zuri's gaze, seeing understanding there. "I guess I'm still adjusting to all of this. It's so different from my life before. Even with Shannon, when she played, the league wasn't as big as it is now. So we didn't get this kind of scrutiny."

"Tell me about it. I've been dealing with this my whole life, and sometimes it still catches me off guard."

"So, what do we do now? About the photo, I mean."

Zuri leaned back in her chair, her expression thoughtful.

"There's nothing to be done. Acknowledging gossip only gives it more legs."

"I appreciate that, but...now I feel like a problem that needs to be handled."

Zuri's eyes widened, a flash of hurt in her eyes. "Gen, that's not-"

"I know, I know," Genesis interrupted, holding up a hand. "That's not your intention. But this is all so new to me. I'm used to being myself. Dancing when I want to dance, laughing when I want to laugh. And now I have to think about how every little thing I do might be perceived."

Zuri leaned forward, her expression earnest. "I understand, babe. Trust me, I do. It's a lot to take in, and it's not fair but this is my reality."

Genesis sighed." I don't want to lose myself in all of this. Or play a part to fit into your world."

Zuri reached across the table, taking both of Genesis' hands in hers. "Listen to me. I fell in love with you because of who you are. Your joy, your spontaneity, your ability to find fun in every moment. I don't want you to change that, but there has to be a balance."

Genesis pulled her hands away. "This isn't us talking about planning our wedding. We're speaking about my behavior being policed. How is that a 'we' thing?"

Zuri flinched at Genesis' sharp tone. She took a deep breath. "Gen, I'm not trying to police you. I'm trying to help you navigate this new world you've entered by being with me. It's not always fair or easy, but it's our reality."

Genesis stood up abruptly. "Our reality? Zuri, this is your reality. I didn't sign up for this. I want you, not your public image or your family's empire."

Zuri didn't respond and her face was unreadable. Genesis had seemingly hit a nerve

"Sit down."

"Excuse me?" Genesis said, startled by the coldness in her tone.

"You heard me, sit down."

Genesis froze and for a moment, she considered refusing, her own stubbornness rising to meet Zuri's command. But something in Zuri's expression made her reconsider. Slowly, she eased herself back into her seat.

Zuri rested her elbows on the table, her fingers steepled beneath her chin. When she spoke, her voice was low and measured, each word carefully chosen.

"Gen, I need you to understand something. This relationship, like any other, comes with compromises. My public image is part of who I am, whether you signed up for it or not. Just like your close friendship with your ex-wife is part of who you are, whether I'm comfortable with it or not."

Genesis' eyes widened at the unexpected turn in the conversation. She opened her mouth to speak, but Zuri held up a hand, silencing her.

"Let me finish. Do you think I enjoy seeing you and Shannon so close? The inside jokes, the casual touches, the history you share? It's not easy for me. But I accept it because she's a part of your life."

Genesis couldn't speak. She hadn't considered how her friendship with Shannon might affect Zuri. It had seemed like something to get over but she hadn't considered the toll it could take. "I didn't realize it bothered you that much," she said.

"I trust you, but it's an adjustment, like this public scrutiny is an adjustment for you."

She took Genesis' hand into her own again. This time, Genesis didn't pull away.

"My point is, relationships require give and take. We both have aspects of our lives that the other needs to adapt to. I'm not asking you to change who you are, Gen. I'm asking you to be aware of the realities of my world."

Genesis nodded, her body relaxing. "I understand. I'm sorry for lashing out. Seeing that photo on a gossip site felt like a violation. Going out that night was so nice, and now this has sullied it."

Zuri's stroked Genesis' hand. "I know, babe. And I'm sorry you have to deal with this. If it was possible to shield you from it, I would. Your carefree spirit is something I love about you."

A smile tugged at the corners of her mouth. "Do you love me even when I'm being stubborn and difficult?"

"Especially then. It keeps me on my toes. But I get the sense that there's more going on here."

Genesis hands played with the table cloth, her eyes downcast. "It's not only about the photo or the public scrutiny. It's wedding stuff too. I want it to be perfect for you, but every time we discuss the plans, there's this pit in my stomach. Your family expects this grand affair, and I know you do too. But it all feels too extravagant. I know you'll cover everything, but I want to contribute to it as well."

Her voice trembled as she continued. "I love you, Zuri. But I'm afraid that one day you'll wake up and realize that I'm not enough. That I don't belong in your world, no matter how hard I try."

Zuri stood up, moving around the table to kneel beside Genesis' chair, taking both her hands.

"Gen," she said, her voice thick with emotion. "My love, my heart. You are more than enough. You're everything." She reached up, wiping away a tear that had escaped down Genesis' cheek. "Are you thinking of that incident that happened at the charity event?"

Genesis nodded. "But there's been others."

"Babe, you don't have to fit into my world. I want us to

create our own world together. A world where we both feel comfortable and true to ourselves. Trust me when I say, most of those pretentious people are miserable and have no right to judge anyone. I've been so caught up in trying to make everything perfect, I didn't realize how overwhelming it all must be for you. The wedding, the social events, the scrutiny - it's a lot. And I'm sorry I didn't see how much it was affecting you."

Genesis gave a small, watery smile. "It's not your fault. I should have said something earlier."

Zuri nodded, a determined look crossing her face. "Well, we're going to change things starting now. Let's rethink our wedding. What if we scaled it back? Something intimate, only close friends and family. We can have it at that little beach you love, the one where we had our first picnic together."

"Really? You'd be okay with that?"

"More than okay," Zuri assured her. "I had a fantasy about what my wedding would be, but I don't need a grand spectacle to show the world how much I love you. All I need is you standing beside me, promising to spend the rest of our lives together."

Genesis grinned. "That sounds perfect."

"My only caveat is that we do it big for the reception."

Genesis let out a hearty laugh. "I wouldn't expect anything less from you, babe."

"Hey, I may be willing to compromise on the ceremony, but you know I can't resist a good party. Plus, it'll give you a chance to show off those killer dance moves."

Genesis rolled her eyes playfully. "As long as there are no paparazzi around to catch me grinding on anyone else."

Zuri pulled back, and bit her bottom lip. "Oh, I'll make sure you're only grinding on me that night."

Zuri's laughter filled the air, lightening the mood. She leaned across the table, cupping Zuri's face in her hands and placing a kiss on her lips. "Perhaps I will, but only if you talk to me the way you did just now, all CEO-like and commanding."

Zuri smirked. "Oh, you like it when I'm commanding, do you?"

A blush creeped up Genesis' cheeks. "Maybe," she said coyly, biting her lower lip.

Zuri stood up, her movements deliberate as she made her way around the table. She towered over Genesis, her presence filling the small balcony. With one finger, she tilted Genesis' chin up, their eyes locking.

"Well," Zuri said, her voice low and husky, "perhaps I should command you more often."

The tension from their earlier conversation had transformed into something else, something electric and charged with desire.

"What would you command me to do?" Genesis asked, her voice barely above a whisper.

Zuri leaned down, her lips brushing against Genesis' ear. "First, I'd command you to stand up."

Genesis obeyed, rising to her feet. She was acutely aware of how close they were, of the heat radiating from Zuri's body.

"Good girl," Zuri murmured, her hands sliding down Genesis' sides to rest on her hips. "Now, I command you to kiss me."

Genesis didn't need to be told twice. She surged forward, capturing Zuri's lips in a passionate kiss. They would have kept going, and oh how sweet it would have been, but the alarm on Genesis' phone began blaring the rap song "Shoop" at full volume.

Genesis jumped at the sudden interruption, breaking away from Zuri with a startled laugh. "Oh my god, I forgot I set that alarm," she said, fumbling for her phone.

Zuri chuckled. "Salt-N-Pepa? Really?"

"What? I like the classics too," Genesis said, silencing the alarm. "I guess we should get ready."

Zuri sighed, her hands still resting on Genesis' hips. "I suppose we should. But I'm not done with you yet, Ms. Malone."

A shiver ran down her spine at Zuri's words. "Is that a promise, Ms. Baker?"

"You bet it is," Zuri said, stealing one more quick kiss before stepping back. "How about you shower first, and I'll clean up out here?"

Genesis paused at the doorway, throwing a playful glance over her shoulder. "We could save time if we showered together."

Zuri's eyes darkened with desire, but she shook her head with a rueful smile. "Nice try, babe. But if we do that, we'll definitely be late. Go on, I'll be right behind you."

Genesis pouted but complied, taking a quicker shower than her norm. When she and Zuri passed each other as Genesis exited the bathroom, there was a charged moment. Zuri's eyes roamed over Genesis' towel-clad form before she disappeared into the steamy bathroom.

As Genesis dried her hair and got dressed, her mind wandered back to their conversation on the balcony. Their conversation and its implications still weighed on her mind, but the way Zuri had handled it, with understanding, patience, and the right amount of firmness, made her feel more secure.

Her life had changed so much since meeting Zuri. The glamor, the public scrutiny, the responsibility - it was all so new and sometimes overwhelming. But then there was Zuri herself - strong, passionate, and loving. Genesis smiled to herself, realizing that despite the challenges, she wouldn't trade this new life for anything.

Zuri stepped into the room wrapped in a towel as Genesis took down her hair to style it.

"You want my help?" Zuri asked, putting on her bra.

Genesis' face lit up. "That would be amazing."

Genesis took a seat and Zuri worked the product through her curls, carefully detangling any knots. She took her time, making sure not to pull too hard, occasionally pausing to massage Genesis' scalp.

"This is nice," Genesis murmured, her eyes closed in contentment.

Zuri's fingers worked their magic through Genesis' curls, each gentle tug and stroke sending waves of relaxation through her body.

When she was done, Zuri stepped back to admire her handiwork. "There you go, beautiful. All done."

Genesis opened her eyes and gazed at her reflection in the mirror. Her curls looked amazing - perfectly defined and full of life. She turned to Zuri with a wide smile. "Thank you, babe. It looks incredible."

Zuri leaned down, kissing Genesis' shoulder. "Anytime, babe. I love your hair."

Genesis caught Zuri's hand, bringing it to her lips for a kiss. "I love you," she said, her eyes meeting Zuri's in the mirror.

"I love you too," Zuri replied, her voice warm with affection. She gave Genesis' shoulder a gentle squeeze before stepping away to finish getting dressed.

As they moved around the room, putting on the final touches of their outfits, Genesis felt a sense of contentment wash over her. Moments like these - quiet, intimate, and filled with love - made it all worthwhile.

# Chapter Eighteen

As Genesis and Zuri exited their rental, they were greeted by the sight of the Evergreen Heights Fitness Complex, a sprawling oasis of luxury nestled in the heart of the city. The club's entrance was framed by towering oak trees, their branches creating a natural archway that seemed to transport them into another world.

The main building, a grand structure of gleaming white stone and floor-to-ceiling windows, stretched out before them. Its façade was adorned with intricate Art déco detailing, a nod to the club's illustrious history dating back to the 1920s. Perfectly manicured lawns rolled out in every direction, dotted with vibrant flower beds that added splashes of color to the verdant landscape.

As they approached the entrance, a valet in a crisp uniform rushed forward to greet them. "Welcome to Evergreen Heights, ladies," he said with a polite bow before whisking their car away to the private parking area.

The lobby was a marvel of opulence. Marble floors, crystal chandeliers, while plush velvet sofas and armchairs invited members to relax in comfort. The air in the lobby carried a subtle scent of jasmine, enhancing the ambiance of refined luxury.

Genesis gaped at the sheer extravagance surrounding them. "Of course, this place is pretentious, just like Rebecca."

"Be nice," Zuri whispered, right as Rebecca and Andrea approached them from across the lobby.

"Zuri! Genesis! So glad you could make it," Rebecca called out, air-kissing both their cheeks in greeting. "Isn't it just divine?"

Andrea rolled her eyes good-naturedly at Rebecca's enthusiasm. "Don't mind her. She's still in the honeymoon phase with this place. We just joined a couple of months ago."

"And I'm already on the events committee," Rebecca added proudly.

"So, what's on the agenda today?" Zuri asked.

"Well, I thought the four of us would be doing some activities today, but the birthday girl over here wanted some alone time with Genesis. I'm thinking Zuri that you and I could tour the place and attend a couple of classes. Maybe get a spa treatment?"

Zuri smiled. "Sounds like a plan." She looked over at Genesis and mouthed, "You owe me," before following behind Rebecca, who was already talking away.

Genesis and Andrea were finally alone, but they both stood awkwardly for a moment, unsure how to begin.

Andrea broke the silence first. "You look surprised. We never get to see each other. I wasn't gonna let you leave without some alone time."

"Thank God," Genesis said, pulling her in for a hug.

Andrea linked her arm through Genesis' and began leading her through the club. "Come on, I want to show you my favorite spot here."

As they walked arm in arm down a long hallway, Genesis

marveled at the opulence surrounding them. The walls were adorned with intricate gold leaf designs, and every few feet stood pedestals displaying priceless works of art. It's as if they were walking through a museum rather than a fitness club.

"This place is ridiculous," Genesis whispered, her eyes wide as they passed a marble statue that looked suspiciously like an original Rodin.

Andrea chuckled. "I know, right? It's like you should be wearing white gloves just to touch the equipment."

Eventually they reached a set of heavy wooden doors. Andrea paused, a mischievous glint in her eyes. "Close your eyes," she instructed.

Genesis complied, her curiosity piqued. She heard the creak of the doors opening, Andrea's hand on her back guided her forward. The air changed, becoming cooler and less humid.

"Okay, open them," Andrea said.

Genesis opened her eyes and gasped. They were standing in an enormous, cavernous room dominated by a towering indoor climbing wall. The wall stretched at least 50 feet high, its surface a patchwork of multicolored holds creating routes of varying difficulty. Ropes dangled from the top, swaying in the artificial breeze created by the room's climate control system.

Genesis' eyes widened as she took in the impressive sight. "Wow, this is amazing! I didn't expect to see something like this here."

Andrea grinned, pleased by Genesis' reaction. "I know, right? It's my favorite part of the club. I come here whenever I need to clear my head or work through a tough problem."

"So you never stopped climbing?"

"Hell no, I just don't do it outdoors anymore. I figured it was a suitable compromise and it's one reason we joined this specific location. Rebecca has connections, so we get a discount."

"Thank god." Genesis threw herself at Andrea, holding her tight. "I thought you had become someone else entirely."

Andrea laughed, returning Genesis' embrace. "Never. I may have upgraded my wardrobe and joined a fancy club, but I'm still me at heart. Just with better shoes."

Genesis pulled back, grinning. "And what fabulous shoes they are," she said, glancing down at Andrea's designer sneakers. "I'm so glad. I was worried."

"That I'd turned into some stuffy socialite?" Andrea finished for her, a wry smile on her face. "I'll admit, this lifestyle took some getting used to. But I've found ways to stay true to myself."

Genesis nodded, relief washing over her. She gazed up at the climbing wall. "You want us to climb this beast, don't you?"

"Hell yeah."

"I don't know, Drea. It's been years since I've climbed anything more challenging than the stairs to my office."

"Come on," Andrea coaxed, already moving toward a nearby locker. "It'll be just like old times. Remember when we used to sneak out to that quarry outside of town?"

Genesis laughed, memories flooding back. "How could I forget? You nearly gave me a heart attack every time you free-climbed those cliffs."

Andrea emerged from the locker with two harnesses and a pair of climbing shoes. "Well, no free-climbing today. We'll stick to the basics. What do you say?"

Looking at Andrea's expectant face, Genesis gave in. "Alright, you win. But if I fall and break something, you're explaining it to Zuri."

"Deal," Andrea said, beaming as she handed Genesis the gear.

As they strapped on their harnesses and laced up their climbing shoes, Genesis a familiar thrill of excitement mixed with trepidation ran through her. Andrea led her to one of the easier routes, a beginner-friendly path marked with large, brightly colored holds.

"Ready?" Andrea asked, clipping herself into the auto-belay system.

"As I'll ever be."

They began their ascent, Andrea moving with practiced ease while Genesis took her time, testing each hold before committing her weight. The cool, textured surface of the wall felt both foreign and familiar under her fingers.

As they climbed higher, the world below seemed to fall away. The soft whir of the climate control system and the occasional click of carabiners were the only sounds that reached them. Genesis fell into a rhythm, muscle memory kicking in as she reached for hold after hold.

Halfway up the wall, they paused on a small ledge to catch their breath. Genesis looked down, marveling at how far they'd come. The floor below looked like a distant patchwork of mats and equipment.

"You're doing great," Andrea encouraged, her face flushed with exertion and joy.

Genesis grinned back, feeling a surge of confidence. "Thanks. It's coming back to me now."

They continued their climb, the route becoming more challenging as they neared the top.

Genesis's arms burned as she reached for the next hold. She paused, taking a deep breath to steady herself.

"You okay?" Andrea called from above.

"Yeah, just give me a sec," Genesis replied, shaking out her arms. She looked up, gauging the distance to the top. Only a few more moves to go.

With renewed determination, Genesis pushed on. Her fingers found purchase on a small crimper, her toes balanced precariously on a tiny foothold. She stretched, reaching for the next handhold, just out of reach.

"You've got this, Gen!" Andrea cheered.

Genesis gritted her teeth, summoning one last burst of strength. Her hand closed around the hold, and with a final push, she hauled herself up to the top of the wall.

Breathing heavily, she slapped the buzzer at the summit, a wide grin spreading across her face. Andrea was already there, beaming with pride.

"We did it!" Genesis exclaimed, high-fiving her friend.

"Like old times," Andrea agreed with a grin.

As they began their controlled descent, there was a giddiness. The exhilaration of the climb, and the joy of reconnecting with Andrea.

Their feet touched the ground, and Genesis unclipped her harness with shaky hands. Andrea enveloped Genesis in a tight hug, both of them still panting from the exertion. As they embraced, the comfort she had been missing between them returned.

They made their way to a nearby bench, collapsing onto it with grateful sighs. Andrea took a long drink from her water bottle before turning to Genesis.

"I know my appearance threw you for a loop," Andrea said with a smirk.

"Was it that obvious?" Genesis said, covering her face.

"Girl, you looked like you saw a ghost!" Andrea chuckled. Genesis joined her, laughing at her accurate description. "I didn't think it'd be such a shock. Did you forget how spontaneous I can be?"

"Yeah, but you've always been my personal Lisa Bonet. The bohemian vibe was your thing. I guess I just always assumed it would be."

Andrea sighed. "Part of me still is that girl, but something shifted when I met Rebecca. She helps me feel... grounded, I guess. Like I can be both free-spirited and responsible at the same time. I needed that after the break up with Natalie."

"I get that. Zuri does that for me too. Helps me find balance."

"Did you get a chance to talk to her about how you've been feeling?"

"Yeah, it wasn't necessarily the ideal time, but it came out when it needed to. Anyway, she's trying her best."

Andrea chuckled. "That's great."

"Yeah, it is. She's always been good about listening and wanting to make things work."

"That's because she loves you," Andrea said. "Anyone can see that."

"I love her too. So much. I just... I worry sometimes about whether we're moving in the right direction, if we want the same things."

"Gen, honey, that's normal. Relationships are always evolving, but from what I've seen, you and Zuri are solid. You communicate, you support each other. That's rare."

Genesis nodded, taking in Andrea's words. "You're right. It's just... sometimes I feel like I'm in over my head with all this."

"I get it. Trust me, I do. When I first started dating Rebecca, I was like a fish out of water in her world. All the galas, the charity events, the networking. It was overwhelming."

"How did you deal with it?" Genesis asked, leaning in closer.

Andrea smiled. "I reminded myself why I was there in the first place. Because I love Rebecca. Everything else - the fancy parties, the designer clothes - that's just window dressing. What matters is us, our relationship."

"And it is nice to be with someone who can spoil you," Genesis said with a smirk.

"You ain't never lied."

Genesis leaned back on her elbows. "Thanks for this. For the climb, for the talk. For everything."

"Of course, you know I love you." Andrea paused, her eyes growing misty. "We've known each other for so long. You were there for me through some of the toughest times in my life. The least I can do is return the favor."

"True, we've always been there for each other, but I'm not gonna lie, it hurt when you two told us about the engagement last night. That's something that you would have shared right away in the past."

Andrea sighed, her expression turning serious. "It happened so fast after Natalie and I split up. I was worried you'd think I was rushing into things or making a mistake. You were there for me so much when that ended, and I didn't want you to think it was in vain. It felt easier to tell you with Rebecca there."

Genesis was truly taken aback. "Was I there for you? I thought I wasn't available enough during your break up."

"We don't have to talk every day to be connected. That's one thing I love about us. You're there when it matters. Those care packages you sent meant the world to me. The herbal teas, the aromatherapy candles, the silly little trinkets - they all served as reminders that I was loved, even when I was at my lowest.

Genesis smiled, remembering the hours she'd spent curating those packages. "I'm just glad they helped. It was hard being so far away." Her eyes began to well up. "God, we're getting sappy in our old age."

Andrea patted her head. "Old age? Speak for yourself. I look damn good."

"Yes, you do," Genesis agreed, giving her friend an appraising look. "The fancy lifestyle seems to agree with you."

"It has its perks," Andrea admitted. "But you know what I

miss sometimes? Our old apartment. Remember that tiny shoebox we shared right after college with Shannon?"

Genesis groaned. "How could I forget? The leaky faucet, the creaky floors, the neighbor who always seemed to be practicing the bagpipes at 3 AM."

"But it was ours. Our first proper home away from home."

"Yeah," Genesis agreed, a wave of nostalgia washing over her. "We had some good times there."

"Remember the Halloween party we threw? When you insisted on bobbing for apples and ended up with your wig in the bucket?"

Genesis burst out laughing. "Oh God, I'd forgotten about that! And you, Miss Smarty Pants, thought it would be hilarious to take a picture instead of helping me."

"That was Shannon's idea. Just like all the pranks she pulled on me," Andrea said with an eye roll. "What is she up to, anyway?"

Genesis hesitated for a moment before responding. "She could be better. Her cancer is in remission but she lost her job and has been having a hard time."

Andre gave her a side eye. "Don't tell me she came to you for help again?"

Genesis closed her eyes and nodded. "She's got evicted and needs a place to stay, so I offered her to stay with me."

"Genesis Malone, when are you going to learn to set boundaries with that woman?"

"I know, I know. But what was I supposed to do? She needed help."

"You were supposed to let her figure it out on her own," Andrea replied. "Gen, you can't keep being Shannon's safety net. It's not fair to you, and it's not helping her in the long run."

Genesis nodded, knowing Andrea was right. "It's just she's

been through so much already with the cancer. I feel guilty not helping when I can. We're family."

"You have to be mindful of your choices. You're with Zuri now. She's understanding, but even she will have her limits."

Genesis thought back to what Zuri said earlier about having to make adjustments at accepting Shannon's place in her life. Her mind whirled with conflicting thoughts and emotions. She pictured Zuri's face from that morning, the vulnerability as she admitted her discomfort with Genesis' closeness to Shannon. Had she been taking Zuri's understanding for granted?

After Shannon's diagnosis and subsequent stay with her, they had reached a different stage in their relationship, one of genuine friendship. Genesis recalled the late-night phone calls during chemo treatments, the financial support when medical bills piled up, the emotional scaffolding as Shannon rebuilt her life. Genesis had always been there, a steady presence amidst the chaos. It was a natural extension of their years together as partners and best friends.

But now, with Zuri in her life, the dynamics had shifted. Genesis realized she'd been trying to maintain her role in Shannon's life while building something new with Zuri. Straddling two worlds, and the strain was showing.

"Alright, I think we've had enough heart to heart time. Let's go find our ladies," Andrea said, standing up and offering Genesis her hand. "I'm sure Rebecca has talked Zuri's ear off by now."

Genesis smiled and placed her hand on Andrea's arm. "So you're happy, right?"

Andrea's face softened, a smile spreading across her features. "I am. Happier than I've been in a long time. Rebecca challenges me, supports me, loves me in ways I never knew I needed. It's not perfect but it's real and it's ours."

"Okay. If you're happy, then I'm happy for you," Genesis

said, squeezing her arm. "But I don't believe for one second you don't drink anymore."

Andrea smiled and continued walking. "My lips are sealed."

Genesis laughed, shaking her head. "Your secret's safe with me."

As they searched for Zuri and Rebecca, Genesis's mind drifted back to her argument with Zuri that morning. It had been their first real fight, and while they had resolved things, it left Genesis unsettled. She loved Zuri, but were they both getting what they needed from each other? Of course, it was normal to have disagreements in a relationship, but Genesis couldn't shake the feeling that there were deeper issues they needed to address.

When they rounded a corner, they spotted Zuri and Rebecca lounging by the indoor pool, sipping colorful mocktails and chatting. Zuri's face lit up when she saw Genesis and Andrea, and she waved them over.

"There you two are!" Zuri called out. "We were starting to wonder if you'd gotten lost."

Genesis leaned down to kiss Zuri, and she pulled her on top of her. She let out a giggle as Zuri trailed kisses on her jaw.

"I love you, beautiful," Zuri whispered into her ear.

And for a moment, all was right in the world.

# Chapter Nineteen

uri and Genesis stepped into the venue for Andrea's birthday and were in awe. The space was a transformed warehouse, its industrial bones softened by cascading white fabric draped from the high ceilings and well-placed light fixtures. Zuri's eyes widened as she took in the sheer opulence of it all. Enormous crystal chandeliers hung at varying heights, their facets catching and refracting light in dazzling patterns across the polished concrete floor.

To their left, a grand bar stretched the length of the wall, its surface obsidian and lined with gold-rimmed glasses that sparkled. Bartenders in crisp white shirts and black bow ties moved with practiced efficiency, crafting colorful cocktails for the guests already mingling about.

Zuri's gaze swept across the center of the room where dozens of round tables were artfully arranged, each draped in shimmering champagne-colored linens and adorned with towering floral centerpieces. The flowers—a lush mix of white orchids, blush roses, and delicate baby's breath—seemed to float above mirrored bases, creating an illusion of endless blooms.

A stage dominated the far end of the warehouse, framed by

thick velvet curtains in a deep purple. A live band had just finished setting up and sultry jazz soon filled the air.

"Damn, you would think this was a wedding. How much money does Rebecca have?" Zuri asked as they looked for their seats.

Genesis chuckled, linking her arm through Zuri's as they weaved through the gathering crowd. "From what Andrea told me, she has amazing connections because of her mother, who's a local politician."

"Ah, that explains it," Zuri nodded, her eyes still roaming the decor. "Politics and money always seem to go hand in hand."

Genesis rolled her eyes. "Not you talking about extravagance after that engagement party you threw."

"Touché," Zuri conceded with a laugh. "I guess I'm not the only one who can be a bit extra."

They found their table, nestled near the dance floor. Genesis pulled out Zuri's chair, earning a playful eye roll and a kiss on the cheek. As they settled in, Genesis scanned the room for Andrea, eager to wish her a happy birthday.

"There she is," Zuri said, nodding towards the entrance.

Andrea stood in the doorway, a vision that commanded attention. Gone was her usual flowing dress or casual attire. Instead, she wore a tailored suit that was nothing short of breathtaking. The jacket, a deep midnight blue, had lapels adorned with intricate silver embroidery that caught the light with every movement. The matching trousers were fitted, falling in a crisp line to where they met a pair of silver stilettos.

A delicate silver chain hung around her neck, disappearing beneath the crisp white shirt that peeked out from under her jacket. Her ears sparkled with new larger diamond studs, a birthday gift from Rebecca, no doubt.

Zuri didn't know Andrea that well, but she remembered the

pictures Genesis had shown her of them over the years. To say she had a glow up was an understatement.

"Wow, I tell you this weekend has been full of surprises," Genesis said, placing her hand over her heart. "She looks so beautiful. Let me go say hi."

Genesis speed walked over to Andrea and it was adorable to see how excited they got around each other. It was a complete 180 from the day before.

Zuri took her seat and quickly checked her messages. They were doing their best to mitigate the situation with Phillip Minor but after some negotiation, they got him to agree to meet with William for the lead role. She was aware that regardless of what she promised Will, Minor would make the audition process challenging. In the end, she hoped all of this was worth it because she needed it to work in order to strengthen their position in the industry. She sighed, pushing the thoughts of work aside. This was Andrea's night, and she wanted to enjoy it.

Genesis returned with a wide grin. "They have a chocolate fountain."

Zuri pretended to gasp. "Not a chocolate fountain."

"Whatever, I love chocolate and strawberries. Come on, let's go check it out before the party gets going."

Zuri allowed herself to be pulled along, Genesis' enthusiasm infectious. As they approached the dessert table, the rich aroma of melted chocolate filled the air. The fountain stood as a centerpiece, a three-tiered marvel of cascading dark chocolate. Surrounding it was an array of fresh fruits, marshmallows, and bite-sized pastries. Genesis grabbed a long skewer and speared a plump strawberry, holding it under the flowing chocolate with reverence. Zuri watched, amused, as Genesis took her first bite, closing her eyes in bliss.

"Oh my god, Zuri, you have to try this," Genesis moaned, offering the half-eaten strawberry to her fiancée.

Zuri leaned in, taking a small bite. The sweetness of the fruit mingled perfectly with the rich, velvety chocolate. She had to admit, it was pretty incredible.

"Okay, you're right. That is amazing," Zuri conceded, reaching for her own skewer. "But I think I prefer you covered in chocolate."

Genesis nearly choked on her strawberry. "Zuri!" she hissed, glancing around to make sure no one had overheard.

Zuri just grinned, unrepentant. She loved catching Genesis off guard with her flirtatious comments. It was a game they often played, seeing who could make the other blush first.

"They look beautiful together, don't they?"

Zuri looked up and saw Andrea and Rebecca dancing while the band played a sultry rendition of "At Last".

"They do," Zuri agreed, munching on a strawberry. "I'm so happy for them and for you. This weekend started off pretty rough."

"It did, but I'm glad we could work through it. Andrea and I have been friends for so long, I couldn't bear the thought of losing that connection."

"I'm glad," Zuri said, pressing a kiss to Genesis's temple. "And I'm glad we could talk as well."

Genesis continued eating, but kept quiet. Zuri could tell from her face she was contemplating what she wanted to say.

She turned to face Zuri, her expression serious. "I've been thinking about what you said, about us needing to communicate better. You're right, and I'm committed to working on that."

"I appreciate that, Gen. It means a lot to me."

"I can be... well, avoidant sometimes," Genesis admitted, fidgeting with her skewer. "It's just, I've always been the one to smooth things over. To keep the peace. But with you, I want to be different. I want to be honest, even when it's hard."

Zuri reached out, taking Genesis's free hand in hers. "That's all I want, baby. For us to be real with each other, no matter what."

Genesis squeezed Zuri's hand. "Well, in the spirit of honesty, I should tell you that I'm considering stealing this entire chocolate fountain and installing it in my kitchen."

"Now that's the kind of honesty I can get behind," Zuri said, leaning in to steal a quick kiss.

As they pulled apart, the music changed, shifting to a more upbeat tempo.

"Dance with me?" Genesis asked, tugging gently on Zuri's hand.

"You don't have to ask twice."

* * *

A couple of hours later, Zuri sat back and watched Genesis as she mingled with some of Andrea's newer friends. Although there was a hint of jealousy at first, her lady was possessive of all the women in her life it seemed. But she had found a few she connected with. Even getting a referral for a potential client.

As Zuri observed Genesis from afar, she admired her fiancée's natural charm. The way Genesis moved through the crowd, her laughter ringing out above the music, was mesmerizing. Zuri traced the curve of Genesis's neck with her eyes, admiring how the light caught the delicate gold chain she wore.

Lost in her thoughts, Zuri almost didn't notice Andrea approaching. The birthday girl slid into the seat next to her, a glass of champagne in hand and a smile on her face.

"Enjoying the view?" Andrea teased, nodding towards Genesis.

Zuri felt a blush creep up her neck but didn't look away from her fiancée. "How can I not?," she admitted. "She's something else, isn't she?"

"She is. I'm so glad you two found each other, Zuri. I've never seen her this happy."

Zuri turned to face Andrea, touched by the sincerity in her voice. "Thank you. I feel the same way"

Andrea's eyes took on a more serious glint. She leaned in closer to Zuri, her voice lowering to ensure their conversation remained private amidst the party's din.

She traced the rim of her champagne glass with a manicured finger, "Genesis is a delightful woman, but also a bit complicated."

Zuri's brow furrowed, her attention fully captured by Andrea's words. "What do you mean?" she asked.

Andrea sighed, her gaze drifting to where Genesis stood, laughing at something a guest had said. "She has always been the strong one. The one who holds everyone else up. But beneath that sunny exterior, she's more fragile than she lets on." Andrea paused, seeming to choose her next words carefully. "I'm know she's told you about her parents passing away."

Zuri nodded, feeling a pang in her chest at the memory of Genesis recounting that painful chapter of her life.

"Well, what she probably didn't tell you is how much it broke her. For weeks after, she would wake up in the middle of the night, crying. But by morning, she'd have that smile back on her face, ready to take care of everything and everyone. Kenzi was a brat, angry at the world and Shannon loved her but was always needy, taking way more than she ever gave."

A lump began to form in Zuri's throat as she listened to Andrea's words. "It always felt like she was holding back when she talked about how much life changed for her. When her aunt appeared at the engagement party, I thought she'd be excited, but the pain I saw on her face was... unbearable. Then just as quickly as she broke down, she was back out there talking to them."

Andrea nodded. "That's Gen, always with a brave face. But that strength comes at a cost." She paused, taking a sip of her champagne. "I'm telling you this because I want you to understand. Genesis needs someone who can see past that smile, someone who can be strong for her when she can't be strong for herself."

A fierce protectiveness welled up inside Zuri. "I understand," she said, her voice thick with emotion. "And I promise you, I will always be there for her. I'll make sure she knows it's okay to lean on me."

Andrea smiled, reaching out to squeeze Zuri's hand. "I believe you. That's why I'm so happy she found you."

As if sensing she was the topic of conversation, Genesis glanced over at that moment, her eyes locking with Zuri's. Even from across the room, Zuri could see the love in her fiancée's gaze. Genesis excused herself from her conversation and began making her way back to their table.

"Hey, you two," Genesis said as she approached, her smile bright but her eyes curious. "What are you conspiring about over here?"

Zuri stood up, wrapping an arm around Genesis's waist and pulling her close. "Just girl talk."

"Yup, I was letting Zuri know that it's possible she might have a new step mom," Andrea said with a glint in her eye.

Zuri laughed and waved her off. "In your dreams, girl! My mom is way too smart to fall for your charms."

Andrea feigned offense. "Excuse you, I'm quite the charmer. Just ask Rebecca."

The three women chuckled as Andrea stood up, smoothing down her suit jacket. "I should go mingle some more. Duty calls," she said with a wink. "You two enjoy yourselves."

As Andrea sauntered away, Genesis turned to Zuri with a raised eyebrow. "So, what were you two really talking about?"

Zuri hesitated for a moment, considering how much to reveal. "Let's just say your friend loves you very much, and wanted to make sure I was aware how special you are."

A mix of emotions flickered across Genesis' face. She leaned into Zuri, resting her head on her shoulder. "Andrea's always been protective of me," she murmured. "I hope she didn't go overboard."

"Not at all. We're on the same page when it comes to you."

Genesis lifted her head, meeting Zuri's gaze. There was a vulnerability in her eyes that Zuri rarely saw. "I hope you know that I can take care of myself."

Zuri cupped Genesis's face gently. "Of course, but that doesn't mean you always have to. It's okay to let someone else be there for you sometimes."

Genesis's eyes welled up with unshed tears. She blinked rapidly, trying to hold them back. "I'm not used to that," she admitted.

"I know," Zuri said, pulling Genesis closer. "But I'm here now, and I'm not going anywhere. You can lean on me, always."

"Good, cause I'm gonna hold you to that, Ms. Baker."

Zuri's phone went off, interrupting their kiss. She had it so only calls from certain contacts came through. After excusing herself, she checked and saw her lawyer's name flashing across the screen.

"Marcus, this is a pleasant surprise."

Zuri stepped away from the party, her heels clicking on the polished concrete as she found a quiet corner to take the call. The muffled sounds of laughter and music faded into the background as she pressed the phone to her ear.

"Zuri, I apologize for disturbing you on a weekend," Marcus's deep voice came through, tinged with an unusual hesitancy. "But I've received some... concerning news that I felt you should be made aware of immediately."

A knot of unease formed in Zuri's stomach. Marcus was always direct, and his careful tone set off warning bells in her mind. "What is it? Is everything alright?"

There was a pause on the other end of the line, filled only by the sound of shuffling papers. When Marcus spoke again, his words fell like lead weights. "It's about your godfather, Francis. He's reached out through his legal team with a... request."

Zuri's grip tightened on her phone, her knuckles turning white. The party around her seemed to fade away, replaced by a dull roar in her ears. "What kind of request?"

Marcus cleared his throat. "He's hoping you'll write a character letter for his upcoming trial. His lawyers believe a glowing recommendation from his well-known goddaughter could sway the jury in his favor."

Zuri felt as if the air had been sucked from her lungs. She leaned against the cool concrete wall, needing its solidity to keep her upright.

"I don't understand," Zuri stammered, her mind reeling. "He's asking me to vouch for his character? After everything?"

"I'm afraid so," Marcus confirmed, his tone gentle but firm. "His team is pulling out all the stops. They're trying to paint a picture of Francis as a misunderstood family man, a pillar of the community who's been unjustly accused."

Zuri's free hand clenched into a fist, her manicured nails digging crescents into her palm. The pain helped ground her, bringing a moment of clarity to her swirling thoughts.

"This is insane," she muttered, more to herself than to Marcus. "After everything he's done, all the lives he's ruined..."

"I know, and I understand this must be difficult for you. You're under no obligation to comply with his request. In fact, I would strongly advise against it."

Zuri closed her eyes, taking a deep breath to steady herself. Memories flooded her mind. Childhood birthdays with her godfather's booming laughter, his proud smile at her college graduation, the devastation on her parents' faces when the truth of his crimes came to light.

"What are our options here?" she asked, her voice regaining some of its usual strength.

"We can ignore the request," Marcus replied. "Or, if you prefer, I can draft a formal response declining to provide a character letter. Either way, you're well within your rights to refuse."

Zuri nodded, even though Marcus couldn't see her. "Draft the response," she said firmly. "I want it on record that I refused. And Marcus? Make it clear that if they try to contact me again about this, we'll pursue legal action."

"Understood. I'll handle communicating with his team. Enjoy the rest of your weekend. And don't hesitate to reach out if you need anything."

As Zuri ended the call, she felt a gentle hand on her shoulder. She turned to see Genesis standing there, concern etched across her beautiful features.

"Baby, everything okay?" Genesis asked, pulling Zuri into a comforting embrace. "You look worried."

Zuri looked into Genesis's concerned eyes and felt a wave of emotion wash over her. The weight of the call with Marcus, the audacity of her godfather's request, and the constant pressure of work all seemed to crash down on her at once. But in that moment, as she gazed at the woman she loved, a different feeling took root.

She was tired. Tired of the drama, tired of the constant interruptions, tired of letting the world dictate how she spent her time. Here they were at a beautiful party, supposed to be enjoying themselves, and once again, reality had come crashing in to spoil it all.

Without a word, Zuri grabbed Genesis's hand. She tugged,

leading Genesis away from the bustling party and towards a quieter area near the back.

The coat room was dimly lit and cramped with rows of jackets and dresses hanging from hooks on the walls. The scent of perfume and cologne lingered in the air. Zuri pulled Genesis inside her, pulse quickening with each step. The moment the door closed behind them, she captured Genesis' lips in a searing kiss.

"Is this your way of avoiding whatever is going on? Genesis asked, her breath unsteady as Zuri nibbled on her neck.

Zuri pulled back, her eyes dark with desire and a hint of mischief. "Maybe," she murmured, her lips ghosting over Genesis's ear. "But it's also me deciding to focus on what matters."

Genesis shivered, her hands coming to rest on Zuri's hips. "Zuri," she breathed, half warning, half plea. "We're at Andrea's party. We can't just..."

Zuri's hands slid down Genesis's sides. "I know," she murmured, pressing a kiss to the sensitive spot just below Genesis's ear. "But I need this. I need you."

With a sigh of surrender, Genesis tilted her head, giving Zuri better access to her neck. "Okay," she breathed. "But we have to be quick. And quiet."

Zuri's response was immediate. Her lips crashed against Genesis's, hungry and demanding. Her hands roamed freely now, slipping beneath the hem of Genesis's dress to caress the smooth skin of her thighs.

Unable to clean her hands, Zuri had to settle for a less direct approach.

Genesis gasped as Zuri's fingers trailed higher, teasing along the edges of her lace underwear. Zuri's fingers danced along the delicate lace, tracing feather-light patterns that made Genesis shiver. She pressed closer, pinning Genesis against the wall as her hand slipped between her thighs.

With exquisite slowness, Zuri stroked Genesis through the thin fabric of her panties. Her touch was light at first, barely there caresses that had Genesis arching into her hand, seeking more friction.

Zuri captured Genesis's lips in another searing kiss, swallowing her moans as she increased the pressure of her fingers. She could feel the heat radiating from Genesis's core, the dampness seeping through the lace.

Her thumb found Genesis's clit, circling the sensitive bundle of nerves with practiced skill. Genesis's hips bucked involuntarily.

Zuri set a steady rhythm, her fingers moving in tight circles as Genesis clutched at her shoulders, nails digging in as she fought to stay quiet. The air in the small coat room grew thick and heady with the scent of their arousal.

Genesis buried her face in Zuri's neck, muffling her cries as the pleasure built. Her whole body trembled, teetering on the edge of release. Zuri could feel how close she was, could sense it in the way Genesis's thighs trembled.

With a final, well-placed stroke, Genesis came undone. Her body went rigid, then shuddered as ecstasy overtook her. Zuri held her close, peppering kisses along her jawline as Genesis rode out the aftershocks.

As their breathing returned to normal, Zuri rested her forehead against Genesis's. "It may not always seem like it, but I choose you, every time."

Genesis's eyes fluttered open, still hazy with desire. She cupped Zuri's face gently, her thumb tracing along her fiancée's cheekbone. "I choose you too, baby. Always."

They stayed like that for a moment, basking in the afterglow and the intimacy of their stolen moment. The muffled sounds of the party filtered through the door, a reminder of the world waiting just outside.

"We should get back," Genesis murmured, though she made no move to leave Zuri's embrace.

"You're right. But first..." She stepped back, her hands moving to smooth down Genesis's dress and fix her mussed hair. "There. Perfect."

Genesis chuckled, returning the favor by adjusting Zuri's necklace and tucking a stray lock of hair behind her ear. "For someone who just ravished me in a coat closet, you look annoyingly put together."

Zuri grinned, a mischievous glint in her eye. "Years of practice, babe. Now, shall we?" She offered her arm to Genesis with an exaggerated flourish.

As they slipped back into the party, the sight of Andrea greeted them twirling Rebecca on the dance floor, both women laughing with pure joy. The energy in the room was infectious, and Zuri happily followed Genesis' lead and joined them.

# Chapter Twenty

Back in Cali the following Friday, Shannon and a couple of her friends brought over what she was moving in with fairly early. Genesis was sure Zuri would be pleased and want to get on with her day. As requested, she was there on Shannon's move-in date to assess the situation, nothing more. Instead, she was still hanging out and seemingly on a quest to interrogate Shannon.

"So, how's that job search going?" Zuri asked, glancing up from her phone.

The tension between the two women was thick and Genesis couldn't tell who was more uncomfortable, Zuri or Shannon. Genesis sighed inwardly, wishing she could ease the awkwardness somehow.

After their time in Colorado, it seemed like she and Zuri were on the right page. They had both spoken about their fears and concerns, and Genesis thought they had made genuine progress. But now, watching Zuri's stiff movements and tight expression, she wondered if they had truly resolved anything.

"She's got an interview next week, right Shannon?" Genesis replied even though it wasn't directed at her.

Shannon looked up from a box she was unpacking. "Yeah, the WNBA is really heating up with Angel Reese and Caitlyn Clark entering the league. The networks are looking for more former players to do commentary. Kind of perfect timing."

Zuri nodded while typing on her phone, her movements careful and controlled. Genesis noticed how when she did look up, her eyes darted around, never quite landing on Shannon, who was unpacking in the corner.

Shannon cleared her throat. "Thanks for supervising," she said, her tone laced with sarcasm.

"Of course," Zuri responded, her tone polite but cool.

Genesis couldn't tell if she picked up on Shannon's tone or just didn't care. The entire morning, she had found herself trapped in the middle, uncertain of how to handle the delicate situation.

"Hey, why don't we take a quick break?" Genesis suggested, forcing cheerfulness into her voice. "I've got some lemonade in the fridge. We could all use a drink, right?"

She headed to the kitchen without waiting for a response, hoping a moment away would help clear the air. As she poured three glasses, she took a deep breath and reminded herself that this was only temporary. They just needed to get through the next three months, and everything would settle back to normal.

Genesis returned to the living room, balancing the glasses of lemonade on a tray. The air was heavy with unspoken words as she set the tray down on the coffee table.

"Here we go," she said, forcing a smile. "Nice and cold."

Zuri and Shannon both reached for a glass at the same time, their fingers brushing against each other. Shannon jerked her hand back, while Zuri's jaw tightened almost imperceptibly.

"Sorry," Shannon murmured, averting her gaze.

"It's fine," Zuri replied, her voice clipped.

Genesis sank onto the couch, and took a sip of her lemonade. The tart sweetness gave her something else to focus on.

"So, Zuri, how's work going? Genesis mentioned you've got a new film coming up," Shannon said.

"It's going well. We're in pre-production." She paused, then added with a hint of challenge, "But I'm sure Genesis has told you all about it."

Shannon's fingers tightened around her glass. "She hasn't fully. I've been a bit preoccupied."

"Right," Zuri said, her tone dripping with false sympathy. "Must be tough, having to move back in with your ex."

Genesis winced, sensing things possibly escalating. She shot Zuri a warning glance, silently pleading with her to dial it back.

"It's not ideal," Shannon admitted, her voice tight. "But I'm grateful for Genesis's help. She's always been there for me, even when we weren't together."

Zuri's eyes flashed, and Genesis could see the muscles in her jaw working. She recognized that look. Zuri was biting back a retort, probably something about how Shannon had taken advantage of Genesis's kindness one too many times.

Before Zuri could say anything, Genesis jumped in. "There's a couple of boxes with house stuff, how about we finish bringing those inside. The sooner we get done, the sooner we can all relax."

She stood up, hoping the others would follow her lead. To her relief, both women set down their glasses and moved toward the door.

As they headed outside, Genesis caught Zuri's arm. "Can I talk to you for a sec?" she murmured.

Zuri nodded, her face relaxing when she met Genesis's eyes. They hung back as Shannon went to grab another box from her car.

"What's going on?" Genesis asked, turning to face Zuri. "I thought you were okay with this arrangement."

Zuri's eyes flashed. "I said I understood, not that I was okay with it. Do you have any idea how hard it is to see you playing house with your ex?"

Genesis sighed, running a hand through her curls. "We're not 'playing house,' Zuri. Shannon needed help, and I couldn't turn my back on her. But we talked about this last week babe, I thought we were good."

Zuri's shoulders sagged, the fight seeming to drain out of her. "I know, I know. I'm sorry. It's just... seeing her here, in your space, it's harder than I thought it would be."

Genesis reached out, squeezing Zuri's hand. "I get it. But you have to trust me, okay? Shannon and I are over. You're the one I want to be with."

Zuri nodded, but Genesis could still see the doubt lingering in her eyes. Before she could say anything else, Shannon appeared, struggling with a large box.

"A little help?" Shannon called, her voice strained.

Genesis moved to assist her, but Zuri was quicker. "I've got it," she said, striding over to Shannon and easily taking the box from her arms.

Shannon blinked in surprise. "Oh, thanks."

Zuri nodded curtly and carried the box inside. Genesis watched her go, a mixture of pride and concern swirling in her chest. She turned to Shannon, who was staring after Zuri with an unreadable expression.

"You okay?" Genesis asked.

"Yeah, I'm fine." She turned and looked into Genesis' eyes. "She's good for you, right?

Genesis' cheeks flushed. "She is. Zuri's amazing."

Shannon nodded. "And a better woman than me, because I

don't think I'd be able to handle my woman living with her ex. Even if it's temporary."

Gazing in the direction of the house, Genesis smiled. "I'm not gonna lie. She is better than a lot of women."

Zuri's voice called from inside the house.

"Where do you want this box, Shannon? It's labeled 'toys.'"

Shannon's cheeks flushed. "I'll get it," she called back, hurrying inside.

Genesis followed, her mind whirling. She found Zuri and Shannon in the guest room, avoiding each other's gaze as they arranged boxes.

"I think that's the last of it," Zuri said, dusting off her hands. "Unless there's anything else you need help with?"

Although the question was directed at Genesis, Shannon was the one who answered. "No, I think we're good. Thanks again for your help, Zuri. I appreciate it."

"No problem. I hope you get settled."

An awkward silence fell over the room. "I'll walk you out, babe," Genesis said, grabbing Zuri's hand.

Once they were outside, Zuri leaned against her car and pulled Genesis in for a hug. She melted into Zuri's embrace, inhaling the familiar scent of her coconut shampoo. For a moment, she let herself forget about the complicated situation inside the house and just enjoyed being in her girlfriend's arms.

"I'm sorry if I made things awkward in there," Zuri murmured against Genesis's hair. "I'm trying."

Genesis pulled back to look into Zuri's eyes. "I appreciate you being here today. I know it wasn't easy."

"The things we do for love, right?" Zuri said with a smirk.

"Mmmm, well, the feeling is mutual."

Genesis leaned in and kissed Zuri, trying to pour all her love and gratitude into the gesture. When they parted, Zuri gave her a small smile.

"I'll call you later, okay?" Genesis said, stepping back.

Zuri nodded, opening her car door. "You better. And Gen?"

"Yeah?"

"I love you. Don't forget that."

"I love you too, baby."

She watched as Zuri drove away, waving until the car turned the corner. With a deep breath, Genesis steeled herself to go back inside. The next few weeks wouldn't be easy, but she was determined to make it work.

As she entered the house, she heard Shannon moving around in the guest room. Genesis paused in the doorway, watching as her ex-girlfriend unpacked a box of clothes.

"Need any help?" she offered.

Shannon looked up, a wistful smile on her face. "I think I've got it. Thanks though."

Genesis nodded, sensing the weight of their shared history in the air between them. "Listen, Shannon, I know this isn't an ideal situation..."

"Gen, stop," Shannon interrupted. "You don't have to explain. I'm the one who should be apologizing. I shouldn't have put you in this position."

Genesis sighed, leaning against the doorframe. "This is on me. I could have said no. Drea said as much."

Shannon laughed out loud. "She's still salty about that Halloween prank, I see."

"Drea can hold a grudge like nobody's business. But seriously, Shannon, you don't need to apologize. We're friends, and friends help each other out."

Shannon nodded. "And I'm grateful, but I also saw the way Zuri looked at me today. I don't want to cause problems between you two."

"Zuri understands. She's just... adjusting."

"She loves you very much. Anyone can see that. Did you get a chance to discuss the issues you mentioned to me."

"We have, and I think we're good for now. We both have some adjusting to do."

"Yeah, compromise. That's a word Melissa likes to use a lot. I'm learning how to give, not just take. Might have learned it later than I should have, but it's never too late, I guess."

"No, it never is."

A moment of silence stretched between them. Shannon was the first to speak.

"Well, I should finish unpacking. Don't want to leave boxes lying around your house forever."

Genesis nodded, pushing herself off the doorframe. "Right. Let me know if you need anything."

As she turned to leave, Shannon called out, "Gen?"

Genesis paused, looking back. "Yeah?"

Gratitude and regret filled Shannon's eyes. "Thank you. For everything."

"You're welcome, Shan."

Genesis retreated to her bedroom, closing the door behind her. Leaning against it, she did her best to sort through a jumble of emotions.

Genesis thought of Zuri's face earlier, the hurt and jealousy barely concealed behind her usual confident facade. Genesis closed her eyes, and thought about Zuri's embrace, the softness of her lips, the strength in her arms. Zuri was her rock, her safe harbor in the stormy sea of life. The thought of causing her pain made Genesis's stomach churn with guilt.

But then there was Shannon, her first love, the woman who had taught her so much about herself. Genesis remembered the early days of their relationship, the giddy excitement, the passion, the dreams they'd shared. Even though that chapter of her life was closed, she couldn't deny the lingering fondness she felt for Shannon.

All along, she had been doing her best to treat this as simply helping her friend, but her history with Shannon carried more weight than that. With everything going on with Zuri, she knew she was playing with fire and if she got burned, she had no one to blame but herself.

# Chapter Twenty-One

Zuri paced in her office, awaiting her assistant's update on William's arrival. He was still figuring out his tour dates but able to work around the shooting schedule for the film. It helped that he was an independent artist who made his own decisions without a label breathing down his neck.

As she read her emails, her mind went back to earlier at Genesis' house. She hated how triggered she was by Shannon's presence, especially when her relationship with Genesis was good. That didn't keep her mind from conjuring up images of Genesis and Shannon together, laughing and sharing inside jokes, their history ever present in the house.

Zuri shook her head, trying to banish the thoughts. She trusted Genesis, she reminded herself. Their relationship was solid. A few months of Shannon living there wouldn't change that.

A knock on her office door startled her out of her reverie. Her assistant, Tanya, poked her head in.

"William's here, Ms. Baker," she announced.

"Send him in," Zuri replied, straightening her blazer and putting on her professional face.

William entered the office with his usual swagger, but Zuri immediately noticed a change in his appearance. Gone was the flashy, larger-than-life persona he often projected on stage and in music videos. Instead, he looked almost normal.

His trademark diamond grill was absent, revealing a sweet, genuine smile that lit up his face. The elaborate chains and designer labels were nowhere to be seen. In their place, William wore a simple white t-shirt that hugged his athletic frame, paired with well-worn jeans that had seen better days. The outfit was a far cry from his usual haute couture ensembles, but it made him seem more approachable, more real. The only hint of his superstar status was a single diamond stud in his left ear, catching the light as he moved.

"Zuri," he said, his voice rich and smooth. "Looking fine as ever."

Even dressed down, William exuded charisma. "You're not looking too shabby yourself," she replied, gesturing for him to take a seat. "I almost didn't recognize you without all the bling."

William chuckled, settling into the chair across from her desk. "Thought I'd tone it down for our meeting. Show you I can do low key when the role calls for it."

"That's great, but it's not me you need to convince. Phillip is... something else, to say the least. You're going to need him to see you as more than just a rapper. How did it go, rehearsing your lines?"

"Not bad. The fellas helped me with it. I'm confident that I got it down."

"Awesome. Phillip should be here shortly but I'm not gonna lie, he isn't sold on you."

William waved her off. "Don't worry about it. I got this."

"Alright, well, let's head to the conference room," Zuri said, gesturing towards the door.

As they walked down the hallway, Reggie came running in behind them. He greeted William as he caught his breath.

"Cuz, you okay?" Zuri asked with genuine concern.

"I wanted to get here before Minor did. He's not pleased about some things."

Zuri's brow furrowed. "What things?"

Reggie glanced at William, then back to Zuri. "Maybe we should discuss this out front."

She nodded to William. "Give us just a moment, please." Out into the hallway, she closed the door behind them. "What's going on?"

Reggie ran a hand over his face. "You know all the stuff he asked for? Well, he said the carnations we got him are cheap, and the masseuse left something to be desired. Also, that Grammy award-winning harpist we found, she's already quit because Phillip yelled at her for not knowing how to play some random song he likes."

Zuri pinched the bridge of her nose. "You've got to be kidding me. We bent over backwards to accommodate his ridiculous demands, and now he's throwing a tantrum over flowers?"

Reggie nodded grimly. "I'm afraid so. And that's not all. He's threatening to walk if we don't replace William."

"Replace Will? But he said he would give him a chance to audition!" Zuri exclaimed, frustration evident in her voice.

"I know, I know. But Minor says he doesn't have the 'gravitas' he's looking for. Whatever that means."

"Okay, here's what we're going to do. You go smooth things over with Phillip. Tell him we'll upgrade the flowers and find a new masseuse. The harpist he's just going to have to deal with it. We can't conjure up Grammy winners out of thin air."

"Got it," Reggie nodded, already turning to leave.

Just then, the elevator dinged, and Phillip Minor himself stepped out, his face set in a scowl. Zuri straightened up, plastering on a smile that didn't quite reach her eyes. Minor strode towards them, his outfit a testament to his eccentric tastes. He wore a pair of fitted salmon-colored chinos, cuffed at the ankles to reveal socks in a bold geometric pattern in orange and purple.

Upon first meeting him, all the rumors they had heard about him were not only true, but almost not exaggerated enough. She wasn't sure if his status as one of the premier directors of Black cinema had gone to his head or he was always such a pompous man, but at this point, she just needed him to use his expertise to get the studio a much needed win.

His very presence seemed to fill the hallway, an aura of self-importance radiating from him like heat from a furnace. With sharp, angular features softened by a layer of well-maintained stubble, his face was a study in contradictions, with piercing hazel eyes that crinkled at the corners when he smiled (which, admittedly, wasn't often). Underneath the fedora, his salt-and-pepper hair was peeking out, styled to give off a "just rolled out of bed" vibe that implied he had put in hours of effort.

As he approached, his cologne, an overpowering mix of sandalwood, citrus, and something exotic, wafted ahead of him. Zuri fought the urge to step back, instead standing her ground as Phillip came to a stop before her.

"Change of plans. Let me talk to him," Zuri said, squeezing Reggie's arm. "Phillip! I heard you had some thoughts. Let's chat in my office, shall we?"

"Ah, Ms. Baker," he drawled, his voice a peculiar blend of British upper-crust and Southern twang. "Just the woman I was hoping to see. Yes, let's chat."

Zuri led Phillip into her office. She gestured for him to sit while she perched on the edge of her desk, arms crossed.

"I understand you have some concerns," she began, keeping her tone neutral.

The director snorted. "Concerns? That's putting it mildly. This production is turning into a disaster before we've even started filming."

Zuri reminded herself to stay calm. "I assure you, we're addressing the issues with the flowers and the masseuse. As for the harpist—"

"It's not just about the damn flowers!" Phillip interrupted, his face flushing. "It's about respect. I'm an award-winning director, and I expect a certain level of professionalism."

"And we've accommodated your every request," Zuri countered, her patience wearing thin. "But let's cut to the chase. I hear you want to replace William."

Phillip's eyes narrowed. "Ah yes, the rapper. Zuri, dear, I'm aware you have a soft spot for this street performer, but this is a serious film. We need gravitas, depth. Not some... hip-hop artist playing at being an actor."

Zuri kept her cool. "William is perfect for this role, Phillip, and he's not a street performer. He's dedicated, talented, and brings authenticity to the character. Plus, he's a huge draw for our target audience."

Phillip scoffed, waving his hand dismissively. "Target audience? I'm not interested in pandering to the masses. I'm creating art here, Zuri. Art requires vision, nuance. Your little rapper friend lacks both."

Zuri paused, reminding herself that throttling the director would be bad for business. "With all due respect, you haven't even seen William perform yet. Why don't we let him show what he can do like you said you would. He's here now, ready to read for you."

"I have already made up my mind," Phillip said, as he jumped up from his seat.

Zuri remembered Genesis's comment about how she was good at commanding others. The memory made her blush a bit, but it was a pleasant reminder for her that she was in control, not Minor.

"There seems to be a misunderstanding here, Mr. Minor." Zuri walked to the other side of her desk and pulled out a folder and slid it across the desk. "Your contract gives you input on casting decisions, but final approval rests with the studio. Which, in this case, is me."

Phillip snatched up the paper, his eyes scanning it. Zuri could almost see the steam coming out of his ears as he realized she was right.

"I don't remember seeing this when I signed. Normally, I'm given full creative control. This is unacceptable," he sputtered. "I won't be strong-armed into working with some amateur!"

Zuri leaned forward, her voice low and intense. "Listen. You have two choices here. You can work with William, who I know will surprise you with his talent and dedication. Or you can walk away from this project, break your contract, and face the legal consequences. Your choice."

Phillip narrowed his eyes as he sputtered incoherently. Zuri remained calm, her gaze steady as she waited for his response.

Finally, he deflated, collapsing back into the chair. "Fine," he muttered. "I'll give the boy a chance. But if he's not up to par, I want him gone. No arguments."

Zuri nodded, relief washing over her. "That's all I ask. Now, shall we head to the conference room?"

Upon entering the room, Zuri found William chatting with Reggie. She cleared her throat, drawing their attention.

"William, this is our director, Phillip Minor. Phillip, meet William."

William stood, extending his hand with a smile. "It's an honor to meet you. I'm a huge fan of your work."

Phillip grunted in response, ignoring the outstretched hand. Zuri shot William an apologetic look, but he seemed unfazed.

"Alright, Will," Zuri said, trying to keep things moving. "Why don't you run through the scene we discussed?"

As William delivered his lines, Zuri watched Phillip's face. At first, the director's expression remained skeptical, but as William continued, she saw a flicker of surprise in his eyes.

His line reading was raw, emotional, and captivating. He'd picked a difficult scene but made it look effortless. Zuri knew he was talented, but even she was surprised.

As William finished his monologue, the room fell into a stunned silence. Zuri's eyes darted between William and Phillip, holding her breath. Reggie was frozen in place, waiting for the director's reaction.

Phillip's face was unreadable for a long moment. Then a begrudging look of respect crept into his eyes. He cleared his throat, shifting in his seat.

"Well," he said gruffly, "that was... unexpected."

William's face broke into a wide grin. "Thank you, sir. I've been working hard on getting into character."

Phillip nodded, his earlier hostility diminished. "Yes, well... it shows. Your interpretation of the scene was... intriguing. Maybe we should talk about your approach to the character further."

A wave of relief washed over Zuri. She caught Reggie's eye, and they shared a quick, triumphant smile.

"That sounds great," William replied. "I'd love to hear your thoughts on the character's motivations."

As William and Phillip discussed the character in depth, Zuri excused herself and slipped out of the conference room. She leaned against the wall in the hallway, taking a deep breath. Crisis averted, at least for now.

Reggie joined her a moment later. "That was impressive,"

he said, a note of admiration in his voice. "How did you get Minor to back down?"

Zuri smirked. "I reminded him of the terms of his contract. And I made it clear to him that his options were limited."

Reggie chuckled. "Remind me never to get on your bad side, cuz."

"As if you could forget," Zuri teased, bumping his shoulder with hers. "William pulled it off. I knew he had it in him."

"You made the right call. Looks like we may get this production together after all."

"Let's not get ahead of ourselves," Zuri cautioned, though she couldn't quite keep the relief out of her voice. "We've still got a long way to go.

As she walked back to her office, Zuri's phone buzzed. She glanced down to see a text from Genesis:

> Hope your meeting went well. Miss you
> already. Dinner tonight?

Zuri smiled, momentarily pushing aside the stress of the day. She typed back:

> Meeting went great. Miss you too. Dinner
> sounds perfect. Your place or mine?

Genesis's response came almost immediately:

> How about that new Thai place downtown? I
> could use a night out.

Zuri's smile faltered. She'd forgotten already that Shannon was at Genesis' place.

Zuri hesitated for a moment before replying,

> Sounds perfect. I'll make a reservation for 7.
> Can't wait.

She put her phone away, trying to ignore the twinge of unease in her stomach. It was just dinner, she reminded herself. There was no reason to read anything into Genesis wanting to go out instead of staying in.

Still, as she settled back into her office chair, Zuri couldn't quite shake the feeling that things were more complicated than she wanted to admit. The situation with Shannon was stirring up insecurities she thought she'd left behind.

Shaking her head, Zuri forced herself to focus on her work. She had a million things to do before dinner, and dwelling on her relationship worries would not help anyone. She pulled up the production schedule on her computer, determined to lose herself in the details of budgets and shooting locations.

# Chapter Twenty-Two

Genesis glanced at the clock on her office wall, the hands inching closer to 6 PM. She stretched her arms above her head, enjoying the satisfying pop as she arched her back. The day had been long, filled with spreadsheets and budget meetings between her business and Beacon, but the thought of hanging with Rain and Zuri brought a smile to her face. They were meeting Rain's new boyfriend, but Genesis was most excited to get out and do something with Zuri.

Some of her excitement was dampened by the tension of Shannon moving in. It had been two weeks but felt longer. She'd been spending more time at Zuri's place for her comfort but Shannon's presence was always hovering in the background.

Genesis grabbed her phone, typing out a message to Zuri. They had barely spoken throughout the day.

> Are you still coming tonight? Can't wait to
> see you.

She hit send and started packing up her things, humming to

herself. Just as she was slinging her bag over her shoulder, her phone buzzed with a reply.

> Sorry, babe. Something came up with work. Raincheck?

Genesis' smile faltered. This was the third time in two weeks Zuri had canceled on her. She took a deep breath, trying to push down the disappointment bubbling in her chest.

> No worries. But you have to tell Rain.

She dropped her phone back into her bag, trying not to let herself get too irritated. Zuri didn't do this on purpose. If she canceled, it was for a good reason. But she thought back to how she had promised to be more present.

Genesis sighed, her fingers hovering over the phone screen. She wanted to type out another message, but she held back, not wanting to come across as needy or clingy.

Instead, she tucked her phone away and began gathering her things, slipping her laptop into its sleek leather case and fishing around in her desk drawer for her car keys.

Just as Genesis was about to switch off her desk lamp, a soft knock at the door made her pause. She looked up to see Kem standing in the doorway, her usually bright eyes red-rimmed and glistening with tears.

"Kem? What's wrong, honey?" Genesis asked, concerned. She beckoned the young woman into her office, watching as Kem's lower lip trembled.

Kem stepped inside, wringing her hands. "Gen, I... I don't know what to do," she said, her voice barely above a whisper. "Lea just fired me."

"What? Why would she do that?"

Kem shook her head, a tear escaping and trailing down her

cheek. "She said that my performance as an instructor has been lackluster." Kem's voice cracked as she spoke, her shoulders slumping.

Genesis let out a deep sigh. Lea could be difficult, but this seemed out of character even for her. "I'm sorry about that but this doesn't make any sense," she said, shaking her head. "You're one of our best instructors. The kids love you."

She got up and stepped around her desk, placing a comforting hand on Kem's shoulder. "Listen, I'm going to talk to Lea, and we're going to figure it out. Okay?"

Kem looked up at her, hope flickering in her tear-filled eyes. "Really? You'd do that for me?"

"Of course," Genesis said firmly. "We're a family here, and we watch out for one another. Now, why don't you go home and get some rest? I promise we'll sort this out."

As Kem left, mumbling grateful thanks, Genesis felt her earlier irritation with Zuri fade into the background. This was more important right now. She sent a text to Rain, explaining that she'd be a little late to the fight. Then she marched out of her office, her heels clicking against the polished floor as she made her way to Lea's office.

The door was closed, but Genesis could see light spilling out from underneath. She knocked, not waiting for a response, before turning the handle and stepping inside.

Lea looked up from her computer, surprise flashing across her face. "Genesis? I thought you'd left for the day."

"We need to talk," Genesis said, her voice steady despite the anger simmering beneath the surface. "Why did you fire Kem?"

"It's complicated. The board has been pushing for changes."

"The board?" Genesis interrupted, her brow furrowing. "Since when does the board get involved in staffing decisions for the dance program?"

Lea's eyes darted away for a moment before meeting Genesis's gaze again. "There have been some... financial concerns. They're looking to cut costs wherever possible."

"Kem is a wonderful instructor. The kids adore her, and she's consistently gotten excellent feedback. I don't understand why you'd let her go without even discussing it with me first. Last time I checked, I was the head of the dance department."

Lea's face hardened. "And last time I checked, I am the head of Beacon. I am not required to go through anyone if I choose to let go of a staff member."

*This bitch.* Genesis sighed and tried to calm herself. She didn't have proof, but she was sure this was a 'fuck you' to her. After she asserted herself about the direction of the program, Lea had gone quiet. It seemed she had been plotting how to screw with her in some other way. Genesis had to keep her cool. Losing her temper wouldn't help Kem, and it wouldn't help her position at Beacon.

"Lea, let's cut the bullshit. This isn't about the board or finances. It's about you trying to assert your power because I dared to challenge you on the dance program."

Lea's eyes narrowed, a flicker of surprise crossing her face before she schooled her features into a mask of indifference. "I'm doing what's best for Beacon. Things change and we all have to adapt."

"Adapt to what?" Genesis pressed, taking a step closer to Lea's desk. "Because from where I'm standing, it looks like you're making decisions based on personal grudges rather than what's best for Beacon."

Lea's eyes flashed. "Are you accusing me of something?"

"You know what? I am," Genesis said, her voice low and steady. She planted her hands on Lea's desk, leaning forward. "I'm accusing you of letting your personal feelings interfere with your professional judgment. This is about Zuri."

Lea's face paled, her composure cracking for a split second

before she regained control. "I don't know what you're talking about," she said, but her voice lacked conviction.

"Don't you?" Genesis pressed, her eyes never leaving Lea's face. "I've seen the way you look at her. The lingering glances, the 'accidental' touches. I'm not blind, and I'm not stupid."

Lea's jaw clenched, a muscle twitching in her cheek. "Your behavior right now is unprofessional."

Genesis felt her anger flare at Lea's attempt to deflect. "Unprofessional? That's rich coming from you. Firing a talented instructor out of spite is about as unprofessional as it gets." She took a deep breath, forcing herself to lower her voice. "Look, Lea, I get it. Zuri is amazing. She's beautiful, talented, and kind. It's natural to be drawn to her, but she's with me. And using your position to lash out at me or the people I care about isn't going to change that."

Lea's face flushed, a mix of anger and embarrassment coloring her cheeks. "This conversation is over. You need to leave my office now."

Genesis stood her ground, crossing her arms. "Not until you agree to reinstate Kem. She doesn't deserve to lose her job because of your personal issues with me."

The two women stared each other down, the air crackling between them. Lea's shoulders slumped and she sneered at Genesis. "Fine," she said through gritted teeth. "I'll reconsider Kem's position. But this doesn't change anything between us. You're on thin ice."

Genesis nodded, knowing this was the best she could hope for at the moment. "Thank you," she said, her voice cool. "I'll expect to see Kem back at work on Monday."

She stepped out of Lea's office, her heart pounding and hands shaking. This wasn't over. Lea wasn't the type to let things go easily, but for now she had secured Kem's job.

* * *

"Yeah baby, kick his ass," Rain yelled, the veins in her neck protruding.

Genesis laughed out loud. Rain was wild, but she hadn't expected her to be quite so bloodthirsty. Despite being late, she had arrived just in time for Brick's match.

"You are enjoying this a little too much, ma'am." Genesis grabbed her large diet coke and winced as a kick landed on Brick's opponent. "I didn't take you to be a lover of MMA."

Rain turned to Genesis with a wicked grin. "Are you kidding? This is better than sex!" She paused, reconsidering. "Well, almost."

Genesis shook her head, amused. "I'll take your word for it."

As the fight intensified, Genesis found her mind wandering. She checked her phone again, hoping to see a message from Zuri explaining her absence. Nothing. The disappointment settled in her chest like a heavy weight.

"Hey, you okay?" Rain nudged her, momentarily distracted by the action in the ring.

Genesis forced a smile. "Yeah, I'm good. Just annoyed that Zuri isn't here."

Rain took a swig of her beer. "She has a good reason, I'm sure. Zuri is crazy about you."

Genesis sighed, shoving her phone back into her purse. "Yeah, most likely another 'emergency' at the studio."

Rain plopped down beside her and chugged her beer. "If that debacle with Jackson taught me anything, it's that you should pay attention to a person's actions and not just their words. So what if Zuri can't always make it to events? She's going to show up in ways that matter."

"I guess you're right." Genesis nudged her. "Look at you doling out romantic advice. Does Brick show up for you?"

"He's got a big dick and money to burn. Your girl loves a generous, well hung king."

Genesis almost spit out her drink. "Always so classy Rain."

"Of course," Rain said with a wink. "Anyway, I'm in my soft girl era. No more chasing men. If they want it, then they need to earn it."

Genesis chuckled, shaking her head at Rain's blunt honesty. "I hear you. I just wish..." She trailed off, her eyes drifting back to the ring where Brick was landing a series of brutal punches.

"Wish what?" Rain prompted, her attention split between her friend and the fight.

Genesis sighed. "I wish I knew where I stood with Zuri sometimes. It's like, one minute we're on cloud nine, and the next... I'm sitting here wondering why she couldn't make time for me."

Rain nodded sympathetically, then jumped up, cheering as Brick executed a perfect takedown. "That's my man!" she hollered, before settling back down next to Genesis. "Look, relationships are tricky. Especially when you're dealing with someone like Zuri who's got a lot on her plate. There are other ways to change the dynamic in your relationship as well."

Genesis raised an eyebrow. "And what might that be?"

"Well, have you tried taking the lead in the bedroom?"

A blush creeped up Genesis' neck. Despite not being too timid to discuss sex, there was an awkwardness when it came to Rain, whom she considered a younger sister.

"Sometimes, but that isn't a role I fall into naturally. Zuri, on the other hand..."

"Gives off top energy."

"What do you know about tops and bottoms?" Genesis said, stifling a laugh.

"From my experiences, very often the people who seem to be more dominant are not or like to switch it up."

"So, you're saying that the solution to our relationship problems is for me to fuck Zuri into submission?" Genesis regretted the words as soon as they left her mouth. She covered her face with her hands, mortified. "Oh my god, I can't believe I just said that."

Rain cackled, slapping her thigh. "Girl, yes! That's what I'm saying. Show her who's boss!"

Genesis peeked through her fingers, still blushing. "Rain, please. I was joking."

"Were you though?" Rain wiggled her eyebrows suggestively. "Come on, Gen. You've got moves. Use 'em!"

Genesis groaned, sinking lower in her seat. "Can we please change the subject? I think I've had enough relationship advice for one night."

Just then, the crowd erupted in cheers. Genesis looked up to see Brick standing victorious, his opponent tapping out on the mat. Rain leapt to her feet, screaming with joy. "That's my man! That's my fucking man!"

Genesis stood up too, clapping but still distracted by thoughts of Zuri. As the crowd dispersed, Rain turned to her, still giddy with excitement.

"Okay, so here's the plan. We're going to celebrate Brick's win, and you're coming with us."

Genesis hesitated. "I don't know, Rain. I should head home..."

"Nuh-uh, no way. You're not going to sit at home moping about Zuri. We're going out, have fun, and you're going to forget about all this drama for one night. Deal?"

Genesis sighed, knowing resistance was futile when Rain set her mind to something. "Fine. But just for a little while."

As they made their way out, Genesis' phone vibrated in her purse. Her heart skipped a beat as she fished it out, hoping it was Zuri. She saw she had a missed call and text. After scanning the text message, she felt confused instead of relieved. Why was Zuri hanging out with Will and his friends again?

Instead of responding, Genesis dropped the phone back in her bag. She was over being an afterthought. When Zuri promised to do better, she believed her. But it didn't take more than a few weeks before they were right back where they started. Maybe she wasn't being fair, as change takes time, but how long was she going to tolerate something that for her was unacceptable?

Genesis shook off the nagging thoughts and followed Rain through the crowded arena. They met up with Brick outside the locker rooms, his face still flushed from the fight but beaming with pride. Rain threw herself into his arms, peppering his face with kisses.

"You were amazing, baby!" she squealed.

Brick grinned, wrapping an arm around Rain's waist. "Thanks, babe. Are you ready to celebrate?"

"Hell yeah! Brick, this is Genesis. Genesis, this is my honey, Brick."

Brick was over 6 feet tall and made of pure muscle. Genesis extended her hand, feeling dwarfed as Brick's massive palm engulfed hers. His skin was calloused and rough, bearing the marks of countless hours of training. Up close, she could see the intricate web of tattoos that covered his arms, a vibrant tapestry of colors and symbols that disappeared beneath the sleeves of his tight-fitting shirt.

Brick's face was a study in contrasts. His strong, square jaw and prominent cheekbones gave him a rugged appearance, but his eyes were gentle, a honey brown that crinkled at the corners when he smiled. A thin scar ran along his left eyebrow, a testament to the brutal nature of his chosen sport.

"Nice to meet you, Genesis," he said, his voice a low rumble that seemed to vibrate in his chest.

"Likewise, and congrats on your win. You did a great job."

"If the amount of wincing she did is any indication, I'd say you did a phenomenal job," Rain added with a grin.

Brick laughed. "Was the violence a bit much for you?"

"Let's just say I prefer my physical activities with a little less... impact."

"Oh, that's right," Brick said, snapping his fingers. "Rain mentioned you're a dancer. Ballet, right?"

"Among other styles, yes," Genesis replied, surprised he'd remembered. "But I doubt my pirouettes would be of much use in the ring."

Brick grinned. "Hey, don't sell yourself short. Footwork is footwork. I bet you've got some moves that could come in handy."

As they bantered, Genesis relaxed. Brick's easy going manner was infectious. She watched Rain and the way she stared up at him in admiration. Despite her bravado earlier, it was clear that she was smitten with him. Brick's calm energy served as a refreshing antidote to Jackson's overwhelming arrogance and self-absorption. Something Rain needed in her life.

"So, where are we headed?" Genesis asked.

Rain did a happy dance. "We're hitting up Onyx," she announced, her eyes glittering with excitement. "It's this new club downtown that just opened. Brick's buddy owns it, so we're VIP all night, baby!"

Genesis hesitated. "I don't know, Rain. I'm not dressed for clubbing." She glanced down at her casual jeans and sweater combo.

"Girl, please. You're fine," Rain insisted, giving Genesis a once-over. "Besides, with that body of yours, you could wear a potato sack and still turn heads."

Brick chuckled, slinging an arm around Rain's shoulders.

"She's right, but if you're not into it, we can always grab a quiet dinner instead."

Genesis appreciated the offer, but she could see how much Rain wanted to go. And if she was honest with herself, another night of dancing and letting go didn't sound bad. Maybe it would help get her thoughts together about everything she was experiencing.

As she climbed into Brick's massive black SUV, a sleek Audi screeched to a halt behind them, its engine purring like a contented cat. Genesis' heart leapt into her throat when she recognized the car. The driver's door swung open, and out stepped Zuri, her dreadlocks swaying as she moved with purposeful strides towards the group.

Zuri wore dark jeans and a white button down, looking every bit the beauty she was. The streetlights caught the glint of her gold jewelry–delicate hoops in her ears and a thin chain around her neck that disappeared beneath her crisp white shirt. Even in the dim parking lot lighting, her caramel skin seemed to glow, and she fixed her dark eyes on Genesis.

"Gen," Zuri called out, breathless.

Genesis froze, her hand still on the car door handle. She felt a mix of emotions swirling inside her. Relief, anger, confusion, and an undeniable surge of attraction at the sight of Zuri. *Damn it.*

"Z, what are you doing here?" Genesis got out.

Zuri closed the distance between them. "I'm so sorry I missed the fight. I got caught up with—"

"William," Genesis interrupted, unable to keep the edge out of her voice. "You texted."

Zuri winced at Genesis' tone. "Come on, don't make it sound like that. It was work related."

Genesis let out a bitter chuckle. "Isn't it always?"

Rain cleared her throat and walked around the car to join

them. She exchanged a quick hug with Zuri before introducing her to Brick. Genesis watched the interaction, her emotions churning. Part of her wanted to throw herself into Zuri's arms, while another part wanted to turn away and climb into Brick's SUV without another word.

"Look," Zuri said, turning back to Genesis, "I messed up, but I'm here now. Can we talk?"

Rain glanced between the two women, then nudged Brick. "Hey, babe, why don't we give them a minute?"

Brick nodded, understanding. "Sure thing. We'll wait in the car."

As Rain and Brick retreated, Genesis crossed her arms, trying to steel herself against the pull she felt towards Zuri. "Talk about what, Z? About how you promised things would be different, but here we are again?"

Zuri stepped closer, her eyes pleading. "I screwed up, and I'm sorry." She inched closer. "Let's go home and talk this out."

Genesis wanted to pull away when she picked up her hands in hers and began caressing her palms. But then she drew her close and kissed the hollow of her neck. A shiver ran through her body at Zuri's touch. She closed her eyes, fighting the urge to melt into the familiar embrace. Then the hurt and frustration of the evening came rushing back.

She gently pushed Zuri away, creating some distance between them. "Fine, we can go back to your place to talk, but that's all we're doing."

Zuri smirked at her response, a knowing glint in her eyes. "Just talk, huh?" she murmured, her voice low and husky. "Sure, we can do that."

After exchanging goodbyes, Genesis berated herself internally for being weak. Then a piece of her conversation with Rain earlier flashed through her mind. Maybe it was time for her to take charge.

# Chapter Twenty-Three

On the drive back to Zuri's house, Genesis remained quiet. She sensed Zuri's eyes on her, stealing glances as she navigated the city streets. Unspoken words and simmering emotions lingered in the silence between them.

When they arrived, Genesis led the way into the house. She kicked off her shoes and turned to face Zuri, who was leaning against the closed door, her eyes dark with a mix of desire and apprehension.

"So," Genesis said, crossing her arms. "We're going to talk, like I agreed, but we're going to do things a little differently this time. When I say so, I want you upstairs, on your knees, with only your bra and panties."

Zuri's eyes widened at her request. "Say that again?"

Genesis took a step closer, her voice low and husky. "You heard me, Zuri. I want you upstairs, on your knees, in your underwear. "

She left Zuri standing there as she called for Kuma. She tended to stay in the bedroom when they were at Zuri's place, so she found a snack to lure her into the living room. When she appeared and finished getting pats from Zuri, Genesis led Kuma to her plush bed in the corner of the living room, giving her a final scratch behind the ears before turning back to Zuri.

"You have five minutes," Genesis said, her voice low and commanding. "I'll be upstairs."

Without waiting for a response, she turned and ascended the stairs, her heart pounding with excitement. This was unfamiliar territory for her, taking charge like this, but Rain's words echoed in her mind. Switching up things couldn't hurt and maybe, just maybe, commanding respect in one aspect of their life would impact other areas.

In her bedroom, Genesis took a deep breath, steeling herself for what was to come. She lit a few candles and put on some music. Unsure of what to change into, she opted for a matching silk short set. It wasn't sexy per se, but this wasn't about seduction - it was about asserting herself.

She perched on the edge of the bed, her heart racing as she heard Zuri's footsteps on the stairs. When Zuri appeared in the doorway, Genesis felt her breath catch. Neither of them spoke as she removed her clothes and placed them on a chair.

Genesis kept her cool despite the nerves fluttering in her stomach. "On your knees."

Zuri dropped to her knees, her hair falling around her face as she looked up at Genesis with anticipation. She stood up, circling Zuri with deliberate steps.

"You've been neglecting me, Z. Making promises you don't keep. Putting work before us."

Zuri opened her mouth to say something, but Genesis held up a hand, silencing her. "No, don't speak. Just listen." She stopped in front of Zuri, looking down at her. "I've been patient. I've been understanding. But I'm tired of being an afterthought in your life."

Genesis reached out, running her fingers through Zuri's dreadlocks, then gripping them gently. "Tonight, you're going to show me just how sorry you are." She tugged on Zuri's locs again, tilting her head back. She leaned down, her lips hovering just above Zuri's. "Do you understand?"

Zuri nodded, her eyes dark with desire and something else - perhaps a hint of remorse. "Yes," she whispered.

"Good," Genesis murmured. She released Zuri's hair and stepped back, sitting on the edge of the bed. "Now, I want you to show me how sorry you are."

Zuri moved forward, her hands sliding up Genesis' thighs. She looked up, seeking permission, and Genesis nodded. Zuri's fingers hooked into the waistband of Genesis' silk shorts, sliding them down.

Genesis' threw her head back as Zuri's lips grazed her inner thigh. She bit her bottom lip, trying to maintain control, but the sensations coursing through her body made it difficult.

"That's right," she said, her voice husky, as Zuri's tongue traced a wet path up her center. Her grip tightened on Zuri's hair as the pleasure intensified.

"Don't stop," she gasped, arching her back as Zuri found her most sensitive spot. "Right there."

The sounds of their heavy breathing and the wet, wanton noises coming from their joined bodies filled the room. Genesis rocked her hips against Zuri's face, lost in the moment, her earlier frustrations melting away in the face of the pleasure coursing through her veins.

Zuri's hands slid up her torso, cupping her breasts, squeezing gently before trailing downwards, teasing the sensitive flesh beneath her navel. Fingers found their way between her cheeks, spreading her open wider, and Genesis arched her back into the touch.

A loud groan escaped her lips as Zuri's tongue dove deeper, lapping up every bit of her juices. She was so close and Zuri didn't relent, her tongue practically devouring Genesis, sending her spiraling over the edge. Genesis cried out, her body tensing as waves of pleasure washed over her.

With her orgasm subsiding, Genesis sank back on the bed, her chest heaving and her heart pounding. She expected Zuri to climb up with her, but when she raised herself up on her elbows, she was still on her knees, watching her.

Zuri licked the wetness from her lips and smiled. "That was only one orgasm. I think I can do better than that."

"Is that so?" Genesis glanced over at the bedside table, then turned back to Zuri. "I think there's something in there that can help you with that."

Zuri laughed, momentarily breaking their role-playing. "We haven't used that thing in months!"

"Well, I think tonight's the night to break it out, don't you?"

"For you, of course. Permission to stand?"

Genesis smirked, enjoying the power she was wielding. "Granted. But don't keep me waiting too long. I'm still owed a proper apology."

Zuri winked before getting up to retrieve the toy from the drawer. Genesis smiled to herself as she watched Zuri's beautiful ass swaying back and forth.

After taking out the harness and dark purple dildo from the drawer, Zuri placed them on the bed, then removed her bra and panties. Genesis licked her lips at the sight of her dark, plump nipples. Although she longed to caress them with her tongue, she remained focused. This was about her pleasure and making a point.

Once she had the harness and dildo in place, Genesis directed Zuri on to the middle of the bed. Now it was her turn to finish removing her clothing. When she climbed on the bed, her breasts swaying as she positioned herself, Zuri attempted to grab her hips, but she forced her hands down.

"Not so fast," Genesis said with a naughty grin. "Hands to yourself until I say otherwise."

Zuri placed her hands behind her head. Her eyes hungrily followed Genesis's every move as she straddled the head of the toy and sunk down on it.

"Oh, God," Genesis moaned, her eyes rolling back in her head. "You have no idea how much I've missed this."

Zuri groaned as she watched her move. "I can imagine," she managed between gritted teeth. "You look amazing."

"Mmm, I know," Genesis purred, running a hand down her body, over her stomach and between her legs, to tease her swollen clit. "Just like I know you don't mean to be thoughtless."

Zuri groaned, her eyes squeezing shut, and Genesis could tell she was on the verge of orgasm. Every move of her hips was causing delicious friction for them both.

She leaned forward, pressing their chests together, and whispered in her ear, "But you won't do that again, will you?"

"No," Zuri gasped, her hips bucking. "I promise... never again."

"Good," Genesis purred, picking up the pace. "Because I don't know if I could handle it if you did."

Zuri's breathing became more ragged. Her hands dropped to the sheets and gripped them tightly.

"Babe," Zuri panted, "I...I'm...I'm gonna..."

Genesis leaned down and caught Zuri's lips in a deep, passionate kiss. Her hands slid through Zuri's hair as she moaned into it. She sat up, grabbing Zuri's hands and placing them firmly on her hips. Zuri gripped Genesis tightly, her fingers digging into her flesh.

It was right there, a release that she knew was going to be so sweet. The sounds of Zuri's orgasm as she jerked up from the force of it sent Genesis over the edge. She allowed herself to succumb as her body trembled from the sheer force.

As their orgasms subsided, they both collapsed onto the bed, panting and spent. Genesis slumped to the side, her head resting on Zuri's shoulder. Zuri stroked her hair, and they lay there in silence for several minutes, catching their breath.

"I love you," Genesis said.

Zuri pulled away to look into her eyes. "I love you too. I'm sorry for tonight. It was a serious misstep."

"I know you didn't mean it, babe," Genesis replied, kissing her forehead. "Just try not to let it happen too much."

"Alright," Zuri said, the corners of her mouth turning up in a small smile. "But I can't make any promises if you keep punishing me like that."

Genesis laughed and swatted her stomach. "You're lucky I'm even sharing the covers with you tonight."

They both laughed, their bodies entwined. As they lay there, basking in the afterglow, Genesis felt a pang of guilt. She knew she needed to tell Zuri about what had happened with Lea earlier that day. The confrontation had been weighing on her mind, and now that they were in this intimate moment, it seemed wrong to keep it from her.

Genesis propped herself up on one elbow, looking down at Zuri's relaxed face. "Z, there's something I need to tell you."

Zuri's eyes opened, a flicker of concern crossing her features. "What is it, babe?"

Genesis took a deep breath, steeling herself. "Earlier today, before the fight, I had a... confrontation with Lea at Beacon."

Zuri sat up, her brow furrowing. "What kind of confrontation?"

Genesis recounted the events of the afternoon. Kem's tearful arrival, the heated exchange in Lea's office, and the accusations she'd made. As she spoke, she could see Zuri's expression shifting from concern to anger.

"She fired Kem?" Zuri exclaimed, shaking her head in disbelief. "She's one of the best instructors we have."

Genesis nodded, relieved that Zuri understood the gravity of the situation. "I know. That's why I couldn't just let it slide. But I might have said something out of line."

"Like what?"

"I might have told her that I knew she fired her because she's unhappy with our relationship."

Zuri's eyes widened in shock. "You said what?"

Genesis sat up, pulling the sheet around her. "You should have seen the way she was acting. It was so clear that this wasn't about Kem's performance or budget cuts. This was personal. But I'm sorry, it's not something I should have brought up."

Zuri ran a hand through her locs, exhaling. "There's nothing to be sorry about, babe. If she wasn't messing with your program, you wouldn't have been pushed to say that." She sat up as well, gathering Genesis into her arms. "I'm going to talk to her like I said I would. Girlfriend or not, her behavior is unacceptable."

Genesis leaned back, searching Zuri's face. "You're not mad?"

Zuri shook her head. "No, I'm not mad at you. I'm frustrated with the situation, but I understand. You were defending someone you care about, and you were calling out behavior that was unprofessional and hurtful. I can't fault you for that."

"I was worried you'd think I was overstepping."

"You're not the type to make accusations without reason. If you felt strongly enough to confront Lea like that, I trust your judgment."

Genesis leaned into Zuri's touch. "Thank you, honey."

"I should have addressed this with Lea sooner, but I guess I was hoping things would smooth over on their own, but that hasn't happened. Don't worry, I'll handle it."

"Just… be careful, okay? I don't want this to blow up into something bigger."

Zuri pulled her closer, pressing a kiss to her forehead. "I will. I promise I'll handle it professionally and discreetly." She paused, her expression growing thoughtful. "I've been thinking I should consider stepping back from Beacon altogether."

Genesis looked up at her, surprised. "Really? But you've put so much into it."

"I have," Zuri agreed, "but maybe it's time to let it stand on its own. I can still support it financially without being involved in the day-to-day operations. It might be better for everyone, especially you."

Genesis felt a flutter of hope in her chest. The idea of not having to navigate the complicated dynamics at Beacon was appealing, but she didn't want Zuri to make such a big decision based solely on her discomfort.

"Are you sure?" she asked. "I don't want you to give up something you're passionate about just because of this situation."

Zuri smiled, running her fingers through Genesis' curls. "I'm not giving it up, just changing my role. And honestly, I've been thinking about it for a while now. This situation with Lea just made me realize it might be the right time."

Genesis leaned in and kissed Zuri. "Whatever you decide, I'm here for you. But let's not make any big decisions tonight, okay? We've had enough drama for one day."

Zuri chuckled and nodded. "You're right. How about we get some sleep and tackle all this in the morning?"

"Sounds perfect," Genesis agreed, snuggling closer to Zuri.

As they settled into bed, Genesis felt at peace. She closed her eyes, breathing in Zuri's familiar scent, and let herself drift off to sleep.

# Chapter Twenty-Four

Zuri stood in front of Beacon a few days later, wishing she smoked. Then at least she would have some way to tamp down the nervous energy running through her. She had promised Genesis she would handle things with Lea, and she intended to keep it, but the thought of confronting Lea made her stomach churn. If it had been anyone else, this would be easy.

They met through a friend of Zuri's dad, who had worked with Lea in another non-profit venture. Her experience made such a difference in the growth of Beacon, and Zuri wasn't sure it would have been as successful with someone else at the helm.

She closed her eyes, memories flooding back of late nights hunched over grant applications, their laughter echoing through empty hallways as they painted walls and assembled furniture. Lea had been there from the beginning, her passion for the arts as fierce as Zuri's own. They'd spent countless hours brainstorming in coffee shops, scribbling ideas on napkins and dreaming up ways to bring creativity to underserved communities.

Beacon had started as a spark, a shared vision between two

women, determined to make a difference. Those early days had been a whirlwind of fundraisers, community outreach, and sheer determination. Zuri could still picture Lea perched atop a ladder, paintbrush in hand, her face streaked with color as she created the mural that would become Beacon's signature. They had celebrated every milestone together. The first class, the first recital, the first time they displayed a student's artwork in a real gallery.

Now those memories were tainted. Lea's recent behavior had crossed a line, and Zuri couldn't ignore it any longer. She took a deep breath, squaring her shoulders. This wasn't just about her anymore; it was about protecting Genesis and the future of Beacon.

Zuri smiled and greeted some of the staff and students as she went in search of Lea.

"Hey Z, what brings you here?"

Zuri turned to face Mrs. Clemons, one of the art teachers. Her silvery hair was pulled back in a bun, her almost wrinkle free brown face belying her 70 years. Known only as Clem among her peers, Clemons was a world-renowned artist, and a welcome addition to Beacon. In her later years, she wanted to give back so that she could nurture the next great artist.

"Hi Clem," Zuri said, forcing a smile. "Just here to talk with Lea about some program changes. How have you been?"

"I'm great, working on a new piece. I have an exhibition coming up at MOCA in a few months."

"Oh, that's wonderful!" Zuri exclaimed, her smile turning genuine. "I can't wait to see your work on display. You'll have to let me know the details so I can spread the word."

"Of course, dear. I'll be sure to send you an invitation. You know Genesis has already been hounding me about it."

Zuri chuckled, of course Genesis was already in the know.

Somehow, despite her part time status at Beacon, she had managed to get close to most of the staff.

"That sounds just like her. She's always so supportive of everyone's endeavors."

Mrs. Clemons nodded, a knowing glint in her eye. "She's a special one, that Genesis. You two make quite the pair."

"Thank you. We're very happy together."

"As you should be," the older woman said with a wink. "Now, don't let me keep you. I believe I saw Lea heading to the garden."

Thanking Mrs. Clemons, Zuri headed to the backyard area where people went to have lunch and take breaks. As she stepped into the garden, she took a moment to appreciate the vibrant space. Colorful murals adorned the surrounding walls, each one a testament to the creativity nurtured within Beacon's walls. Raised beds overflowed with herbs and vegetables, tended by students as part of their sustainability program. In the center, a small fountain bubbled, its gentle sound adding to the peaceful surroundings.

She spotted Lea near the back, kneeling beside a raised bed of vegetables, her hands deep in the soil.

"Lea," Zuri called out.

Lea looked up, surprise flickering across her face before it settled into a smile. "Zuri! What a pleasant surprise."

"What are you up to down there? I'm pretty sure we have gardeners for that."

Lea brushed her hands off on her jeans as she stood up, her smile still in place. "Oh, you know me. I like to get my hands dirty sometimes. Helps me think."

Zuri nodded, trying to keep her expression neutral. "I see. Well, I was hoping we could talk. Do you have a moment?"

"For you? Of course," Lea replied, gesturing toward a nearby bench. "What's on your mind?"

As they sat down, Zuri took a deep breath, steeling herself. "It's about the dance program. I've heard there have been some... issues with the changes Genesis has implemented."

Lea's smile faltered. "Ah, yes. Well, you know how change can be. It takes time for everyone to adjust."

"That's true," Zuri agreed. "But I've also heard that you've been resistant to these changes."

Lea's face hardened, her earlier kindness evaporating. "I see. And may I ask who has been feeding you this information?"

"That's not important," Zuri said firmly. "What matters is whether it's true or not."

"Why don't we go to my office? This conversation might be better had in private," Lea said, getting up and not waiting for an answer.

Zuri followed behind her, trying not to let her irritation show. Lea had to have known that she was going to confront her. So then why had she been pushing against Genesis so hard? Was she hoping to get Zuri to react, and to what end?

Inside Lea's office, the familiar space now felt oddly claustrophobic. Lea settled behind her desk, while Zuri remained standing, her arms crossed.

Lea settled behind her desk, gesturing for Zuri to take a seat. "So, you want to talk about Genesis and the changes she's been making?"

Zuri sat, her posture straight, hands folded in her lap. "Yes, I do. I've heard your resistant to her ideas. Care to explain?"

Lea's eyes narrowed. "I thought we agreed when we started Beacon that major program changes would be a joint decision. Genesis seems to think she can overhaul everything without consulting anyone."

"She's not overhauling everything, Lea," Zuri countered, trying to keep her voice level. "She's introducing new techniques, expanding the repertoire. It's growth, not destruction."

"Growth?" Lea scoffed. "Is that what we're calling it now? She's dismantling years of carefully crafted curriculum."

"The curriculum needs to evolve. We can't keep doing the same things year after year and expect to stay relevant."

"Relevant?" Lea's voice rose. "We've been more than relevant. We've been successful, Zuri. Our students have gone on to prestigious dance companies, won competitions. Why fix what isn't broken?"

Zuri leaned forward. "Because the world is changing. Our students deserve to be exposed to new styles, new perspectives. Genesis brings that fresh energy, that diversity we've always talked about."

Lea's jaw clenched. "And I suppose you're not at all biased in your assessment of her contributions?"

"What's that supposed to mean?" Zuri asked, though she knew exactly what Lea was implying.

"Oh, come on, Zuri. You're dating her." Lea's tone dripped with disdain. "Your judgment is clouded by your personal feelings."

Zuri felt her anger flare. "My relationship with Genesis has nothing to do with this. She's a wonderful director. The teachers love her and the students love the additional classes."

"Of course they do," Lea scoffed. "She lets them do whatever they want, calling it 'artistic expression.' There's no discipline, no structure."

"That's not true, and you know it," Zuri countered. "Genesis pushes the teachers just as hard as anyone else."

Lea got quiet. "Ever since she came into the picture, things have been different between us. You used to value my opinion."

"I still value your opinion," Zuri insisted. "But that doesn't mean I'll always agree with it. And right now, I think you're the one who is letting your personal feelings cloud your judgment."

Lea's eyes flashed with a mix of hurt and anger. "My

personal feelings? You want to talk about personal feelings, Zuri? Let's talk about them. Do you remember the night we opened Beacon? The celebration we had right here in this very office?"

Zuri nodded. She remembered it vividly - the champagne, the laughter, the feeling of accomplishment that had filled the air like a tangible thing.

"We danced," Lea continued, "Right there, by the window. You were wearing that red dress, the one with the open back. You wore that perfume you always have on, and it smelled so damn good."

Zuri shifted in her seat, memories flooding back.

"That night, I thought maybe we were on the verge of something more. And when we kissed all those months later, I was sure that was it. But you never gave me a chance. You never even saw me."

"Lea, I was in a toxic relationship and desperate for attention. I would have been using you if we took it there."

"Maybe I wanted you to use me," Lea said, staring deep into Zuri's eyes. "I've imagined it, you know. Late nights in this office, paperwork forgotten as I push you up against the desk. My hands in your hair, your lips on my neck."

Startled by her confession, Zuri was speechless. Spurred on by her silence, Lea continued.

"I think about that kiss all the time and I touch myself, wishing it was you."

"Lea, that's enough," Zuri said, rising from her seat. "I'm going to stop you before you say something you'll regret."

Lea's eyes flashed with determination. She stepped around the desk, closing the distance between them. "I won't regret it. I've held this in for too long."

Before Zuri could react, Lea leaned in and pressed her lips against hers. For a split second, Zuri froze, shocked by the suddenness of it all. Then, as if jolted by electricity, she pushed Lea away.

"What the hell do you think you're doing?" Zuri exclaimed, her voice trembling with anger.

Lea stumbled back, her face a mix of hurt and confusion. "I thought... I thought maybe if you felt it again..."

"Felt what?" Zuri snapped. "Lea, I'm with Genesis. I love her. What happened between us was a mistake, a moment of weakness."

Lea's expression hardened. "A mistake? Is that what I am to you? After everything we've built together?"

Zuri took a deep breath, trying to calm herself. "Beacon is important to me, Lea. Our friendship was important to me. But this crosses a line."

"So that's it then?" Lea's voice was bitter. "You're choosing her over everything we've created?"

"This isn't about choosing," Zuri said firmly. "This is about respect. I've ignored your behavior for far too long and that's on me, but this is a step too far."

Lea's face flushed with embarrassment and anger. "You can't just dismiss me like this, Zuri. We built Beacon together. You owe me more than that."

"I don't owe you anything," Zuri replied coldly. "Especially not after the way you've been undermining Genesis and making her feel unwelcome here. Your behavior has been unprofessional and, frankly, after that stunt you just pulled, unacceptable."

Lea laughed bitterly. "You're the one who brought your girlfriend in and gave her free rein over my program."

"Your program?" Zuri's voice rose. "Beacon doesn't belong to you. It belongs to the community, to the kids we serve. And if you can't see that, if you can't put your personal feelings aside for the good of this place we built together, then maybe..." She trailed off, the weight of what she was about to say hitting her hard. Lea's eyes widened, a flicker of fear crossing her face.

"Maybe what, Zuri?" Lea spit out.

Zuri smoothed down her blazer and looked her straight in the eye. "Your actions have made it clear that you can no longer be trusted in a leadership position at Beacon."

Lea's eyes widened in shock. "What are you saying?"

"I'm saying you're fired, Lea. Clean out your office and leave your keys with reception. I'll have HR send over the necessary paperwork."

Without waiting for a response, Zuri turned and walked out of the office, her heart pounding. She didn't stop until she reached her car, hands shaking as she gripped the steering wheel. Only then did she let out a long, shuddering breath, the weight of what had just transpired hitting her all at once.

Zuri drove in a daze, her mind replaying the confrontation with Lea over and over. The shock of the kiss, the anger in Lea's eyes, the finality of her own words as she fired her long-time friend and colleague. It all swirled in her head, making her feel dizzy and nauseous.

As she pulled into her driveway, she realized she had no recollection of the drive home. She sat in her car for a moment, trying to gather her thoughts. The enormity of what had just happened was sinking in. Beacon would never be the same without Lea. Despite her recent behavior, she had been integral to the organization's success. Zuri wondered if she had made the right decision.

With a heavy sigh, she got out of the car and headed inside. As she opened the front door, the smell of something delicious wafted through the air. For a moment, she was confused. Then it hit her - Genesis. They had plans tonight.

"Babe, is that you?" Genesis called from the kitchen. "I hope you're hungry because I've outdone myself this time!"

"Damn it," Zuri muttered under her breath. With the whole Lea situation, she had completely forgotten about her dinner plans with Genesis. She took a deep breath, plastered on a smile, and walked into the kitchen.

Genesis was standing at the stove, stirring something in a large pot. She turned when Zuri entered, her face lighting up with a radiant smile. "There you are! I was starting to worry. How did everything go with Lea?"

Zuri wanted nothing more than to collapse into Genesis's arms and spill everything, but she couldn't bring herself to ruin this moment. Genesis looked so happy, so excited about their evening together.

"It was... intense," Zuri said, trying to keep her voice steady. "But it's handled now. Let's not talk about work. What smells so amazing?"

Genesis raised an eyebrow, sensing there was more to the story, but she didn't push. Instead, she gestured to the pot with a flourish. "Behold, my grandmother's famous gumbo! I've been simmering it all afternoon. Granny Lee and I have been talking on the phone and she's shared so much with me."

Zuri managed a genuine smile, touched by Genesis's effort. "That sounds incredible, babe. Thank you for doing this. And I'm so glad you're reconnecting with your family."

Genesis beamed at Zuri. "Well, that's all thanks to my amazing girlfriend." She turned back to the stove, giving the gumbo another stir. "Now, why don't you freshen up while I finish up here? Dinner will be ready in about 15 minutes."

Zuri nodded, grateful for the chance to compose herself. She headed to the bedroom, her mind still whirling with the events of the day. As she changed out of her work clothes, she glimpsed herself in the mirror. The woman staring back at her looked tired, conflicted.

She splashed some cold water on her face. As she patted her

skin dry, she heard Genesis humming in the kitchen, the sound warm and comforting. Zuri closed her eyes, letting the melody wash over her. She wasn't going to let what happened with Lea taint this evening with Genesis.

When she returned to the kitchen, Genesis was ladling the gumbo into bowls. The rich aroma filled the air, making Zuri's mouth water despite her churning emotions.

"Perfect timing," Genesis said, carrying the bowls to the dining table. "Come on, let's eat before it gets cold."

They settled at the table, and Zuri took a spoonful of the gumbo. The flavors exploded on her tongue.For a moment, she forgot about everything else.

"Oh wow," Zuri said, her eyes widening. "This is incredible, babe."

Genesis beamed, her smile lighting up the room. "I'm so glad you like it. Granny Lee would be proud."

As they ate, Genesis chattered about her day, the students she'd worked with, and her plans for upcoming performances. Zuri tried to focus, to be present, but her mind kept drifting back to Lea.

"Zuri? Earth to Zuri," Genesis said, waving her hand in front of Zuri's face. "Where'd you go just now?"

Zuri blinked, realizing she'd zoned out. "I'm sorry, babe. I guess I'm more tired than I thought."

Genesis reached across the table, taking Zuri's hand in hers. "Are you sure that's all it is? You've been off since you got home. Did something happen with Lea?"

Zuri hesitated, torn between wanting to protect Genesis from the ugliness of the situation and needing to share the burden she was carrying. She looked into Genesis' concerned eyes and felt her resolve crumble.

"I fired her," Zuri blurted out, her voice barely above a whisper.

Genesis's eyes widened in shock. "Really? I hope you didn't do it because of me."

Zuri took a deep breath, her fingers tracing the pattern on the tablecloth. "It wasn't about you, Gen. It was... everything. The way she's been resisting change, undermining your authority, creating a toxic environment. When I confronted her about it, she just... she couldn't see reason."

Genesis listened intently, her brow furrowed with concern.

"She started talking about the old days, about how we built Beacon together," Zuri continued. "And I realized she's been living in the past. She can't see that Beacon needs to grow, to evolve. When I tried to explain, she got defensive, angry even."

Zuri paused, the memory of Lea's lips on hers flashing through her mind. She pushed it away, guilt gnawing at her insides. "Things escalated. Words were said... harsh words on both sides. And in the end, I realized she couldn't continue in her role. Not if we want Beacon to thrive."

Genesis reached across the table, taking Zuri's hand in hers. Her touch was comforting. "Oh, babe. That must have been so hard for you. I know how much Lea meant to you, how important she's been to Beacon."

Zuri nodded, tears pricking at the corners. "It was hard but necessary. I'll be fine, as long as I have you," she said, squeezing Genesis' hand.

Genesis stood up, tugging Zuri to her feet. "Come here," she said, pulling Zuri into a tight embrace. Zuri melted into her girlfriend's arms, burying her face in the crook of Genesis's neck. The familiar scent of her shea butter lotion was comforting, grounding.

They stood like that for a long moment, Genesis rubbing Zuri's back. When they pulled apart, Genesis cupped Zuri's face in her hands, her thumbs wiping away the tears that had escaped.

"You did what you had to do," Genesis said firmly. "Beacon is your baby, and sometimes being a good parent means making tough decisions. You're protecting the future of the organization, and the kids it serves."

Zuri nodded, feeling some of the weight lift from her shoulders. "You're right. It feels like the end of an era."

"It is, but I'm sure the next one will be better than ever." Genesis stepped back smiling. "How about I draw you a nice bath so you can relax?"

"Mmm, I'm down, but only if you join me."

"Well, if you insist..." She leaned in, pressing a kiss to Zuri's lips. "You go get the bath started, and I'll clean up here."

Zuri nodded, feeling a flutter of anticipation in her stomach. As she headed to the bathroom, she could hear Genesis humming again, the sound bringing a smile to her face.

In the bathroom, Zuri turned on the faucet, adjusting the temperature until it was just right. She added a generous pour of lavender-scented bubble bath, watching as the tub filled with fragrant foam. The stress of the day seemed to melt away as steam filled the room.

She had just slipped out of her clothes when Genesis appeared in the doorway, a bottle of wine and two glasses in hand. "I thought we could use a little something extra to help us unwind," she said with a wink.

Zuri felt her heart swell with love. "You think of everything, don't you?"

Genesis set the wine and glasses on the edge of the tub before undressing. Zuri drank in the sight of her curves as she sank into the water with a contented sigh. Genesis slid in behind her, wrapping her arms around her.

They were both quiet, only the sounds of Mozart drifted in from the speaker in Zuri's bedroom. Genesis loved to put classical music on in the evenings. It was something Zuri looked forward to, something that made her house feel more like a home. Sometimes when her love wasn't there, she would put it on herself and let the sounds envelope her.

Zuri felt her mind drift, no longer replaying the confrontation with Lea, but imagining the possibilities that lay ahead for Beacon. Her decision to let Lea go and to keep what happened to herself was for the best. It was a necessary sacrifice to preserve the peace and harmony that she and Genesis had worked so hard to establish. She felt a tinge of guilt for selfishly wanting to protect what they had created together. But in that moment, surrounded by thoughts of hope and ambition, she pushed the guilt away. Genesis was right, sometimes you had to make hard decisions to protect what you hold dear.

# Chapter Twenty-Five

"Shit, shit, shit."

Genesis looked up from her book and did her best not to chuckle. Zuri was running around attempting to finish the meal she insisted on making herself. It was Genesis' birthday and although she never did much to celebrate, Zuri had decided that was unacceptable. Since they'd already done the engagement party and Genesis wasn't interested in another big event, she agreed to let Zuri cook dinner. The woman was a whiz with breakfast foods, but somehow still hadn't mastered more complex meals.

"Babe, do you need any help?" Genesis called out from her seat on the couch.

Zuri poked her head around the corner. "Absolutely not. I told you I've got this." Her dreadlocks swung as she shook her head. "You just sit there and look pretty."

Genesis raised an eyebrow. "I can do that, but are you sure? That smoke coming from the kitchen tells a different story."

Zuri's eyes widened in panic. "Smoke? What smoke?" She disappeared back into the kitchen, a string of colorful curses following her.

Genesis chuckled, setting her book aside. She couldn't resist anymore. Rising from the couch, she padded barefoot into the kitchen, following the trail of Zuri's muttered expletives.

The scene that greeted her was pure chaos. Pots and pans littered every surface. A thin haze of smoke hung in the air, and in the center of it all stood Zuri, looking defeated. Flour dusted her usually pristine dreadlocks, and a smear of something that might have been tomato sauce decorated her cheek.

"I might have been a bit too ambitious with this whole 'cooking a gourmet meal' thing," Zuri admitted sheepishly, gesturing at the surrounding disaster.

Genesis laughed as she crossed the kitchen, navigating the mess, and wrapped her arms around Zuri's waist. "Oh, baby. You tried so hard."

Zuri leaned into the embrace, a rueful smile tugging at her lips. "You're always cooking these amazing meals, and I thought I could return the favor."

Genesis planted a kiss on Zuri's flour-dusted cheek. "You impress me every day, just by being you. No gourmet meal required."

Zuri's smile widened. "How do you always know what to say?"

"It's a gift," Genesis teased, then glanced around the kitchen. "Now, how about we salvage what we can of this meal and order takeout for the rest?"

Zuri nodded, relief evident in her expression. "That sounds perfect. But first..." She leaned in, capturing Genesis's lips in a tender kiss. When they parted, both women were grinning.

"Alright, let's assess the damage. What were you trying to make?"

Zuri grimaced. "Coq au vin. Ambitious, right?"

Genesis whistled low. "Damn, baby. You don't do anything halfway, do you?"

"Go big or go home, right?" Zuri shrugged, then frowned at the smoking pot on the stove. "Though in this case, maybe I should have started with something simpler. Like spaghetti and meatballs."

Genesis laughed, moving to turn off the stove. "Let's see what we can save and clean up this disaster zone."

Zuri laughed, the sound light and carefree. "That sounds perfect." She reached out, swiping a dollop of whipped cream from a nearby bowl and dabbing it on Genesis's nose. "There. Now we're both a mess."

Genesis gasped in mock outrage. "Oh, it's on now, Baker!" She grabbed a handful of flour, ready to retaliate.

Zuri squealed, ducking behind the kitchen island. "Don't you dare, Malone! This is designer!"

Genesis paused, flour-filled hand poised to throw. "Oh, so now you care about messing up your clothes? A little late for that." She gestured at Zuri's stained apron and flour-dusted shirt.

Zuri peeked over the counter, a mischievous glint in her eye. "Truce?"

"Hmm," Genesis pretended to consider it, lowering her hand. "What's in it for me?"

In a flash, Zuri was up and around the island, pressing Genesis against the counter. "How about..." she murmured, her lips hovering just inches from Genesis's, "a proper thank you for coming to my rescue?"

Genesis's breath caught in her throat. Even covered in food and surrounded by kitchen chaos, Zuri was beautiful. "That could work," she managed to say, her voice husky.

Zuri closed the distance between them, her lips insistent against Genesis's. Genesis melted into the kiss, pulling Zuri closer. The flour in her hand forgotten, it dusted both their clothes as they lost themselves in each other.

"Now that's what I call a proper thank you," Genesis said, her voice low.

Zuri laughed, resting her forehead against Genesis's. "I aim to please."

"Oh, you do," Genesis replied with a wink. She glanced around the kitchen, taking in the mess once more. "But as much as I'd love to continue, we should deal with... all of this."

Zuri groaned, burying her face in Genesis's neck. "Do we have to? Can't we just, I don't know, set the kitchen on fire and collect the insurance money?"

Genesis chuckled, running her fingers through Zuri's flour-dusted locs. "Pretty sure that's illegal, babe. Besides, I kind of like this kitchen. When it's not a disaster zone, that is."

Zuri lifted her head, pouting. "Fine, fine. You're no fun."

"Oh, I can be fun," Genesis retorted. "But first, clean up. Then food. Then we'll see where the night takes us."

"Well, when you put it that way..." Zuri stepped back, surveying the kitchen with newfound determination. "Alright, let's do this. What do you say we divide and conquer?"

Genesis nodded, already rolling up her sleeves. "Sounds like a plan. I'll tackle the dishes if you want to wipe down the counters and stove."

"Deal," Zuri agreed, grabbing a sponge.

They worked in comfortable silence for a few minutes, the only sounds were the clinking of dishes and the swish of the sponge. Genesis stole glances at Zuri as they cleaned, admiring the way her girlfriend's brow furrowed in concentration as she scrubbed at a stubborn spot.

"You know," Genesis said, breaking the silence, "this isn't how I imagined spending my birthday evening, but I don't hate it."

Zuri paused her scrubbing, looking up with a grimace. "God, I'm so sorry. I wanted tonight to be special."

Genesis set down the plate she was washing and crossed the kitchen, pulling Zuri into her arms. "Any time I get to spend with you is special."

Zuri melted into the embrace, burying her face in Genesis's neck. "Even when I nearly burn down the kitchen?"

"It's not every day I get to see the great Zuri Baker, film mogul extraordinaire, covered in flour and looking utterly adorable."

Zuri pulled back, her eyes narrowing. "Adorable? Sexy sounds way more appropriate."

Genesis laughed. "Sexy, huh? With flour in your hair and tomato sauce on your cheek?"

"Absolutely," Zuri replied with a confident smirk. "I make this look good."

Genesis reached out, wiping the sauce from Zuri's cheek with her thumb. "Weirdly enough, you do."

Their eyes locked, the playful atmosphere shifting into something more intense. Genesis's hand lingered on Zuri's face, her thumb tracing the curve of her cheekbone. Zuri leaned into the touch, her eyes fluttering closed for a moment.

"Gen," Zuri murmured.

"Yeah?"

"The kitchen can wait."

Before Genesis could respond, Zuri's lips were on hers, demanding. Genesis responded, her arms wrapping around Zuri's waist, pulling her closer. The kiss deepened, months of love and desire pouring into it.

Zuri's hands found their way into Genesis's curls, tugging as she nipped at her lower lip. Genesis gasped, the sound swallowed by Zuri's eager mouth. They stumbled backward, Genesis's back hitting the refrigerator with a soft thud.

"Wait," Genesis said, breaking the kiss. "Are we really doing this here? In the messy kitchen?"

Zuri pulled back, her eyes dark with desire. "Why not? It's your birthday, after all. And I promised to make it special."

Genesis bit her lip, glancing around at the flour-dusted counters and piles of dishes. "But the mess..."

"Will still be here later." She leaned in, trailing kisses along Genesis's jawline. "Right now, I want to focus on you."

Genesis's resolve crumbled as Zuri's lips found that sensitive spot just below her ear. She tilted her head, giving Zuri better access. "Well, when you put it that way..."

Zuri chuckled against her skin, the vibration sending shivers down Genesis's spine. "That's what I thought."

With a playful growl, Genesis spun them around, pressing Zuri against the fridge. Zuri gasped in surprise, her eyes widening with delight.

"If we're doing this," Genesis murmured, her hands sliding under Zuri's flour-covered shirt, "we're doing it my way."

Zuri's breath hitched as Genesis's fingers traced patterns on her skin. "And what way is that?"

Genesis smirked, leaning in to nip at Zuri's earlobe. "Slowly," she whispered. "Very, very slowly."

Zuri groaned, her head falling back against the fridge.

* * *

A couple of hours later, Genesis and Zuri lay tangled together on the living room floor, empty takeout containers scattered around them. The rich aroma of pad thai and green curry still lingered, mingling with the faint scent of their lovemaking. Genesis caressed Zuri's bare arm, her head resting on her girlfriend's chest, listening to the steady rhythm of her heartbeat.

"This might be my best birthday yet," Genesis murmured, pressing a kiss to Zuri's collarbone.

Zuri chuckled, the sound vibrating through her chest. "Even with the kitchen disaster?"

"Especially because of the kitchen disaster," Genesis replied, lifting her head to meet Zuri's eyes. "It was perfectly imperfect, just like us."

Zuri's moved in for another sweet, lingering kiss. When they parted, Zuri's eyes widened. "Oh! I almost forgot!"

She disentangled herself from Genesis, ignoring her girlfriend's playful protests, and hurried to the kitchen. Genesis propped herself up on her elbows, watching as Zuri rummaged through the fridge.

"Cover your eyes!" Zuri called out.

Genesis complied, a mix of excitement and apprehension fluttering in her stomach. She heard Zuri's bare feet padding across the hardwood as she returned.

"Okay, you can open your eyes now."

Genesis could hear the excitement in Zuri's voice as she removed her hands from her eyes, blinking against the return of light. She admired Zuri's naked body, so much so she almost overlooked what was in her hands. Zuri cradled a beautifully crafted cake that seemed to be too perfect to eat. It had ornate frosted gold roses and delicate sugar art twirled around its edges in an intricate pattern, glistening under the dim lighting.

"I made this for you," Zuri said, her voice full of pride. "There's a bakery in Crenshaw called Melba's Place, and she teaches classes on how to make cakes. It runs for several weeks."

"You learned how to bake a cake for me?"

Zuri nodded, her smile widening as she walked closer. "Not just any cake, but a champagne-infused one." She held it out to Genesis, pride written all over her face. "It's your favorite. You remember New Year's Eve?"

Genesis laughed at the memory, recalling the way they had devoured an entire champagne cake between them until all that was left was a plate full of crumbs. She took the cake from Zuri's hands, tracing her fingers along the expertly crafted roses and sugar art.

"Surprised?" asked Zuri, her voice barely above a whisper as she stepped closer to Genesis.

Genesis blinked against the rush of emotions that threatened to spill over. She swallowed hard and nodded, realizing that words had abandoned her.

"I wanted to do something different for your birthday. I'm always buying you stuff but this is from the heart..."

"It's perfect," Genesis said, cutting her off.

Zuri stopped rambling and looked at her, brown eyes wide with relief. "Yeah?"

Genesis nodded, tears threatening to fall. She blinked them back, not wanting to ruin the moment with her sudden outburst of emotion. She placed the cake back into Zuri's hands, their fingers brushing against each other.

"More than perfect," she whispered, reaching up to tuck a stray dreadlock behind Zuri's ear, tracing the curve of her jaw with her fingertips before cupping her face gently.

Zuri closed her eyes and let out a contented sigh. Genesis leaned forward then, capturing those sighing lips with hers. It was a gentle kiss filled with gratitude and unspoken words of love.

When they pulled back, Zuri was the first to speak. "I'm glad you liked it. The cake, I mean." She tried to hide the nervousness in her voice, but Genesis picked up on it.

Genesis responded by making a joke. "Oh, I haven't tasted it yet." She glanced at the cake, still nestled in Zuri's hands. "It could be terrible."

Zuri gasped at the accusation, placing a hand over her heart in mock offense. "How dare you? Melba herself said I was a natural."

They walked over to the table and Zuri laid the cake on top. There were plates and cutlery sat out already, along with a bottle of champagne.

"I used a pink champagne to go along with the strawberry flavor of the cake," Zuri said while she filled up their flutes.

Genesis grinned. "Oooh, you know I love strawberry cake."

Zuri locked eyes with her. "I do know that, my love."

A jolt of desire shot straight into her core and it took everything in her not to grab Zuri's hand and drag her into the bedroom to continue what they started earlier.

Zuri approached Genesis, the champagne flutes held out in front of her. Genesis took one and clinked it against Zuri's. The sound echoed in the room.

"To your birthday," Zuri toasted.

"To us," Genesis replied, looking at her as she took a sip.

They stayed like that for a minute, just savoring the taste of the champagne. Zuri was the first to break the silence.

"I suppose we should get on with cutting the cake?"

Genesis set down her glass and did a little happy dance. The cake was beautiful; she thought to herself again, taking in its intricate details. She still couldn't believe Zuri had learned to make this for her.

Zuri handed over a knife to Genesis, who gave her a sidelong glance. "You're not going to do it?"

"Consider it as another part of your birthday gift," Zuri replied, gesturing to the cake. "The honor of the first slice is all yours."

Genesis smiled, accepting the knife. She positioned it over the top of the cake, looking up at Zuri for approval. Receiving a nod of encouragement, she pressed the blade into the spongy surface with a sense of reverence. The knife slid smoothly through it, releasing a puff of sweet aroma that was intoxicating.

Genesis pulled out a sizable piece and laid it onto the plate

Zuri had put aside. The inside was as beautiful as the outside, the layers of pink champagne-infused cake sandwiched between swirls of creamy frosting.

After slicing another piece for herself, Genesis handed Zuri a fork and took one for herself. They both sat down and dug into their slices, bringing them to their mouths almost simultaneously.

The champagne soaked through every inch of the cake, creating a perfect symphony with the strawberry flavor and the creaminess of the frosting. Every bite had a delightful crunch, thanks to the outer layer of sugar art. Genesis savored each mouthful, her eyes closing in bliss.

Zuri watched her reaction, an expectant look on her face as Genesis savored her first mouthful. "Well?" she asked after a moment, unable to keep the anxious excitement out of her tone. "How is it?"

Genesis took one more bite before answering, wanting to relish the wonderful blend of flavors longer. "It's... sensational," she declared, grinning from ear to ear.

A wave of relief washed over Zuri's face, and she let out a small laugh. "Really?"

Genesis nodded emphatically. "This is easily the best cake I've ever eaten."

"Thanks, baby." Zuri breathed out, her eyes shimmering with joy. "I'm glad you like it." She took another bite, her own eyes closing as she savored the flavors.

Genesis watched her, feeling a warmth spread through her chest that had nothing to do with the champagne or cake. She wiped a smudge of frosting from the corner of Zuri's mouth, chuckling when Zuri tried to nip at her fingers.

"You're incredible," Genesis said.

"Only for you," Zuri replied, looking at her with such intensity that it made Genesis' squirm in a pleasant way.

"You keep looking at me like that and we won't be finishing this cake."

Zuri smiled and slid another piece into her mouth. Her eyes didn't leave Genesis as she placed her plate and fork down and waited for her to do the same.

"Are you proposing we leave the rest of this divine creation behind?" Genesis teased. However, her gaze didn't leave Zuri's, and the corner of her lips twitched upwards into a provocative smile.

Zuri playfully took hold of Genesis' hand and brought it to her lips, kissing the knuckles before stating, "I have another surprise for you," she said, her voice low. "Let's get dressed and I'll show you."

Genesis raised an eyebrow, intrigued. "Another surprise? You're spoiling me."

Zuri grinned, standing up and pulling Genesis with her. "It's your birthday. You deserve to be spoiled."

They dressed quickly, stealing glances and trading touches as they did. Genesis marveled at how, even after all this time, the simple act of getting dressed together felt so intimate.

Once they were ready, Zuri led Genesis upstairs. As they approached the bedroom, a sweet, floral scent wafted through the air, growing stronger with each step. Zuri paused at the closed door, turning to Genesis with a mischievous smile.

"Close your eyes one more time for me," she whispered.

Genesis obliged, her eyelids fluttering shut as she heard the click of the door opening. Zuri's hand, warm and gentle, guided her forward. The scent intensified, enveloping her senses in a cloud of fragrance.

"Okay. Open them."

Genesis opened her eyes, blinking as they adjusted to the soft glow that filled the room. Her breath caught in her throat as she took in the sight before her. The bedroom had been transformed into a romantic oasis, bathed in the flickering light of dozens of candles strategically placed around the room.

But what captured her attention were the roses. Zuri had scattered a trail of deep red rose petals leading from the doorway to the bed, creating a sensual pathway that beckoned them forward. On the nightstands, elegant crystal vases held small bouquets of roses in various shades of pink and red, their delicate petals unfurled in full bloom.

"Zuri," Genesis said, voice shaking. "This is... it's beautiful."

Except Zuri wasn't there face to face but kneeling. Her hand held a small velvet ring box.

"Genesis," Zuri began, her voice trembling slightly. "From the moment I met you, you brought so much joy into my life. Your kindness, your passion, your unwavering support - they've all shown me what true love really means."

She took a deep breath, steadying herself before continuing. "I can't imagine spending another day without you by my side. You're my best friend, my lover, my soulmate. I want to wake up next to you every morning, dance with you in the kitchen, argue over who forgot to buy milk, and grow old together. We're already engaged, but I wanted to show you I'm committed to this, too. "

Genesis's hand was shaking as Zuri placed the ring on her finger. It was a deep blue sapphire with small diamonds around it. Nothing fancy, but it was the type of jewelry she liked.

"It belonged to my grandmother, but on my dad's side, Grammy Cecelia," Zuri said as she stood up.

Genesis looked up from the ring and stroked her face. "You've never mentioned her before."

"She passed away when I was 5, but the one thing I remember was her kind spirit. You remind me of her."

Genesis' eyes filled with tears as she locked eyes with Zuri. Without a word, she wrapped her arms around Zuri's body.

"I love you so much," Genesis whispered, her voice thick with emotion. "This has been the most incredible birthday. The cake, the roses, and now this..." She glanced down at the ring sparkling on her finger. "I can't believe you did all this for me.

"You deserve it all and more. I just want to make you as happy as you make me."

So many thoughts flowed through Genesis' mind but she chose to just kiss Zuri in gratitude.

"So," Zuri said, a playful glint in her eye. "What do you say we put this romantic setting to good use?"

Genesis laughed, the sound light and joyful. "I thought you'd never ask."

# Chapter Twenty-Six

**O**ne **Month Later**

Zuri's reflection stared back at her as she adjusted one of her waist-length dreadlocks, tucking it behind her ear as she cleared her throat.

"I'm thrilled to discuss our latest project," she practiced, her voice steady but tinged with an undertone of nervousness. "Our film company has always strived to tell authentic stories, and this one is no exception."

She shuffled through her notecards, brow furrowing as she read over key talking points. The weight of her family name and the expectations that came with it pressed down on her shoulders. Despite her job, she wasn't someone who craved the spotlight. She much preferred being behind the scenes, orchestrating, but over time she had to get comfortable with all aspects of her job, including interviews.

This one was with Apex Magazine for their Power 30 edition, which featured the 30 most powerful women in the film industry. It was an honor to be included and anything that brought positive light to Ellis Films was a win in Zuri's book. She took a deep breath, smoothing down her silk blouse and adjusting her blazer. The sharp rap on her office door made her jump.

"Ms. Baker? The reporter from Apex is here," her assistant called through the door.

"Send her in," Zuri replied, plastering on her most welcoming smile.

The door opened, revealing a petite woman with a shock of red hair and a notebook clutched to her chest. "Ms. Baker, I'm Cassandra Wells. Thank you for taking the time to meet with me."

Zuri extended her hand, her smile open and professional. "Please, call me Zuri. It's a pleasure to meet you, Cassandra."

The journalist shook her hand firmly. "Thank you, Zuri. Shall we get started?"

They settled into the plush leather chairs in Zuri's office, the Los Angeles skyline stretching out behind them through floor-to-ceiling windows. Cassandra pulled out a voice recorder, placing it on the sleek glass coffee table between them.

"Do you mind if I record our conversation?"

"Not at all," Zuri replied, leaning back in her chair. "I'm an open book."

Cassandra smiled, pressing the record button. "Excellent. Let's start with your journey in film. How did you get your start?"

Zuri relaxed, grateful for the softball question. "Well, I grew up surrounded by the industry. My family has been in film for the last two generations. But I wanted to carve my path, so I studied business and finance in college. It wasn't until after graduation that I realized my passion lay in storytelling through film, just like my parents and grandmother before me."

The interview progressed, with Cassandra asking thoughtful questions about Zuri's career trajectory and the challenges she faced as a young, Black woman in the film industry.

Zuri relaxed into the conversation, her initial nervousness fading as she spoke about her work and vision for Ellis Films.

"You also have a nonprofit, Beacon. I've heard great things about the work you do there."

"Oh, Beacon is my pride and joy," she said, leaning forward with enthusiasm. "We started it several years ago with the goal of empowering young women through the arts, particularly those from underserved communities."

She paused, collecting her thoughts before continuing. "Growing up, I was fortunate to have access to incredible resources and mentors in the arts. But I realized that not everyone has those same opportunities. Beacon aims to bridge that gap."

Cassandra smiled. "It's an amazing way to give back. I don't doubt we'll have some Zuri Baker proteges running around."

Zuri chuckled. "That would be incredible. We've already seen some of our girls go on to do amazing things in the arts. It's very rewarding."

Cassandra nodded, jotting something down in her notebook. Then, her expression shifted, a slight tightness appearing around her eyes. "Now, Zuri, I'd like to touch on something a bit more... sensitive."

Zuri's smile faltered, but she maintained her composure. "Of course. What would you like to discuss?"

Cassandra cleared her throat. "There have been some recent allegations made against you by a former employee, Lea Thompson. She claims you and your girlfriend harassed her during her time at Beacon. Can you comment on these allegations?"

Zuri felt as if all the air had been sucked out of the room.

"I'm taken aback by this information," Zuri said, doing her best to be careful with her words. "Lea and I parted ways professionally over a month ago. There were never any complaints or allegations during her time at Beacon. I pride myself on maintaining a safe and respectful work environment for all our employees."

Cassandra's pen scratched across her notepad. "So you deny the allegations of retaliation towards Ms. Thompson for not getting along with Ms. Malone, who I believe runs the dance program?"

"There was no retaliation, but I would rather not discuss this further until I've spoken with my attorney."

Cassandra leaned forward, her green eyes sharp. "Are you aware of any reason Ms. Thompson might make such claims?"

Zuri clenched her jaw, the muscles in her neck tightening as she fought to maintain her composure.

"Ms. Wells, I understand you have a job to do, but I'm not comfortable speculating about Ms. Thompson's motivations," Zuri said, her voice cool and measured. "These allegations are unfounded. I've always conducted myself with the utmost professionalism and respect towards all of my employees and colleagues."

Cassandra nodded, scribbling in her notebook. "Yes, you've said that twice now. Do you think that these allegations, along with the trial of your godfather, might further tarnish the reputation of the studio?"

Zuri's temper flared at the mention of Francis. She leaned forward, her eyes narrowing. "I'm going to stop you right there. My godfather's legal troubles have nothing to do with me or my work. I won't be commenting on that situation and I would appreciate it if you didn't draw false parallels."

Cassandra opened her mouth to speak, but then seemed to think better of it. She placed the notebook down and raised her hands up. "I have a lot of respect for any woman who has managed to get a foothold like you have in such a male domi-nated industry. The journalist in me wants the scoop, but I also understand the need for discretion. Let's move on to something more positive, shall we?"

Zuri relaxed, but she remained on guard. "I appreciate that, thank you. What else would you like to discuss about Ellis Films or Beacon?"

Cassandra smiled, picking her notebook again. "Tell me about your latest project. I hear it's generating quite a buzz in the industry."

Grateful for the change in topic, Zuri launched into a passionate description of their upcoming film, a coming-of-age story set in New Orleans. She did her best not to let her mind wander, but she couldn't shake the knot of anxiety in her stomach over the questions about Lea's allegations.

Zuri was relieved as the interview wound down.

"Thank you for your time, Zuri," Cassandra said, gathering her things. "This was illuminating."

Zuri forced a smile, standing to shake Cassandra's hand. "Thank you for the opportunity. I look forward to reading the article."

As soon as the door closed behind Cassandra, Zuri slumped back into her chair, her head in her hands. She took several deep breaths, trying to calm her racing heart. The allegations from Lea had blindsided her, and she was sure this was only the beginning. She needed to get ahead of this before it spiraled out of control.

With trembling fingers, she pulled out her phone and called Marcus.

"Yo Z, everything okay?" He answered in his usual upbeat manner.

"Marcus," Zuri said, her voice tight with tension. "We've got a situation."

She filled him in on the interview and Lea's allegations, her words tumbling out in a rush.

"Whoa, slow down," Marcus interrupted. "Take a breath. We'll handle this."

Zuri inhaled, trying to calm her racing thoughts. "What do we do?"

"First things first, don't panic," Marcus said, his tone reassuring. "Have you received any formal notice of a complaint or lawsuit?"

"No, nothing," Zuri replied, rubbing her temple. "This came out of nowhere during the interview."

"Alright, that's good. It gives us some time to prepare. These are just allegations at this point. We need to gather all the facts before we make any moves."

"But what about the article? It's going to be published soon," Zuri pressed, her free hand fidgeting with a pen on her desk.

"I'll reach out to Apex's legal team," Marcus assured her. "We'll request to review any mentions of these allegations before publication. In the meantime, I need you to send me everything you have on Lea Thompson. Her employment records, any correspondence, everything."

Zuri nodded, despite Marcus being unaware of it. "I'll have HR send it over right away."

"Good. Now, is there anything, any interaction at all, that could be misconstrued as inappropriate?"

Zuri told him about their encounter a few years ago and how Lea made a pass at her the day she fired her.

Zuri's stomach churned as she recounted the events to Marcus. "I rejected her advances. Both times. But what if she twists it around?"

Marcus was silent for a moment, processing the information. "Okay, this might work in our favor. We need to be prepared for Lea to use these interactions against you, but it does bring into question her character. Did anyone else witness either of these encounters?"

Zuri wracked her brain. "No, we were alone both times. God, Marcus, this looks bad, doesn't it?"

"It's not ideal," Marcus admitted, his voice steady. "But remember, Zuri, you didn't do anything wrong. We'll fight this. For now, I need you to lie low. Don't speak to anyone about this, not even your family. And no contact with Lea."

"Okay. What's our next move?"

"I'm going to start building our defense. We'll need character witnesses, people who can vouch for your professionalism and integrity. I'll also look into Lea's background, see if there's any pattern of behavior we should be aware of. I'll also need to speak with Genesis about their interactions since she is mentioned as well."

After going over a few more things, Marcus reassured her and set up a time for them to meet once he knew more. As Zuri hung up the phone, she felt a wave of exhaustion wash over her. She glanced at the clock. It was barely noon, and already the day felt long.

Zuri tried to center herself. She couldn't let this situation derail her entire day. There was still work to be done, projects that needed her attention. With a determined set to her jaw, she turned to her computer and pulled up the latest script revisions for their New Orleans project.

The words swam before her eyes at first, her mind still reeling from the interview. But as she forced herself to focus, she gradually became absorbed in the story. The screenplay, a coming-of-age tale about a young jazz musician in the vibrant streets of New Orleans, was a passion project for Zuri. She lost herself in the vivid descriptions of the French Quarter, almost able to smell the heady scent of beignets and hear the sultry notes of a saxophone floating on the humid air.

As she worked through the script, making notes and suggestions, the knot in her stomach loosened. This was why she loved her job. The ability to bring stories to life, to transport audiences to different worlds and experiences. She spent the next few hours immersed in the world of jazz clubs and steamboats, of crawfish boils and second-line parades.

By late afternoon, Zuri had made significant progress on the script notes. She stretched, her back popping as she arched it, and glanced out the window. The sun was beginning to set, so she shut everything down and gathered her things.

She made the decision to see Genesis and discuss what was going on. Normally she would have told her she was coming, but Zuri knew if she mentioned it, then she would have to tell Genesis about the situation with Lea. That was something she preferred to discuss in person.

The drive across town gave her time to process, but her mind kept replaying the interview, analyzing every word and gesture. While Cassandra claimed she wasn't interested in the salacious nature of the allegations, Zuri was aware how these situations went. It was hard to resist a scoop as a journalist.

There was no way to tell what would come of the situation, but Zuri had only one thought in her mind; she was fucked.

# Chapter Twenty-Seven

When she arrived at Genesis' house, Zuri saw Shannon's car parked out front. A twinge of irritation flared in her chest, but she pushed it down. Shannon's stay would soon come to an end, so she had to let it go. After taking a deep breath, she plastered on a smile and knocked on the door.

Genesis opened it, her wild curls framing her face as she beamed at Zuri. "Hey, babe! I wasn't expecting you tonight. Everything okay?"

Zuri stepped inside, pulling Genesis into a tight hug. "Just a rough day. I needed to see you."

Genesis pulled back, concern etched on her face. "What happened?"

Before Zuri could answer, Shannon's voice floated in from the kitchen.

"Yo Gen, you want me to pop this garlic bread in the oven?"

"Yes, thanks Shannon. By the way, Zuri is here. She's going to join us."

Zuri's stomach clenched when Shannon sauntered into the living room, wearing a faded Spelman College t-shirt and yoga pants. She had a messy bun and a dish towel slung over her shoulder. The casual, at-home look struck Zuri like a physical blow.

"Hey, Zuri," Shannon said, her tone friendly but with an undercurrent of something Zuri couldn't quite place. "Good to see you. Joining us for dinner?"

Zuri forced a smile, her jaw clenching. "Looks like it," she replied, trying to keep her voice light.

As she watched Shannon move back to the kitchen, Zuri noticed how at home she seemed. The way Shannon confidently reached for the cabinet where the plates were kept without hesitation, how she was fully aware of Genesis' wine glasses' storage location–it all spoke of a deep familiarity that Zuri found unsettling. She'd lived there before. Of course she would be comfortable, but that didn't make it any less irritating.

Genesis turned back to Zuri and pulled her into the house, her brow furrowed with concern. "Come on, let's sit down and you can tell me what's going on."

They made their way to the living room, settling onto the plush couch. Zuri sank into the cushions as Genesis wrapped an arm around her shoulders.

"So, what happened?" Genesis asked as she stroked Zuri's hair.

Zuri leaned into Genesis' touch, drawing comfort from her presence. She took a deep breath, steeling herself to recount the day's events.

"I had that interview with Apex Magazine today," she began, her voice low. "It started off fine, but then..."

She trailed off as Shannon entered the room, a glass of wine in each hand. "Thought you ladies might need this," she said, offering the glasses with a smile.

Genesis accepted both glasses with a nod of thanks, handing

one to Zuri. Shannon lingered for a moment, her gaze flicking between them.

"I'll just... check on that garlic bread," she said, retreating to the kitchen.

Zuri took a long sip of wine, grateful for the heat that spread through her chest. She lowered her voice further. "The journalist blindsided me with questions about Lea. She's made allegations of harassment against me and named you as well in the suit."

Genesis' eyes widened in shock. "What? That's ridiculous!"

"That's what I said," Zuri sighed, running a hand through her locs. "But now it's out there. The journalist even tried to connect it to Francis' case, like there's some pattern of misconduct surrounding me."

Genesis squeezed Zuri's hand. "That's unfair. You're nothing like Francis, and you've always been professional with your employees."

"Yeah, but to the outside world, it will look like something else." Zuri blinked back tears. "Damn it, I've worked so hard for this Gen."

"I know, my love, we'll figure this out together, okay?"

Zuri nodded and leaned in to kiss Genesis, drawing strength from her support.

Shannon interrupted their moment, calling from the kitchen, "Dinner's ready!"

Zuri suppressed a sigh as they made their way to the dining room. The table was set for three, with a steaming dish of lasagna in the center surrounded by a crisp salad and golden garlic bread. Despite her stress, Zuri's stomach rumbled at the enticing aroma.

"This looks great, Shannon," Genesis said as they took their seats. "Thanks for cooking."

"No problem," Shannon replied with a smile. "It's the least I can do while I'm crashing here."

A pang of irritation washed over Zuri upon hearing Shannon's casual reference to staying at Genesis' place. She tried to push the feeling aside, reminding herself again that it was temporary.

As they ate, an awkward silence settled over the table. Zuri sensed Shannon's eyes on her, curious and a little wary. She focused on her food.

"So," Shannon said, breaking the silence, "how was everyone's day?"

Genesis glanced at Zuri, clearly unsure how much to share. Zuri forced a smile. "It was... eventful. How about yours, Shannon?"

Shannon shrugged, twirling pasta around her fork. "Mostly job hunting. It's difficult out there."

Zuri had almost forgotten that Shannon's presence was due to her financial situation. "I'm sure something will come up soon. You're talented."

Shannon's eyes snapped to Zuri's, a flicker of surprise in them. "Thanks, that's nice of you to say."

Zuri took another bite of lasagna, searching for a neutral topic of conversation.

"Genesis, how are the dance classes going at Beacon?" she asked, turning to her girlfriend.

Genesis' face lit up. "Oh, they're amazing! The girls are so talented and eager to learn. We're working on a showcase for next month."

As Genesis launched into an enthusiastic description of the upcoming performance, Zuri allowed herself to relax a little. She loved seeing Genesis so passionate about her work with the young dancers.

Shannon chimed in with questions about the choreography

and music choices, and Zuri found herself grudgingly impressed by her genuine interest and knowledge. It made sense. At one point they were together when Genesis was pursuing dance as a career.

As the meal progressed, the conversation flowed more easily. They discussed recent films, shared funny stories from their college days, and debated the merits of various Los Angeles neighborhoods. Despite her initial reservations, Zuri enjoyed the evening.

When they finished eating, Shannon stood to clear the plates. "I've got this," she said, waving off Genesis' attempt to help. "You two relax."

As Shannon disappeared into the kitchen, Genesis turned to Zuri. "See? It's not so bad having her here, is it?"

Zuri sighed. "I suppose not," she admitted. "But it's still… weird. It's like I'm intruding in my girlfriend's house."

Genesis waved her off. "You could never intrude, babe. This is your space, too. It's not ideal, but remember, it's temporary." She stood up and offered her hand. "How about we go upstairs and relax? I've got some episodes of Bones for us to watch."

"That sounds perfect," Zuri said, taking Genesis' hand and allowing herself to be led upstairs.

Once in the familiar space of Genesis' bedroom, Zuri calmed down. She kicked off her heels and shed her blazer, draping it over a chair.

As she pulled out the pajamas she kept there, Genesis went into the bathroom to brush her teeth but then returned, toothbrush in hand. It buzzed in her mouth as she watched Zuri change.

"Babe," Genesis began, her voice tinged with concern, "Why would Lea accuse you of harassment? I get that she's bitter about being fired, but you gave her a great severance package."

"Her anger goes deeper than just being mad at being fired. I never mentioned it, but at one point, she and I were pretty close."

"No, you never mentioned that. What do you mean by 'close'?"

Zuri sighed, sinking onto the edge of the bed. She patted the space beside her, inviting Genesis to join her.

"Lea and I have a history. There was always some flirtation, but we never went there. Then one night we were working late at her place, going over some grant proposals. There was this energy between us."

Genesis listened intently, her toothbrush forgotten in her hand. Zuri continued, her eyes fixed on a point in the distance as she recalled the memories.

"It started with innocent touches. A hand on the shoulder, knees brushing under the table. But that night, we kissed. It was electric. We both got caught up in the moment. This was while I was still dating Tracy, and you remember how messy that situation was."

Zuri paused, glancing at Genesis to gauge her reaction. Genesis's face was unreadable, but she nodded for Zuri to continue.

"Tracy and I weren't exclusive, so I allowed things to progress."

"Progress? Did you two have sex?"

Zuri shook her head. "No, I came to my senses, given our professional relationship. I made it clear to Lea that nothing was going to happen between us ever again, and I assumed we had both moved on."

Genesis was quiet for a long moment, processing this new information. When she spoke, her voice was controlled. "I see. And it never occurred to you to bring this up earlier?"

Zuri winced at the hint of hurt in Genesis' tone. "I should

have told you. It just... it seemed like ancient history. I never imagined it would come back to haunt me like this."

With a look Zuri couldn't read, Genesis got up and returned to the bathroom. She could hear her as she finished brushing her teeth and washing her face. This was, of course, her usual routine, but Zuri was aware that she was using that time to gather her thoughts.

When she was done and returned, the look on her face was no longer unreadable; Genesis was angry.

"You let me work with that woman for over a year and didn't think it was important to inform me about the nature of your relationship? When I mentioned her liking you, you played it off like I was being silly."

Zuri looked away when she saw the hurt and anger in Genesis' eyes. "It just seemed like it would complicate things. Lea and I had moved past it, and I didn't want to create any awkwardness between you two at work."

Genesis crossed her arms. "That wasn't your decision to make, Z. I had a right to know, especially if I was going to be working with her. Do you have any idea how hurtful this is? Like I've been made a fool of all this time."

"That was never my intention, I swear. I didn't want to hurt you or damage what we've been building."

Genesis sighed. "I understand that, but keeping secrets like this it does damage our relationship, Zuri. Trust is everything, and right now, I'm not sure I can trust that you've been honest with me about other things."

"Are you kidding me?" Zuri's heart was beating a mile a minute. "You say that to me while your ex-wife is living in your home. A little tidbit you shared with me after you decided to let her stay."

Genesis' eyes flashed with anger. "That's not the same thing, and you know it. Shannon and I have been divorced for years, and I've been upfront about our history and why she's staying here."

Zuri stood up, her own temper rising. "And I've been upfront about my past relationships, too. This was meaningless."

"Meaningless?" Genesis scoffed. "Clearly it wasn't if Lea is now suing you. This could impact your career, Zuri."

"I'm well aware of that. This whole Lea situation is because I was trying to protect you."

Genesis' eyes widened. "I never asked you to do that. In fact, I remember asking you to stay out of it, but you insisted."

"After you told me how she was treating you, what else could I do? When she made a pass at me, I realized she would never respect our relationship. So I let her go. I chose you."

Genesis let out a frustrated breath. "You inserted yourself into this situation because you need to be in control. I was handling Lea. It's just like when you took it upon yourself to offer to pay for my sister's schooling without even talking to me about it. You take up so much space and don't even think about who you might crush in the process. You can't be the orchestrator of everything. Life isn't one of your movies."

"Life isn't one of my movies? What the hell does that even mean?"

"It means you can't script everything, Zuri. You can't control every situation or person to fit your ideal narrative. Real life is messy and complicated."

"Is that how you see me? That I'm some kind of control freak who doesn't care about anyone else's feelings?"

"You care, but sometimes you act without considering the consequences."

"Wow." Zuri rubbed her hands over her face.

"Wait, did you say she made a pass at you?"

"Yes, that's what I said," Zuri replied, her voice tight. "The day I fired her, she tried to kiss me. I rejected her advances, of course."

Genesis threw her hands up in disbelief. "And you didn't think to mention that either? Zuri, this is what I'm talking about. You keep these important details to yourself, trying to protect me or handle things on your own, but all it does is create more problems. I got chastised for not mentioning dancing with some woman I met once, but you hid this whole situation from me."

Zuri's eyes flashed with anger. "I've been dealing with the stress of running a multi-million dollar company, trying to navigate the minefield that is Hollywood, all while supporting your dreams and ambitions. And now, on top of everything else, I'm facing these allegations. But sure, let's focus on the fact that I didn't tell you about a kiss that happened years ago!"

"Don't you dare try to trivialize this. And your career choice doesn't have anything to do with you being honest."

Zuri did her best to remain calm. "Everything I've done is for us! Can't you see that?"

"Lying to me was for us?" Genesis shot back. "All it's done is help create this mess we're in now. "

Zuri gripped the bedsheets to assuage her anger, but it bubbled over, anyway. "Nothing I do is ever good enough, is it? You want me to be present, but not too much. I'm supposed to show my love to you, but only in how you approve. If you decide on something, like letting your ex live with you in the home you shared as a married couple, I'm supposed to just smile and say 'of course babe, whatever you want,' without batting an eyelash. Who's the real control freak here, Gen? You won't even finalize a date for us to get married." She jabbed her finger toward the room Shannon was staying in. "When the hell will I stop paying the price for what she did to you?"

Genesis recoiled as if she'd been slapped. "That's not fair.

My hesitation about marriage has nothing to do with Shannon, and bringing her into this conversation is a low blow."

Zuri second-guessed what she was about to say, but her frustration overrode it. "Is it? Because from where I'm standing, it seems like she's always there, lurking in the background of our relationship. And now she's literally here, in your house."

Genesis opened her mouth to retort, but then seemed to change her mind.

"Z," she said, her voice low, "We both need to take a step back. It's been a long, emotional day for you, and now for both of us. Maybe we should just... go to bed. Get some rest. We can talk more in the morning when we're both calmer."

Zuri nodded, suddenly aware of how exhausted she felt. "Okay."

They prepared the bed, removing the extra pillows and pulling down the layers of the sheet and quilt. When Genesis turned off the lights, plunging the room into darkness save for the moonlight shining through the sheer curtains.

"Goodnight Z."

"Goodnight," Zuri replied, settling onto her side of the bed.

The silence between them was heavy, charged with unspoken words. Zuri stared at the ceiling, her mind racing despite her exhaustion. She could hear Genesis' breathing beside her, slightly uneven, and was sure she wasn't asleep either.

For the first time since they'd begun dating, they slept on opposite sides of the bed. The space between them felt like a chasm, wide and imposing. God only knew how they were going to cross it back to each other.

# Chapter Twenty-Eight

"Hey sis, you okay?"

Genesis looked over at Kenzie and gave her best smile. They'd arrived in Virginia shortly after 11am, ready for the family reunion their aunt and uncle told them about at the engagement party. They would be staying with them and were waiting on Lenny to pick them up.

Zuri had been on her mind, consuming her thoughts for the past week. The argument they had at her house replayed in her mind over and over, each word cutting deeper than the last. She wasn't sure how to process all the emotions that were still swirling inside of her.

They'd made promises to discuss what happened, but the following morning a crisis popped up at the office for her and Zuri was busy trying to keep the peace between Phillip Minor and, well, everybody. Before they knew it, the time for her trip had arrived and they still hadn't had their sit down. A small part of her hated to admit it, but she was happy to be away with something else to occupy her. The potential demise of her relationship with Zuri was too painful to dwell on.

"Yeah, I'm fine," Genesis replied, forcing a smile. "Just

thinking about work stuff. Most specifically, finding your replacement."

Kenzie raised an eyebrow, not buying Genesis's attempt at deflection. "Uh-huh. Work stuff. That's why you've been staring at your phone every five minutes, like it might sprout wings and fly away." They both laughed. "Whatever it is, let yourself enjoy this time. We're home sis."

"Yeah, we are."

As if on cue, a car horn honked outside. Genesis peered out the window to see their Uncle Lenny waving from his beat-up Chevy. They rolled away from the airport waiting area, and Lenny greeted them with open arms. As he helped get their bags in the back of the truck, Genesis ran her hands over the sides.

"How is it possible that you still have this beat up old truck?" Genesis turned to Kenzi. "He's owned this since I was a kid."

Genesis settled into the worn leather seat, the familiar scent of tobacco and pine air freshener washing over her. Uncle Lenny's hearty laugh filled the cab as he pulled away from the curb.

"This old girl has got plenty of life left in her," he said, patting the dashboard. "Ain't that right, Betsy?"

As they drove through the winding Virginia roads, Genesis relaxed for the first time in days. The lush green landscape and rolling hills were a pleasant change of pace. She closed her eyes, letting the breeze from the open window caress her face.

"So, what's new with you girls?" Uncle Lenny asked, his eyes meeting theirs in the rearview mirror. "Any exciting city life stories to share with your old uncle?"

Genesis hesitated, her mind going to Zuri. She opened her mouth to speak, but Kenzie beat her to it.

"I'll be attending law school, hopefully in the Fall. I got a high score on the LSAT," Kenzie said, unable to hide the excitement in her voice.

"That's fantastic news, Kenzie!" Uncle Lenny exclaimed, his face beaming with pride. "Your mama would've been so proud of you. She always said you had a sharp mind."

A sad smile appeared on Genesis's face at the mention of their mother. She'd been thinking about her a lot, wondering what advice she might have given about the Zuri situation.

"What about you, Gen?" Uncle Lenny asked, jolting her from her thoughts. "How's accounting treating you?"

Grateful for the distraction, she shared about her latest venture. "It's going great. We've been doing free tax prep for low income families as a way to give back. So many get scammed or end up paying money for simple tax returns that should be free. It's been rewarding, helping people navigate the system and get the refunds they deserve."

"That's my girl," Uncle Lenny said with pride. "Always thinking of others. Your mama had that same giving spirit."

Did she really think of others? It had been Zuri who inspired her to make the service available, and when she thought about it, the woman she loved very much resembled her mom in nature. *How have I never realized that before?*

The conversation flowed as they drove, catching up on family gossip and reminiscing about childhood summers spent in Virginia. By the time they pulled up to the old family home, Genesis felt more at ease.

As they climbed out of the truck, Genesis stopped in her tracks when she saw their grandmother sitting on the porch. Granny Lee sat regally on the swing, her silver hair catching the early afternoon sun like a halo. At 90 years old, she was still a striking figure, her deep mahogany skin smooth save for the laugh lines etched around her eyes and mouth. Those eyes, a rich amber color, were full of wisdom as they landed on Genesis and Kenzie.

She wore a vibrant yellow dress adorned with intricate African patterns, the fabric draping over her slender frame. Her hands, weathered by years of hard work but still graceful, rested on a carved wooden cane propped against her knees. A string of amber beads hung around her neck, a family heirloom passed down through generations.

As Genesis approached, she could smell the familiar scent of cocoa butter that always seemed to surround her grandmother. Granny's lips curved into a smile, revealing a set of perfectly maintained dentures.

"Well, look what the cat dragged in," she called out, her voice strong despite her advanced age. "Come, give your granny some sugar, girls."

They rushed up the creaking porch steps, enveloping their grandmother in a gentle but enthusiastic hug. As Genesis pulled back, she noticed the way Granny Lee's eyes lingered on her face, as if searching for something.

"What's troubling you, child?" Granny Lee asked. "I can see it in your eyes."

Of course, her grandmother could see right through her. "It's nothing. Just some work stress."

Granny Lee raised an eyebrow, not buying the excuse either. "Mm-hmm. Well, when you're ready to talk about it, I'll be here."

Genesis nodded, grateful for her grandmother's understanding. As they settled onto the porch, the scent of fried chicken and collard greens wafted from inside the house.

"I hope you girls are hungry," Uncle Lenny called out as he carried their bags inside. "Your Aunt's been cooking up a storm all day."

As if on cue, Aunt Rachel appeared in the doorway, wiping

her hands on her apron. "There are my favorite nieces!" she exclaimed, pulling them both into her embrace. "Come on in and get settled. Dinner will be ready soon."

As Genesis followed her aunt inside, a sense of comfort washed over her. The familiar sights and smells reminiscent of her childhood wrapped around her like a blanket. She hoped that coming home would bring the comfort Kenzie promised because she needed it now more than ever.

* * *

After they changed and settled into the guest room, Kenzie and Genesis made their way downstairs. Their cousins were coming by for an early dinner. Genesis was excited to see Grace, her one cousin that had been around when they were still close to the family. Having similar personalities and being of the same age, they had been as close as siblings, imitating the bond between their mothers.

The aroma of Aunt Rachel's cooking filled the house, making Genesis's mouth water as she descended the stairs. Laughter and chatter drifted from the kitchen, and she felt a flutter of excitement. Kenzie smiled back at her as they entered the large space.

When they stepped inside, two young women turned in their direction. They looked like Rachel at different ages. Genesis recognized them from the pictures her aunt and uncle had shared. Sophia was 30 with long gorgeous locs and a spattering of tattoos and piercings adorned her mocha colored face and arms. Lynn was a couple years younger and wore a chic short bob along with a more traditional style, not a tattoo or piercing to be found, other than the small hoop earrings in each of her ears.

Sophia stepped forward, arms outstretched.

"Well, if it isn't our long-lost cousins!" Sophia exclaimed, pulling Genesis into a hug. "It's about time you two made it down here."

Lynn joined in, embracing Kenzie with equal enthusiasm. "We've heard so much about you guys. It's like we already know you!"

As they exchanged greetings and introductions, Genesis relaxed into the easy camaraderie. The kitchen buzzed with activity as Aunt Rachel bustled around, putting the finishing touches on dinner.

"Alright, ladies," Aunt Rachel called out, "make yourselves useful and set the table. Dinner's almost ready."

They fell into an easy rhythm, laughing and chatting as they worked. Genesis shared stories about her life in the city, omitting any mention of Zuri. She wasn't ready to open that can of worms just yet.

As they settled around the large dining table, heaped with steaming dishes of soul food, Genesis gazed adoringly at her family. This was how dinners used to be when her mother was alive. Loud, chaotic, and filled with love.

Just as they began serving up the food, their cousin Isaac strolled in with his girlfriend, Isabel. He and Lynn were twins, but you'd never know it by looking at them. They were fraternal so where Lynn was petite and light-skinned, Isaac was tall and dark brown, with a muscular build that spoke of hours spent in the gym.

"Sorry we're late," Isaac said, flashing a charming smile. "Traffic was a nightmare."

Isabel, pretty with long dark hair, waved shyly. "I hope we didn't hold everyone up."

"Nonsense," Aunt Rachel said, ushering them to their seats. "We were just getting started. Grab a plate and dig in."

Isaac hugged Genesis and Kenzie as he introduced Isabel.

"It's amazing ya'll are here. I almost didn't believe Ma when she said your fiancée had reached out to her."

"That's right. You're engaged to a movie mogul, right?" Sophia asked as she bit into her chicken.

Genesis cleared her throat. "Uh, yes, Zuri. She wanted to come down as well, but had some work obligations."

Happy when the conversation moved on, the sound of a car playing rap music caught Genesis's attention. "Is that Grace?" she asked.

Lenny nodded. "Yup, Grace always has to make an entrance."

Genesis excused herself and hurried to the front of the house. She yanked the door open and bounded down the porch steps. Just as she got to the bottom, Grace slammed her car door shut and turned to her with flowers in hand.

Instead of the young girl that stood firm in Genesis' memory, a beautiful stud stood before her. Grace had a stylish fade haircut, with short sides and longer twists neatly styled on the top. She wore fitted jeans, a crisp white button-down shirt, and a sleek blazer that accentuated her athletic build. A gold watch glinted on her wrist, matching the small hoop earrings in her ears.

"Gen!" Grace exclaimed, her face lighting up with a wide smile. She rushed forward, enveloping Genesis in a tight hug. "God, it's been way too long!"

Genesis melted into the embrace. "Grace! Look at you, all grown up and looking fly!"

Grace pulled back, grinning as she handed Genesis one bunch of flowers. "I always get for mom, but I had to get you some too."

They linked arms and started walking towards the house.

"I can't believe the girl who wouldn't be caught dead without a dress is looking so dapper."

Grace chuckled, running a hand through her short hair. "Yeah, well, a lot's changed since we were kids. Turns out, I clean up pretty nice when I get to wear what I want. Mom was the main reason for my wardrobe back then. I hit my teens and decided it was time to be true to myself. Speaking of which, I hear you got yourself not one but two famous women under your belt."

Genesis felt her cheeks grow warm at Grace's comment. She swatted her cousin's arm. "Oh hush, you make it sound so scandalous. It's not like that at all."

"Oh? I want all the juicy details this weekend."

As they stepped onto the porch, Genesis paused, turning to face her cousin. "It's so good to see you. I've missed you."

Grace's expression softened, a hint of sadness flickering in her eyes. "I've missed you too, Gen. When we lost touch after... well, after everything, it was like I lost a sister."

Genesis nodded, understanding the weight of those words. "I should have reached out when I could, but so much time had passed. Somehow I'd convinced myself that Kenzie and I had been forgotten."

Grace squeezed Genesis's hand. "Never. You and Kenzie were always in our hearts. We just didn't know how to bridge that gap."

They shared a moment of silent understanding before Grace grinned and nudged Genesis's shoulder. "But hey, we're here now, right? Let's make up for lost time."

As they entered the house, the buzz of conversation and laughter enveloped them. Grace greeted everyone, hugging her parents, Kenzie and siblings, and Isabel.

Throughout dinner, Genesis stole glances at Grace, marveling at how much her cousin had changed yet remained the same. Grace's easy laugh and quick wit were just as she remembered, but there was a new confidence in her demeanor that Genesis admired.

As the meal wound down, Granny Lee cleared her throat, drawing everyone's attention. "Now that we're all here together, I want to say a little something."

The matriarch's amber eyes shone with emotion as she continued.

"Genesis, Kenzie, you two have been away from us for far too long. Your mother would be so proud of the women you've become." Granny Lee's voice wavered. "I know losing her was hard on all of us, but especially you girls. I want you to know that you've always had a home here, and always will."

Genesis blinked back tears, squeezing Kenzie's hand under the table. The room was silent, Granny Lee's words settling over everyone.

"Now," Granny Lee said, her tone lightening, "since y'all are here, we're going to make the most of this reunion. Welcome home, my babies."

The love in the room was palpable, and for a moment. She caught Kenzie's eye and saw her sister wiping away a tear.

"Thank you, Granny," Genesis said, her voice thick with emotion. "We've missed you all so much."

Aunt Rachel clapped her hands together. "Alright, who's ready for dessert? I made your favorite, Genesis, sweet potato pie!"

"Aunt Rachel, you didn't have to go to all that trouble!" Genesis said, trying not to cry.

"Nonsense," Aunt Rachel waved her off with a smile. "It's no trouble at all for my girls."

As Aunt Rachel bustled off to the kitchen to fetch the pie, conversation resumed around the table. Genesis found herself drawn into a discussion with Grace and Sophia about their careers and life in the city.

"So, Gen," Grace leaned in, "tell me more about this fiancée of yours."

Genesis hesitated at the mention of Zuri. She glanced around the table, noticing that several family members were now listening in curiously.

"Well," she began, trying to keep her voice steady, "Zuri is... she's amazing. She runs a film production company with her cousins. She's passionate, driven, and has the biggest heart."

Grace nodded. "Sounds like quite the catch. How'd you two meet?"

Genesis smiled, remembering their first encounter. "I went on vacation and ended up staying at the guest house on her estate. Things just... clicked between us."

Sophia chimed in, "And now you're engaged! That must be exciting. Have you set a date yet?"

Genesis felt her smile falter. The memory of how enthusiastic Zuri had been for the wedding and her reluctance seemed so ridiculous when she thought about it.

"We, uh, we're taking things slow. No date set yet."

She could see the curiosity in her cousins' eyes and knew they sensed there was more to the story. Grace, ever perceptive, gave her a knowing look.

"Well, whenever it happens, you better believe we'll all be there to celebrate," Grace said, changing the subject. "Not like any of us are getting married anytime soon, except for maybe Isaac."

Isaac looked up from kissing Isabel and gave Grace the stank eye. "Now why are you bringing me into this?"

"I'd love to get married," Isabel said with a big smile.

Sophia chuckled and began singing. "Isaac and Isabel sitting in a tree..."

"K-i-ss-ing," Lynn finished for her.

Isaac looked mortified, but Isabel was tickled. "Look, our names even go together, babe."

The family erupted into laughter as Isaac threw a dinner roll at Sophia. Genesis relaxed, grateful for the shift in conversation. Rachel returned with the sweet potato pie, the aroma filled the room, bringing back a flood of childhood memories.

Conversation shifted to plans for the rest of the weekend. There was talk of a family barbecue, a trip to the lake, and even whispers of karaoke night at the local bar.

"Oh, you have to come to karaoke!" Lynn exclaimed. "Grace here is the reigning champion. You should hear her belt out some Aretha."

Grace rolled her eyes good-naturedly. "Please, I'm not that good."

"Don't be modest," Sophia chimed in. "You've got pipes, girl."

Genesis looked over at Grace. "Is that so? I seem to remember a certain someone who used to be too shy to even sing in the shower."

Grace laughed, a slight blush creeping up her neck. "Yeah, well, things change. Maybe I'll even convince you to get up there and sing with me for old times' sake."

As the evening wore on, Genesis relaxed more and more. Her family's love and acceptance wrapped around her like a comforting blanket. She laughed at Isaac's corny jokes, swapped stories with Sophia about city life, and listened intently as Lynn shared about her latest art projects.

As the night grew late, the family dispersed. Sophia and Lynn headed home, while Isaac and Isabel retreated to his old room upstairs. Genesis found herself on the back porch with Kenzie, nursing a glass of sweet tea and watching fireflies dance in the yard.

"So," Genesis said, nudging Kenzie's shoulder. "I think it's my turn to ask why you've been so quiet tonight, Kenz?"

Kenzie sighed deeply, her fingers tracing the condensation on her glass. The chirping of crickets filled the silence between them as she gathered her thoughts.

"I've been... processing," Kenzie said, her voice barely above a whisper. "Being here, surrounded by all this love... it's beautiful, but it also hurts."

Genesis turned to face her sister, concern etched on her features. "What do you mean?"

Kenzie's eyes glistened with unshed tears in the porch light. "I'm angry at Mom for letting Dad take us away from all of this."

The words hung heavy in the air between them. Genesis felt her breath catch in her throat, unprepared for the raw emotion in her sister's voice.

"Every hug from Aunt Rachel, every laugh with Grace, every story from Granny Lee... it's like a knife twisting in my gut," Kenzie continued, her voice gaining strength. "We could have had this all along. We should have had this."

She stood up abruptly, placing her glass down and pacing the length of the porch. The old wooden boards creaked beneath her feet, a counterpoint to the intensity of her words.

"Do you remember how Dad used to talk about Mom's family? How he'd say they were 'too country,' 'too set in their ways'? They were heathens who didn't know how to serve the Lord?" Kenzie's hands were clenched at her sides. "And Mom just... let him. She let him dictate everything about our lives."

Genesis felt a wave of emotion wash over her as she listened to Kenzie's words. She reached out and took her sister's hand, guiding her back to sit on the porch swing.

"I remember," Genesis said. "I remember how Dad would get so angry whenever Mom mentioned visiting. How he'd quote scripture and talk about 'worldly influences.'"

Kenzie nodded, wiping away a stray tear. "And now we're here, and I can see how much we missed out on. All those years of family gatherings, holidays, just... being loved. How could she let him take that away?"

Genesis wrapped an arm around her sister's shoulders, pulling her close. "I don't think it was that simple, Kenz. You know how controlling Dad could be. And Mom... she wanted to keep the peace, to keep our family together."

"But at what cost?" Kenzie's voice cracked. "We lost so much time, Gen. So many memories we'll never get back."

Genesis pulled her sister into a tight embrace, Kenzie's body shook with silent sobs. She stroked her hair, just as she used to do when they were children and Kenzie had nightmares.

"I don't know, sis," Genesis whispered, her own voice thick with emotion. "I wish I had answers for you. For us."

They sat in silence for a moment, the weight of their shared history hanging between them. Genesis thought back to their childhood, to the rare moments when their mother would speak of her family with a wistful smile. She remembered the way Mom's eyes would light up when she told stories of summers spent in Virginia, only to dim again when Dad entered the room.

"I think," Genesis chose her words carefully, "that Mom did the best she could with the situation she was in. At some point, I'm sure she felt like she was in too deep to just leave. We'll never know the truth, but we're here now. You and Zuri did this and I'm so glad you weren't a coward like me."

Kenzie pulled away, wiping at her eyes. "You're not a coward, Gen. You were just trying to protect yourself, like Mom was."

"I should have been braver for both of us."

They sat in companionable silence for a few moments, letting the sounds of the night wash over them.

"You know, being here, surrounded by all this love, it makes me think about Zuri."

Kenzie turned to her, eyebrows raised. "Oh? How so?"

Genesis sighed, running a hand through her curls. "It's just... the way Aunt Rachel fusses over everyone, how Uncle Lenny always has a joke ready, how Granny Lee seems to see right through you... it reminds me of Zuri's family. Of how it felt to be around them."

"But that's a good thing, isn't it?" Kenzie asked.

Genesis felt tears prick at her eyes. "Yes, but it scares me," she admitted. "I haven't just been falling in love with Zuri. I've fallen in love with the idea of belonging to a family like this again."

Kenzie rubbed her arm. "And the other family you built fell apart as well. It must be scary to think about getting attached and then losing it all."

Startled, Genesis looked at Kenzie and felt a sudden rush of tears. Her sister was right. She had lost every family she had, including the one she made with her and Shannon. Sure Shannon was in her life again, but that didn't change that she felt like a failure.

Genesis nodded, wiping at her tears. "You're right. I'm terrified of losing it all again. With Zuri, with this family... I keep waiting for the other shoe to drop."

Kenzie squeezed her hand. "Gen, you can't live your life waiting for disaster. You deserve love and happiness."

"But what if I mess it up again?" Genesis whispered. "What if I'm not good enough?"

"Hey, look at me," Kenzie said, turning to face her sister. "You are more than good enough. You're kind, and one of the strongest people I know. Zuri is lucky to have you."

Genesis gave a watery smile. "Thanks, Kenz. You know, being here, seeing how welcoming everyone is... it makes me realize how much I want this with Zuri. A family, a home, a place to belong."

Kenzie nodded. "So, what are you going to do about it?"

Genesis took a deep breath, a sense of clarity washing over her. "I'm going to fight for it. For us. No more running away."

Just then, Grace poked her head out the back door. "Hey, y'all down for a game of Monopoly? Isaac's talking trash and we need to put him in his place."

Genesis and Kenzie shared a look, a silent understanding passing between them. The heavy conversation of moments ago dissipated like mist in the morning sun.

"You know what? That sounds perfect," Genesis said, standing up and offering a hand to her sister. "Ready to show these country folk how we do it in the city, Kenz?"

Kenzie grinned, taking Genesis's hand and pulling herself up. "Oh, you know it. Isaac won't know what hit him."

As they walked back into the house, laughter enveloped them. This weekend was already proving to be what she needed - a reminder of where she came from and the future she hoped to build with Zuri by her side.

# Chapter Twenty-Nine

Zuri's car glided through the bustling streets of downtown LA, the tinted windows a shield against the world outside. Her manicured fingers tapped an anxious rhythm on the steering wheel as she navigated through traffic, her mind a whirlwind of thoughts. Lea's lawsuit hung over her like a dark cloud, threatening to tarnish everything she'd worked so hard to build.

As she pulled into the parking garage of the towering glass and steel building that housed Marcus's law firm, Zuri's phone chimed. Her heart leapt, hoping it might be Genesis, but it was just a calendar reminder. She sighed, the ache in her chest intensifying. Other than a brief message letting her know she'd arrived in Virginia, Gen was M.I.A. It didn't surprise her; they had parted on shaky ground. Despite saying they would talk about what happened, they'd chosen to tiptoe around it and ultimately left things unresolved.

Having a disagreement wasn't the sign of a poor relationship, but Zuri wondered if Genesis was happy. It was like everything she tried to do just wasn't good enough and while she was doing her best to make work less of a priority; it would always be an issue. What was she supposed to do about that? Film was her life, and she needed someone who didn't always need to be the center of her world. She loved Genesis with all her heart, but maybe that love just wasn't enough.

Zuri's heels clicked against the polished marble floor as she strode through the lobby of Marcus's law office. The crisp air conditioning was a welcome respite from the sweltering Los Angeles heat outside, but it did little to cool her anxiety.

As the elevator ascended, Zuri's mind drifted back to Genesis. The memory of their argument still stung, sharp and raw. They had both said hurtful things, but Zuri remembered the look of betrayal on Genesis' face and the memory made her ill. The foolishness of hiding anything from her girlfriend now seemed glaringly obvious. Genesis valued honesty above all else, and Zuri had broken that trust.

The elevator dinged, jolting Zuri from her reverie. She smoothed her tailored blazer and stepped into the reception area, where Marcus's assistant greeted her with a sympathetic smile.

"He's ready for you, Ms. Baker," the young woman said, gesturing toward the corner office.

Marcus rose from behind his imposing mahogany desk as Zuri entered. His charcoal suit was impeccable, and his salt-and-pepper hair neatly trimmed. He exuded an air of calm competence that Zuri desperately needed right now.

"Zuri," he said, extending his hand. "Always a pleasure. Though I wish it were under better circumstances."

Zuri shook his hand and sank into the plush leather chair across from his desk. "What's the latest, Marcus? Please tell me you have good news."

Marcus's expression tightened, and Zuri's heart sank. "I'm afraid Lea's legal team is pushing hard. They're claiming breach of contract and emotional distress. The numbers they're throwing around... well, let's just say they're astronomical."

Zuri closed her eyes, the weight of it all pressing down on her. "This could ruin everything," she said, feeling defeated.

"It's not over yet. We have some strong counterarguments, and I've got a few tricks up my sleeve. Is there anything else that could come out during this process?"

"No, I told you everything. All I can add is that Lea continued to be flirtatious with me over the years and I just brushed it off. The work environment was uncomfortable for me, if anyone. She was fine until Genesis started working there."

"This is good," Marcus said, typing into his computer. His fingers flew across the keyboard, brow furrowed in concentration. "This information about Lea's behavior could be useful. It paints a different picture than the one she's trying to present."

Zuri felt a glimmer of hope. "So, what comes next?"

Marcus leaned back in his chair. "We need to gather more evidence to support your side of the story. Witness statements from other employees who might have observed Lea's behavior would be invaluable. And we need to prepare you for a potential deposition. Genesis already gave me her statement about their interactions."

The word 'deposition' sent a chill down Zuri's spine. The thought of having to relive every uncomfortable moment, every misunderstanding, under the scrutiny of Lea's lawyers was daunting.

Zuri's heart clenched at the mention of Genesis. "How did that go?" she asked, trying to keep her voice steady.

"Genesis was very thorough and professional. Her statement corroborates your account of events, which strengthens our case."

Zuri nodded, a mix of relief and longing washing over her.

Even now, with everything going on, Genesis was still supporting her. The realization made her chest ache with renewed intensity.

"That's good," she managed, blinking back the sudden moisture in her eyes.

"Hey Z, I'm confident that we will make this go away quick. I've dealt with situations like this before and quite frankly, there isn't much money can't solve."

Zuri nodded, forcing herself to compartmentalize her emotions. "You're right. What do you need from me?"

"I need you to go through your emails, text messages, any communication you've had with Lea. We're looking for anything that might support our claim that her behavior was inappropriate, or that you were uncomfortable. The more we can turn this into a case of she said-she said they'll be more open to settling."

For the next hour, Zuri and Marcus pored over documents, strategizing their approach. By the time she left his office, Zuri was exhausted. The legal battle ahead would be grueling, but at least she had a plan.

* * *

That evening, Zuri had dinner with her parents, grateful for the invitation from her mother. As soon as she pulled into the driveway, the front door swung open before she could even knock, revealing her mother's warm smile.

"There's my girl," Veronique said, pulling Zuri into a tight hug as soon as she made it to the door. "Come in, come in. Dinner's almost ready."

Zuri followed her mother into the house. The aroma of jerk chicken and rice and peas made her mouth water. Her father, Frederick, looked up from his newspaper in the living room.

"Hey, baby girl," he said, rising to give her a hug. "How are you holding up?"

Zuri forced a smile. "I'm managing, Daddy. One day at a time."

Veronique bustled around the kitchen, adding the finishing touches to the meal. "Zuri, honey, set the table, would you? How's Genesis? I'm sorry she couldn't come. We always enjoy having you girls over."

Zuri winced as she reached for the plates. "She's in Virginia for a family reunion."

"That's right. I remember her mentioning it. I look forward to hearing about it when she gets back."

The affection between her mom and Genesis was incredibly heartwarming, surpassing all her wildest dreams. While her mom had been indifferent about Tracy, she embraced Genesis with open arms and took her in as if she were another daughter. Knowing Genesis' history, Zuri was aware that it meant a lot to her.

After arranging the plates on the table, Zuri helped her mom plate the food. They all sat and ate. Having skipped lunch, Zuri devoured the food and got up to get seconds.

"This is so good," she said as she took her seat.

Veronique refilled their wine glasses. "Your father has been taking cooking classes for the past month."

Zuri smiled at the thought of her father in a cooking class, apron on and wooden spoon in hand. "Well, it's paying off. I might have to start coming over for dinner more often."

Her father chuckled. "You're always welcome, baby girl. Though I suspect you might have other dinner plans these days," he said with a knowing look.

The mention of her relationship triggered a small pang in her chest. She took a sip of wine and changed the subject. "I've been having quite a time working with Phillip Minor. He agreed to the lead actor I wanted, but in so many little ways he's being difficult. I've had to get him back in line several times."

Frederick sipped his wine and sighed. "Phillip has always been eccentric. He's a brilliant director, but insufferable. You're handling him well. The only thing he responds to is directness. Once you've earned his respect, all the nonsense will calm down."

Zuri nodded in agreement, grateful for the change of subject. "You're telling me. I thought he was going to walk out when I insisted on keeping William. But once he saw him perform, even he couldn't deny his talent."

"That's wonderful, honey," her mother said, reaching over to pat Zuri's hand. "I'm so proud of you. Running a film company isn't easy."

Zuri blushed at the compliment. "Thanks, Mom. It's challenging, but I love it. Even when I have to deal with diva directors and their ridiculous demands."

Her father chuckled. "Speaking of demands, your mother here has been making some of her own lately. She wants me to take ballroom dancing classes with her next."

"Oh, Fred," Zuri's mother said. "Stop acting like you aren't excited about it."

Zuri smiled at her parents' banter. It was moments like these that made her miss Genesis even more. She wondered what Gen was doing right now, if she was thinking about her, too.

"So, when is Genesis coming back?" her mother asked, as if reading Zuri's thoughts.

Zuri hesitated, pushing her food around on her plate. "I'm not sure. We haven't talked much since she left."

Her parents exchanged a glance filled with concern.

"It's okay to admit if you're going through something. Your mother and I aren't going to judge," Frederick said.

"God knows, we've been through our fair share of ups and downs," Veronique added, her lips turned down. "But that's relationships."

Zuri sighed, setting down her fork. Her parents meant well, but discussing her relationship troubles wasn't how she'd planned to spend the evening. Still, maybe talking about it would help.

"It's just... complicated," she began. "Genesis and I, we love each other, but sometimes it's like we're speaking different languages. She wants me to be less focused on work, but my career is such a big part of who I am. And now with this new film project.."

Her mother nodded. "It's always a challenge to balance work and relationships, especially in our industry. Have you talked to Genesis?"

Zuri shook her head. "Yes. She told me how she felt about it and I promised to do better. But then I hid something from her and we got into this huge argument. I threw in her face how frustrated I was that she wouldn't plan our wedding. Anyway, we've been tiptoeing around each other. And now, with her being away, there's this growing distance between us."

Her father leaned forward, his expression serious. "Zuri, communication is key in any relationship. You can't expect Genesis to understand your perspective if you don't share it with her. And vice versa."

"We have talked but there's still so much to be said. What if we talk and realize we want different things? What if this is all just too much for her?"

"Then at least you'll know," her mother said gently. "Honey, you can't live in fear of what might happen. You should be honest with Genesis and with yourself."

After dinner and dessert, Zuri cleaned up the kitchen while

her parents relaxed. Once finished, she proceeded to the living room to say goodnight, only to discover her father alone.

"Hey dad, where's mom?"

Frederick looked up from his phone, his glasses tilted on the bridge of his nose. "She's lying down. I was thinking we could go into the backyard and smoke a couple of cigars. My buddy Wendell got me a new batch and they are perfect."

"I can't say no to you, old man," Zuri replied with a smile.

Zuri followed her father out to the backyard, the evening air enveloping them as they stepped onto the patio. Frederick retrieved two cigars from a small humidor on the outdoor table, handing one to Zuri.

As they settled into the comfortable patio chairs, Frederick lit his cigar, then passed the lighter to Zuri. She took a moment to savor the rich aroma before lighting her own.

Zuri stared at the end of the cigar as it lit up and burned. "It's like my world's on fire right now, Dad." She told him about the issue with Lea. "Did I do the wrong thing getting rid of her?"

Frederick took a long draw on his cigar, the ember glowing in the twilight. He exhaled, the smoke curling up into the evening air.

"That's a complicated situation, baby girl," he said, his voice low and thoughtful. "But from what you've told me, it sounds like you made the best decision you could with the information you had. Lea's behavior was unprofessional and created a hostile work environment. You had to protect yourself and Beacon."

Zuri nodded, taking a puff of her own cigar. The rich, earthy flavor helped calm her nerves. "I understand that logically. But now with this lawsuit... I can't help but second-guess everything."

Frederick reached over and patted her knee. "That's

natural. But don't let it consume you. You're a smart, capable woman, Zuri. You've built something incredible with Beacon. Don't let one setback make you doubt yourself."

They sat in companionable silence for a few moments, the only sound the gentle chirping of crickets and the occasional puff of their cigars.

"I have to ask you," Frederick began, puffing contentedly, "is the issue you're having with the woman at Beacon part of why you and Genesis are on the outs?"

Zuri shook her head vigorously. "That issue is just a symptom of my need to control things, according to Genesis anyway."

"Genesis might have a point there. You've always had a strong need for control, even as a little girl. Remember when you used to organize your stuffed animals by size and color?"

Zuri chuckled, the memory bringing a smile to her face. "Yeah, I guess some things never change."

"But some things do," her father said, his tone growing serious. "Zuri, relationships require compromise and flexibility. You can't control everything, especially not another person's feelings or actions."

Zuri took a long drag on her cigar, letting the smooth smoke fill her lungs before exhaling. "It's just... hard sometimes. I'm used to being in charge, but with Genesis, it's different. I want to make her happy, but I also need to be true to myself."

Frederick reached out and patted her hand. "That's the challenge, isn't it? Finding that balance. But let me tell you something. The most rewarding things in life often come from letting go a little. Your mother and I, we've had our share of disagreements but we've learned to bend without breaking."

Zuri nodded, considering her father's words. "How do you do it? When do you stand your ground and when do you compromise?"

Frederick chuckled, taking another puff of his cigar before answering. "There's no simple answer, sweetheart. It's something you learn over time, through trial and error. But I can tell you this - when you love someone, compromise doesn't feel like losing. It feels like growing together. Your way isn't always going to be right, sometimes it's necessary to change your approach."

Zuri mulled over what was said, the smoke from her cigar curling in the night air. "I do love her, Dad. I'm so scared that I'm going to mess this up."

"That's how you know it's real. Love isn't always comfortable. It challenges us, pushes us to be better versions of ourselves." Her father put his cigar down and folded his hands. "Speaking of better versions of ourselves, I got a call from Francis' lawyer."

"I'm guessing the same one I got?"

Frederick chuckled bitterly. "That fool wanted me to write a character letter for him. I guess he's trying to get the people he knows to vouch for him being a good guy."

"It's crazy that he thinks any of us would support him."

Frederick shook his head, his expression a mix of disbelief and disgust. "The audacity of that man never ceases to amaze me. I told his lawyer in no uncertain terms that I would do no such thing."

"Good," Zuri said firmly. "He doesn't deserve any help, especially not from you."

Her father nodded, taking another puff of his cigar. "It got me thinking, though. About forgiveness, about the choices we make and the consequences we face."

Zuri raised an eyebrow. "You're not considering forgiving him, are you?"

Frederick laughed, a deep, rumbling sound that echoed in the quiet night. "No, baby girl. Some things are beyond forgiveness. But it reminded me of how important it is to cherish the good people in our lives. Do not take them for granted."

Zuri thought of Genesis. "I hear you, Dad. I do."

After saying goodbye to her parents, Zuri drove home, her father's words echoing in her mind. As she entered her empty house, the silence was oppressive.

Exhausted, the only thing she wanted to do was sleep, but after a quick shower, her mind was still racing.

She picked up her phone, ready to call Genesis and end the torture, but then thought better of it. Sometimes, like her dad had said, it was necessary to try a different approach. So, she picked up the notebook and pen she kept beside her bed and began to write.

# Chapter Thirty

The family reunion kicked off early Saturday morning with a flurry of activity. The aroma of bacon, eggs, and freshly brewed coffee wafted through the house, drawing sleepy-eyed relatives from their beds. Genesis found herself in the kitchen, laughing with aunt Rachel as they flipped pancakes and swapped stories.

As the day progressed, more family members arrived, filling the house and spilling out onto the sprawling backyard. Colorful tents dotted the landscape, providing shade from the Virginia sun. The air was thick with the scent of barbecue, the sound of soulful music, and the joyous laughter of children playing.

Genesis watched in awe as her family tree came to life before her eyes. There were cousins she hadn't seen since childhood, now with families of their own. Great-aunts and uncles regaled the younger generation with tales of their youth.

Mingling with her relatives was fun for Genesis. The sense of belonging she'd been missing for so long was seeping back in. She laughed at inside jokes, marveled at how much the kids had grown, and found herself drawn into heated debates about everything from politics to the best way to make potato salad.

Throughout the day, Genesis kept finding herself gravitating towards Grace. They fell back into their old rapport, finishing each other's sentences and cracking up over shared memories. During a lull in the festivities, they snuck away to the old treehouse in the backyard, a sanctuary from their childhood days.

"Remember when we used to hide up here for hours?" Grace asked, running her hand along the weathered wood.

Genesis nodded, a wistful smile on her face. "Yeah, it was our secret clubhouse. No boys allowed."

Grace chuckled. "Well, that rule stuck for both of us.

They shared a look and broke into a fit of laughter.

After a quick knock, Kenzie popped her head inside. "Hey, can ya'll come out here and redeem me because Renee and I aren't vibing, "Kenzie said with a grimace.

Genesis and Grace exchanged a mischievous glance. "Oh, we got your back, little cuz," Grace said, a competitive glint in her eye.

"Come on, let's go show these amateurs how it's done," Genesis added, already climbing down from the treehouse.

They made their way back to the main gathering, where a heated Spades game was in full swing. Ricky, one of their second cousins, was gloating over his latest win.

"Alright, alright," Genesis called out, rolling up her sleeves. "Time for some actual competition. Grace and I are about to school you all."

A chorus of "oohs" and playful trash talk erupted as Genesis and Grace took their seats. She and Grace had spent countless summer evenings perfecting their Spades strategy, developing a near-telepathic connection in the game.

Several hands in the tide turned. Grace's strategic bidding

and Genesis's ability to read her opponents had Ricky and Marcus on the defensive. The crowd around their table grew as word spread about the intense game. Genesis and Grace were in their element, exchanging subtle nods and winks as they dominated hand after hand.

"Boom! That's game!" Grace exclaimed, slapping down the last card with a flourish. The onlookers erupted in cheers and good-natured ribbing as Ricky and Marcus conceded defeat. Genesis high-fived Grace, their faces flushed with excitement.

As the day wore on, Genesis drifted towards the quieter corners of the gathering. It was overwhelming, although she was more than happy to be there. She just wished her mom could have been as well.

"What's up, you okay?" Grace asked, plopping beside her on the grass.

Genesis picked at the grass underneath her hand. "Yeah, lots of emotions right now."

"Mom said they could use some more drinks. Want to head into town with me, take a breather?"

"Yes, please."

Grace jumped up and pulled Genesis with her. In their search for Kenzie, they found her dancing the electric side to the cookout favorite Before I Let Go by Frankie Beverly and Maze.

"Kenz, we're going to the store."

Kenzie waved them off, too engrossed in her dance moves to respond verbally. Genesis and Grace chuckled as they headed to Grace's car.

The drive into town was quiet, both women lost in their thoughts. As they pulled into the parking lot of the local grocery store, Grace squeezed Genesis' hand.

"You know, I'm glad you came. It wouldn't have been the same without you."

Genesis smiled. "I'm glad I came too. It's been... healing, in a way."

They grabbed a couple of twelve packs of soda and a few more items people had requested. When they finished paying and got back into the car, Grace turned to Genesis with a mischievous grin.

"There's a local bar we can stop into for a drink. It's a dive, but I know the owner and she'll give us at least a couple of drinks on the house."

Genesis chuckled. "Won't they notice we're missing?"

"Please, there's like a hundred relatives at the house. We can be gone for an hour or two."

"Sure, why not?"

Grace pulled off and drove for several minutes before pulling up to a small juke joint with a flashing sign that said Terry's. It was tiny and didn't look like much on the outside, but when they stepped inside, they were met by a wooden interior with decorations and plants everywhere. There were a few bar stools, an occupied pool table, and several booths and tables. The place was packed.

"Ay yo Terry," Grace called as she stepped up to the bar.

Genesis expected a man to respond, but a tall, slender woman with salt-and-pepper hair turned around, her face lighting up at the sight of Grace.

"Well, if it isn't my favorite troublemaker!" Terry exclaimed, reaching over the bar to give Grace a hug. "And who's this lovely lady you've brought with you?"

"This is my cousin Genesis," Grace introduced. "Gen, this is Terry. She owns this fine establishment and makes the best damn cocktails in the state."

Terry extended her hand to Genesis. "Any family of Grace's is family to me. What can I get you ladies?"

"Two of your special margaritas, please," Grace requested, winking at Genesis. "Trust me, you're gonna love it."

As Terry bustled away to mix their drinks, Genesis leaned in close to Grace. "So, how do you know Terry? She seems cool."

Grace chuckled. "Terry's been like a second mom to me since I came out. This place is kind of a safe haven for queer folks in the area. I started coming here when I was barely legal, and Terry always looked out for me."

It was touching to see this side of Grace's life, to know she had found support and community.

Terry returned with two vibrant, salt-rimmed glasses. "Here you go, ladies. On the house, of course."

Genesis took a sip and her eyes widened. The margarita was perfectly balanced, with a hint of spice that lingered on her tongue. "Wow, this is amazing," she said, taking another sip.

Grace grinned. "Told you. Terry's a magician behind the bar."

They settled into a cozy booth, sipping their drinks and chatting. The familiar sounds of the jukebox and clinking glasses created a soothing backdrop.

"So," Grace said, leaning forward with a glint in her eye. "Tell me about Zuri."

Zuri took another sip of her margarita, savoring the flavors as she gathered her thoughts.

"She is incredible. Passionate, driven, and so giving. And she listens, like no matter what I want to talk about, she wants to hear it."

Grace leaned in, intrigued. "Sounds like someone's smitten. How did you two meet?"

Genesis shared their love story in more depth than she had the night before. Before, it was like she needed to hide how everything went down, but the messiness of it all was one element of it. She no longer felt shame. They were human and had learned from it all.

"Wow," Grace said, leaning back with a low whistle. "That's quite a story. Sounds like you two have been through a lot already."

Genesis nodded, tracing the rim of her glass. "We have. But it's worth it, you know? Zuri... she makes me feel alive in a way I haven't in a long time. How about you? Anyone special in your life?"

A hint of sadness creeped into her eyes. "There was someone," she began, her voice low. "Her name was Amara. We met at a photography exhibit in Richmond about a year ago. She was this vibrant, free-spirited artist with wild curls and the most captivating laugh I'd ever heard."

Grace paused, taking another sip of her drink. "I fell hard and fast. For six months, it was pure bliss. We'd have picnics in the botanical gardens, feeding each other strawberries and reading poetry. She painted my portrait once, capturing me in swirls of blues and purples. Said it represented the depth of my soul." She let loose a sad chuckle. "Then one day she didn't show up for a date, and blamed it on getting caught up with her art. That 'art' turned out to be a woman named Danielle."

Genesis reached across the table, squeezing Grace's hand. "Oh Grace, I'm so sorry. That must have been devastating."

"It was, but I've gotten used to the heartbreak at this point. I just haven't found the right person," Grace sighed, finishing her drink. "But enough about my sad love life. Tell me more about Zuri. You two are still going strong?"

Genesis hesitated, her fingers tracing patterns on the condensation of her glass. "We had a bit of a rough patch recently. Coming here is helping to clear my head."

Grace's eyebrows shot up. "Oh? What happened?"

"It's complicated. There was a misunderstanding, some

trust issues. We both said things we didn't mean. I feel silly right now even talking about it. Here you are still searching and I'm complaining about finding someone who loves me."

"Hey, don't do that. Your feelings are valid, no matter what anyone else is going through. Relationships can be a lot even when you've found the right person."

Terry interrupted their conversation when she appeared with two more full glasses. "I saw you two were running low."

"See, that's why I love this woman," Grace said, pulling Terry in for a kiss on the cheek.

"Hey now, I don't want anyone else getting ideas. I'm looking for my next wife."

"Next one?" Genesis asked.

Grace raised up two fingers, indicating Terry had been married twice already.

"Yup, I'm ready for number 3," Terry said with a grin.

"How can you be so optimistic if you've already done it twice?" Genesis slapped her hand over her mouth. "I'm sorry, that sounded awful."

Terry shook with laughter. "No offense taken, honey. Love is like good whiskey - it gets better with age, and sometimes you gotta try a few different brands before you find the one that hits you just right. Life's too short to give up on love. Each relationship teaches you something, even when it ends. My first wife taught me patience, my second taught me forgiveness. Who knows what the third will bring?"

Grace nodded, raising her glass. "To lessons learned and love yet to come!"

They clinked glasses. Genesis thought about Zuri, about the difficulties they'd weathered together. Maybe their recent rough patch was just another lesson, another opportunity to grow stronger together.

* * *

When they returned to the house, the party was still in full effect. Genesis mingled some more, catching up with a few of the elders who shared stories with her and Kenzie about their mother.

Late in the evening, Genesis sat on a bench facing a large oak tree in a corner of the backyard. A plaque with her mother's name and birth and death dates was attached. The distant sounds of laughter and music created a comforting backdrop as she lost herself in thought. She barely noticed when Granny Lee settled beside her.

"You ready to talk now, child?" Granny Lee said, her voice gentle.

Genesis turned to her grandmother, seeing the wisdom and understanding in those deep brown eyes. "I was just thinking about... everything. How much I've missed, how much has changed."

"Well, this is a time for reflection if there ever was one." Granny Lee nodded towards the tree. "Your mama was sprinkled around this tree. I like to think the flowers that bloomed around are a part of her."

After her parents were cremated, Genesis had sent her mother's ashes to Granny Lee. It seemed only fair that her mother should go home in death.

Genesis gazed at the tree, imagining her mother's essence nourishing its roots. "I wish she could see us now," she whispered.

Granny Lee patted her hand. "Oh, she sees, honey. She sees."

They sat in comfortable silence for a moment before Granny Lee spoke again. "So, what's really troubling you. I can see it in your eyes, just like I could with your mama."

Genesis took a deep breath, the weight of her worries pressing down on her. "It's... it's about Zuri," she admitted, her voice barely above a whisper.

"Ah, the movie mogul," Granny Lee nodded. "What's going on with you two?"

Genesis poured out the entire story. The argument, the miscommunication, the fear that she might lose the woman she loved.

Granny Lee listened, her weathered hands clasped in her lap. When Genesis finished, she turned to face her grand-daughter.

"Love ain't easy," she said, her voice filled with years of wisdom. "It's messy and complicated and sometimes it hurts like hell. But when it's real, when it's worth fighting for, you don't give up at the first sign of trouble."

Genesis nodded, tears pricking at the corners of her eyes. "I know, Granny, everyone keeps saying that. But what if I've already messed things up beyond repair?"

Granny Lee shook her head. "Child, if there's one thing I've learned in my 90 years, it's that nothing is beyond repair if both people are willing to put in the work. You love this woman?"

"More than I've ever loved anyone," Genesis admitted.

"Then fight for her," Granny Lee said firmly. "Your mama didn't raise you to run from your problems. She taught you to face them head-on."

Her grandmother was right, running away had solved nothing.

Granny Lee let out a deep sigh. "You know I don't want to speak ill of the dead, but your daddy took my Lynn away from here and it took me a long time to forgive him for that. But what I came to understand is that she was looking for someone outside of herself for love." Her eyes took on a faraway look. "Lynn was always searching for something, even as a little girl.

She had so much love to give, but she didn't know how to love herself first. When your daddy came along, all charm and big dreams, she thought he could fill that emptiness inside her."

Genesis recognized some of herself in that description. "But it wasn't real, was it?"

"Oh, your daddy loved her in his own way," Granny Lee whispered. "But love built on shaky foundations can't weather the storms of life. Your mama learned that the hard way."

Genesis nodded, remembering the volatile relationship her parents had. There had been passionate highs and devastating lows.

"I'm afraid of making the same mistakes," Genesis said, her voice trembling.

Granny Lee squeezed her hand. "Then don't. Learn from them. Love yourself first and let that love overflow to others. You'll be able to know and receive the right kind of love for you. That's the kind that lasts."

Tears welled up in Genesis's eyes as she thought about her mother's journey. "Do you think she was happy in the end?"

Granny Lee smiled, a bittersweet expression on her face. "I like to think that she found peace. And I know she loved you girls more than anything in this world."

Genesis hugged Granny Lee from the side, drawing comfort from her presence.

"Thank you," she whispered. "For everything."

"That's what family's for, sweetheart. Now why don't you go to your room? There's something waiting there for you."

Genesis looked at her grandmother in surprise. "How did you—"

Granny Lee just winked and shooed her away with a wave of her hand. "Go on now. Don't keep love waiting."

With a small laugh and a quick hug, Genesis made her way to the house. She climbed the stairs to the guest room, her heart pounding with anticipation. On her pillow was an envelope addressed to her. She recognized Zuri's handwriting right away.

Her hands trembled as she picked up the envelope. She traced her fingers over Zuri's elegant handwriting, her heart racing as she opened the envelope and unfolded the letter inside.

*My dearest Genesis. I hope this letter finds you well and enjoying your time with family. I know we left things unsettled, and the weight of our unfinished conversation has been heavy on my heart.*

Genesis sank onto the bed, her fingers tracing the curves of Zuri's handwriting as she continued to read.

*These past days, without you, have been a stark reminder of how integral you've become to my life. The silence in my home is deafening, and I find myself turning to share a thought or a laugh, only to remember you're not here.*

Tears welled up in Genesis's eyes as she read on, her heart aching with each word.

*It's not possible to go back to the beginning, but maybe if we go back to where it started, we can find each other again. Will you meet me in Barbados?*

Genesis didn't hesitate and dialed Zuri's number right away.

As soon as she picked up, she yelled her answer, "Yes, I'll meet you in Barbados?"

Zuri's soft laughter spilled out of the phone. "Really? You'll come?"

"Of course I will," Genesis replied, her voice thick with emotion. "I love you, Zuri. I don't want to lose what we have."

There was a pause, and Genesis could almost hear Zuri's smile through the phone. "I love you too, Gen. More than I can put into words."

They spent the next few minutes discussing logistics - when Genesis would fly out, where they'd meet. She was taken aback when Shannon's voice came from the background, asking if Zuri wanted something else to drink.

"Are you with Shannon?"

"Yeah, I came by the house so she and I could talk. I figured if she's going to be in your life, then I need to get to know her better. She's pretty cool."

The fact that Zuri was attempting to connect with Shannon, despite their rocky start, meant more than she could express.

So, Genesis simply said, "Thank you, baby."

"Of course. I want to be a part of every aspect of your life," Zuri replied. "How's the reunion going?"

Genesis settled back against the headboard, recounting the day's events. She told Zuri about Grace and their trip to Terry's bar, about Granny Lee's wisdom, and about the oak tree where her mother's ashes were scattered.

The conversation flowed easily between them, the sadness of their recent argument dissolving with each laugh and tender word. Genesis relaxed, the familiar comfort of Zuri's voice washing over her. Finally, she was at ease; they were going to be okay.

# Chapter Thirty-One

As the sun ascended over the blue Caribbean skies of Barbados, Zuri scrolled through her social media feeds. She nibbled on her bottom lip, reading through the news of Ellis Films' latest bomb. According to projections, Crimson Shore, a sci-fi thriller that Zuri had backed wholeheartedly, would only make back half of the money they put into it. Of course, they had contingency plans in place for this sort of thing, but that didn't make the loss sting any less.

"There are more fun things you could do this early in the morning." Genesis slid in closer to her from behind, the touch of her naked skin eliciting a groan of pleasure. "Please tell me you aren't doom scrolling again?"

Zuri put her phone down and turned to face Genesis. "What would make you think that?" She did her best to keep her face straight.

"Experience with you, perhaps?" Genesis cupped her cheek. "It's not good, is it?"

"No, it isn't, but it's also not the worst thing. I want our studio to keep putting out the best films we can. I just would have appreciated a win after this ordeal with Francis."

Once her godfather went to trial, people had been coming out of the woodwork to air his past transgressions. Francis had been victimizing women for years, starting before he met her father and gained a foothold in the film industry. She was still reeling from what was coming to light as the trial continued. The sooner the courts convicted him, the quicker she hoped they could all move on.

Genesis ran her fingers through Zuri's locs. "Revelations like these... they change you, baby. They test your resilience. And for what it's worth, I think you're doing an admirable job handling it all."

Zuri attempted a smile, though she knew it didn't quite reach her eyes. The pain of the recent revelations was still raw. "So have you," she murmured, leaning into Genesis' touch. "You've been right here with me, every step of the way."

Genesis chuckled, the sound of it like sweet music to Zuri's ears. "Well, where else would I be?"

"Mmmm, nowhere. You're right where you belong," Zuri said, a sigh escaping her lips as she nuzzled closer into Genesis' embrace. "Right here with me."

Genesis brushed a gentle kiss on Zuri's forehead, her hands tracing comforting circles on her back. "Always," she whispered, their bodies entwined in the light of dawn.

Zuri closed her eyes, breathing in the scent of Genesis's skin. Coconut oil and something uniquely her. It was hard to believe that just one week ago, she'd wondered if they'd ever find their way back to each other. Those days after Genesis left for Virginia had stretched endlessly, each hour feeling like a small eternity. She'd thrown herself into work, tried to lose herself in meetings.

The nights had been the worst. She'd lie in their bed, reaching across the cool sheets to where Genesis should have been, her fingers finding only emptiness. She'd replay their argument over and over, wincing at the sharp words they'd both hurled like weapons.

But then she'd thought about Barbados. About the beginning. So she'd written the letter. Poured her heart onto paper and been open like her father had told her to be. The call from Genesis after reading it had made that moment of vulnerability worthwhile.

They laid in silence for a while, the only sounds being the gentle hum of the morning outside and the rhythmic beating of their hearts. The serene moment shattered when Genesis' stomach growled loudly, causing both women to burst into laughter.

"Alright, alright," Zuri said, pushing herself up on her elbows. "Let's go find some breakfast before you starve." She pulled on the joggers she abandoned the night before beside the bed.

Genesis stretched and yawned. "I've been dying for you to say that. I'm starving. Someone kept me up half the night."

Zuri laughed out loud while slipping on a tank top. "Well, that someone can't help themselves because you are so delicious." She climbed back on the bed and nipped at Genesis's bare breasts.

"Don't you dare," she yelled out, pushing Zuri away.

Zuri tumbled off the bed, landing with a thud on the plush carpet. She feigned a pained expression, clutching her chest. "Such violence from my sweet Genesis," she exclaimed, her voice filled with mock horror.

Genesis pulled herself out of the bed, standing tall with her hands on her hips. "You should know better than to tease me when I'm hungry," she countered, her lips curving upward in a mischievous grin.

Zuri pushed herself up from the floor, brushing imaginary dust off her joggers. "Noted," she said with a nod, moving to pull Genesis into a hug. But Genesis nimbly sidestepped her advance, heading for the door in swift strides.

"We are not postponing breakfast again just because you can't keep your hands to yourself."

Zuri motioned to her naked body and asked, "Aren't you forgetting something?"

With a smile, Genesis continued her walk to the kitchen unabashed, her bare feet padding against the cool marble floors. "I don't believe I am," she called back over her shoulder, leaving Zuri standing alone in the bedroom.

The days they spent apart had been enough to convince her she didn't care what it took. They were going to figure out their issues. Life was too short, and she wanted to spend the time she had loving Genesis and being happy.

They still needed to talk things out, but she figured they would get to it when the time was right.

Barefoot herself and still half-asleep, she padded down the hallway after Genesis. The aroma of brewing coffee wafted through the air as she entered the kitchen. Genesis couldn't start her day without coffee, so she had set the very expensive machine that Zuri hardly used on a timer to ensure some would be ready when they woke up.

She placed Zuri's favorite mug in front of her and held up two different creamers. "Caramel or French vanilla?"

Zuri licked her lips and did her best not to let her eyes drop. "Caramel," she said, her eyes never leaving Genesis. The sunlight filtering through the kitchen windows accentuated the natural copper highlights in her hair, and Zuri found herself momentarily lost in admiration.

Genesis handed her the container, then turned to the fridge, providing an unobstructed view of her toned back and bottom, catching the morning light. Fingers light on the porcelain handle of her mug, Zuri watched with something akin to awe as Genesis made their breakfast.

She turned around, catching Zuri's gaze and blushed under the scrutiny, but held her gaze steady. "What is it?" she asked, trying to sound casual.

Zuri smiled and shook her head. "Nothing... Just admiring the view."

Genesis snorted at that, feigning annoyance. "Go sit down. You're distracting me."

Chuckling, Zuri complied, dragging a chair from the island counter to sit by one of the oversized windows overlooking the golden beach. "Breakfast is my domain Ms. Malone."

"Oh, I'm well aware of that, Ms. Baker. That first morning after we met, watching your cute little ass flit around this kitchen, I'm pretty sure that's when I fell in love with you."

Zuri raised an eyebrow. "I'm not sure if I'd call what I'm working with little, but finish your story."

Genesis let out an exasperated sigh and flung water in her direction, which Zuri deftly dodged.

"Anyway, as I was saying," Genesis began, rolling her eyes playfully. "You were so focused on making your amazing waffles, you didn't notice me watching you. You had flour smeared across your cheek, your hair was a mess, and I thought I had never seen anyone more beautiful."

Zuri blushed at the memory. "I wanted to impress you. And I was flirting with you hard."

Genesis laughed, a sweet, tinkling sound Zuri loved. "Oh, you impressed me alright," she said, with a wink. "But not with your cooking skills."

"Hey!" Zuri protested, laughing. She took a sip of her coffee. The caramel flavor was delightful with the rich dark brew. Genesis had the ability to create a flawless cup of coffee.

"All teasing aside," Genesis said, her voice growing softer.

"That morning was special for me, too. It was the first time I thought I wanted to spend more mornings with you. As many as life would allow."

Zuri's chest constricted at Genesis' confession. "Genesis," she said, her voice thick with emotion.

They didn't talk often about the time they spent apart. While Genesis seemed to understand why Zuri made the choices she did, there was still some residual resentment and that was fair. She had unintentionally strung Genesis along, knowing that Tracy was still in the picture. If she had to do it all over again, she would have chosen Genesis without hesitation, but as the saying goes, hindsight is 20/20.

Genesis broke their eye contact and turned back to the stove, scraping the scrambled eggs on two plates. She moved with a grace and elegance that was not lost on Zuri. "Sometimes, love is about timing. We needed that time apart to grow and understand what we wanted.," Genesis said, placing a plate of toast, eggs, and a couple of crisp bacon strips in front of Zuri. "Breakfast is served," she announced, a smile pulling at her lips.

Zuri nodded, her eyes never leaving Genesis. A breeze blew in through the open window, causing a few loose curls to flutter around her face. God, Zuri loved that face.

"Looks delicious," Zuri said, her words carrying more weight than just the breakfast. Genesis, who chuckled, didn't miss the implication.

"I hope you're referring to the food." Genesis teased.

With a chuckle, Zuri dug into her breakfast, appreciating the comfort of their shared space and the woman sitting across from her. Breakfast conversations with Genesis were always fun and deep all at once. Sometimes they talked about their dreams and aspirations; other times they discussed favorite foods or films.

This morning's conversation steered toward work. After

grabbing a silk robe she kept by the breakfast nook, Genesis sat down. She began talking about one of her young dance students who showed so much promise but wouldn't have been able to afford dance classes if not for Zuri's organization.

"Babe, Keisha is amazing, like, naturally gifted. The way she moves is so fluid and always on point. She's going to be a star one day."

"With you as a guide, I don't doubt it."

Genesis blushed under the praise, rolling her eyes to downplay the compliment. "You're biased," she teased, though the smile tugging at her lips betrayed her feigned indifference.

"Perhaps, but I am also able to recognize talent when I see it. And you, my love, are incredibly talented."

A tender smile replaced her playful smirk. "Thank you," she said, bringing Zuri in for a kiss.

It started off innocently enough, but Zuri's hand was soon rising to ease Genesis's robe off of her shoulder. She stood and placed a kiss on the spot where the silky material had once rested.

Genesis gasped as Zuri moved to her neck. Her hands settled on Genesis' waist, pulling her closer.

"Zuri," Genesis breathed out, her fingers tangling in Zuri's dreadlocks. "We haven't finished breakfast..."

"True," Zuri whispered against Genesis' skin, her hands making their way up Genesis' back. "But I'm gonna make sure I get my fill."

Zuri's lips traced a line of fire down Genesis' neck, her hands roaming up the smooth expanse of her back, feeling the delicious shiver running through her body. She gently pushed Genesis up against the kitchen counter, an almost imperceptible moan escaping from between her lips.

"Zuri..." she whispered again, her fingers tangling more insistently in Zuri's locs. Her legs wound around Zuri's waist, granting her better access to explore the curves concealed beneath the thin silk robe.

She reveled in the feel of Genesis squirming beneath her touch. The heat radiating off of her was intoxicating. Moving away from her neck, she unknotted Genesis' robe, revealing the body she had been coveting earlier. "God, you're beautiful," she breathed out huskily.

Her fingers trailed downwards, skimming over Genesis's skin as she arched into her touch. The tips of her fingers traced teasing circles on Genesis' hard nipple, eliciting muffled sighs from between Genesis' parted lips. She leaned down and replaced those skilled fingers with her mouth, tracing a wet path from collarbone to breast. Her tongue played with Genesis' nipple while her hand slipped below to tease at the trim line of hair leading further south.

Genesis whimpered as Zuri found and teased at her throbbing clit. A low growl resonated deep within Zuri's chest as she continued to lavish attention onto Genesis' sensitive nipple with one hand while teasing between her slick folds with the other.

"Can I taste you?" Zuri asked, taking a step back to look into her eyes.

"God, yes," she murmured through heavy breaths. Her fingers tightened their grip on Zuri's dreadlocks, pulling her closer. This was a dance they both knew well.

Zuri's dark eyes shone with lustful delight as she eased Genesis out of her silk robe, laying bare the body that had been hinted at beneath the thin material. With a last glance into Genesis' eyes full of desire, she lowered herself onto her knees before her lover.

Slowly placing feather-light kisses down Genesis' belly, started by exploring Genesis' lower folds with the tip of her tongue; teasing, prodding, tasting every inch of sweetness that dripped from within. She savored the distinct taste of Genesis — raw honey laced with delirious desire.

Genesis held onto her, gripping her head just enough to make sure she stayed in place.

Encouraged by Genesis' reaction, Zuri slipped two digits inside her slick heat while continuing to flicker and swirl her tongue around Genesis' engorged bundle of nerves. She curled those fingers upwards where Genesis liked it most — right against the spot that made stars explode behind her eyes.

"Oh god,...don't... don't stop," Genesis moaned out, her voice strained with pleasure. Her body moved rhythmically against Zuri's face and fingers, her legs opening wider to accommodate the simultaneous assault on her senses.

Zuri was relentless, alternating between pleasuring Genesis' clit using different patterns of pressure and speed with her tongue and thrusting those skillful fingers in and out of Genesis. She loved to hear her beg beneath her touch, the raw and primal need in her voice invigorating as much as it was intoxicating.

Her tongue focused on her sensitive nub while she continued working inside her depths. Genesis screamed out in ecstasy as her orgasm washed over her. Zuri kept up the pace until every tremor had subsided — each one accompanied by a sweet whimper from Genesis' lips.

As Genesis came down from her high, panting heavily and basking in the afterglow, Zuri emerged from between her thighs. The sight of Genesis unraveled and spent because of her sent an all-consuming desire shooting through Zuri's veins.

"Was that a good enough breakfast?" Zuri asked smugly as she offered a taunting smirk to the breathless woman above her.

Genesis chuckled weakly, pulling Zuri up into a ravenous kiss. "I think I'm more than satisfied," she gasped out between heavy breaths. "But who said we're finished?"

# Chapter Thirty-Two

"Yes, Mr. Richards, everything was done as you asked. Lucy has already taken.. yes, I understand that you want me to handle it but I'm out of the country. Lucy is a trusted colleague and can more than handle..."

Genesis did her best to let her client talk, but his insistence that he only deal with her was grating. Having rich clientele meant more money to be made, but it also meant more demands.

She sipped her lemonade, the condensation running down her skin in rivulets. The pool behind her ate up the sounds of both their voices as she tried to placate him. It was calling her name. She couldn't wait to plunge in as soon as the call ended.

"I hear you but I won't be back until next week... Mr. Richards, I assure you that everything... Hmmm, yes, I'm listening" She looked at the beach. "Alright, I'll call you back after I speak with her. Yes. Bye."

Genesis hung up with a sigh and tossed her phone onto the table beside her. The phone call had been about the last thing she wanted on this much needed vacation, but alas, work had a habit of finding her now that she was in business for herself. She had no right admonishing Zuri when she was becoming just as bad.

"Well, that didn't sound like fun," Zuri said, strolling out onto their balcony in a skimpy yellow bikini that showed off her caramel skin to perfection.

"Lucy can handle it," Genesis said as she reclined against the lounge chair.

"Uh huh," Zuri scoffed, sipping her drink. "You keep telling yourself that."

Genesis let out a groan. "Remind me why I went into business for myself again?"

Zuri chuckled. "I warned you."

"You sure did, but I don't think it hit me until six months into it."

"You're doing a great job and pretty soon you are going to be the go-to person in Hollywood. Reggie talks about you to everyone when he has the chance."

"Yes, I've gotten most of my referrals from him. I appreciate the love, and of course you, for even having him take me on."

Zuri got up and straddled Genesis on her chair. "All the better to keep you close to me."

"Hmm, is that so?" She kissed the top of Zuri's chest. "This yellow bikini is making me feel some kind of way," Genesis teased as she groped Zuri's ass.

"I mean, what do I wear that you don't love?"

Genesis laughed as Zuri's lips found her own. "You're so full of yourself."

"Mmm, true," Zuri smirked as she put her drink down. "But what are you gonna do about it?"

Laughing, Genesis braced Zuri's body with her arms and walked to the pool, gingerly dropping her in after planting a kiss on her lips. She jumped in after her and they began splashing each other with water.

Ever since they had arrived in Barbados, they'd been all smiles. All the heaviness that had been weighing down their relationship was gone. It was nice not only to spend time together, but to do so without the constant interruptions of work and other obligations, even if it was temporary. Genesis felt truly relaxed for the first time in months.

Zuri leaned with her back to the pool, allowing the sun to kiss her skin, drying the droplets of water that clung to her. Genesis swam over to her, resting her arms on either side of her, looking into her face. Zuri's hands found Genesis' curls, running her fingers through the damp tresses.

"Are you ready for all this?" Genesis asked, gesturing between them.

Zuri gazed adoringly at Genesis. Her hands gently stroked along the side of Genesis' face. "I've never been more ready for anything in my life," she replied, her voice full of emotion.

A smile spread across Genesis' lips. "Good," she murmured, "because I can't wait to be your wife."

"Same here, baby," Zuri said, holding Genesis close.

Genesis leaned in, pressing her lips against Zuri's in a languid kiss that tasted of sunlight. They stayed like that for a while, wrapped up in each other, letting the water cradle them.

The sun dipped, casting a soft golden glow around the two women. Zuri looked up at the sky, its colors shifting from cobalt blue to hues of orange and pink. "We should head inside and get ready," she suggested, loosening her hold on Genesis.

Genesis nodded, casting one last glance at their peaceful paradise before helping Zuri out of the pool. They wrapped each other in oversized beach towels, their fingers interlacing.

They had plans to attend a folk concert and art festival happening as part of the Crop Over Festival. Zuri was excited for Genesis to attend the Grand Kadooment carnival parade the following day. While Rihanna would not be attending, much to Genesis's chagrin, it was something she was excited for. Every bit of Barbados that Zuri shared with her was a sweet glimpse into her life. One that Genesis was now a part of.

"What do you think about this?" Zuri asked, holding up a yellow jumpsuit.

"Oh, you're in a yellow type of mood today." Genesis stepped back to give it a once over. "I like it, but I'll need to see it on you."

"Your wish is my command. Let me just take a quick shower." Zuri turned to her as she slipped out of her bathing suit. "Care to join me?"

Genesis smirked, a spark igniting in her eyes. "You're lucky I'm a woman who loves to conserve water," she retorted, following Zuri into the bathroom.

After their shared shower filled with giggles, light touches and lingering kisses, they dressed for the night. Upon seeing Zuri in the yellow jumpsuit, Genesis whistled. It was off the shoulder and had a pretty tie in the middle off to the side. When Zuri did a little spin, she saw her back was out, the opening dipping just low enough to be sexy but not indecent.

"Wow babe, you are absolutely breathtaking," she professed as she approached Zuri.

Zuri turned around to face her. "Not too shabby yourself," she complimented, her eyes roaming over Genesis's figure, clad in a flowing white dress.

Genesis pressed a kiss onto Zuri's lips, whispering in her ear right after, "I love you."

"I love you too, Gen," Zuri replied before adding with a teasing grin, "Now come on, we can't keep Barbados waiting."

They hopped into one of Zuri's sports cars, a dark blue Aston Martin, and headed into Bridgetown.

The streets of Barbados were alive with music and people having a good time. While the atmosphere on the island was always invigorating, during carnival season, it was electric. The rhythms of calypso, soca and reggae pulsated through the air, as vibrant as the island itself.

"Listen to that," Genesis said, letting the music wash over her as Zuri navigated through the bustling streets of Bridgetown. "It's like you can feel the heartbeat of the island."

Zuri glanced at Genesis. "Told you there's no place quite like home," she said, pulling up to a makeshift parking space near Queen's Park where the folk concert was taking place.

*Home.* All this time she had been thinking about Barbados as Zuri's place and she was just a visitor, but now this would be a part of her life. Whenever she wanted a break, she could visit, with or without Zuri. She had come to know her staff well and even some locals. They were building a life together and that included this beautiful island along with its culture and the people on it.

As they walked hand in hand towards the park, Genesis was swept up by the surrounding energy.

The folk concert was an explosion of color and sound. There were dancers swaying to the beat of drums, their bodies moving with a grace and fluidity that left Genesis in awe. Musicians strummed on guitars and beat on tambourines, their voices blending together in perfect harmony.

Zuri led Genesis to an area where they could sit down and enjoy the show. They settled onto a blanket that Zuri had brought with them, leaning into each other as they watched the performers on stage.

"This is surreal," Zuri said, breaking the silence between them. "I've been coming to this festival since I was a kid."

Genesis looked over at her. "Is that right?"

Zuri nodded, pointing towards a group of children who were attempting to dance along with the performers

"Do you see that group there?" Zuri asked, pointing towards an ensemble of dancers dressed in vibrant clothes. "That's the Landship crew. They're a famous Barbadian folk dance group."

Genesis turned her attention towards the ensemble Zuri was pointing at. The dancers moved with such synchrony and rhythm it was mesmerizing to watch.

"They're incredible," she murmured, clapping along with the upbeat tempo of the music.

"They really are! I used to dream about being part of their crew when I was young."

Genesis looked at Zuri in surprise. "Really? You never told me you used to dance!"

Zuri laughed lightly at Genesis's astonishment. "Well, I never danced like you. I was an amateur all the way, but I loved the music so much I just wanted to vibe with it, I guess."

Genesis stood up and put out her hand. "How about you vibe with me now?"

Zuri, looking surprised, hesitated for a moment, but then she took Genesis's hand and rose to her feet. "You're not going to let me sit this one out, are you?"

Genesis winked at her as the music shifted to a slower, sensual beat.

"Are you sure?" Zuri stammered.

"Get your butt up here. If you can dance in a club, you can dance to this."

Zuri was a force to be reckoned with, but at times she turned into the shy, insecure girl Genesis imagined she must have been as a young woman. It was charming, made her more human.

Genesis leaned in close to whisper into Zuri's ear, her curly hair falling haphazardly over her face. "You're with me, aren't you? There's nothing to be nervous about."

Even with all the noise surrounding them, their world seemed to shrink down to just the two of them. Genesis put one arm around Zuri's waist while taking Zuri's hand with the other. "Just follow my lead, okay?" Genesis instructed.

Genesis started moving first, swaying side-to-side with Zuri following suit. As they got more comfortable with the rhythm, Genesis started introducing turns and small spins into their dance. They moved as one under the beautiful night sky.

When the song ended, they collapsed in a happy heap on the blanket.

"See, you're not so bad at this, "Genesis teased.

Zuri looked away, a blush forming on her cheeks. "Well...you're an excellent teacher."

Genesis chuckled, tilting Zuri's chin towards her. "Give yourself some credit. I didn't have much to teach. You're a natural."

Zuri grinned at the praise, her blush deepening as she leaned in to kiss Genesis. "Thank you," she said when they separated. The words were simple, but Genesis could sense the depth of feeling behind them.

As the festival went on, they enjoyed more performances, ranging from dance offs to singing competitions. They laughed at the antics of the performers and clapped, for every winner announced. It was a beautiful night filled with joy that was infectious.

At some point, Zuri's phone rang, disrupting their peace. It was business, as usual, interrupting their "us" time. Zuri sighed apologetically, but Genesis waved off her apologies.

"Don't worry about it, love."

With that Zuri moved a little away from where they were sitting to take the call while Genesis remained seated, watching as a group of children attempted to imitate the movements of the dancers. They were awkward and fell over each other a lot, but their laughter filled the air, making everyone around them smile.

Genesis looked at the time and decided to visit some of the art stalls. She was hoping to find some original pieces to take home.

After gathering up the blanket and her purse, she indicated to Zuri where she was going. Zuri, phone pressed against her ear, gave Genesis a small wave, the corners of her mouth tilting upwards in a smile.

The stalls stretched out in front of Genesis like colorful puzzle pieces scattered across the grass. She stopped at each one, taking in the vibrant canvases full of dreamy landscapes and portraits steeped in emotion. Despite her love for dance, she held a deep admiration for artists who could capture life's beauty with just a few strokes.

She was drawn towards a particular stall where the artwork seemed to speak to her. The paintings had a mythical quality to them, each one telling a story about Barbadian folklore. The artist, an old man with wrinkles etched deeply into his skin, had a calming aura about him. He saw Genesis admiring his work and walked over to join her.

"The beauty of our land is infinite," he said, looking at one of his paintings.

Genesis nodded in agreement. "Your work is beautiful."

"Thank you, miss." His eyes smiled with appreciation. "That one there is inspired by Bajan folk tales. It's about the Heartman who is said to be a creature that steals the hearts of disobedient children."

Genesis shuddered slightly at the myth but admired the painting, nonetheless. It was then that her eyes fell on a piece that took her breath away. It was an abstract painting of two women dancing under the night sky with music notes swirling around them.

She felt a sharp tug towards the painting. It was them–her and Zuri–captured so perfectly on canvas that she could almost hear their laughter filling up the quiet night and feel their bodies swaying to the rhythm of their own song. She had to have it. "How much for this one?" she asked, tracing the figures with her fingers.

He studied her for a moment, then, as if making up his mind, he said, "For you, I'll make it a special price." He named a figure that was generous, considering the mastery of the piece.

Without a second thought, Genesis agreed to the price and paid for the artwork. With a broad smile on his face, the old man carefully wrapped up the painting and handed it over to her. "I hope it brings you joy," he said.

"I'm sure it will," Genesis replied. She held the painting close to her chest as if cradling something precious. With a final wave to the old man, she turned back towards where she left Zuri.

As she walked back, she saw Zuri still on her call, but this time pacing around. She looked frustrated as she ran a hand through her long dreadlocks. It was a look Genesis knew well.

She approached Zuri gingerly, not wanting to startle her. When Zuri noticed her, she sighed and shook her head apologetically. "I'm sorry about this, Gen," she said apologetically.

Genesis just smiled at her, shaking her head. "It's okay, love; I understand." She held up the painting to distract Zuri from her obvious frustration. "Look what I got. It's perfect for the house."

"I can't wait to see it. I'm almost done, let's see what food they got, then we can head home."

"Sounds like a plan," Genesis agreed, watching as Zuri returned to her call.

As she waited, her eyes wandered over the crowd again. There was a palpable energy around the festival that was contagious. The laughter and joy of people celebrating their culture seeped into her, making her feel at peace with herself.

When Zuri finished her call and turned off the stressful part of her world for the night, she looked visibly relieved. She walked over to Genesis, wrapping an arm around her waist. "I am so sorry about that."

Genesis just waved it away. "Stop apologizing, Zuri. I'm okay."

Zuri flashed a grateful smile towards Genesis as they walked together towards the food stalls. The delicious smell wafting from the various vendors made Genesis's mouth water. They found a stall selling jerk chicken and plantains, which they both loved and bought enough for an indulgent late-night dinner.

They found an empty table and opened up the food. Zuri did a happy dance as she took her first bite, eliciting a giggle from Genesis. Her woman loved to eat and the fact that she wasn't afraid to show it was one thing Genesis adored about her.

As they indulged in the food, their conversation flowed. They talked about work, art and everything in between. From time to time, Zuri would reach over to swipe a piece of plantain from Genesis' plate, earning herself a playful swat on the hand and a protest from Genesis.

"Hey there, thief! Get your own," Genesis exclaimed, trying to shield her plate from Zuri's roving hand.

Zuri just laughed at that. "Oh, come on, sharing is caring, babe," she replied with a wink.

Genesis laughed, shaking her head at Zuri's antics. "Anyway, if you could go anywhere else in the world, where would it be?"

Zuri's eyes lit up at the question, a dreamy smile spreading across her face. "Oh, that's easy - Tahiti," she said without hesitation. "I've been dreaming about visiting there for years."

Genesis leaned in, intrigued. "Really? Tell me more."

Zuri's excitement was palpable as she began to gush. "Tahiti is like paradise on Earth. Picture crystal clear turquoise waters so pure you can see straight to the bottom, even in the deep parts. The beaches have this incredible white sand that feels like powder between your toes." She closed her eyes for a moment, as if visualizing it. "And the overwater bungalows! Can you imagine waking up every morning to the gentle lapping of waves right beneath you? You can step right off your private deck into that warm, pristine water."

Genesis found herself captivated by Zuri's vivid description. "It sounds magical."

"It really does," Zuri agreed fervently. "And the culture is so rich and beautiful. The Tahitians have this incredible tradition of hospitality called 'Mana' - it's like this spiritual life force that is not just about being welcoming. It's a deep spiritual belief that flows through everything they do. The way they connect with nature, with each other. It's truly magical."

Zuri continued eating but stopped when she noticed Genesis just watching her. "What?" she asked. "I have something on my face?"

Genesis smiled and looked away. "You're beautiful, especially when you talk about something you're passionate about. It gets me every time."

Zuri ducked her head and fluttered her eyelashes, causing Genesis to laugh.

By the time they finished eating, it was getting late. The festival was winding down, the vibrant energy of earlier transitioned into a more relaxed, reflective mood.

"Ready to go home?" Zuri asked.

Genesis nodded and stood up, folding their blanket and helping Zuri gather up their trash to throw away. They walked hand in hand towards Zuri's car parked just outside the festival grounds.

Once they reached home, Zuri insisted on carrying the painting inside herself. She admired Genesis's choice after unwrapping it. "It's beautiful," she said. There was a softness in her eyes as she studied the artwork.

"It reminded me of us tonight. Now we have something to remember it by. When we're home and feeling stressed..."

"We can look at this and remember what it's like to be in each other's arms under the stars." Zuri placed it down on the mantle and embraced Genesis. "I love it baby."

They walked to the bedroom and began removing their clothes. After their outing, neither one of them could muster up the energy to do anything besides shower and lay down.

After putting on her bonnet, Genesis slipped into bed beside Zuri, feeling the cool sheets against her skin. The gentle sea breeze drifted in through the open balcony doors, carrying with it the faint sound of waves crashing on the shore. She snuggled closer to Zuri, breathing her in.

"Tonight was so nice."

Zuri hummed in agreement. "It was. I'm so glad you're here with me, experiencing all of this." She paused. "That was Marcus on the phone earlier. He's trying to negotiate a settlement with Lea's lawyer."

"Are you serious?" Genesis sat up and leaned on her elbow. "But you didn't do anything wrong."

"I know, but this isn't worth the bad publicity it will bring to Beacon and myself. But, Marcus is great. He'll make sure it doesn't hurt too much."

"I'm sure he will, but how are you feeling?"

In response, Zuri pulled Genesis into her arms tighter. "I'll be fine, love. It's just a hurdle we'll overcome together, like we always do. Now what was I going to do? Oh yeah."

She flipped Genesis onto her back, causing her to let out a small yelp of joy. A giggle bubbled up from Genesis's throat and Zuri joined in, her laughter mixing with Genesis's in a melody that filled the room.

"I love you," Zuri said between kisses.

Genesis stared up at the woman straddling her, a content sigh slipping past her lips. "I love you too," she said, and meant it with every fiber of her being.

# Chapter Thirty-Three

The following day, Zuri stared at the flowers she had placed on the kitchen counter. They were beautiful, but something about the vase wasn't doing it for her. The doorbell rang, and she went to let in her cousin Christopher.

"Hello my darling. Are we ready for the carnival or are we ready?" He danced his way into the house.

"Ready as we'll ever be," Zuri answered, a broad smile spreading across her face at his infectious energy. Christopher pulled her into a tight hug, his cologne filling her nostrils. "Gen's just finishing getting ready. Would you help me with this arrangement?" Zuri asked, leading him towards the beautiful bouquet.

"Oooh, this is nice," Chris said, admiring the colorful display.

"I wanted to surprise Gen, but something about it looks off. Is it the vase?"

Chris rolled his eyes. "You think she's going to be worried about a vase when she sees these gorgeous azaleas? You are too much."

"I just want things to be perfect for her. She deserves it."

Placing his hand over his heart, Chris smiled. "Okay, that is sweet but this is more Keith's area, however I know how to make things look good too, so let me take a look."

Christopher approached the arrangement, tilting his head to the side. His eyes scanned the flowers, the vase, and the way it all sat on the countertop. He reached out, tweaking a couple of stems here, adjusting some petals. Finally, he stepped back with a satisfied nod.

"There you go. It was just a matter of balance and a touch of love."

Zuri looked between Christopher and the arrangement then smiled. The minor changes had made such a difference. The flowers no longer appeared as if they were thrown in the vase, but seemed to be happily nestled inside.

"Thanks cuz."

Just as Zuri exhaled a sigh of relief, Genesis stepped into the kitchen, looking exquisite. She wore a lime green top and shorts that made her long, voluptuous legs appear even longer. Her wild curls tumbled over her shoulders.

She gasped in delight as she took in the glorious arrangement of azaleas in varying hues of pink and white against lush, green leaves. "Oh Zuri, they're beautiful!"

"Something beautiful for someone beautiful."

Genesis bent down to sniff them, a bright smile lighting up her face. She caressed Zuri's cheek and kissed her, then made her way over to Christopher.

"Chris, I've missed you," she said, opening her arms for a hug.

He squeezed her close and kissed her cheek. "You two have been extra busy. I expected to see way more of you."

"Well, we might have gotten a bit caught up in our love bubble," Genesis admitted with a sheepish smile. "But work has also been intense for both of us. This is the first long weekend we've taken in a minute. What a year, right babe?"

Zuri came up behind her and wrapped her arms around her waist. "Yes, it's been a very long year. We've been making sure to take advantage of this short-lived freedom."

Chris grinned. "So you mean you've been sexing each other all over this house?"

"Christopher!" Genesis admonished with her own smile.

"What? Did I lie?" he persisted playfully.

Zuri shook her head, unable to keep a grin off her face. "We should get going. Keith is meeting us there right?"

"Yeah, he has to work, but he'll find us to say hello."

After gathering their belongings, the three of them headed out. Chris was driving, so Zuri happily jumped in the backseat with Genesis. Anticipation coursed through her veins, knowing that Gen was about to experience something she had never seen before. Being with her allowed Zuri to experience Barbados anew and it endeared her to her even more.

"You excited, babe? Cause I know I am," Zuri asked, leaning into her.

"Absolutely. I've always dreamed of attending a Caribbean carnival."

"Then prepare to be blown away," Zuri promised, squeezing her hand.

* * *

The carnival was just as lively as Zuri had said. People danced in elaborate costumes on the streets of Bridgetown, and the air was filled with the scent of frying fish cakes and sweet coconut bread. Stands selling sugarcane juice and rum punch lined the sidewalks, their owners shouting out for visitors to come and try their drinks.

367

"Zuri, look!" Genesis pointed at a group of stilt walkers in radiant costumes depicting mythical creatures. They moved with such grace that they seemed unreal.

"Here you go ladies," Chris said, handing them some rum punch he purchased from a stand behind them. "To Bajan culture and unforgettable memories!"

Zuri and Genesis raised their cups, then they all took a healthy sip.

"Oh, that is good," Genesis said, raising hers to drink some more.

"Slow down babe, that stuff packs a punch," Zuri warned with a chuckle, a protective hand resting on Genesis's arm.

She winked and took a sip. "Got it, honey."

Zuri chuckled and shook her head in amusement. Chris tapped her arm to get her attention.

"There's Kevin," he said, waving him down.

Kevin walked up to them in his formal police outfit, all smiles.

"Hello, beautiful ladies!" He said as he gave them hugs. "And hello to you too, Chris," he added as an afterthought, the corners of his mouth twitching in amusement.

Christopher folded his arms. "Oh, you're tryna play in my face. I see how it is."

"Aww, don't be like that." Kevin pulled him into a hug and whispered something in his ear that made him laugh.

Zuri was happy to see them being openly affectionate. Barbados finally struck down laws that criminalized homosexual behavior a couple of years ago. Slowly, people were becoming more comfortable being themselves out in the open. Kevin still had to play it cool because of his job, but they weren't hiding the way they had to in the past.

"You got here right when things started getting good," Kevin said, pointing towards the crowd. "The real show is about to start."

As if on cue, the first beats of a rhythmic drum sequence echoed through the streets. The crowd cheered and clapped, moving in time with the pulsating rhythms. A wave of dancers burst onto the scene, their bodies adorned in costumes of vibrant colors. They moved like shimmering waves, their bodies telling stories of love and life through their motions.

Beside her, Genesis gushed with excitement. Her eyes were wide with delight as she gripped Zuri's hand. "Oh my," she breathed out, enchanted by the spectacle before them.

The parade of dancers continued to stream through the streets, captivating the audience with their intricate choreography and dazzling attire. Each group had their own theme and style, showcasing different aspects of Caribbean culture and history.

Genesis was swept up in the lively atmosphere, her toes tapping rhythmically to the music as she watched each performance unfold. She turned to Zuri with a radiant smile plastered on her face. "This is incredible! Why didn't we come sooner?"

Zuri shrugged with a playful smirk, tugging at her lips. "I don't know, but we're here now."

For hours they watched the grand spectacle of colors, laughter and artistic expression that made up the Kadooment Day Parade. After some time, they joined in the revelry. Chris got them each a bright feathered headband from a vendor selling carnival gear.

"You can't attend a carnival without looking like you belong," Chris said with a wink.

Zuri and Genesis laughed and helped each other put on their flamboyant accessories, drawing approving nods from passersby.

As darkness fell, the carnival transformed. Colorful lights

illuminated the streets, and the energy of the crowd seemed to intensify. Genesis and Zuri danced close, their bodies moving in sync with the pulsating soca rhythms. The rum punch had loosened them up, and they laughed, caught up in the moment's joy.

"I can't believe I've never experienced this before," Genesis shouted over the music. "It's like... pure joy incarnate!"

Zuri grinned, pulling Genesis closer. "I'm so glad I get to share this with you," she said, her lips brushing Genesis's ear. "Seeing it through your eyes is making me fall in love with it all over again."

Genesis and Zuri danced until their feet ached, laughing and twirling beneath the starry sky. The rum punch had left them buzzed, inhibitions lowered just enough to immerse themselves in the celebratory atmosphere.

"I need a break," Genesis said while fanning herself. "And maybe some water, ooh, and food?"

A nearby stall was bustling with people. The enticing smell of jerk chicken and roti permeated the air, making Zuri's stomach grumble in response.

"Sure thing, babe," Zuri responded, pulling Genesis towards the stand.

When their turn came, they ordered a variety of dishes. Fried flying fish sandwiches, spicy jerk chicken, and piping hot roti stuffed with curried goat. They found a spot on the crowded sidewalk to sit down and devour their feast along with Chris, who had gotten them more drinks.

Genesis took a bite from the sandwich and moaned. "This is so good!" she said through a mouthful of food. Zuri watched with amusement as Genesis continued to savor each bite as if it was her last.

After finishing their meal, they wandered some more through the streets. They ended up near a stage where a steel band was playing an upbeat calypso tune, which had everyone within earshot tapping their feet or dancing along.

Chris jumped into the throng of dancers, and it wasn't long before Genesis pulled Zuri in as well, her hips swaying to the music. Zuri laughed at Genesis' enthusiasm, but she allowed herself to be led, the energy of the crowd infusing her with a sense of exhilaration. They danced until the music ended, their bodies moving in time with the rhythmic pulse of the drums.

By the time they made it home, exhaustion had once again descended on them. But this time, she wasn't willing to let the night end just yet. As Genesis flopped onto the couch with a contented sigh, Zuri headed to the kitchen.

"What are you up to?" Genesis called out, her voice tinged with curiosity.

"You'll see," Zuri replied.

A few minutes later, she returned with two glasses of rum punch and a plate of leftover coconut bread from earlier.

Genesis smiled as Zuri handed her a glass. "Mmm, more rum punch. You're spoiling me."

"Only the best for you, my love," Zuri said, clinking her glass against Genesis's.

They ate in silence, listening to the ocean outside of the house. When they were done, Genesis placed her glass down and tilted her head to look at Zuri.

"It's only a few hours before the sun rises." She leaned in close, her eyes dropping to Zuri's lips. "And I'm not tired."

Those words echoed through the room as Genesis leaned in for a kiss. Their lips touched lightly, but even that simple act ignited a firestorm inside.

Zuri pulled away despite the desire to keep going. "As tempting as you are, I think we should go to bed."

Genesis poked out her lips. "You're turning me down? Lesbian bed death, here we come."

Zuri laughed and swatted Genesis. "You're so silly. I just want us to get some rest so we can enjoy the rest of our time here. Plus, I have plans for us tomorrow."

Genesis raised an eyebrow, intrigued. "Oh? What kind of plans?"

She leaned into Genesis, pulling her close. "I was thinking we could take a catamaran cruise along the coast. There's this secluded cove I know about. Crystal clear water, white sand. We could go snorkeling, have a picnic on the beach.."

"That sounds heavenly."

"And then," Zuri continued, her voice low and teasing, "We'll end the day with a private sunset dinner at the restaurant The Cliff. Just you and me, candlelight, the sound of the waves..."

Genesis sighed. "You know how to treat a girl, don't you?"

"Only the best for you, my love."

Zuri hoped the tranquil setting would be the place for them to air out their grievances so they could move forward, but she prayed it wouldn't backfire.

# Chapter Thirty-Four

Genesis waited for Zuri as she spoke to the owner of the company they were renting the catamaran from. A gust of wind threatened to snatch away her big floppy hat. The sun beat down on her skin, and she was grateful for the cool breeze coming off the water. She watched Zuri's animated gestures as she chatted with the owner.

Zuri jogged back to Genesis, a wide grin on her face. "We're all set, babe! Are you ready for an adventure?"

"I sure am," Genesis said as she watched the owner and some helpers load their bags. She expected one of them to stay on board to steer the boat, but they walked off, leaving the two of them alone. "Who's going to sail with us?"

Zuri smiled sheepishly. "Yeah, I guess I forgot to mention that I can sail."

Genesis's eyes widened in surprise. "You sail? How come you never mentioned it?"

Zuri shrugged, a glint in her eye. "I'm full of surprises, babe. My dad taught me and my cousins when we were kids. It was his way of bonding with us."

Genesis shook her head in amazement as Zuri untied the ropes and guided them away from the dock. The catamaran glided across the crystal-clear water, and Genesis felt a thrill of excitement course through her body.

"So, where are we headed, Captain Baker?" Genesis asked, settling into a comfortable spot on the deck.

Zuri's dreadlocks whipped in the wind as she adjusted the sails. "That secluded cove I mentioned isn't too far off. I didn't want to go anywhere that required too much sailing."

Genesis leaned back, letting the sun warm her face as she watched Zuri maneuver the catamaran. The gentle rocking of the boat and the sound of water lapping against the hull lulled her into a peaceful state.

"You're good at this," Genesis called out, admiring Zuri's confidence as she adjusted the sails.

Zuri flashed her a bright smile. "Thanks, babe. It's been a while, but it's like riding a bike. You never forget."

"You make it look so easy," Genesis called out, her curiosity piqued. She stood up, making her way across the deck to where Zuri stood at the helm. "Do you think you could teach me?"

"Of course! I'd love to show you the ropes–literally!" She laughed, gesturing to the intricate network of lines and pulleys around them.

Zuri began explaining the basics, pointing out the different parts and showing how to adjust the sails. Genesis listened and tried not to focus on just how hot Zuri was, especially when she was in her element like this.

"Want to try steering?" Zuri asked, breaking Genesis out of her reverie.

"What if I mess something up?"

Zuri gave her an encouraging smile. "Don't worry, I've got you. Come here."

She guided Genesis to stand in front of her , wrapping her

arms around her from behind to place Genesis's hands on the wheel. Zuri's closeness made her want to lean in further.

"Just hold it steady," Zuri instructed, her breath against Genesis's ear. "Feel the wind and the current. Let the boat guide you."

Genesis closed her eyes for a moment, moving with the gentle push and pull of the water beneath them. She could sense Zuri's steady presence behind her, their bodies swaying together with the motion of the boat.

"This is amazing," Genesis breathed, opening her eyes to take in the vast expanse of blue stretching out before them.

Zuri pressed a kiss to her shoulder. "You're doing great, babe."

They sailed on in comfortable silence for a while, Genesis growing more confident under Zuri's watchful guidance. The sun climbed higher in the sky, beating down on them.

"I think I see the cove up ahead," Zuri said, pointing to a small inlet in the distance. "Why don't you let me take over the approach?"

Genesis nodded, stepping aside as Zuri took the helm. She watched in awe as her fiancée guided the catamaran into the secluded cove, skillfully maneuvering around rocky outcroppings and shallow areas.

When they entered the cove, Genesis gasped at the beauty surrounding them. Lush greenery spilled down steep cliffs, framing a pristine white sand beach. The water was so clear she could see colorful fish darting beneath the surface.

"Honey, this is breathtaking," Genesis said, drinking in the view.

Zuri beamed with pride. "I'm glad you like it. I stumbled upon this place years ago and have been wanting to share it with someone special ever since."

She anchored the catamaran in the calm waters of the cove.

As they gathered their things to head to shore, Genesis noticed dark clouds gathering on the horizon.

"Uh, Z? Those clouds look a little ominous," Genesis said, pointing.

Zuri frowned, looking in the direction where Genesis pointed. "Hmm, that's odd. The forecast didn't call for any storms today." She shrugged it off. "It's probably nothing to worry about. Let's get to the beach and enjoy ourselves."

They lowered themselves into the small dinghy, and Zuri rowed them to shore. As they set up their beach blanket and umbrella, the wind picked up. As if on cue, a loud crack of thunder echoed across the water, making Genesis jump.

"Damn it, the weather can change so fast here. There's a small cave system in the cliffs. We can wait out the storm there."

Genesis nodded, helping Zuri gather their belongings as the wind whipped around them. They hurried across the beach, the sand stinging their legs as it blew in the strengthening gusts.

Zuri led them to a narrow opening in the cliffs, barely visible unless you knew where to look. They ducked inside just as the first heavy drops of rain fell. Inside, the cave was cool and damp, but provided welcome shelter from the sudden storm.

"Well, this is quite the adventure," Genesis said with a nervous laugh, trying to lighten the mood.

Zuri didn't respond right away. She was staring out at the turbulent water, a troubled look on her face.

"What's wrong?" Genesis asked, touching her arm.

"This isn't what I planned. I was hoping we'd be able to relax and talk about everything. I don't want to leave this island and go back home the same way we left." Zuri looked at Genesis, her eyes pleading. "I'm so scared of losing you."

Genesis wanted nothing more than to comfort her as she looked into Zuri's eyes. She reached out and took her hands in her own. "I'm scared too, baby. I tell you what, let's eat and talk, just like you planned. We're here, and we have time."

They settled onto the blanket they'd brought from the beach, spreading out their picnic supplies. Rain and crashing waves echoed through the cave, creating a strangely intimate atmosphere.

Genesis opened the wicker picnic basket, revealing an array of gourmet delights Zuri had packed. The aroma of freshly baked bread wafted through the air as Genesis pulled out a crusty baguette, still warm from the bakery. Beside it lay an assortment of artisanal cheeses.

Zuri produced a small wooden cutting board and a knife, slicing the baguette into perfect rounds. The knife glided through the bread, releasing more of its heavenly scent. Genesis arranged the cheese alongside the bread, creating a rustic charcuterie board right there on the cave floor.

Next came a container of plump, juicy strawberries, their vibrant red color a stark contrast to the cool, damp cave walls. Genesis arranged them next to a small jar of local honey, its golden hue catching what little light filtered into their shelter. She couldn't resist dipping her finger into the honey, savoring its sweet, floral notes on her tongue.

From the depths of the basket, Zuri produced a bottle of chilled white wine and two glasses. She poured them each a generous serving, the pale golden liquid glinting in the dim light of the cave.

"To unexpected adventures," Zuri said, raising her glass.

Genesis clinked her glass against Zuri's. "And to facing our fears together."

They sipped the crisp wine, letting the flavors dance on their tongues. The tension between them was palpable, like a living thing coiled in the small space.

Zuri drew in a long breath. "So maybe I should go first."

She bit into some bread and cheese before continuing. "Why have you been so distant about the wedding planning? Every time I bring it up, you brush it off or change the subject."

Genesis looked down, unsure of how to respond. She hadn't realized how her behavior had been affecting Zuri. "I'm sorry, that wasn't my intent. It's just..." She paused, struggling to find the right words.

"It's just what?" Zuri prompted.

"I know you believe that Shannon is the reason I'm scared of getting married again, and I'd be lying if I said that wasn't part of it." Genesis' fingers twisted the stem of her wine glass. "But it's more than that. I'm scared of failing again, of disappointing you like I disappointed her."

Zuri's eyes filled with understanding. "Baby, you could never disappoint me. I love you for who you are, not for some idealized version of a perfect wife."

Tears pricked at the corners of her eyes. "I hear you, but there's this voice in my head that keeps telling me I'm not good enough, that I'll mess things up somehow. Like I'm not meant to have a proper family."

"Gen, you didn't make Shannon cheat on you. You both were young when you got together and from what you told me, she wasn't the best wife herself."

"It's still hard to shake those feelings of inadequacy sometimes." She took a deep breath, gathering her courage. "And I guess... I've been avoiding wedding planning because it makes everything more real. Like once we start planning, there's no turning back."

Zuri's brow furrowed in concern. "Do you... not want to marry me?"

"No! That's not it at all," Genesis said, squeezing Zuri's hand. "I want to marry you more than anything. But it's like...

the closer we get to the wedding, the more I worry about messing things up."

Zuri scooted closer, wrapping an arm around Genesis's shoulders. "Baby, I need you to hear me. You are not going to mess this up. We're in this together, okay?"

"Okay." Genesis drizzled some honey onto a strawberry before taking a bite. "Why were you scared to tell me how much my attitude bothered you?"

Zuri twisted the ring on her finger. "I guess I was afraid of pushing you away. I didn't want to come across as some bridezilla obsessed with wedding details." She paused, biting her lip. "And... I thought that if I pressed too hard, you might decide you didn't want to get married after all."

"Oh, Z, I never meant to make you doubt my commitment to us."

"I know, babe. I've wanted so long to find someone I could build a life with, and when I found you, it was like everything clicked into place. But I'll admit, I made it more about me than anything. Your needs matter, too."

Genesis felt her heart swell with emotion at Zuri's words. She leaned in and pressed a kiss to her fiancée's lips. "It's the same for me. You're everything I've ever wanted, and I'm so grateful we found each other."

Rain pounding against the rocks outside filled the silence as they gazed into each other's eyes.

"My turn." Genesis said as she poured them some more wine. "There are times when I feel like one of your projects."

Zuri's brow furrowed as she considered Genesis' words. She took a sip of wine, buying herself a moment to gather her thoughts. "What do you mean by that?"

"Well, you have this whole life that you've built. Your family, your business, Beacon, your routines. It's like I'm being slotted into your existing life, rather than us building something new together. Like I'm an addition to your world, but not changing it."

Zuri's eyes widened in surprise. "Gen, you've changed everything for me. Before you, I was just going through the motions. Sure, I had my family and my work, but something was always missing. You filled a void I didn't even realize was there."

"Really?"

"Really," Zuri affirmed. "My parents were always working, together, apart, it didn't matter. Business came first. I've internalized that more than I realized."

Genesis nodded, understanding dawning on her face. "That explains a lot. But honey, we're building a life together. I want to be part of your world, not just an afterthought."

"You're right and I'm so sorry. You're not an afterthought, Gen. You're everything to me." She paused, gathering her thoughts. "And you are right about my need for control. I've always felt like I had to be in charge, to make everything perfect. But I realize now that I've been trying to control how you see me and how much of myself I give, but expecting you to be open. That's not fair."

"I appreciate you saying that. Honestly, I think we're both a bit guilty of that. But I fell in love with you, not some perfect version of you. I want all of you, the good and the messy parts."

"Are you sure about that?"

Genesis laughed. "I'm sure. In fact, I love your messy parts. Like how you always leave your towel on the bathroom floor, or how you can't resist buying every new gadget that comes out."

Zuri grinned. "Hey, those gadgets are investments!"

"Sure they are, babe," Genesis said, rolling her eyes playfully. She grew serious again. "But I want us to be partners in everything. That means sharing the good and the bad."

Zuri nodded. "You're right. I want that too. I promise I'll do better at including you in all aspects of my life. No more forgotten date nights."

"And I promise to be more open about my fears and not shut down with wedding planning. We're in this together, right?"

"Of course we are," Zuri said, rubbing her leg. "Listen, I want to ask you something, but I'm afraid it will make you uncomfortable."

Genesis raised an eyebrow, curiosity piqued. "You can ask me anything, Z. What's on your mind?"

"Well," Zuri began, her voice tentative, "I've been thinking about family a lot. Not just the family we're building together, but our roots, where we come from. You don't talk about him much, but I was wondering... about your father."

Genesis' heart sped up at the mention of her father. She inhaled the salty sea air that wafted into their shelter. The cave walls seemed to close in, the rough texture of the rock a stark contrast to the softness of the blanket beneath them.

Zuri sensed her discomfort because she added, "I'm sorry, we don't have to talk about it if you're not comfortable."

"It's okay," Genesis said with a sad smile. "I talk about my mother most and it's because she was the more loving of the two. Dad was not a kind man, and he often seemed agitated by our presence. Almost like he would forget he had children and then we'd do something to remind him, and he'd be angry about it."

"That must have been hard for you growing up."

"It was. He wasn't physically abusive, but his words... they cut deep. He had a way of making you feel insignificant. Like you were a burden he never asked for."

"Oh, Gen," Zuri whispered.

"I remember this one time around eight or nine, I'd just won a dance competition at school. I was so excited to tell him, thinking maybe this time he'd be proud. But when I showed him the trophy, he just looked at it and said, 'What good is that going to do you in the real world?'" Genesis's voice cracked slightly. "I stopped showing him my achievements after that."

Zuri swiped at her cheeks and Genesis realized she had started to cry. She gripped Zuri's hands and kissed them.

"When you said during our fight, that nothing you do is ever good enough…"

Zuri cut her off. "I was angry honey. I didn't mean it."

Genesis held up her hand. "No, you were right. Except it hasn't been Shannon that you've been going up against, it's my dad and my mom. My parents… they set the template for what I thought love was supposed to be. Mom was always trying to please, to be perfect. Dad was never satisfied, always finding fault. I didn't realize how much that affected me until now."

"And you've been afraid of falling into that same pattern with me."

"I've been holding back, afraid that if I let myself commit, I'd end up like my mom, trying to prove my worth to someone who could never be satisfied. So I became like my dad, looking for something to be wrong. Now I'm not saying that you don't have some things to work on, but expecting perfection is a recipe for failure."

Zuri pulled Genesis into a tight embrace, her arms wrapping around her fiancée protectively. "Oh, baby," she murmured, her voice thick with emotion. "I'm so sorry you had to go through that. No child should ever think they are a burden to their parents."

Genesis melted into Zuri's embrace. She hadn't realized how much she needed to share this part of herself, how much of a relief it would be to voice these long-buried feelings.

"Thank you for telling me," Zuri said, running her fingers through Genesis's curls. "And you are never a burden to me."

They shared a tender kiss and as they pulled apart, the sound of the rain outside seemed to lessen.

"I think the storm might be passing," Zuri observed, glancing towards the cave entrance.

Genesis nodded, but made no move to get up. Instead, she snuggled closer to Zuri, resting her head on her shoulder. "Can we stay here a little longer? I'm not ready for this moment to end just yet."

Zuri smiled, wrapping her arms tighter around Genesis. "Of course, baby. We can stay as long as you want."

# Chapter Thirty-Five

Zuri sipped coffee as she looked out the window of the conference room in her lawyer's office. After much debate between their respective counsel, Lea had agreed to withdraw her lawsuit for a sizable settlement. Although it wasn't ideal, Zuri much preferred to be done with it before things got out of hand. So far, there had been some gossip in the blogs, but no major outlet had picked up the story, and she hoped to keep it that way.

The past three weeks since Zuri and Genesis had gotten back from Barbados were showing signs of things returning to normal for them. For a while, it was like a cloud was following them around, raining down whenever things looked up. But now, with this last hurdle cleared, the sun was breaking through. Zuri was grateful for the reprieve.

She turned away from the window as Marcus entered the room with a stack of papers.

"Well, it's done," he said, placing the documents on the table. "Lea has signed the agreement and the funds have been transferred. You're officially in the clear."

Zuri nodded, her shoulders relaxing. "Thank you, Marcus. I appreciate your hard work on this."

"Of course. That's what I'm here for. And you made the right call, Zuri. This could have dragged on for months, maybe even years."

Zuri nodded, her mind already moving on to the next challenge. "What's the damage to our reputation?"

Marcus paused, choosing his words carefully. "Nothing irreparable. We'll put out a statement emphasizing that no wrongdoing was admitted, and that you settled to avoid a protracted legal battle."

"Mm," Zuri murmured, unconvinced. She turned from the window. "I want to be crystal clear about our messaging. We can't afford any ambiguity that could be misconstrued by the media."

Marcus nodded, pulling out his tablet to take notes. "Absolutely. We'll craft a statement that leaves no room for misinterpretation."

They shook hands and Zuri pulled out her phone while settling into a chair so she could respond to a few messages before heading out. She didn't notice that someone else had entered the room after Marcus left until she smelled a familiar perfume.

"Hi Zuri," Lea said, standing by the door.

Zuri composed herself, her expression shifting to one of cool professionalism. "Lea," she said, her voice even. "I didn't expect to see you here."

Lea took a hesitant step into the room, her fingers fidgeting with the strap of her purse. "I wanted to talk to you. Without our lawyers present."

Zuri leaned back in her chair, crossing her arms. "I'm not sure that's a good idea. We've just settled everything."

"Right," Lea said, moving closer. "But I needed to say something. To you directly."

There was a vulnerability in Lea's eyes that made Zuri pause. Against her better judgment, she gestured to the chair across from her. "Alright. I'm listening."

Lea sat down across from her, her posture tense as she met Zuri's gaze. "I wanted to apologize for everything. The lawsuit, the accusations... I let my anger and hurt feelings cloud my judgment."

Zuri's eyebrows rose, but she remained silent, waiting for Lea to continue.

"I acknowledge that our parting wasn't ideal," Lea continued, her voice quivering slightly. "But I never meant for it to go this far. I must confess, there was a sense of betrayal that consumed me when I learned about your relationship with Genesis, and the anger grew over time. And then even our friendship fizzled out. So when you came in that day and took away the one thing that gave me purpose, I lashed out. I'm not proud of it, and I regret my actions."

Zuri sat back, processing Lea's words. "But not enough to retract your claims without taking a pay out?"

Lea's eyes dropped to her hands, which were clasped in her lap. "I'm aware it looks bad, but the settlement wasn't about the money, not really. It was about..." she trailed off, searching for the right words.

"About what?" Zuri pressed.

Lea took a deep breath. "It was about closure, I guess. And maybe a little about saving face. I was wrong, but there was no way for me to back down without losing everything."

"Hmm, but you sure seemed okay with having me possibly lose what I've built."

Lea looked down at her hands, then back up at Zuri with tears in her eyes. "I'm sorry for putting you through this. I hope that someday we can move past it. Not be friends, but at least be civil."

Zuri studied Lea for a long moment, taking in the genuine remorse etched across her face. She leaned forward.

"Lea," she began, her voice low and measured, "I appreciate your apology, but I'm not going to let you play victim here." She stood, smoothing the wrinkles from her tailored suit. "You didn't just put me through a legal battle. You put Beacon and all the kids and teachers there at risk. And now you waltz in here, after taking a hefty settlement, to do what? Ease your conscience?"

Lea flinched, her eyes dropping to the table.

Zuri continued, her words precise and cutting. "You say you want closure, but it seems to me you're just looking for absolution. I'm not in the business of handing out forgiveness just because you've decided you're ready for it."

Zuri gathered her things, slipping her phone into her designer bag. She paused, her hand on the door handle, and turned back to Lea.

"I'm glad you regret your actions. Perhaps you've grown. But actions have consequences. And sometimes 'sorry' isn't enough to undo the damage."

Lea nodded, her eyes glistening. "I understand. I hope someday..."

"Someday is a long way off," Zuri cut in. "For now, I think it's best if we keep our distance. Stick to the terms of the settlement. No contact. Seeing you for who you really are, I hope the money you stole from me keeps you warm at night because even without Genesis in the picture, I would never have chosen you."

Zuri stepped out of the conference room, letting the door click shut behind her. Her words had been harsh, but it needed to be said. Once inside the elevator, she pressed the button for the lobby, leaning against the cool metal wall as the car descended.

Her phone buzzed in her bag, and she fished it out, grateful for the distraction. A smile tugged at her lips when she saw Genesis's name on the screen.

"Hey, baby," she answered with a smile. "How'd the auditions go?"

Genesis's melodic laugh filled her ear. "Oh, you should've seen these kids, Zuri. So much talent! I think we've found our lead for the Fall showcase."

As she listened to Genesis's excited chatter about the young dancers, her body relaxed. By the time she reached her car in the parking garage, her entire mood had been lifted. Another call came through just as theirs ended. She pulled out of the garage and put it on her Bluetooth.

"Eli, what's going on?"

Her cousin stumbled over his words before he got out what he wanted to say. "Z, William is threatening to walk."

They were in pre production on the film and so far Phillip had been behaving, other than a few diva moments here and there. She didn't expect to be getting an emergency call so early on.

"William is as chill as it gets. What the hell happened that he's making threats?"

Zuri's grip tightened on the steering wheel as she listened to Eli's exasperated sigh on the other end of the line.

"It's Phillip," Eli explained. "He's been pushing Will's buttons all week, but today he crossed a line. He showed up drunk to the costume fitting and started making crude comments about Will's girlfriend."

Zuri cursed under her breath. "Damn it. I thought we were past this with him. Where is he now?"

"Reggie's got him sobering up in his trailer. But Will's furious. He says he won't work with Phillip unless we make some changes."

Zuri pinched the bridge of her nose, a headache was coming on. "Okay, I'm on my way. Don't let either of them leave. I'll handle this."

She ended the call and made a quick U-turn, heading towards the studio. As she drove, her mind raced with potential solutions. They couldn't afford to lose William. He was perfect for the role and his name carried weight, but Phillip was also crucial to the project, despite his behavior.

When she arrived at the studio, she found Eli pacing outside William's trailer.

"Where's Will?" she asked, striding up to her cousin.

"Inside." Eli jerked his thumb towards the trailer. "He's calmed down a bit, but he's still pretty pissed."

Zuri nodded. "Alright, I'll talk to him first. You go check on Phillip, make sure he's sobered up enough to have a conversation."

She knocked on William's trailer door and entered when she heard his muffled, "Come in."

William was sitting on the small couch, his usual easygoing expression tight with anger. "Zuri," he greeted her, standing up. "I'm sorry about this, but I can't work with that man."

Zuri held up a hand. "I understand, Will. And I'm sorry this happened. Can you tell me what he did?"

William ran a hand through his hair, frustration evident in every movement. "Look, Zuri, I've been patient. I'm aware that Phillip's got a reputation, and I figured I could handle it. But today..." He shook his head. "He stumbled into the fitting room, reeking of booze, and started making these disgusting comments about Aisha. Asking if she was as 'flexible' as she looked in her yoga videos, if you know what I mean."

Zuri's jaw clenched. "I'm so sorry, Will. That's unacceptable."

"Damn right it is," William agreed, his voice rising. "I've put up with his antics, his mood swings, even his 'method acting' nonsense. But I draw the line at disrespecting my girlfriend."

"I understand," Zuri said, her tone sincere. "And I promise you, this won't happen again. We'll make whatever changes necessary to ensure a safe and respectful set."

William's shoulders relaxed slightly. "I appreciate that. But what does that mean? Keeping it 100, I don't see how I can work with this dude after this."

Zuri took a deep breath. "Give me a chance to have a conversation with him. If he's willing to make some serious changes - including getting help for his drinking - would you be open to giving it another shot?"

William hesitated, then nodded. "Maybe. But he'd have to make a genuine effort. If he doesn't get his shit together, I'm out."

"That's fair," Zuri agreed. "I'll go talk to him now. Thank you for being willing to work with me on this. I promise I'll make it right."

As she left William's trailer, her relief gave way to anger. She marched towards Phillip's trailer, hoping that he was sober enough to understand the gravity of the situation. Eli stood nearby, arms crossed, a look of disgust on his face.

"This man is out of control. Why did we want him again?" Eli said once she reached the trailer.

Zuri let out a heavy sigh. "Because when he's on, he's brilliant. But you're right, this behavior is not okay." She squared her shoulders. "Let me handle this."

She rapped on the trailer door before entering. Phillip was on the couch, sprawled out and looking disheveled and bleary-eyed. He sat up when he saw Zuri attempting to smooth his rumpled shirt.

"Ah, the boss lady herself," he slurred, a lopsided grin on his face. "Come to join the party?"

Zuri's eyes narrowed. "This isn't a party, Phillip. This is your career going up in flames."

His grin faltered. "What? Come on, it was just a bit of fun..."

"Fun?" Zuri's voice was sharp as a whip. "You call harassing your lead actor's girlfriend 'fun'? Showing up drunk to work 'fun'?"

Phillip had the decency to look ashamed, but Zuri wasn't finished.

"Let me be crystal clear," she continued. "You're on thin ice. William is ready to walk, and I'm considering letting him."

"What? No, you can't do that. This is my film," he said, his words slurred.

Zuri snapped her fingers in front of his face. "Hey, wake the fuck up."

Phillip's eyes fluttered open, struggling to focus on Zuri's stern face. She leaned in close.

"Listen to me very carefully, Phillip. We wanted you because you have directed some of the best films of our generation. But we are not obligated to put up with all of your bullshit. You signed a contract, and it says any violation of that contract means we have the right to remove you from this film. You agreed to that."

That sobered Phillip up quickly. "Yes, I recall."

"Good. Now, here's what's going to happen. You're going to sober up, and then apologize to William and Aisha, in person, and sincerely. After that, you will enter a rehab program. We'll delay production for two weeks to accommodate this."

Phillip's eyes widened, but he shook his head in agreement.

She turned to leave, but Phillip's hand shot out, grabbing her wrist. Zuri froze, looking down at him with a mixture of surprise and irritation.

"Wait," Phillip said, his voice clearer. "I... I need to tell you something."

Zuri hesitated, then turned to face him, arms crossed. "What is it?"

Phillip released her wrist. "I wasn't just drinking for no reason," he admitted, his eyes downcast. "This film... it's not just another project for me. It's everything."

He leaned forward, elbows on his knees, his voice dropping to a near whisper. "My last three films were flops. The critics loved them, but they didn't make their money back. Studios don't care about awards. They want to make money on their investment."

"That's why you were looking for a smaller studio," Zuri said, understanding. "You need a hit."

Phillip nodded, his eyes glistening. "If this film doesn't succeed, my career is over. I'll be washed up at 50." He laughed bitterly. "Can you imagine? The top director of my generation and I'll be lucky if they'll let me direct episodes of Law and Order."

"That's a bit dramatic, don't you think?"

"No, I don't think so. I'm a Black film director, Z. Not only am I rare, but I don't get endless chances like everyone else."

Zuri knew all too well the pressure of being a Black professional in an industry that often seemed stacked against them.

"Phillip, I get it. I do. But drowning your fears in alcohol and acting like an asshole isn't going to help."

Phillip nodded, wiping at his eyes. "I panicked. The weight of it all just hit me the last few days and... I couldn't handle it."

Zuri shifted into movie exec mode and let out a sigh. "This film will be amazing. We've got a stellar cast, a brilliant script, and you at the helm. Your talent hasn't gone anywhere. This is going to work, got it?"

Phillip looked up at her, a glimmer of hope in his bloodshot eyes. "You believe that?"

"I do," Zuri said firmly. "But I need you at your best. No more of this," she gestured around, indicating his drunken state. "We need you to be focused and clear-headed. Can you do that?"

Phillip nodded, straightening up slightly. "Yes, I can. I promise, Zuri. No more screw-ups."

"Good. Now, get some rest. We'll talk more tomorrow when you're sober."

As she turned to leave, Phillip called out, "Zuri?"

She paused at the door, looking back at him.

"Thank you," he mumbled. "For everything. I've been an asshole to you and your cousins. You took a chance on me when a lot of other studios didn't want to. I don't deserve your kindness."

Zuri gave him a small, tired smile. "Don't mistake my kindness for weakness. I expect a return on my investment."

As she closed the door behind her, Zuri leaned against it for a moment, exhaling slowly. The weight of the day pressed down on her shoulders. The good news was she had an in with Phillip, which she hoped would translate into an easier film shoot.

Elijah walked up to her with a steaming cup of coffee in hand. "Thought you might need this," he said, offering her the mug.

Zuri accepted it, inhaling the rich aroma. "You're a lifesaver, Eli."

"How did it go?"

"Better than expected," Zuri replied, taking a sip of the hot brew. "I may have gotten through to him."

Elijah chuckled as they walked back towards her car. "If this isn't 'be careful what you wish for' in action."

Zuri hugged him tight and opened her car door. "There's a reason they say never meet your heroes."

They exchanged goodbyes and Zuri hesitated after turning on the car. Her instinct was to head home and veg out, but she had been working on not closing herself off when she had a rough day. So, she pulled out her phone and dialed Genesis' number. The line rang twice before Gen's voice filled her ear.

"Hey baby, is everything okay?"

Zuri sank into the driver's seat, letting out a long sigh. "It's been a really long day. Are you still at Beacon?"

"Just finished up. Was about to head home and heat up some leftovers. Want me to swing by your place instead?"

"That would be amazing. I'll pick up some wine on the way. I think we both deserve a glass after today."

"Sounds perfect. I'll see you soon, love."

Zuri ended the call, excited to go home. As she navigated through the city streets, a sense of gratitude washed over her. Despite the chaos of the day, she had Genesis to go home to.

She stopped at their favorite wine shop, selecting a rich red wine that Genesis loved. As she waited in line to pay, her phone buzzed with a text from her cousin Reggie:

"Heard about Phillip. You okay? Need backup?"

Zuri smiled, appreciating her family's support. She typed back a quick reply:

"Handled. Fill you in tomorrow. Thanks, cuz."

By the time Zuri pulled into her driveway, she could see Genesis' car already parked out front. The sight of it brought a wave of comfort. She grabbed the wine bottle and her bag, making her way to the front door. When she entered, the aroma of spices and vegetables filled the air.

"Gen?" Zuri called out, kicking off her heels with a sigh of relief.

"In the kitchen!" Genesis' melodic voice rang out.

Zuri padded into the kitchen, where Genesis stood at the stove, stirring something in a large pan. She was wearing one of Zuri's old t-shirts and a pair of leggings, her wild curls piled high on her head. The sight of her made Zuri's heart swell.

"I thought you were just heating up leftovers," Zuri said, wrapping her arms around Genesis from behind and planting a kiss on her neck.

Genesis leaned back into the embrace. "Changed my mind. Figured you could use some comfort food after the day you've had. I'm whipping up that spicy shrimp and vegetable stir-fry you love."

Zuri was touched by Genesis' thoughtfulness. She tightened her arms around her girlfriend's waist, burying her face in Genesis' neck for a moment.

"You're amazing."

Genesis chuckled. "So I've been told." She grabbed her phone and showed a headline to Zuri. "Looks like this is finally over."

Zuri's eyes widened as she scanned the headline on Genesis' phone: "Media Mogul Francis Baker Found Guilty on All Charges." Her breath caught in her throat as she read further, taking in the details of the verdict. Multiple counts of sexual assault, harassment, and abuse of power - her godfather had been convicted on every single one.

"Oh my God," Zuri whispered, her hands shaking slightly as she took the phone from Genesis. She sank onto a nearby stool, her mind reeling.

Genesis turned off the stove and moved to Zuri's side, placing a comforting hand on her back. "Are you okay?"

Zuri nodded slowly, still staring at the screen. "I... I think so. It's just... I never thought I'd see the day, you know?" She looked up at Genesis, her eyes glistening. "After everything he did, all the women he hurt... I was starting to think he'd never face justice."

"Now you and your cousins can move forward without this hanging over you."

Zuri nodded, taking a deep breath. "You're right. It's finally over." She looked up at Genesis with a small smile. "Thank you for being here with me for this."

Genesis cupped Zuri's face gently. "Always, baby. That's what partners are for."

Zuri leaned into Genesis' touch, feeling a wave of gratitude wash over her. After a moment, she straightened up and wiped her eyes. "Okay, enough heavy stuff for one day. Let's eat that amazing dinner you made and open this wine. I want to hear all about those talented kids you auditioned."

Genesis grinned, pressing a quick kiss to Zuri's forehead before turning back to the stove. "You got it. And don't think I didn't notice that fancy bottle you brought home. You're spoiling me, Ms. Baker."

Zuri smirked and shrugged her shoulders. "Maybe just a little. Only the best for you, my love."

As they settled in to eat, Zuri felt a sense of peace settle over her. The day had been a rollercoaster of emotions, from the tense meeting with Lea to the drama on set with Phillip, and now the news about her godfather. But here, in her kitchen with Genesis by her side, she felt grounded.

In that moment, surrounded by the aroma of sizzling stir fry and their love, Zuri finally understood what it meant to be at peace.

# Chapter Thirty-Six

"Hey Gen, do you have any more boxes? I used all the ones in the garage?"

Shannon leaned into Genesis' office, her tank top damp with sweat. She was moving into her new apartment. Her girlfriend had helped her secure a lease and after several interviews, she had a new job as an analyst at a smaller network. The pay would not be as high, but it was something she could work with and get back on top.

Genesis looked up from her computer, a smile spreading across her face. "I think there might be a few more in the closet. Let me check real quick."

As she rummaged through the shelves, she called out, "How's the packing coming along? Need any help?"

Shannon let out a dramatic sigh. "It's going. Slowly but surely. Somehow, I managed to accumulate even more stuff in the short time I stayed here."

Genesis chuckled, emerging from the closet with a handful of folded boxes. "That's always how it goes. You think you're a minimalist until you have to pack your life into boxes."

She handed the boxes to Shannon, who accepted them

gratefully. "Thanks, Gen. You're a lifesaver. By the way, Kenzi told me that you went dress shopping a few days ago."

"Yeah, I've been putting it off, but I was kind of excited. You and I didn't get to wear anything fancy when we got married."

Shannon laughed out loud. "Right? I had my rented tux that was way too big, and where did you get that dress again?"

Genesis laughed too. "Oh my god, that dress! I found it at that little thrift shop on 5th Street. Remember how the hem was uneven, and I had to use a safety pin?"

Shannon shook her head, grinning. "And yet, you still managed to look stunning."

"Flatterer. But seriously, I'm excited to try on something new."

"That's great. I'm excited for you. You deserve to be happy."

"Thanks, Shan. That means a lot coming from you." She glanced at the clock on her desk. "It's almost time for me to get ready for the party. Are you coming?"

"Am I coming? Your girl rented out the Kitty Kat Club. Of course I'll be there. Melanie can't wait either."

Shortly after they returned home from their Barbados mini vacay, Genesis settled on a time frame for their wedding. Within a month and a half, everything had come together. Zuri was on it as if she had just been waiting to be given the green light. It was Zuri's idea to have a joint bachelorette party and rent out the infamous lesbian lounge for a night of sensuous but classy fun.

Genesis rubbed her hands together. "Oh, it's going to be a good time. Zuri's gone all out for this one."

Shannon raised an eyebrow, a mischievous glint in her eye. "I bet she has. Your woman doesn't do anything halfway, does she?"

Genesis shook her head, laughing. "Not a chance. Go big or go home."

"I bet," Shannon said, adjusting the bags in her arms. "Well, I better get back to packing. See you tonight."

"Don't be late!"

After Shannon left, Genesis turned back to her computer, trying to focus on the last bit of work she needed to finish before the party. But her mind kept wandering to thoughts of Zuri, of the upcoming wedding, of the life they were building together.

A couple of hours later, she closed her laptop, deciding that work could wait until tomorrow. Tonight was about celebration and fun.

As she stood to leave her office, her phone buzzed with a text from Zuri:

"Can't wait to see you tonight, beautiful. I have a surprise for you. ;)"

Zuri's surprises were always memorable. She texted back:

"Ooh, I love your surprises. Can't wait! See you soon, babe."

She hurried to her bedroom to get ready, her mind buzzing with excitement. As she showered and styled her hair, she hummed, unable to contain her joy. She slipped into the slinky red dress she'd bought, admiring how it hugged her curves in all the right places.

Just as she was applying the finishing touches to her makeup, her doorbell rang. She didn't know who it was since she was supposed to be meeting Kenzie and her friends at the club.

When she got downstairs and looked through the peephole, she screamed in delight and yanked the door open.

"Drea, what are you doing here?" she said as she pulled her into a hug.

Andrea laughed, returning the hug with equal enthusiasm. "Surprise! You didn't think I'd miss my bestie's bachelorette party, did you?"

Genesis pulled back, her eyes wide with joy. "But I thought you could only come down for the wedding next weekend."

"That was a little white lie. I work from home, so I'll be able to take care of things while I'm here. Besides, Zuri convinced me while you all were visiting that I could make it work and she was right. Rebecca sends her love, by the way."

Of course, Zuri would do something like this. "She didn't tell me a thing," she said, shaking her head in amazement.

"Well, it wouldn't be a surprise if she did, would it? Now, are you going to let me in, or are we having this reunion on your doorstep?"

Genesis laughed and stepped aside, allowing her to enter.

"So," Drea said, turning to face Genesis and placing her bags down. "I hear we're in for quite a night. Kitty Kat Club, huh? Zuri doesn't mess around. And neither do you Miss Red Dress. You look hot!" Andrea exclaimed, giving Genesis a twirl. "Zuri's not gonna know what hit her."

Genesis laughed. "That's the plan. I'll let you freshen up, then we can get the car and head out."

Andrea gathered her bags. "I know where the guest room is. And I saw our ride waiting for us when I got here. You might want to check outside."

Genesis went back to the door and pulled it open to reveal a sleek black limousine parked at the curb, Drake standing at attention by the open door.

Her jaw dropped. "Oh my god," she breathed, taking in the sight of the luxurious vehicle. She turned back to Andrea, who was grinning from ear to ear. "Did you...?"

"Nope, this is all Zuri," Andrea replied, joining Genesis at the door. "She texted me earlier to let me know it would be here. Your girl knows how to kick off a celebration."

Genesis smiled. "She never ceases to amaze me."

Drake approached them with a polite nod. "Good evening, ladies. Are you ready to depart?"

"Hi Drake, just give us a few minutes," Genesis said, still a bit dazed. "We'll be right out."

As they closed the door, Andrea squeezed Genesis' arm. "I'm going to freshen up real quick. Don't leave without me!"

While Andrea got ready, Genesis took a moment to text Zuri:

> A limo? You're too much, babe. Thank you. I love you.

The response came almost immediately:

> Only the best for my queen. Love you more. See you soon.

Genesis felt her heart swell with love and excitement. She couldn't wait to see what other surprises the night had in store.

Fifteen minutes later, Genesis and Andrea settled in the back of the limousine, sipping champagne and giggling like schoolgirls. Shannon decided to meet them there.

"So, spill," Andrea said, leaning in. "How are you feeling about tonight? Nervous? Excited?"

Genesis took a sip of her champagne, considering. "A little of both, I guess. Zuri's always full of surprises, and I know she's gone all out for this. But mostly, I'm just excited to celebrate with everyone."

"And to see some hot dancers, right?" Andrea winked.

Genesis laughed, a slight blush creeping up her cheeks. "Well, that's a bonus. But I'm more excited about marrying Zuri than anything else."

"I'm glad you two figured things out. I knew you would."

As they chatted and caught up, the limo glided through the city streets. Before long, they pulled up in front of the Kitty Kat

Club. The neon sign cast a pink glow over the sidewalk. Normally there would be a crowd waiting to get in, but tonight, the entrance was clear except for a few familiar faces waiting by the door.

When Drake opened the door, Genesis and Andrea stepped out to a chorus of cheers and whistles. Kenzie, Lucy and Rain rushed forward to greet them.

"Look at you, hot mama!" Kenzie exclaimed, pulling Genesis into a tight hug. "That dress is fire!"

Genesis laughed, twirling for everyone. "Thanks, babe. You all look amazing, too!"

Once inside, Genesis' eyes wandered over the space. It was as if she had stepped into a sensual dream. Anticipation filled the air, mingling with a heady mix of perfume, alcohol, and something deeper, more primal. A sultry, slow rhythm replaced the usual thumping bass of the club, pulsing through Genesis's body and making her skin tingle.

A rosy glow bathed the main stage, while sheer curtains were artfully draped around its edges, promising tantalizing glimpses of what was to come. To the left, a champagne fountain bubbled, surrounded by an array of delicate flutes and an assortment of chocolates and strawberries.

As they moved further into the club, Genesis noticed small, intimate alcoves tucked away in corners, each lit by flickering candles and adorned with plush cushions in rich hues. Flowing fabrics in shades of burgundy, purple, and gold covered the walls, creating an atmosphere of opulent sensuality.

A circular bar dominated the center of the room. Behind it, bartenders in sleek, form-fitting outfits moved with fluid grace, mixing cocktails with a flair that was almost hypnotic.

A hand touched her arm and she turned to see Lucy, her eyes wide with excitement. "Can you believe this?" she whispered, gesturing around the transformed space. "Zuri outdid herself."

Genesis nodded, still taking it all in. "It's incredible," she breathed.

More guests started filing in as Genesis found a seat. They'd kept the guest list small, only people within their inner circle. She watched as Shannon and Melanie entered, hands clasped together, their eyes widening as they took in the transformed space. Alma followed soon after with a couple of mutual friends of hers and Zuri's.

Several more people arrived, filling in the seats. They had set up the seating to create a more intimate space despite the size, exactly the atmosphere that she and Zuri preferred.

Genesis looked around, wondering where her fiancee was, when suddenly, the lights dimmed and a hush fell over the crowd. A spotlight illuminated the stage, and a sultry voice purred over the sound system.

"Ladies and gentlemen, please welcome one of our guests of honor, the soon-to-be Mrs. Zuri Baker-Malone!"

Genesis' heart skipped a beat as Zuri emerged from behind the curtain, looking stunning in a fitted black jumpsuit. Her dreadlocks were piled high on her head in an intricate updo, and her smile was radiant as she scanned the room, her eyes landing on Genesis.

"Welcome, everyone," Zuri said. "Tonight, we're here to celebrate love, friendship, and the beginning of a beautiful journey." Her gaze locked with Genesis's. "My love, this is for you."

With a snap of her fingers, the curtains parted, revealing a burlesque dancer in silhouette. The room erupted in cheers and whistles as Zuri made her way down the stage steps. She stopped in front of Genesis and leaned down to give her a kiss.

"You look breathtaking," Zuri murmured into her ear before sitting beside her.

"So do you," she whispered back. "I can't believe you did all this."

"Oh, baby, this is just the beginning."

As the spotlight intensified, the silhouette of the dancer came into sharp focus. She was a vision of curves and grace, her deep ebony skin gleaming under the lights. Her hair was a glorious crown of tight coils, adorned with sparkling pins that caught the light with every movement.

She moved, her hips swaying hypnotically to the slow, sensual beat of the music. Her costume, a dazzling creation of red sequins and black lace, hugged every luscious curve of her body. With each step, the fringe on her skirt shimmered and swayed, drawing the eye to the mesmerizing movement of her hips.

Her hands, adorned with long, crimson nails, traced the contours of her body, teasing the audience with the promise of what was to come. She moved with a confidence that was both powerful and alluring, her eyes scanning the room with a smoldering gaze that made each person feel as if she was performing just for them.

As the music swelled, she peeled away layers of her costume with tantalizing slowness. First, she removed a long glove, sliding each finger free with deliberate sensuality. Then she unhooked the skirt, and it fell to the floor in a pool at her feet.

The audience was entranced, their eyes following every movement, every reveal. Zuri's hand tightened in hers, both of them caught up in the spell the dancer was weaving.

With a flourish, the dancer spun, revealing an intricately designed corset that accentuated her hourglass figure. She arched her back, running her hands through her hair, her expression one of pure ecstasy.

When the music hit its crescendo, she made her way down the stage steps, moving through the audience with feline grace.

She paused at their table, locking eyes with Genesis and Zuri. With a wink and a blown kiss, she twirled away, leaving behind a trail of glitter and the lingering scent of her perfume.

The performance concluded with a final, breathtaking pose, the dancer's body silhouetted against a burst of red light. Thunderous applause followed, with Genesis and Zuri on their feet, cheering louder than anyone.

"Now that was sexy," Rain said from behind them, clapping vigorously.

As the applause died down, Zuri leaned in close to Genesis. "What did you think, baby?"

Genesis turned to Zuri, mouth agape. "That was incredible!"

Zuri grinned, pride evident in her expression. "Only the best for you, my love. But the night is still young."

As if on cue, the lights dimmed once again, and a new beat started pulsing through the speakers. This time, a masculine voice announced, "Ladies, get ready for some more eye candy!"

The curtains parted to reveal a lineup of muscular studs, each dressed in different fantasy outfits - a firefighter, a police officer, a construction worker, and more. They moved in perfect synchronization, their bodies rippling with each choreographed motion.

Genesis cheeks flushed as she watched the performance unfold. She glanced around the room, noting the mixed reactions of their friends. Some, like Rain and Lucy, were whooping and hollering, while others, like Shannon and Alma, watched with amused smiles.

As the studs made their way into the audience, Zuri leaned in again. "I wanted to make sure there was something for everyone," she said with a wink.

Genesis laughed, squeezing Zuri's hand. "You succeeded there."

The night continued in a whirlwind of performances, each more impressive than the last. There were acrobats who twisted and turned in silks suspended from the ceiling, drag kings who lip-synced to classic rock anthems, and even a magician who incorporated sensual illusions into her act.

Between performances, Genesis and Zuri mingled with their friends, sipping on crafted cocktails and indulging in the decadent spread of appetizers. The atmosphere was electric.

At one point, Rain dragged Genesis over to the bar and convinced her to do some shots.

"God, I wish I was a lesbian," Rain said after throwing back the first one.

"How many of these have you had?"

Rain grinned, her eyes unfocused. "Enough to make me question my life choices, apparently. But seriously, you and Zuri are so lucky. This party is insane!"

Genesis laughed, shaking her head. "We are lucky. And you're drunk, sweetie."

"Maybe a little," Rain admitted, swaying. "But can you blame me? Those dancers were hot!"

"Brick not taking care of business, or.."

"Brick and I are no more."

Genesis's eyes widened in shock. "What? When did this happen?"

Rain shrugged, her carefree demeanor slipping for a moment. "About a month ago. I just... I realized I was trying to force things, you know? And I didn't want to settle."

Genesis pulled her friend into a tight hug. "Oh, Rain. I'm so sorry. Why didn't you tell me?"

Rain hugged her back, sniffling a little. "I didn't want to bring down the mood with all the wedding excitement. Plus, I'm okay. It was the right decision."

Genesis pulled back, studying her friend's face. "Are you sure? You know you can always talk to me, right?"

Rain nodded, wiping at her eyes. "I know. Thanks, Gen. I promise I'm good. Tonight's about celebrating you and Zuri. We'll talk later."

After downing two more shots in solidarity, Genesis guided Rain back to her seat, then plopped down beside Zuri.

"Hey you," she said with a giggle.

"Hmm, those drinks seem to have you feeling good." Zuri kissed her, nibbling on her bottom lip. "You taste delicious."

"Ahh, ahh, ahh. Remember, no nookie until the honeymoon."

Zuri smirked. "Who said anything about nookie? I'm just appreciating my beautiful fiancée."

A flush spread across her cheeks, partly from the alcohol and partly from Zuri's intense gaze. She leaned in close, her lips brushing against Zuri's ear. "Well, keep looking at me like that and we might have to bend the rules a little."

Zuri's breath hitched, her hand tightening on Genesis's waist. "Don't tempt me, baby."

Just then, a spotlight illuminated the stage. The sultry voice from earlier announced, "Ladies and gentlemen, it's time for our guests of honor to take center stage!"

Zuri stood up, tugging her towards the stage. "What's happening?" she whispered, a mixture of excitement and nervousness bubbling in her stomach.

Zuri rubbed her hands together.. "One last surprise, my love."

As they ascended the steps to the stage, the crew brought out two ornate chairs. Zuri guided Genesis to sit in one, then took her place in the other. Two dancers - one femme, one stud - emerged from behind the curtains as the music shifted to a slow, sensual rhythm.

The dancers moved with fluid grace, circling Zuri and Genesis like big cats stalking their prey. With a seductive smile, the femme dancer, her curves highlighted by a shimmering gold bodysuit, approached Genesis. Meanwhile, the stud, sporting tight leather pants and a vest that showed off sculpted arms, moved over to Zuri.

Genesis' dancer moved around her, her body undulating to the beat. She caught Zuri's eye across the stage, seeing her fiancée's amused and flustered expression as the stud dancer performed similar moves for her.

The dancers never touched them directly, but their proximity and the heat of their movements were intoxicating. Genesis found herself caught between laughter and a very real surge of arousal as the performance continued.

As the song reached its climax, the dancers finished with a flourish, striking poses on either side of Zuri and Genesis. There were cheers and applause, as their friends whistled and shouted encouragement.

Dazed, Genesis stood up, reaching for Zuri's hand. They thanked the dancers, who bowed before exiting the stage.

As Genesis and Zuri headed back to their seats, the energy in the room shifted. The pulsing music faded into a softer, more melodic tune, and the lighting dimmed to a more intimate glow. The frenetic excitement of the performances gave way to a gentler, more reflective mood.

Genesis sank into her seat, her heart still racing from the exhilarating performance. Zuri slid in next to her, wrapping an arm around her waist and pulling her close.

"So, what did you think of that last surprise?" Zuri asked.

Genesis turned to face her fiancée, a mix of emotions swirling in her eyes. "It was... intense. And sexy. You never cease to amaze me, Zuri Baker."

Zuri's smile was tender. "I just want to give you everything, Genesis. You deserve the world."

Genesis cupped Zuri's face gently, stroking her thumb across her cheekbone. "You are my world, Zuri. All of this is amazing, but you're the best gift I could ever ask for."

They leaned in, sharing a deep, passionate kiss that seemed to make the rest of the room fall away.

Genesis smiled, because unlike the past few months, there was no doubt in her mind she had found her forever love.

# Chapter Thirty-Seven

Zuri stood in the opulent bridal suite of the Montague Estate in Napa Valley and did her best to calm her breathing. Her heart pounded as she paced back and forth on the plush cream carpet. She paused in front of an ornate mirror to scrutinize her reflection.

"This is it," she whispered to herself.

Her dress was exactly what she wanted, a vision in ivory silk that clung to her curves like a second skin before cascading to the floor in a river of fabric. Intricate lace patterns adorned the bodice, delicate swirls and flowers across her chest and shoulders. The seamstress painstakingly sewed tiny seed pearls and crystals into the lace, so that they caught the light with every movement and gave the gown an ethereal shimmer.

The off-shoulder neckline accentuated Zuri's elegant collarbone and drew attention to her flawless caramel skin. A hairstylist expertly styled her waist-length dreadlocks into an elaborate updo, interweaving strands of pearls and sprigs of baby's breath. A gossamer-thin veil, edged with the same lace as her dress, cascaded down her back, adding an air of romance and tradition to the ensemble.

As Zuri turned, the dress moved with her, the silk sliding against her skin. The back of the gown dipped low, revealing a tantalizing expanse of smooth skin before cinching at her waist with a row of tiny, covered buttons. The skirt flared out from her hips, layers of tulle and silk creating a voluminous silhouette that seemed to float around her.

She reached down to smooth an invisible wrinkle, her fingers brushing against the hidden pockets seamlessly integrated into the dress–a practical touch she had insisted on. Her engagement ring, a stunning oval-cut diamond set in rose gold, glinted on her finger, a constant reminder of the love that had brought her to this moment.

Taking a deep breath, Zuri closed her eyes and tried to still her racing heart, reminding herself that today was the day she had been waiting for, the day she would finally marry Genesis.

Zuri gazed out the window and clutched her grandmother's pearl necklace around her neck. It was a family heirloom she wore as her something old. She smiled at the view outside. It was beautiful. The rolling hills of the vineyard were a patchwork of emerald and gold, stretching as far as the eye could see. Rows upon rows of grapevines stood in perfect symmetry, their leaves rustling in the California breeze. The late afternoon sun bathed the landscape in light, casting long shadows across the verdant fields.

The estate's gardens were a riot of color, with roses in every hue imaginable, climbing trellises and archways. Lavender bushes lined the pathways, adding a touch of purple to the already stunning scene.

Although they agreed to do something small, Genesis changed her mind and decided having a big wedding wasn't such a bad idea. Zuri knew it was to please her, but she appreciated Gen was willing to overcome her discomfort to do this for her.

With her thoughts on the decor outside and her bride to be, Zuri didn't hear the door to the suite creak open, but she smelled her mother's perfume as she entered the room, holding a beautiful bouquet bursting with fragrant roses and peonies. A proud smile spread across her face as she took in the sight of Zuri, her eyes glistening with unshed tears.

"Zuri, my darling, you are absolutely radiant," Veronique said, crossing the room to envelop her in a tight embrace.

"Thank you, Mama," Zuri murmured into her mother's shoulder, enjoying the comfort of her mother's arms. "I just want everything to be perfect."

"Sweetheart, perfection is what you make of it," her mother replied, stepping back to make eye contact with Zuri. "You and Genesis have worked so hard to make this day special, and I know that no matter what happens, you will be happy."

Zuri's eyes welled up with tears hearing her mother's words. She knew deep down that her mother was right. True perfection lay in the love she and Genesis shared, a solid foundation that would carry them through their life together.

"Thank you, Mama," Zuri said again, her voice full of gratitude.

Her mother brushed away a stray tear that had escaped from Zuri's eye, her own eyes full of love. "I am so excited for you and Genesis to start your lives together. You did good, my love."

As if on cue, a soft knock sounded at the door, and Alma, her maid of honor, poked her head in. "Is it safe to come in?" she asked with a playful grin.

"Of course," Zuri replied, gesturing for her to enter.

Alma glided into the room, her bridesmaid dress flowing around her. She glanced at Zuri and gasped. "Oh my goodness, Z! You are breathtaking!"

A blush creeped up Zuri's cheeks. "Thank you," she said.

Alma approached and pulled Zuri in for a hug. "So, are you ready to become Mrs. Baker-Malone?"

At the mention of her soon-to-be shared last name, a flutter of nervous excitement rippled through Zuri's stomach. She took a deep breath, trying to calm her racing heart. "I think so," she replied, her voice wavering slightly. "I can't believe this day is finally here."

Alma reached out and squeezed Zuri's hand reassuringly. "You've got this, girl. Genesis is probably just as nervous as you are right now."

The thought of Genesis, her beautiful bride-to-be, waiting for her at the altar, brought a smile to Zuri's face. She pictured Genesis's wild curls tamed into an elegant updo, her radiant smile lighting up the room. The image calmed her nerves somewhat.

"You're right," Zuri nodded, squeezing Alma's hand back. "I just want to see her already."

Veronique chuckled. "Soon enough, my dear. But first , we need to make sure everything is perfect."

She reached for the delicate veil draped over the back of a nearby chair and carefully arranged it atop Zuri's head, securing it with a pearl-encrusted comb. As she stepped back to admire her handiwork, Zuri glimpsed herself in the full-length mirror.

"Oh, Zuri," Alma breathed, coming to stand beside her. "You look like a queen."

Zuri's eyes welled with tears again, threatening to ruin her carefully applied makeup. "Don't you dare cry," Veronique warned, though her own eyes were misty. "We don't have time to redo your face."

Zuri laughed, blinking rapidly to keep the tears at bay. "I'm just so happy," she whispered. "But also nervous and excited. Is it normal to be all these things at once?"

"Of course," Alma assured her, rubbing her back. "You're about to marry the love of your life. It's a big deal."

A knock on the door interrupted their moment. Zuri's father poked his head in. "Ladies, it's time," he announced, his deep voice filled with emotion.

Zuri's heart skipped a beat. The strains of a violin drifted through the air, mingling with the distant laughter of arriving guests. Zuri's heart swelled with anticipation as she listened to the sounds that heralded the approaching ceremony. It was happening–she was about to marry the woman who had captured her heart so thoroughly.

Zuri breathed deeply, steadying herself. She turned to her mother and Alma. "Thank you both for being here with me," she said. "I wouldn't be able to do this without you."

Veronique cupped her daughter's face gently. "We wouldn't be anywhere else, my love. Now, let's go make you a married woman."

With a last glance in the mirror, Zuri took her father's arm. The small bridal party made their way through the winding corridors of the vineyard's main house, the scent of flowers growing stronger with each step. As they approached the double doors leading to the garden, Zuri's heart raced.

"Ready?" her father asked, giving her arm a reassuring squeeze.

Zuri nodded, unable to speak past the lump in her throat. The doors swung open, revealing a sea of smiling faces turned towards her. But Zuri only had eyes for one person.

Genesis stood at the end of the aisle, a vision of ethereal beauty that took Zuri's breath away. Her wedding dress was a masterpiece of modern elegance, perfectly complementing her dancer's body. The gown accentuated Genesis's rich, dark brown skin with its champagne hue, crafted from the finest silk charmeuse.

The dress featured a plunging V-neckline that showcased Genesis's graceful collarbones and drew the eye to a delicate diamond pendant nestled at her throat. Intricate beadwork adorned the bodice, creating a shimmering pattern that caught the light with every subtle movement. The beads, a mix of crystals and tiny pearls, formed abstract swirls reminiscent of the fluid movements of a dancer.

The gown's sleeves were sheer, made of the finest tulle and embroidered with the same beaded pattern as the bodice. They clung to Genesis's toned arms before flaring out at the wrists, giving the impression of delicate wings.

The skirt of the dress was a marvel of engineering, appearing to float around Genesis as if she were walking on air. Multiple layers of gossamer-thin silk flowed from her hips, creating a subtle A-line silhouette that moved with grace and fluidity. A thigh-high slit on one side offered tantalizing glimpses of Genesis's leg as she walked, adding a touch of sensuality to the otherwise ethereal gown.

Genesis's wild curly hair had been styled into a loose, romantic updo, with tendrils framing her face. Tiny white flowers were woven throughout, matching the delicate blooms in her bouquet. Her makeup was understated yet glamorous, emphasizing her natural beauty with a subtle smokey eye and a glowing complexion.

As Zuri's eyes met Genesis's, she saw all the love and joy she felt reflected back at her. Genesis's radiant smile lit up her entire face. In that moment, everything else faded away and all Zuri saw was the woman she loved, waiting to begin their life together.

Zuri's feet carried her forward, each step bringing her closer to her future. The soft grass beneath her feet, the gentle breeze carrying the scent of roses and lavender, the melodic strains of the string quartet – everything blended into a perfect backdrop for this moment.

When they reached the altar, Zuri's father placed her hand in Genesis's. This was where she belonged.

"Hi," Genesis said with a grin. "You're so beautiful, baby."

A blush crept up Zuri's neck. "So are you, my love."

The officiant cleared her throat, drawing their attention. "Shall we begin?" she asked with a smile.

Zuri and Genesis nodded in unison, their hands still clasped tightly together. As the ceremony began, Zuri found herself lost in Genesis's eyes, barely hearing the words being spoken. She was aware of the rustling of the gathered guests, the music playing in the background, and the gentle breeze that flowed over them. But she was most aware of Genesis - her radiant smile, the feel of her hands, the love in her eyes.

"Dearly beloved," the officiant's voice rang out, "we are gathered here today to witness the union of Zuri Baker and Genesis Malone in holy matrimony."

The ceremony continued, a beautiful blur of words and emotions. When it came time for the vows, Zuri willed her voice not to shake.

"Genesis, from the moment we met, I knew there was something special about you. You've taught me the true meaning of love, and I promise to cherish and support you for the rest of our lives."

A tear slipped down Genesis' cheek as she responded, her voice equally tender and heartfelt. "Zuri, you are my rock, my inspiration, and my joy. I promise to stand by your side through everything life throws our way, and to always make you laugh when times get tough."

Simple but sweet, exactly how they both wanted.

The officiant's voice rang out, clear and resonant. "By the

power vested in me, I now pronounce you married. You may kiss your bride."

"Finally," Genesis whispered, her lips curving into a tender smile. As they leaned in for their first kiss as a married couple, time seemed to slow down, each second stretching into an eternity. Their lips met, a gentle reassurance that they were now bound for life.

The crowd erupted in applause and cheers, the sound washing over them like a tidal wave of love and support. With beaming smiles, Zuri and Genesis entwined their hands and walked back down the aisle, basking in the love of their friends and family.

Once outside the ceremony site, Zuri tugged Genesis towards a quiet corner of the venue, hidden beneath the dappled shade of an old oak tree. The rustle of leaves and the distant hum of laughter from their guests provided the perfect backdrop for this stolen moment.

"We did it," Zuri whispered, as she gazed at Genesis. "We're married."

Genesis beamed back at her, reaching up to cup Zuri's face. "I can hardly believe it myself. Mrs. Baker-Malone."

The sound of their shared last name sent a thrill through Zuri's body. She leaned in, pressing her forehead against Genesis's. "I love you so much," she murmured.

"I love you too," Genesis replied, her voice thick with emotion. "More than I ever thought possible."

They stood there for a moment, savoring the quiet intimacy of this stolen moment. The sounds of the reception starting up drifted towards them.

"We should get back," Zuri said, not quite ready to end their private moment.

Genesis nodded, but her eyes sparkled with mischief. "We

should," she agreed, "but first..." She pulled Zuri close, capturing her lips in a deep, passionate kiss.

When they broke apart, Zuri had to catch her breath. "Wow," she breathed, her heart racing. "Are you trying to get me to skip our party?"

Genesis chuckled. "Tempting as that sounds, I think our guests might notice if we disappear." She brushed a gentle kiss against Zuri's cheek. "Besides, I can't wait to show off my beautiful wife on the dance floor."

Hearing the word "wife" in reference to herself was surreal. She laced her fingers through Genesis's, marveling at how perfectly they fit together. "Well then, Mrs. Baker-Malone, shall we make our grand entrance?"

"Lead the way, my love," Genesis replied with a grin.

Hand in hand, they walked back to the reception area. The sun was setting. Lights in the trees, creating a magical atmosphere. It was exactly what Zuri wanted and had pictured for many years. Once they began planning for the event, Genesis agreed to all of her suggestions, only adding some of her own for small things. Zuri knew it was her way of apologizing for holding back with getting the planning started. While she may have been nonchalant about the ceremony, Genesis cherished one thing, and that was Zuri.

As they approached the reception area, the strains of music grew louder. Zuri recognized the opening notes of their chosen first dance song - a romantic ballad that had become "their song" early in their relationship. Her heart swelled with emotion as she remembered all the times they had swayed to this melody in their living room, lost in each other's arms.

"Ladies and gentlemen," the DJ's voice boomed over the speakers, "please welcome for the first time as a married couple, Mrs. and Mrs. Baker-Malone!"

The crowd erupted into cheers and applause as Zuri and

Genesis stepped onto the dance floor. Genesis pulled Zuri close, one hand resting on the small of her back, the other clasping Zuri's hand against her heart. As they moved to the music, their eyes only on each other, it was as if no one else was there.

"So, you're still not going to tell me where we'll be going for our honeymoon?" Zuri asked with a grin.

Genesis rolled her eyes. "You planned this entire wedding and our bachelorette party. It's my turn to surprise you."

Zuri laughed and rolled her eyes playfully. "Fair enough. But unlike you, I'm not big on surprises."

"I know, but trust me," Genesis whispered, pulling her closer. "You'll love this one."

As the song ended, their guests applauded, some wiping away tears. Zuri and Genesis parted, but kept their hands intertwined as they made their way to the head table.

The reception was everything Zuri had dreamed it would be and more. Zuri couldn't stop smiling as she watched her friends and family mingling, dancing, and celebrating their union. The speeches were heartfelt and touching, with Alma and Andrea's maid of honor toasts bringing both brides to tears.

Afterwards, Andrea came to their table and Zuri smiled as she embraced Genesis.

"You're getting some of this too," Andrea said, pulling Zuri into a hug.

"Now that the excitement has died down, I've got a special surprise for you." Zuri looked behind Andrea's back so that she would turn around.

Veronique appeared at the table. "Hi Andrea, I hear you've been waiting to meet me."

Andrea's eyes widened in disbelief once she saw Veronique Baker, the legendary actress, standing before her. She opened her mouth to speak, but no words came out. Zuri giggled at Andrea's starstruck expression. Although she had been privy to such behavior over the years, there was something especially sweet about being able to make Andrea's dream come to life.

"I... I... Oh my God," Andrea finally stammered, her hands trembling as she reached out to shake Veronique's hand. "Mrs. Baker, I'm such a huge fan. I can't believe I'm meeting you!"

Veronique smiled, enveloping Andrea in a gentle hug instead of shaking her hand. "Please, call me Veronique. Any friend of my daughter's is family."

Andrea looked as if she might faint from sheer joy. "Veronique," she repeated, her voice filled with awe. "I... I've seen all your movies. Multiple times. Your performance in 'Midnight in Harlem' changed my life. The way you portrayed Josephine Baker was just... it was transcendent."

Veronique's eyes were filled with amusement and appreciation. "Thank you, dear. That role was very special to me."

"Oh, and 'The Color of Love'!" Andrea continued, her words tumbling out in a rush of excitement. "The scene where you confront your character's father about his prejudice? I cry every single time I watch it. The raw emotion in your eyes, the way your voice breaks when you say 'Love doesn't see color, Daddy. Why can't you?' It's just... it's perfection."

Zuri and Genesis exchanged amused glances as Andrea continued to gush, her initial nervousness giving way to unbridled enthusiasm.

Veronique listened, a gracious smile on her face as Andrea rambled on, listing scene after scene, performance after performance. She spoke of the subtle nuances in Veronique's expressions, the way she conveyed entire paragraphs of emotion with just a look or a gesture.

"Oh, and your comedy roles!" Andrea exclaimed, barely pausing for breath. "People always focus on your dramatic performances, but your timing in 'Love on the Rocks' was impeccable. The way you delivered that line about the lobster and the champagne? I laughed so hard I fell off my couch!"

As Andrea continued her enthusiastic monologue, Zuri felt a surge of pride. This was her mother, this incredible woman who had touched so many lives through her art. And now, here she was, patiently listening to Andrea's passionate praise with grace and kindness.

"Andrea, darling," Veronique interjected, placing a hand on Andrea's arm. "I'm flattered by your kind words. It means the world to me that my work has touched you ."

Andrea blushed, suddenly realizing how long she had been talking. "I'm so sorry," she stammered. "I never thought I'd actually get to meet you. I must sound like a complete fangirl."

Veronique laughed, a rich, melodious sound that put Andrea at ease. "Never apologize for passion, my dear. It's what drives us, what makes life worth living." She winked at Zuri and Genesis. "These two understand that, don't they?"

Zuri felt her cheeks warm as she squeezed Genesis's hand under the table. "Mom," she protested half-heartedly, but she couldn't keep the smile off her face.

"Now then," Veronique continued, turning back to Andrea. "Come along with me. I'd love to hear your thoughts on 'Tour de Force'. The critics hated it, but I always thought it was a hidden gem."

"Oh my gosh, me too," Andrea gushed.

Zuri and Genesis watched them disappear into the crowd.

Genesis placed her hand on top of Zuri's. "Your mom is such a sweetheart. Andrea is never going to get over this."

"Something tells me Rebecca and Andrea are going to be visiting California a lot more often."

They both laughed. Genesis noticed Kenzie with her grandmother and signaled for them to come over. When they made it to the table, Zuri was stunned at how much she resembled Genesis.

"Granny was just letting me know she's surprised at how good the food is for such a formal venue," Kenzie said with a smile.

Genesis laughed and shook her head. "Gran, you're terrible. This is a five-star vineyard."

Granny Lee waved her hand. "Fancy places serve tiny portions that leave you hungry. But I must say, that prime rib was divine."

Zuri smiled at the older woman. "I'm so glad you're enjoying yourself, Mrs. Baker. It means the world to us that you're here."

Granny turned to Zuri, narrowing her eyes. "And that's all thanks to you. I'm not surprised you stole my Gen's heart.

"It's a pleasure to meet you, Mrs. Smith. I've heard so much about you."

To Zuri's surprise and relief, Genesis' grandmother broke into a wide smile that was similar to her granddaughter's. "Please, call me Granny Lee. You're family now."

She pulled Zuri into a hug that smelled of lavender. When she pulled back, her eyes were misty. "I want to thank you, Zuri," she said. "For loving my Gen the way she deserves to be loved. For seeing her true self and cherishing it."

"It's my pleasure, ma'am," Zuri said, looking at Genesis over her shoulder. "It's what she deserves."

Granny Lee nodded. "It's what we all deserve."

"May I ask Granny Lee, why do you use your name instead of just having the kids call you Granny?"

Granny Lee chuckled. "Oh, that's a funny story, my dear. You see, when Genesis was just a little thing, maybe three or four years old, she couldn't quite wrap her tongue around

'Grandmother.' It always came out as 'Granny,' which I found adorable. But there was already a 'Granny' in the family, my husband's mother. So, to avoid confusion, I became 'Granny Lee.'"

She leaned in, lowering her voice. "Between you and me, I think it suits me better than just plain 'Granny.' It's got a bit more pizzazz, don't you think?"

Zuri laughed out loud. "It does," she agreed. "It's unique, just like you."

Granny Lee beamed at her. "Oh, I like you," she declared. "You've got a good head on your shoulders, and you make my Gen happy. That's all I want for her."

Genesis, who had been listening to the exchange with a fond smile, wrapped an arm around Zuri's waist.

"You two are just adorable," Granny Lee said, squeezing Genesis' arm. "Now, Genesis, you better take good care of this one. She's a keeper."

Genesis smiled, pulling Zuri closer. "I intend to, Granny. For the rest of our lives."

As Granny Lee gripped Kenzie and moved on to greet the other guests, Zuri turned to Genesis, her heart full of love. "Your grandmother is amazing. I can see where you get your charm from."

Genesis chuckled. "She's one of a kind, that's for sure. I'm so glad you two hit it off."

The rest of the evening passed in a blur of dancing, laughter, and love. As the last song faded away and their guests began leaving, Zuri and Genesis stood hand in hand, thanking everyone for coming. When the last guest had left, they turned to each other, both glowing with happiness.

Genesis grabbed onto Zuri's hand. "Ready to tackle the world together?"

"With you," Zuri said, stroking her cheek. "Definitely."

"Good," Genesis said with a smirk. "First stop, the South Pacific.

# Chapter Thirty-Eight

Pineapple juice. Rum. Orange juice. Grenadine.

Genesis licked her lips as she gingerly sipped the cocktail she whipped up before lounging poolside. The villa she rented was on the beach, but she couldn't resist the allure of the private infinity pool overlooking the crystal-clear waters of the Pacific. The gentle lapping of waves provided a soothing soundtrack as she basked in the Tahitian sun.

She stretched on her lounge chair, her deep brown skin glistening with a light sheen of sunscreen and sweat. She wiggled her pedicured toes, admiring the bright coral polish that matched the tropical flowers dotting the lush landscape around her.

"Now this," she murmured to herself, "is what I call paradise."

A year of planning, saving, and anticipation had led to this moment. Their honeymoon - a week of pure bliss in Tahiti with her new wife. Being able to call Zuri her wife made her happy. Their wedding had been a few days ago, but it still seemed like a surreal experience.

Genesis closed her eyes, reliving the moment Zuri had

appeared at the end of the aisle. Her dreadlocks adorned with white flowers, and her caramel skin glowing in the soft light of the sunset ceremony. The way Zuri's eyes had locked onto hers, filled with such love and promise, had taken Genesis's breath away.

Her phone buzzed, alerting her to an email message. When she saw it was from Kenzie, she let out an excited gasp and opened it up. Kenzie was now attending law school at Yale University.

Genesis beamed with pride as she read through Kenzie's enthusiastic email about her first week at Yale Law. Her little sister had come so far, and Genesis couldn't be happier for her. She made a mental note to share it with Zuri later.

Just then, a shadow fell across her face, blocking out the sun. Genesis cracked open an eye, a smile already forming on her lips.

"There you are," Zuri said, her voice teasing. "I was wondering where you'd disappeared to."

Genesis sat up, drinking in the sight of her wife. Zuri was a vision in a white bikini. Her dreadlocks were piled high on her head, a few escaped tendrils framing her face.

"Just soaking up some sun and sipping on this delicious cocktail," Genesis replied, holding up her glass. "Care to join me?"

Zuri grinned as she plucked the cocktail from Genesis's hand. "Don't mind if I do," she said, taking a sip. Her eyebrows raised in appreciation. "Mmm, that is good. You might have missed your calling as a bartender."

Genesis laughed, the sound light and carefree. "I'll stick to numbers and dancing, thank you very much. But I'm glad you approve. I have many hidden talents."

Zuri set the drink down on the small table beside the lounge chair and then straddled Genesis.

"Oh, I'm well aware," Zuri purred, leaning down to place a kiss on Genesis's lips. The taste of rum and fruit lingered between them.

Genesis reached up, cupping Zuri's face in her hands. "I still can't believe we're here. That we're married. That you're my wife."

"Same here. And Tahiti? This was the best surprise ever, baby."

"Well, you always take care of me. I wanted to do something nice for you, especially since you and Daphne did such an amazing job planning the wedding."

"With your help."

"Sure, but you two handled all the details."

"And you handled the most important detail of all. You showed up and said 'I do.'"

"I'd say 'I do' a thousand times over," Genesis whispered.

Zuri smiled, kissing Genesis on the forehead. "So, what's on the agenda for today, Mrs. Baker-Malone?"

Genesis grinned at the sound of their hyphenated last name. It still gave her a thrill to hear it. "Well, Mrs. Baker-Malone, I was thinking we'd start with a swim in this gorgeous pool, then I scheduled a guided tour through the rainforest. There's this hidden waterfall that's breathtaking. The locals call it 'Faaroa Falls.' It's tucked away in a secluded valley, and the water cascades down these massive black volcanic rocks. Later, we get to have dinner on the beach while the sun sets."

"Mmm, that sounds perfect," Zuri murmured, nuzzling Genesis's neck. "But first, I think we should christen this lounge chair."

Genesis's breath hitched as Zuri's lips trailed along her collarbone. "I like the way you think," she whispered, her fingers threading through Zuri's locs.

Their lips met in a passionate kiss, tropical fruit and rum

mingling between them. Genesis savored the touch of Zuri's skin against hers, the weight of her wife's body a delicious pressure. Her fingers traced the familiar curves of Zuri's hips, eliciting a moan from her partner.

Zuri's heated kisses trailed down to the top of the swimsuit that barely contained her breasts. She nipped at the fabric, causing it to stretch taut before beginning a slow descent towards the valley between them. Genesis let out a gasp as Zuri pulled her top down, exposing her to the sun.

"You taste delicious," Zuri said as she traced her tongue across one of Genesis' nipples.

Genesis moaned, arching into her mouth. The waves crashed onto the shore mixed with the rustling of the palm trees in the distance created a sensual soundtrack for their intimate moment.

Zuri's hand slid down Genesis's stomach, teasing at the wet fabric before slipping underneath to stroke her bare flesh. She groaned, her hips lifting off the lounger in invitation. Zuri's fingers found their way to Genesis's core, already wet with anticipation. She gave a slow, teasing stroke, making Genesis gasp and whimper.

"Oh, Zuri," she breathed out, arching into the touch. "More."

Zuri chuckled, her fingers circling Genesis's clit before dipping inside her. Genesis moaned and did her best to be quiet. While their villa was very private, she was still conscious of them being outside.

Zuri's fingers moved with practiced skill, making it hard for her to maintain any decorum. She curled her fingers inside, hitting that perfect spot that made Genesis see stars. Her thumb circled Genesis' clit in time with her thrusts, building the pleasure.

"That's it, baby," Zuri said in between kisses. "Let go for me. I want to hear you."

Genesis gasped, her hips rocking against Zuri's hand. The coil of pleasure inside her wound tighter and tighter until she thought she might burst. With a cry of ecstasy, she came undone, waves of bliss washing over her as Zuri continued to stroke her.

As she came down from her high, Genesis opened her eyes to see Zuri gazing at her with adoration. "You're so beautiful when you come," Zuri said, her hand gripping her.

Genesis blushed at Zuri's words. She still had the ability to make her feel like a love struck teenager.

"Your turn," Genesis purred, flipping their positions so Zuri was now beneath her on the lounge chair. She trailed kisses down Zuri's neck, savoring the salt on her skin from the ocean breeze.

Zuri's breath hitched as Genesis's hands roamed her body, teasing and caressing. Genesis took her time worshiping every inch of her wife's beautiful form. She loved the way Zuri's caramel skin contrasted with the white of her bikini, how her muscles flexed beneath Genesis's touch.

"Stop being a tease," Zuri whimpered, her hips lifting in search of more contact.

Genesis smiled against Zuri's skin. "Patience, my love," she said, her fingers dancing along the edge of Zuri's bikini bottoms.

She dragged the fabric aside, exposing Zuri to her hungry gaze. Genesis's mouth watered at the sight of her wife, glistening with arousal.

Genesis dipped her head, kissing Zuri's inner thigh before moving to where her wife needed her most. She ran her tongue along Zuri's folds, savoring her and reveling in the moan it elicited.

Zuri's fingers tangled in Genesis's curls, urging her closer.

Genesis obliged, her tongue circling Zuri's clit before dipping inside her. She set a steady rhythm, alternating between long, languid strokes and suckling her into her mouth that had Zuri gasping and writhing beneath her.

Soon sensed Zuri getting close, her thighs trembling on either side of Genesis's head. With a few more well-placed licks and the addition of two fingers curling inside her, Zuri came undone. She cried out Genesis's name, her back arching off the chair as waves of ecstasy washed over her.

Genesis licked Zuri through the aftershocks of her orgasm, savoring the taste of her on her tongue. When Zuri's trembling subsided, Genesis placed a kiss on her inner thigh before moving up to lie beside her on the lounge chair.

"Mmm," Zuri hummed as she nuzzled into Genesis's neck. "I think we've thoroughly christened this chair."

Genesis laughed, wrapping her arms around Zuri and pulling her close. "I'd say so. Though we might need to test out a few more spots around the villa, just to be sure."

They lay there for a while, basking in the afterglow. The gentle lapping of waves against the shore and the rustling of palm leaves in the breeze created a soothing melody around them.

Genesis glanced at her phone on the table. It was time for them to get ready and meet their guide into the rainforest, but she was reluctant to leave this perfect moment. So she held Zuri tighter and let them have a few more minutes of bliss.

* * *

A couple of hours later, they were enjoying their tour. As they stepped into the lush Tahitian rainforest, Genesis and Zuri were enveloped by a world of vibrant green. The canopy above filtered the sunlight, creating a dappled pattern on the forest floor. Their guide, a local man named Teva, led them along a narrow path that wound through the dense vegetation.

"Watch your step," Teva warned, pointing out a gnarled root system that snaked across the trail. "The forest floor can be treacherous, but it's also full of life."

Genesis marveled at the diversity of plant life surrounding them. Massive ferns unfurled their fronds, reaching towards the sky, while delicate orchids clung to the bark of towering trees. The air was thick with humidity, carrying the earthy scent of damp soil and fragrant flowers.

Zuri squeezed Genesis's hand as they navigated the path. "This is incredible," she whispered, her eyes wide with wonder. "It reminds me of Barbados, but with its own special flair."

Teva paused, gesturing to a nearby tree. "This is the Mape tree," he explained. "Its wood is sacred to our people. We use it to make canoes and traditional drums."

As they continued their trek, the sound of rushing water grew louder. Teva led them off the main path, pushing aside a curtain of vines to reveal a hidden clearing. There, cascading down a wall of black volcanic rock, was the Faaroa Falls. Genesis was left breathless by the sight. With a drop of at least fifty feet, the waterfall created a misty veil that shimmered in the dappled sunlight. The pool at its base was a crystal-clear turquoise, inviting and serene.

"It's even more beautiful than I imagined," Genesis breathed, squeezing Zuri's hand.

Teva smiled. "This is a sacred place for our people. The mana - the spiritual energy - is very strong here."

As if to emphasize his point, a gentle breeze rustled through the clearing, carrying with it the sweet scent of tropical flowers. Genesis closed her eyes, breathing in deeply. She felt a sense of peace wash over her, as if the worries and stresses of the world were unable to reach them in this magical place.

"Can we swim?" Zuri asked, already toeing off her hiking boots.

Teva nodded. "Of course. The water is refreshing. Many believe it has healing properties."

They needed no more encouragement. Genesis and Zuri stripped down to their swimsuits, leaving their clothes in a neat pile on a nearby rock. Before they waded into the pool, hand in hand, Genesis captured some pictures, gasping at the initial shock of the cool water against their sun-warmed skin.

She dipped under the surface, relishing the sensation of the pure water enveloping her. When she resurfaced, she saw Zuri swimming towards the waterfall, her dreadlocks streaming behind her like a dark river. Genesis followed, cutting through the water with graceful strokes.

They met beneath the thundering cascade, the mist creating a veil around them. Zuri's eyes were bright with exhilaration as she pulled Genesis close.

"This is magical," Zuri shouted over the roar of the falls. "It's like we've stepped into another world."

Genesis nodded, unable to find words to express her awe. Instead, she wrapped her arms around Zuri's waist and kissed her. The taste of fresh water mingled with the familiar sweetness of Zuri's lips.

When they broke apart, Genesis noticed Teva discretely busying himself with examining some nearby plants, giving them privacy. She smiled gratefully, even though he couldn't see it.

"Race you to that big rock over there?" Zuri challenged, pointing to a moss-covered boulder jutting out of the water near the edge of the pool.

"You're on," Genesis grinned, pushing off and swimming with powerful strokes.

They laughed and splashed as they raced across the pool,

their competitive spirits coming alive. Genesis reached the rock first, but only by a hair's breadth. She hauled herself up onto its slippery surface, then reached down to help Zuri up beside her.

They sat there for a moment, catching their breath and taking in the breathtaking view. The waterfall thundered before them, its mist creating a haze in the air. Colorful birds flitted between the trees surrounding the pool, their calls echoing through the clearing. Genesis leaned against Zuri, their legs dangling in the cool water.

"I can't believe we're here," Zuri murmured, wrapping an arm around Genesis's waist. "It's like a dream."

Genesis nodded, resting her head on Zuri's shoulder. "I know what you mean. But it's real. We're here, together, as wives." She lifted her left hand, admiring the way her wedding band glinted in the dappled sunlight.

Zuri took Genesis's hand in hers. "I love you so much, Gen," she said, placing Gen's hand on her heart.

"And I love you," Genesis replied, tilting her head up to place a gentle kiss on Zuri's lips.

They sat in comfortable silence for a while, basking in the beauty of their surroundings and the joy of being together. The cool mist from the waterfall caressed their skin, providing relief from the humid air.

Eventually, Teva called out to them, reminding them they needed to head back if they wanted to make it to their beach dinner reservation on time. With a shared look of reluctance, Genesis and Zuri slid off the rock and swam back to shore. As they emerged from the water, Genesis admired the way the droplets glistened on Zuri's skin.

They dried off and changed back into their hiking clothes, both refreshed and invigorated from their swim. As they began the trek back through the rainforest, Genesis paid even more attention to the lush beauty around them. She wanted to commit every detail to memory - the way the light filtered through the canopy, the vibrant colors of the exotic flowers, the chorus of bird calls echoing through the trees.

"Thank you for this," Zuri said as they walked along the narrow path. "For planning this entire trip. It's more than I ever imagined."

Genesis squeezed her hand. "You deserve it all and more. I just want to make you as happy as you make me."

They shared a tender smile before turning their attention back to navigating the uneven terrain. By the time they emerged from the rainforest, the sun was dipping towards the horizon, painting the sky in brilliant shades of orange and pink.

Teva bid them farewell at the trailhead, and they caught a ride back to their villa. They had just enough time to shower and change for dinner.

"That was amazing, babe. One of the top five things I've ever done," Zuri gushed while she tied up her hair.

Their adventure in the rainforest had been everything Genesis hoped for, and more. "I'm so glad you enjoyed it," Genesis said, holding Zuri as she finished fixing her hair. "You looked so beautiful standing there in front of the waterfall. I couldn't stop staring at you."

Zuri turned in Genesis's arms. "Is that why you insisted on taking so many pictures?"

Genesis grinned. "Can you blame me? I wanted to capture every moment of our honeymoon. Plus, you know how much I love photographing you."

"True, didn't you have to buy more storage on your phone or something like that?"

Zuri dodged Genesis' playful slap and walked over to the closet.

Genesis followed her to the closet. "So, what are you thinking of wearing tonight?"

Zuri hummed as she perused their options. "How about this?" she asked, pulling out linen short set.

"Perfect," Genesis agreed. "That looks so good on you."

As Zuri slipped into her outfit, Genesis chose a flowy sundress in a vibrant tropical print. The colors complemented her skin, and the light fabric would be perfect for a beachside dinner.

Genesis stepped into her sandals and turned to find Zuri watching her. "What?" she asked, suddenly self-conscious.

"Nothing," Zuri said, crossing the room to wrap her arms around Genesis's waist. "I just can't believe how lucky I am to call you my wife."

Genesis felt her heart swell with emotion. She cupped Zuri's face in her hands and kissed her. "I'm the lucky one," she whispered against Zuri's lips.

They walked hand in hand down to the beach, where someone had set up a private table for them. Tiki torches illuminated the area, casting a glow over the sand. The sun was just beginning to set, painting the sky in brilliant hues of orange and pink.

As they settled into their seats, a server appeared with a bottle of champagne. "Compliments of the resort," he said with a smile, pouring them each a glass.

Genesis raised her glass, clinking it against Zuri's. "To us," she said.

"To us," Zuri echoed, taking a sip of the bubbly drink.

As they perused the menu, Genesis stole glances at her wife. Genesis found herself mesmerized by the elegant line of Zuri's neck as she tilted her head to read the menu.

"See something you like?" Zuri teased, catching Genesis staring.

Genesis blushed but didn't look away. "Just admiring my beautiful wife," she replied with a wink.

The server returned, and they ordered some fresh seafood and local delicacies. As they waited for their food, Genesis and Zuri fell into easy conversation, reminiscing about their wedding day and sharing their favorite moments from their honeymoon so far.

"I still can't believe you managed to keep this trip a secret," Zuri said, shaking her head in amazement. "How did you pull it off?"

Genesis grinned, feeling a surge of pride. "It wasn't easy, let me tell you. I kept wanting to ask you your opinion on what I was choosing, but I decided to trust that I would know what you like."

Zuri laughed, the sound carrying on the evening breeze. "Well, you did a fantastic job. This has been perfect. Thank you."

"You don't have to thank me, honey."

"No, but I do. We've gone through some things these past few months and I questioned whether we were right for each other."

"I know," Genesis said, reaching across the table to take Zuri's hand. "But we made it through. We're stronger for it."

Zuri nodded. "We are. And you've shown me that while love isn't perfect, it is worth fighting for. You've taught me that it's okay to be vulnerable, to let someone in completely. I'm so grateful for you, for us."

Tears pricked at Genesis' eyes. "I'm grateful for you too, baby."

They shared a tender kiss across the table. As they pulled apart, their food arrived, an array of colorful dishes that smelled divine.

"Oh wow, this looks amazing," Zuri said, her eyes widening at the spread before them.

They dug in, savoring the fresh flavors and exotic spices.

"You're in post-production with Minor's film right?" Genesis asked as she sipped her drink.

Zuri grinned. "I love it when you use film jargon. Yeah, everything is pretty much done and babe, it's really good. William pulled out a hell of a performance and I could be biased, but it is one of Phillip's best films."

Genesis beamed with pride. "Not surprised, he's fighting for his status in Hollywood. But that's fantastic, love. I can't wait to see it. You've worked so hard on this project."

"We all have," Zuri nodded. "The whole team really came together. It's been amazing to see it all come to fruition."

"Any word on festival submissions yet?" Genesis asked, knowing how important that step was for the film.

"Actually, yes. We just got word yesterday that we've been accepted into the Cannes Film Festival. I was waiting for the right moment to tell you."

Genesis gasped, nearly choking on her champagne. "Cannes? Babe, that's huge! Why didn't you tell me sooner?"

Zuri laughed, reaching across the table to squeeze Genesis' hand. "I wanted to wait for a special moment. And what's more special than our honeymoon dinner?"

"Oh my god, we have to celebrate!" Genesis exclaimed, waving to catch the waiter's attention. "Can we get another bottle of champagne, please? We're celebrating!"

As the waiter hurried off to fetch more champagne, Genesis couldn't contain her excitement. "I'm so proud of you, Zuri. You've worked so hard for this."

Zuri's eyes shimmered with unshed tears. "Thank you, babe. It means everything to have your support. You've been my rock through this whole process."

"Always," Genesis promised, lifting Zuri's hand to her lips and kissing her knuckles. "I'll always be here to support you, in everything you do."

The waiter returned with a fresh bottle of champagne, pouring them each a glass before discreetly stepping away. Genesis raised her glass, her eyes locked on Zuri's.

"To my incredible wife," she toasted. "May this be the first of many successes. I can't wait to see where your talent takes you."

They clinked glasses, the sound mingling with the gentle lapping of waves on the shore. As they sipped their champagne, the sun finally dipped below the horizon, painting the sky in deep purples and blues. The tiki torches cast an intimate glow over their table.

The conversation continued to flow easily between them, punctuated by laughter and lingering looks. Genesis' thoughts went back to their first dinner in Barbados and she realized that despite the years that had passed, they still felt at ease with each other. This was her person, and she couldn't wait to see what life had in store for them.

# About the Author

Ava Freeman loves romance, the steamier the better. It was that love, and her penchant for storytelling, that inspired her to start writing.

When she's not crafting her next story, Ava can be found reading (of course) or watching horror movies (have to balance out those energies). That is when her daughter lets her get a quiet moment (usually when she's sleeping). She currently lives in New York with her partner and little rebel.

www.authoravafreeman.com

9 798988 751670